**He turned at the sound of her approach,
his eyes alive with raw emotion. . . .**

Jenna's heart pounded painfully as she stepped close to him. "You left before I could share a family birthday tradition," she said softly, praying her courage would not desert her.

"What's that?" he asked hoarsely.

"The Riordan birthday kiss." She stood on tiptoe, her lips brushing his beard-stubbled cheek.

He closed his eyes. For the space of a heartbeat he didn't move, and then with a low, throaty groan, he reached for her, sweeping her into a melting embrace.

He rained kisses across her forehead, her cheeks, her eyes. And then his mouth found hers, his lips velvet-soft yet hard and demanding.

Never had she felt like this. Never had she known she could. She reveled in his taste, his smell, all sagebrush and leather—powerful, primitive, and achingly masculine.

"Jenna. Sweet God, Jenna." His growl of pleasure sent white heat searing through every part of her being. His hands roamed her back until they buried themselves in her hair, and she knew then she was lost forever. . . .

Also by Jessica Douglass from Dell:
SNOWFIRE

All
My Heart Can
Hold

JESSICA
DOUGLASS

A DELL BOOK

Published by
Dell Publishing
a division of
Bantam Doubleday Dell Publishing Group, Inc.
666 Fifth Avenue
New York, New York 10103

ISBN: 0-440-20649-9

Printed in the United States of America

Published simultaneously in Canada

September 1991

10 9 8 7 6 5 4 3 2 1

RAD

Prologue

New Mexico Territory, 1867

Caleb Harper knew he wasn't going to make it. The big roan gelding beneath him was being pushed beyond its endurance. Yet keeping the horse at a dead run was Harper's only chance for survival. He stretched low over the horse's neck, speaking encouragement—whether for the horse or for himself he couldn't have said.

A glance over his right shoulder told him his three pursuers were closer now. He gauged their distance at less than half a mile. Across the canyon floor he could see nothing nearby that offered the slightest cover. His closest hope was a craggy spire of rocks still some five miles off. Under this killing pace the horse would go down long before that.

He hefted his carbine from the saddle boot. They would be in the Spencer's range soon. He would have to be ready to make a stand.

Three against one. The odds were not encouraging.

But somehow he would have to win. It wasn't just his own life at stake. If he lost, these men would find Jenna. The thought redoubled his determination to stay alive.

The roan's motions were no longer smooth. The horse labored against the scorching heat and the relentless demands of its rider. Harper felt the gelding miss a step, then another. The battle site was being chosen for him.

He jerked hard on the reins, swerving the horse in a wide arc to the right, his gaze all the while tracking his pursuers. Two of the riders sawed back on the reins of their own tired mounts. The third kicked his horse in the sides and charged.

Harper leapt from the heaving gelding, knowing he could not get a steady shot from its back. Before the oncoming rider could adjust, Harper had him sighted. He squeezed the trigger. The bullet slammed home. The rider made a violent attempt to right himself in the saddle before he pitched headlong into the dirt, his horse coming to a stumbling halt some hundred yards away.

Harper dared nurture a flicker of hope. If he could finish Valdez's two other hirelings, he just might pull this off.

A bullet kicked up dirt near his boots. At once Harper forced the roan to its knees. A hard twist left the horse lying exhausted on the ground. Its body would be his only barricade. "Easy, Buck," he soothed, patting the sweating gelding's neck. "We'll—"

A bullet thudded into the roan's body. The weary animal trembled, then lay still.

Harper swore low under his breath and levered another cartridge into the Spencer's chamber. Rising up, he fired off four quick shots, hitting nothing, but able to pinpoint where Gravshaw and Mitchell had scrambled for cover behind Gravshaw's bay. The slack-jawed killer had slit his own horse's throat to keep it from bolting.

For a moment the firing ceased and Harper caught the mutter of voices—Gravshaw and Mitchell plotting how best to kill him.

He peeled off his black Stetson, threading his fingers through thick, dark hair straggling damply across his forehead. "Can't we talk about this, Ike?" he called, inching a hand across the roan's barrel to retrieve his saddlebags and the extra ammunition they contained. "Maybe work some kind of deal?"

"Here's your deal!" Gravshaw sneered, firing off several shots that whistled past Harper's head.

Methodically Harper reloaded his Spencer, then checked the Colt he wore strapped to his right thigh. Any other time he would have relished this chance to rid the world of Ike Gravshaw, but every minute's delay jeopardized the life of the woman he loved.

She was out there somewhere. Scared and on the run. And it was his fault, all of it. Nor had he forgotten Iron Fist. If the vengeance-crazed Comanche found her first . . .

"You're dead, Harper!" Gravshaw yelled. "You hear me? Dead! I promised you'd answer fer makin' me look bad in front of Valdez."

"You didn't need my help for that," Harper said, a grim smile tugging at the corners of his mouth as Gravshaw responded with a string of curses and another hail of bullets.

Harper knew he was playing a dangerous game. Gravshaw was a cold-blooded killer a dozen times over. That was precisely why Valdez kept him around—the two were cut from the same bloody cloth. Who the two ultimately took orders from was the unknown Harper had yet to discover. And now perhaps never would. And yet if he could goad Gravshaw into trying something reckless, maybe he could lengthen the odds enough to count.

"You shouldn't have tried to take the woman, Harper," Gravshaw was saying. " 'Tweren't none of your business."

It was more my business than you'll ever know, Harper thought bitterly but said nothing.

"You crossed me for the last time," Gravshaw went on. "Now I'm gonna gut shoot you and leave ya for the buzzards."

"It's you who's going to be giving the buzzards indigestion, Ike," Harper muttered, thumbing back the hammer on his Colt. "And I can't wait—"

He reacted instantly, instinctively to the scrape of a boot to his left, cursing his stupidity that he had in fact allowed Gravshaw to distract him. Twisting, he fired at the approaching Mitchell, but not before he felt a biting sting in his left shoulder, felt the warmth of his own blood trail down his sweat-soaked shirt.

Mitchell grunted and doubled over, stumbling back to the dead bay, all the while Gravshaw was laying down a steady stream of cover fire. Harper yanked loose the blue bandanna from around his neck and shoved it against the blood oozing from his shoulder.

As a unit Gravshaw and Mitchell rose, firing. Harper winced at the sound of a dozen bullets thudding into the roan. He burrowed closer to the animal's body. Under this murderous blanket of bullets they would be on top of him in seconds. He drew in a deep breath and let it out. They would kill him, but he wouldn't die alone. Gravshaw would never find her.

One of the outlaw's rifles misfired. From his huddled position behind the roan Harper could only guess which. He flexed his fingers around the walnut handle of the Colt. This would be his only chance. Diving past the horse's rear legs, he rolled, twisted, fired. White heat seared his right leg. He kept firing.

Mitchell went down, unmoving. With a bellow of rage Gravshaw fired on.

Harper pulled the trigger on the Colt. Empty. He grabbed up the Spencer. Two bullets, three, he was certain he had hit Gravshaw again and again.

Another bullet drove Harper back, a searing pain erupting in his right side. He stumbled over the dead gelding, falling hard, his arms splayed wide. His rifle was empty. He had no time to reload.

Gravshaw lumbered forward, a wounded grizzly on a death charge.

Harper's vision grew blurred, hazy. Everything seemed to be happening in slow motion.

Gravshaw lurched closer, weaving, unsteady, blood a solid mass on his shirt, but still bringing his six-gun to bear. Harper groped downward, dragging his knife free of the sheath in his boot. With his last ounce of strength he threw it. Gravshaw clawed at the bone handle where the knife buried itself to the hilt in his chest.

Then he pitched forward and lay still.

Harper tried to staunch the flow of blood in his leg, but his fingers refused to obey him. His shoulder and side grew numb. He could feel his life ebbing into the dirt. Valdez would win. The son of a bitch would come to gloat over his bones.

Worse, Iron Fist could be close now, searching. Maybe he'd already found her.

Caleb saw her then—in his mind's eye as she had been. Corn-silk hair and the bluest eyes he had ever seen. The pain cut him, but it was no longer from the bullets. It was the pain of what might have been, and it hurt far more than all of what Valdez had done.

He murmured her name as the darkness claimed him.

* * *

The woman rode furtively, keeping to what cover she could find in this barren stretch of land. She'd been without water since just after dawn, but even if she'd seen another human being, she would not have approached. She had the babe to consider. She could take no chances.

The beaded fringe of the doeskin dress she wore clicked in time with the plodding step of the dun gelding beneath her, the matching leggings protecting her from the coarse blanket draping the horse's back. Her blond hair seemed all the more pale against the sun-darkened flesh of her arms and face. But it was her eyes that would have arrested the attention of even the most casual observer—for they were a most startling blue.

A muffled whimper from the cradleboard secured to her back brought a wan smile to her lips. "Be patient, little one. Just a few more minutes. I promise."

Her eyes never stopped moving. It had been three days since she'd crept away from Iron Fist's camp. That he hadn't yet found her attested to how much she had learned this past year. Sometimes she even found herself thinking like a Comanche.

She managed a rueful grimace. She was not so foolish as to believe she could indefinitely hide her trail from a Comanche warrior.

Shutting her mind to the thought, she rode on, staying close to the canyon wall, refusing to acknowledge a prickle of despair as she stared out at an endless sea of sagebrush and mesquite. It was out there somewhere. It had to be. A white settlement. A fort.

Suddenly she jerked back on the reins, an odd movement ahead catching her attention. Squinting, she shaded her eyes against the oppressive glare of the soon-to-be setting sun. Black specks dipped and glided against the crimson streaked sky.

Buzzards.

She scanned the plain far ahead, not sure what she was looking for. No doubt some animal had died or been killed by coyotes. The buzzards merely wanted their share.

Something prodded her to move away from the safety of the canyon wall, a feeling she couldn't have named. She nudged the dun into a trot, speaking soothingly to her restless passenger. The babe would need to be fed. She should stop. But still she rode on.

It was no animal. But men. White men. Four of them. Dead. She stared at the grisly scene, feeling nothing. Over the past twelve months she had grown inured to violent death. In spite of the stench she dismounted and moved swiftly among the bodies. They had water, weapons. She would take them.

When she found a canteen, she poured water into one of the men's hats for her horse. When the animal finished, she drank deeply from the canteen herself. Then she stilled, her senses alert. Had she heard something? She did not let down her guard, even as the baby began to fuss. With practiced ease she slid the cradleboard to the ground and lifted the baby to her breast, trailing a finger along the tiny face.

She stiffened. This time there was no mistake. A grunt? A moan? Stealthily she checked the bodies. Bloated and stinking, three were very dead. But the fourth? The one sprawled on his stomach near the dead roan? She resettled the babe on the cradleboard and pulled the stolen six-gun from the rawhide belt that banded her slender waist. Crossing to the body, she cautiously nudged it in the side with her moccasined foot. Nothing.

She kicked him harder. Still no response. Her eyes narrowed. If he wasn't dead, he soon would be. Dried blood stained one leg of the denims he wore. With her foot she turned him over, his right arm slack across his face. But she wasn't looking at his head. She noted the two dirt-encrusted splotches of blood on his shirt, one high on the left shoulder, the other low on his right side. Three bullets. He had to be dead.

Yet he wasn't bloated like the others. Maybe the sound she heard had been the last he would ever make.

She guessed from the position of the other men that this was the one the others had been fighting. Three against one. He had taken them all with him.

Kneeling beside the wounded man, she pressed her free hand against his whisker-stubbled throat. She couldn't suppress the surge of disappointment that swept through her when she discovered a thin threading of life. Neither did she dwell on the callousness of her reaction.

As if he sensed her touch, he groaned.

Resolute, the pale-haired woman finished plundering what supplies she could find. She had her child to consider. The white man would die soon. No one could survive the loss of so much blood.

She clutched the collected canteens. With all four of their water supplies, though they too had been low, she should be able to make it several days if she was frugal. But a sick man would require much water. He would slow her down, jeopardize her chance to escape.

She took up the reins of a stray horse. The man was nothing to her.

He moaned again, the fingers of his left hand shifting, groping, as though seeking something. Water? A low rasp sounded deep in his throat. Seeing him so helpless tugged at a part of her she'd long since given up for dead, buried along with—

No. She shook off the thought, then with a resigned sigh stepped back over to him. She considered the bitter irony. How long she had waited to see white men, to hope for rescue. Now that she had effected her own escape, this white man could well become the cause of her recapture.

She tugged the cork from the canteen, then caught the man under the shoulders and positioned his head on her lap. The arm that had sagged across his face fell away. She held the canteen to his lips and took her first real look at his face.

With an anguished cry she shoved him off of her, slamming to her feet.

God in heaven! She stared at him, stared at the face that had taunted her dreams and cursed the savage twist of fate that had put his life at her feet. How dare God or anyone expect her to save *him?*

But then she knew.

She jerked the knife from the sheath on her belt. He was alive not so that she could save him. But so she could pay him back for a year in hell.

The Comanche in her raised the knife.

I

One year earlier
Council Grove, Kansas

Jenna Riordan paced anxiously back and forth across the sparsely furnished lobby of the Council Grove Hotel, the hem of her simple blue cotton day dress swirling in time to her agitated movements. Dr. Ira Vinson had been in with her sister now for nearly half an hour. What on earth could be taking him so long? Jenna had been certain Bess was getting better.

Her gaze swept up the polished oak stairs to the second-floor landing. She resisted the urge to go storming up to their room, to demand to know Vinson's opinion of Bess's progress. The medical man's imperious glower and his refusal to even examine Bess until Jenna had left the room had forced her grudging retreat.

Jenna hugged her arms tight against her. Bess was fine. She had to be. It was her own helplessness that nagged at Jenna, chafed her like an itch she couldn't quite reach.

Jenna Riordan was many things, but in all of her twenty-two years helpless had rarely been one of them. It was a feeling that ate at her as nothing else could, a feeling that conjured memories of another time and place when she had been all too helpless as well. Against her will she saw again her mother's pale features twisted with pain, her slight frame bent against the unending spasms of coughing that racked her. Doctors had fussed and conferred then too. And her father had grown into an old man before her eyes. But in the end there had been only the black wreath upon the door.

At fourteen, the eldest of the three Riordan children, the responsibilities of their Spring Hill, Virginia, home had fallen to her. She had done her best to run the household, to be mother to an ever frail Bess, then seven, and their three-year-old brother, Timmy, but she had not reckoned with taking on the responsibilities of *both* her parents. Ilsa Riordan's death and the coming of the War Between the States had combined to crush the spirit of a man who had once found joy in every living thing. Increasingly withdrawn, Kyle Riordan allowed less and less time for family matters, spending upward of a hundred hours a week in his print shop. Those long hours, Jenna knew, had done much to contribute to his own death last year. That and—

"Are you sure there isn't anything I can help you with, Miss Riordan?" The bespectacled clerk interrupted her painful musings as Jenna crossed in front of his desk for the two-dozenth time.

"I'm fine, really," Jenna assured him again. "I'm just worried about my sister."

"Doc Vinson is a crotchety ol' coot, but he's the best there is west of the Mississippi. Miss Bess will be fine."

"Thank you, Percy." She gave him a wan smile. "If I

haven't said so recently, I truly appreciate your kindness toward me and my family these past four weeks."

" 'Tweren't no bother at all, Miss Riordan." His thin chest puffed out. "It ain't often I get the privilege of helping a lady as beautiful as yourself."

Jenna managed a polite nod, then turned and resumed her pacing. Did he mean he wouldn't have helped if he hadn't found her looks appealing? She found the thought unsettling, even irritating, though she'd grown oddly used to the fawning attention of the opposite sex these past few years. Hair the color of corn silk and mountain-lake eyes often made men look twice when she passed.

In truth she found such male fascination a puzzlement. She viewed her coloring as a whim of nature, nothing more, a trait passed down from her mother's Scandinavian heritage. Great-granddaughter to a one-time indentured servant, Ilsa Anderson Riordan had been born into a world far removed from servitude, a world of wealth and privilege in antebellum Virginia. Raised on Thousand Oaks, a sprawling plantation just outside of Richmond, Ilsa had long been regarded one of the most beautiful women in all of the South.

But she was a woman never impressed by her own beauty, or by men's reaction to it. She eschewed a score of handsome, besotted swains to marry the gawky, plain-featured son of a printer. "All the beaus, with all their pretty words didn't turn my head one whit as much as when Kyle Riordan brazened his way into my cotillion on Thousand Oaks, asked me to dance, and then asked my opinion of slavery."

Jenna gave her head a wry shake. Her mother had told her it was years before her parents forgave her brash pronouncement that owning other human beings was an abomination.

"But it didn't matter," her mother said. "What mat-

tered was being with Kyle, knowing always that he respected my opinions, my intelligence, as much as any
man's. Don't ever settle for less, Jenna. Ever."

Jenna had assured her mother that she would not,
though after her mother's death the vow seemed irrele-
vant at best. With Bess and Timmy to care for, Jenna
allowed precious little time for suitors.

Real flesh-and-blood suitors anyway.

Jenna's mouth twisted ruefully. Her maternal responsibilities hadn't stopped an occasional indulgence
in romantic fantasy. Evenings spent in front of a crackling fire with *Jane Eyre, Pride and Prejudice, Wuther-
ing Heights,* and other favorites, had gifted her with a
more-than-fanciful notion of the sort of man with
whom she wanted to spend her life. A man at once
dashing, sophisticated, but with a touch of the rogue.
She smiled. And perhaps just a hint of mystery about
him.

The smile faded. There was little use conjuring romantic fantasies in Council Grove, Kansas.

Or perhaps anywhere.

Even in Virginia real flesh-and-blood men had been
hard pressed to live up to a dream. Not that she could
blame them after four years of war. Her abolitionist
leanings had scarcely endeared her to many of them
anyway. Even so, she clung stubbornly to her notion of
one day finding a man who could make "her heart
sing," as her mother had so often described her own
courtship.

Marching over to the front window, Jenna drew
aside one heavy red velvet curtain. Her mood was not
improving. It was time for a distraction, any distraction.
She stared out at the frontier town's bustling main
street. Even through the glass she could hear the bawl-
ing of oxen, the shouts of freight haulers coming in off

the trail, the clang of hammer against anvil at the smithy's down the street.

The sights and sounds of the Santa Fe Trail town had taken on a strange, even comforting familiarity this past month. Even so, Jenna couldn't wait to be gone. She wanted a home again for Bess and Timmy. Roots. She wanted the new life Uncle William had offered them in California.

The son of an earlier marriage, William Riordan had left Virginia when Jenna's father was barely ten. But William never lost touch with the life he'd left behind. A letter every four or five years kept Kyle Riordan abreast of his half brother's fiddle-footed adventures. And so when her father died, Jenna had written to William in care of his last known address in Los Angeles. Surprisingly he had answered, his reply sympathetic. He'd even invited them to join him at his "simple hacienda, nestled under the bluest skies you will ever see."

The chance to free Bess and Timmy from the aftermath of Appomattox was irresistible. Jenna had accepted his invitation at once. But just as they were making ready to depart this past spring, she had received another letter. Uncle William was pulling up stakes again. "A recurrence of gold fever," he'd called it. He was heading north to the Sacramento Valley, but agreed to wait until their late summer arrival.

Bess's debilitating attack of dysentery had put that scheduled arrival in jeopardy, as well as forced them to bid farewell to the two-hundred-wagon caravan with which they'd been traveling since they'd left St. Joe in early May. Jenna had assured her sister that nothing mattered so much as her getting well, but Jenna knew Bess's condition was compounded by worry over the delay.

Jenna's gaze flicked toward the stairs. What if Bess had fretted herself into a relapse? Though Jenna tried her best to shield her sister, they had both heard enough about the Santa Fe Trail to know that the optimum time for decent weather and adequate forage for the livestock was rapidly running out. They would have to leave within the next two weeks or postpone the rest of their journey until next spring, not only incurring the unplanned-for expense of wintering in Council Grove, but perhaps missing connections with their uncle.

Jenna bit her lip, recalling how her mere hint that staying over might be the wiser choice had made Bess frantic. "Uncle William won't wait for us! We'll be all alone!" Bess's pale features had seemed almost ghostly against the stark white of the bed linens, her ash-blond hair hanging limply about her narrow face.

"We've been alone for nine months now," Jenna had gently reminded her. "Whether we go or stay, we'll be fine." Her own heart had been hammering painfully, uncertainty niggling at her, even as she had forced calmness into her words. But her reassurances had not lessened the fear in her sister's pale blue eyes. Jenna had not brought up the subject again.

Nor was she going to now. She was being absurd. They were not staying over, and Bess was not having a relapse. Her sister had been growing stronger by the day. All Jenna wanted was for the doctor to confirm it. Then she, Timmy, and Bess could reload the few belongings they'd removed from their wagon and be on their way. Maybe even by week's end.

All they really needed was a guide.

And that Bart Jacobs had promised to provide. Jacobs was a bachelor traveling to Fort Union in the New Mexico Territory to take up residence as the fort's new sutler—civilian provisioner for the army post. Though possessed of an often irritating personality, the man had proved unexpectedly solicitous when circumstances dictated that the Riordans and two other families—the Holts and the Kovels—be abandoned by the wagon train. When all three families were again ready to travel, Jacobs assured them he would have no difficulty hiring a trail-savvy scout to take them the final leg of their journey to California.

Jenna peered up the street, hoping to catch some sign of the wiry sutler. He'd said he would stop by this morning with word on his search. If he'd found someone, she would have some good news to relay to Bess. But he was nowhere in sight.

And neither, she frowned ruefully, was Timmy, though she'd told her youngest sibling to stay close by the hotel today. As usual, he had bolted from their room just after dawn. He had made it a habit to spend his entire day exploring the burgeoning frontier town. Normally Jenna had no objections. In fact, Timmy's relentless curiosity had proved an unexpected boon. Whenever she needed anything to make Bess more comfortable, eleven-year-old Timmy knew right where to find it and how much it cost.

Today, though, she could have used his company. His antics would have helped keep painful memories at bay. But there was no help for it now. Besides it was time to confront Vinson. She'd given the medical man more than enough time with Bess.

Jenna started to turn away from the window, then unaccountably turned back, her attention caught by two riders reining in at the hitch rail in front of the barber shop across the street. Their trail dusty clothes suggested it had been days, even weeks, since they'd last come in contact with civilization.

One of the men wore the blue uniform of a cavalry major. Sandy-haired, mustachioed, perhaps in his early thirties, he dismounted and flexed his shoulders as though to ease the tension of a long ride. He gave

Council Grove what amounted to a dismissing look, though his mouth curved into an amused grin.

But Jenna's gaze didn't linger on the officer, her attention caught and held instead by the man who stood at his side. A little older than the soldier and not in uniform, the man exuded a quiet authority that exceeded any military rank. He was tall, though not overly so, his dark trousers and fringed buckskin jacket well suited to his lean, broad-shouldered frame. A black hat with what looked to be a snakeskin band sat atop dark hair that shagged just below the nape of his neck. But it was his face that mesmerized her—all hard angles softened by a generous mouth and several days' growth of dark beard. Even from this distance she could sense the strength in those features, the character.

Her pulses quickened, despite the deep breath she took. She wished fervently she could see his eyes, discern their color as his gaze tracked up one side of the street and down the other. It was as if he was making himself aware of every doorway, every window, every tiny part of his surroundings. Jenna had seen a similar wariness once—in soldiers returned from the war. But in this man it was different somehow—a watchfulness not spawned of war, but part of his very nature.

When he seemed briefly to glance toward the hotel, Jenna took an unconscious step back, then grimaced. The man could hardly see her through the curtain. And what would be the harm if he did? Annoyed at her foolishness, she yanked the curtain aside—only to watch both men disappear into the barbershop.

An odd disappointment rippled through her. She found herself hoping she would see the man again, and soon. She wanted to know what effect a haircut and a shave might have on the peculiar fascination he seemed to have roused in her.

"You've been reading too many romantical books, Jenna," she mumbled aloud, grateful to hear a door opening abovestairs.

"You may come up now, Miss Riordan." She recognized Ira Vinson's no-nonsense tones.

Jenna all but ran up the steps. Before, she had wanted to be distracted from worrying overmuch about Bess. Now she couldn't wait to see her sister, to take her mind off the imposing stranger.

The door to their room stood ajar and Jenna hurried inside. Vinson was busying himself at Bess's bedside table, returning various instruments and potions to his medical bag. Jenna whisked by him, crossing to Bess, who was sitting up in bed, two pillows propped behind her. Her complexion still seemed much too pale, though it was better by half than it had been lately. "I was getting worried," Jenna said. "This morning you told me you felt so much better—"

"I *do* feel better." Bess's gaze flicked toward Vinson, as though fearing he would contradict her. "Much better."

Vinson turned, peering at Jenna over the rim of his spectacles. "Your sister is doing very well," he conceded, his bushy white eyebrows arching over sage brown eyes. "But . . ."

He let the word hang tellingly in the air.

Jenna waited.

"I've told you before, and I'll say it again, I don't think it's wise that she travel on to California this season."

"The good doctor and I have been arguing that point for over twenty minutes," Bess said.

Jenna worried her lower lip. "Maybe he's right, Bess. I don't want to risk your getting sick again. Next spring isn't really so far away. Maybe Uncle William—"

"No," Bess put in firmly. "You want to go on as much as I do. You haven't been fooling me one bit."

Jenna made an exasperated sound. Despite her tender years, Bess had ever possessed an uncanny knack for knowing others better than they knew themselves, and Jenna was no exception. "You're missing the point, Bessie," Jenna managed. "Continuing our journey has nothing to do with what you or I want. What matters is your health. I will not jeopardize it. Not for Uncle William's convenience, or anyone else's."

"But I'm fine!" Bess said. "Please, Jenna, don't make me be the reason we stay behind. Please . . ."

Bess's voice trailed off and her lower lip quivered. Jenna knew what the girl was thinking. So many times Bess's delicate health had caused her to miss out on things. Never hale and hardy, she had often been confined to bed. At times Jenna had had to cancel social events to stay home and care for her. No matter how much Jenna had assured her she was glad to do it, she knew Bess was often consumed by guilt.

And now those pale blue eyes watched Jenna with a kind of quiet desperation. In that moment Jenna saw her options vanish. To stay in Council Grove and miss connections with Uncle William would be far more damaging to Bess's well-being than any bodily discomfort could ever be.

Rising to her feet, Jenna faced Vinson. "I thank you for stopping by, Doctor. Your care these past weeks has saved my sister's life, and I'm grateful."

"But you're going on to California," Vinson said. It was not a question.

"We are. We must."

Bess visibly relaxed, her color seeming to improve before Jenna's very eyes. Jenna too felt a certain calm now that a decision had finally been made. She just prayed it was the right decision.

"I wish you folks good luck, then," Vinson said. "You'll need it." With that he grabbed up his medical bag and showed himself out the door.

Jenna returned her attention to Bess. "I'm so glad you're feeling better."

"It means we can leave soon, doesn't it?" her sister asked hopefully.

"We'll see. Bart Jacobs should be here any minute. He'll let us know if he's found a scout."

"The Holts are getting anxious to be under way again too. Millie stopped by for a visit yesterday afternoon. I didn't get a chance to tell you. She's fine, and she says Emmet and Mary are doing much better."

Jenna thought of the ever cheerful Millie Holt. She, her husband, Emmet, and ten-year-old daughter, Mary, had all been dysentery victims. Only her thirteen-year-old son, Sam, had been spared.

"Millie says Lem Kovel is fit to travel too," Bess went on.

Jenna frowned. "His leg can't possibly be healed yet." The Pennsylvania farmer had suffered a severe fracture of his left leg some four weeks before. The setback had done nothing to improve his already foul temperament. A bitter, alienated couple, Lem and Nelda Kovel had lost three sons to the war. They were traveling to California to start over.

"Mule-stubborn. That's what Millie calls him."

Jenna could think of a more apt description, but decided to change the subject instead. "I wish that brother of ours were here. I could send him to find Mr. Jacobs."

"Maybe it's Timmy who should be looking for a scout. He seems to know everything and everyone in town."

Jenna came over to fluff her sister's pillows. "I just hope he isn't getting into any mischief."

"I still haven't recovered from that lizard he brought in here last week."

Jenna chuckled. "At least it brought some color to your cheeks."

"It was good to see Timmy so excited," Bess admitted. Her voice grew wistful. "Even though Pa wasn't around home too often, his death hit Timmy pretty hard." She sighed. "It hit all of us pretty hard. Sometimes I still can't believe he's gone."

Jenna looked away.

Bess caught her hand. "Oh, Jenna, please don't tell me you're still blaming yourself for what happened."

"If I hadn't put my name on that blasted pamphlet . . ." Jenna didn't finish. There was no need. It could never change what had happened.

To spend time with her father Jenna had resorted to visiting the print shop, helping him after hours with some of his clandestine antislavery leaflets. One evening she'd even typeset and run off one of her own essays on the subject. Unfortunately she'd also proclaimed her authorship. Her father, realizing the danger, had destroyed the pamphlets. But somehow a copy made its way around Spring Hill. Vigilantes burned the print shop to the ground. Three days later Kyle Riordan was dead of a heart attack.

"You didn't kill him," Bess said softly. "You must know that. Dr. Perry said Papa's heart could've failed him anytime."

Jenna let out a shuddery breath. "I know." At her sister's continued worried look Jenna gave Bess's hand a reassuring squeeze. "I'm all right, Bessie. Honestly."

A knock sounded. Jenna looked gratefully toward the door. "Maybe Mr. Jacobs has some good news," she said too brightly.

"Jenna . . ."

"I'm fine." And she was. She had to be. Her sister and

brother depended on her. Schooling her features into an expressionless mask, she crossed to the door and swung it wide. "Mr. Jacobs, I've been wondering what was keeping you. Come in. Please."

The sutler sauntered in and closed the door behind him. Jenna did not protest, though propriety would have been better served had he left it open. She couldn't take her eyes off the man's attire. Instead of his usual range clothes he was dressed in a natty dark frock coat and trousers. The suit was finely cut, though it did not exactly conform to his bony frame. But though he had upgraded his clothing, it was distressingly apparent that he had not deemed it necessary to bathe before doing so.

"Take you to an early lunch, Miss Riordan?" he asked, crossing over to her.

Jenna breathed through her mouth, as she sidestepped both the question and Jacobs. "Have you found us a guide?"

"Not yet. But I know it won't be long."

"You've been saying that for three weeks now. In a town of this sort why should it be so difficult to locate a man who knows the territory?" Her thoughts leapt to the buckskin-clad stranger, but she said nothing. He likely worked for the military in some capacity and would be unavailable to escort civilian wagons.

"It's late in the season," the sutler grumbled. "At least that's what they tell me. But I'm thinkin' it's somethin' else."

"And what might that be?"

"Comanche." Jacobs's full lips twisted with disgust. "There's a peace treaty, but I coulda told 'em you can't trust savages."

Jenna frowned, hoping Jacobs wasn't about to launch into one of his diatribes against Indians. She had little opinion one way or the other, never having met an

Indian herself. Still, Jacobs's vitriol reminded her of nothing so much as the closeminded bigotry of her own grandparents.

"How about that lunch, Miss Riordan? You remember how good the special is at Hays Tavern."

"I remember, but I really should stay with Bess."

"If it'll help find us a guide," Bess put in, "please don't stay on my account. I should rest anyway."

"Your sister's right," Jacobs said. "Besides there's someone I'd like you to meet. He's not a guide. But he does know the territory. His name's Elliot Langston. He's a good man, even if he is an Injun agent."

Jenna hesitated, partly because she doubted she could eat should she be seated downwind of Jacobs. And partly because she didn't want to give him any false notions. They'd shared a meal or two already this past month and his interest in her was becoming less than subtle.

But she *was* hungry. And there was going to be a third party joining them. Besides Bess did need to rest.

And—the thought came from nowhere—*maybe, just maybe, that handsome stranger would be out in search of a meal too . . . in this very small town.*

Her pulses quickened as she thought of bumping into him, discovering for herself the color of those eyes. She smiled. "Mr. Jacobs, I'd be pleased to have lunch with you. But first I would like to change clothes. I can't wear hoop skirts and crinoline on the trail, and I do miss them. Could you come back in half an hour?"

Jacobs ran a hand along his cheek. "Sure thing, Miss Riordan. Maybe I can get me a shave." He gave her a look that lingered a pulsebeat past polite, then left the room.

Maybe the barber will douse him with a little extra bay rum, Jenna thought hopefully.

She stood there then, a strange excitement stirring within her, a feeling she welcomed, embraced.

What color were those eyes?

For once in her life Jenna Riordan deliberately set about to look her very best.

Caleb Harper settled himself into one of the cane-back chairs that lined the inside wall of Titus Wilson's barbershop and stretched his long legs out in front of him, crossing his scuffed boots at the ankle. "How is it you always end up in the barber chair first, Gallagher?" he drawled.

Major Keith Gallagher grinned. "You should know by now, Caleb old man—rank has its privileges."

Caleb scowled good-naturedly, reaching for a dog-eared newspaper lying atop the spur-scarred footstool to his right. "If you lop off one of his ears, Wilson," Caleb told the barber, "there's a two-bit tip in it for you." He didn't look at the paper, his eyes still adjusting to the room's dim interior after the stark sunlight of the open trail.

Gallagher was chuckling, the cheroot he held clamped between even white teeth teetering precariously close to a cheekful of shaving lather.

Unfazed by either of them, the portly barber continued to daub more lather onto the soldier's well-carved jawline. "You gents headin' for Fort Larned?"

"Fort Bascom," Gallagher said. "New Mexico Territory. I'm taking over command there."

"Don't envy you, Major. I hear the Comanch' may be actin' up again soon."

Caleb's gaze flicked briefly to Gallagher's, but the major was already deflecting Titus Wilson's observation with feigned disinterest. "I'm not worried about the Comanche. Eagle Dancer will honor his people's treaty. It's my wife I'm worried about."

"Your wife?" the barber queried, confused.

"I sent the missus on ahead without me," Gallagher said, the cigar waggling as he spoke. "With a full military escort. Figured to overtake her after Mr. Harper and I took care of a little business. But he and I were delayed. If my calculations are correct, Marian has already been at Fort Bascom for three weeks without me."

Wilson's confusion mounted.

"Don't you see, my good man? Mrs. Gallagher is daughter to a general, granddaughter to another general, and great-granddaughter to a third general. I may never be able to wrest control of the fort from her once I arrive."

Wilson hooted, slapping his thigh.

Caleb did not smile. Marian Gallagher was indeed a woman with a mind of her own, but that had nothing to do with Gallagher's mentioning her to Wilson. It was just that neither he nor Gallagher wanted to confront the subject of Comanches. Not now.

Not yet.

His mood darkening, Caleb opened the weeks-old newspaper only to find it filled with stories recounting a quarter century of Comanche atrocities. Nowhere in the article was there a single word about what had sparked the various episodes of bloodletting. The writer's only interest seemed to be fanning the flames of hate already burning hot between whites and Indians.

A tiny bell above the doorjamb jingled, announcing the arrival of a new customer. Caleb studied the man through hooded eyes. Medium height, expensive though ill-fitting clothes, and a body odor ripe enough to offend a sheepherder, the man carried himself with an exaggerated swagger that reeked of self-importance.

Caleb disliked the man at once.

Gallagher rose and gave the barber a solid pat on the back. "Good job, my good man." He rubbed a hand along his clean-shaven jaw and neatly trimmed mustache, then reached into his pocket to extract a dollar, which he handed to Wilson. "Keep the change."

The barber's balding head bobbed in appreciation. "Thank you, sir."

Caleb stood. He scratched at the stubble framing his cheeks, eager now for his own turn with the barber's hot towel, to rid himself, in part at least, of the grubby feel of the trail. And to let someone else do the work for a change. He started toward the barber's chair.

"You wouldn't mind if I went ahead of you now, would you, mister?" The foul-smelling stranger stepped in front of him.

"I would."

The stranger seemed not to hear, turning to take the seat Gallagher had just vacated.

Caleb stared at the man.

"Meeting a lady," the man said. "You understand."

"You've got three seconds to move." Caleb's voice was soft, but his gaze was steel-hard.

"I don't want no trouble in here," Wilson said nervously. "Mr. Jacobs, maybe you'd best wait your turn." Wilson was looking at the .45 slung low on Caleb's right hip.

Jacobs stayed put.

Caleb hooked his thumbs in the waistband of his trousers. His negligent stance belied the tension coiling inside him. "Two seconds."

"Better move, mister," Gallagher put in mildly. "I've seen him skin men alive for less."

Jacobs's gaze slid to the .45.

"One second."

Jacobs swallowed hard. The hand that rested on one arm of the barber's chair began to tremble slightly. He cleared his throat. "If it means that much to you . . ." He rose, forcing his chin forward, though no defiance showed in his watery brown eyes. "Be my guest."

Caleb sat down, his gaze never leaving Jacobs.

"Maybe I don't need that shave after all," Jacobs said. "The lady doesn't mind a little stubble." The laugh that followed was leering, suggestive. He backed toward the door, jerked it open, and hurried outside.

"Have you really skinned men alive, mister?" the barber asked in an awestruck voice.

Caleb rolled his eyes at Gallagher, then leaned back. "I haven't had any occasion to for quite a while, actually," he said. "I think the last time was when a barber got a little careless with his razor . . ."

Wilson swallowed, looking from Caleb to Gallagher and back again. Only when Gallagher burst out laughing did the barber relax.

Minutes later, his shave finished, Caleb joined Gallagher out on the boardwalk, where the major had gone to finish his cigar.

"Do you have to say things like that?" Caleb groused. "I thought the idea was *not* to draw too much attention to ourselves. The whole town'll be buzzing by the time Wilson gets through frosting your little tale."

"Got you your shave, didn't I?"

"I would have gotten it without your help."

"But this way Wilson didn't get his shop rearranged —at least not with that stinking little weasel's head."

"Jacobs would have moved."

"Maybe. But we've got more important things to concern ourselves with. Like that little matter we need to discuss."

The little matter, Caleb knew, was a shipment of Spencers bound for Fort Bascom and how best to get them there without risk of Comanche attack. "We can hardly work out details in the middle of the street," he said. "Besides Jacobs reminded me how much I was looking forward to peeling off a few layers of prairie dust. I'm heading up to that bath house we passed riding in."

"I'll get us some rooms at the hotel."

"Good. We'll hash things out over—" Caleb stopped. A woman had come out of the hotel across the street. He stared at her, stunned. In his life he had never seen anyone so beautiful. Dressed in emerald-green silk, her light blond hair done up in a crown of soft curls, the woman seemed almost too beautiful to be real.

He closed his eyes, certain his mind was playing tricks on him after long weeks on the trail. But when he opened them, the vision remained. Watching her, unable now to take his eyes off her, he recalled a picture he'd seen once that had belonged to a visiting missionary in a Cheyenne village. The only difference Caleb could discern between the picture and this woman was that the visage in the picture had had a halo and wings.

Almost unconsciously he lifted his black Stetson and raked a hand through his unruly mane of shaggy dark hair. In the barbershop he hadn't felt the need for a haircut. Now he found himself wishing he had. Disconcerted, he forced his attention back to his uniformed companion.

But Gallagher's brown eyes were focused across the

street as well. A low whistle escaped his lips. "That is one pretty lady."

"And what would Marian say if she heard you?"

Gallagher grinned. "She wouldn't say anything." He paused. "For about a week."

Caleb grimaced. "I guess that's the price a man pays for being married."

"A price you'll never pay, eh?"

Caleb stiffened slightly, unpleasant memories jabbing him.

"Sorry," Gallagher said. "I didn't mean to remind you of Laurel. I thought you'd gotten over that."

"Forget it." Caleb only wished he could.

"I've got a way with the ladies, you know," Gallagher went on cajolingly. "Perhaps I could find a way to introduce you. Maybe she's the sort that would take a fancy to a flea-bitten army scout."

"Dammit, Keith. Enough."

Gallagher snorted. "You can be so damned touchy, you know that?"

"And you're like a dog on a bone. You never know when to let go."

"All right, all right." Gallagher held up his hands in mock surrender. "She's probably spoken for anyway. A lady that beautiful can't be on her own."

Caleb's gaze again tracked to the woman. He stared in disbelief as the malodorous Jacobs approached her, proprietarily reaching up to touch her elbow and guide her up the street. A surge of unreasoning disgust tore through him, whether at the woman for her obvious poor taste in companions or at himself for giving a damn, he didn't know.

"Now I've seen everything," Gallagher said wonderingly. "He must be a relative. That's the only thing that makes sense. I can't believe—"

"I'm heading for that bath," Caleb cut in.

For once Gallagher took the hint. "I'll check in with the local law. See if they've heard any news about Iron Fist. Eagle Dancer isn't going to be able to keep that buck reined in forever."

"Eagle Dancer is chief. Iron Fist will listen." Caleb said it, though he scarcely believed it himself anymore. But he wasn't going to think about that now. Now he only wanted to take that bath and forget old wounds that at times seemed never to heal.

As Gallagher ambled toward the sheriff's office, Caleb pulled his saddlebags from his mount's back, hefted them over his right shoulder, and headed in the opposite direction. It would be worth the two bits to feel clean again, if only until they rode out in the morning. Somehow the shave had only made him more aware of how grimy the rest of him felt. Or maybe it was the immaculate beauty of the woman in the green silk dress.

He swore softly. Silk. And hoop skirts. An absolutely absurd combination for Council Grove at midday. Obviously, the gods had opted for beauty over brains in that one. But then, he thought cynically, it wouldn't be the first time.

At the bath house, he stripped off his clothes, his lean, hard-muscled body adorned only by the beaded amulet he wore suspended by a rawhide thong about his neck. Briefly his hand rested on the intricately worked circle of doeskin. He didn't have to look at it to see the soaring eagle painted on its surface, to feel a rush of pain at the memory of its giver.

His face grim, Caleb tugged off the amulet and laid it across his saddlebags, then stepped over to a wooden tub half filled with clean though tepid water. He climbed in and sat down, the tub's small circumference forcing him to sit with his knees jutting up almost to his chin. But he endured it, reaching for a cake of lye soap left over from a previous occupant.

Despite his intentions to relax, think of nothing, his mind drifted inexorably to what had brought him and Gallagher to Council Grove.

They had been to Washington, summoned there by the Secretary of War himself. Ostensibly they were to discuss a new, rising tide of Indian attacks along the Santa Fe Trail. It seemed there were young braves in various tribes who dared to view peace treaties with the same contempt as whites. Too well Caleb recalled the afternoon he and Gallagher had spent in the office of Edwin McMasters Stanton.

Caleb and Gallagher had seated themselves in the two chairs fronting the Secretary's massive mahogany desk, while the Secretary himself paced furiously back and forth across the width and breadth of his finely appointed office.

"You know these savages, Harper," Stanton had said, puffing mightily on a Cuban cigar. "What they want, how they think. Though heaven knows how any civilized man could understand how savages think."

A muscle in Caleb's jaw jumped, but he did not interrupt.

"Someone is running guns to them and we need to know who. And it's not just some jack-string outfit, it's organized. It's big. If we don't stop them"—he paused for emphasis—"it's just possible the Indians will be able to fight us for years longer than they would otherwise. Heaven help us, they could even win."

"Win their own land?" Caleb said, uninterested in the quelling look Gallagher sent him.

Momentarily taken aback Stanton gathered himself and continued, "By all rights, gentlemen, you should be dealing with the Bureau of Indian Affairs on this issue. But with the continuing hostilities between the red man and the white on our vast western frontier, there are those with strong sentiments toward turning the Indian problem back over to the Department of War. In part, that is why you are both here."

Stanton's tone grew patronizing. "Let me assure you that no one wants the killing stopped more than I do. On both sides, of course. And it will stop, if savages like Eagle Dancer and Santanta and other chiefs are willing to make the effort it takes to control their people."

Caleb leaned back in his chair and put his feet up on Stanton's desk. "If you'll excuse me, sir—you're a damned fool. The killing will never stop. Not until the Indians are living on a piece of land so worthless that no white man anywhere would ever want it."

His face purpling, Stanton stalked toward Gallagher. "Who the hell is this man, Major? Other than an obvious Indian lover. I would have thought you had better judgment. After all, you are General Thurgood's son-in-law, are you not?"

Gallagher squirmed in his seat. "My friend might *seem* overly sympathetic to the Indian cause, sir. But he knows where his loyalty lies, and he's the best scout I've ever seen. He speaks several Indian dialects and is accepted as a member of more than one tribe."

"All the more reason to doubt his loyalty, Major."

Caleb shot to his feet. "Stanton, you can go straight—"

Gallagher was in Caleb's face. "Sit down. Please. Let me handle this."

Stiff with rage, Caleb sat.

"Sir," Gallagher said, turning a placating gaze to Stanton, "hear me out, please. I met Caleb three years ago when I was a captain assigned to Fort Union. I'd been sent there to help prevent the Confederates from setting up a supply line from California."

"An assignment you weren't too fond of, as I recall," Stanton interjected disapprovingly.

"I would have preferred to be fighting for the Union back here, sir, on the front lines. Not on the frontier. But that's not the issue. I—"

Stanton held up a hand, looking toward Caleb. "And what was your opinion of the war, Harper?"

"The war wasn't any of my business. The West is my home."

Stanton stiffened. "This country is your home. One country, undivided."

"Preferably without Indians, right?" Caleb was trying very hard to gain control of his temper, not out of any deference to Stanton, but for Gallagher. Caleb liked the young major, even when the man was being too naive for his own good. He didn't want to get Gallagher into trouble, but neither was he going to sit there and pretend to believe Stanton's bull about his abiding concern for "savages."

"Mr. Secretary," Gallagher hurried on, "let me assure you Caleb taught me more in six months about life on the plains than I could have learned in sixty years on my own. He's saved my life. Twice. If there's a man in the Southwest who knows how to get into a gunrunners' camp and out again—alive—it's Caleb Harper."

Stanton drilled a look at Caleb. "Ah, yes, the gunrunners. That is what brings us all here today, isn't it? It's your opinion, I believe, Mr. Harper, that we're dealing with *comancheros?* I had thought they had been wiped out in the forties."

"All *comanchero* means," Caleb said, with more patience than he knew he had, "is Comanche trader."

"Then why," Stanton said, "does the very word seem to evoke such fear and revulsion throughout the Southwest?"

"Maybe because the *comancheros* aren't exactly the

kind of men you'd bring home to marry your sister. Ten, twenty years ago most of them were legitimate Mexican traders making an honest living. Then somebody saw a way to get rich."

Caleb rose, stalking toward the far end of the room. Somehow the effect of putting distance between himself and Stanton settled his temper, if only a little. "Today's *comancheros* are mostly Mexican bandits who get the Comanche and the Kiowa to steal cattle for them from the herds going over the Goodnight-Loving Trail. The *'cheros* make money selling the cattle. And the Indians get what they want from the *'cheros.*"

"Guns," Stanton muttered.

"Exactly," Caleb said.

"That's why we have to deal with the problem where it starts," Gallagher put in, "with the *comancheros,* not the Indians. And gunrunners like Enrique Valdez."

"Valdez." Stanton shuffled through a sheaf of papers on his desk. "I have a report here somewhere on a man named Valdez. A cold-blooded killer, I believe."

"Valdez would murder his own sister," Caleb said, "if there was an extra peso in it for him. And he'll trade guns and whiskey for anything the Indians bring him— cattle, animal hides, white captives, anything he can sell or ransom for a profit."

Stanton stubbed out his cigar in a buffalo-hoof ashtray atop his desk. "And you think you can get into this Valdez's camp and out again alive, Harper?"

"I do."

"And just how do you propose to do so?"

Caleb hesitated, not sure just how much he wanted to tell the Cabinet official. Eagerly Gallagher hurried to fill the silence. "Caleb will pass himself off as a *comanchero* himself, sir."

Stanton snorted. "Then he's a bigger fool than I

thought." To Caleb he said, "What makes you think you can pull off such a deception?"

"I'll manage."

"Valdez will think Caleb is a traitor," Gallagher explained, "that he's turned his back on the army and all it stands for."

Stanton pulled a fresh cigar from the inside pocket of his jacket but made no move to light it. "This had best not have anything to do with that shipment of Spencer carbines you've procured for Bascom, Major."

"No, sir!" Gallagher assured him. "The Spencers will be safe. Valdez won't get near them."

"I should hope not," Stanton said. "He'd trade them to the Comanche as fast as a savage could lift a scalp. A hundred Spencers in Indian hands would mean the wholesale slaughter of new settlers."

"The Spencers will be safe, sir," Gallagher said again. "I guarantee it."

"There can't be any guarantees with the likes of Iron Fist on the loose. I've seen the reports on him too. Raping and murdering women and children. He's no better than a rabid dog."

"Iron Fist is a warrior," Caleb gritted. "More than that, he's a Comanche warrior. Fighting to a Comanche is like breathing to you and me. They live to fight. The Utes gave them the name *Comanche,* because it means 'the people who fight us all the time.' " Caleb stepped toward Stanton, forcing a deference he in no way felt. "I believe even Iron Fist would lay down his weapons and live in peace with the whites if you, if President Johnson, would just—"

"Get this straight," Stanton interrupted. "If the Indians are going to survive, they're going to surrender. And do what they're told. It's that simple."

"Then maybe they won't want to survive."

Obviously weary of arguing, Stanton turned to Gallagher, his voice terse. "Get the job done, Major. Get it done and there's a promotion in it for you, a substantial promotion."

Gallagher extended his hand toward Stanton. "It'll be done, sir."

While Gallagher went on to thank the Secretary for his time, Caleb pointedly showed himself out. Minutes later Gallagher joined him in the deserted hallway.

The major's usual even temper slipped a notch. "That was stupid," he snapped. "I thought you wanted this assignment."

"I want it because I thought I could get the Indian side of this heard."

"And you will. But ride Stanton like that and he'll find someone else. And then we just might see that bloodbath we both want to avoid."

Caleb stalked to the stairs as Gallagher hurried to keep pace. "Speaking of bloodbaths," Caleb bit out, "I don't know how bright it was to tell Stanton about my joining up with Valdez."

The major's brown eyes widened. "You're not saying Stanton can't be trusted?"

"I'm saying I don't trust anybody when my life's on the line."

"Not even me?" Gallagher actually looked hurt.

Caleb halted midway down the marble staircase, exasperation replacing outrage. "You know what I mean. Valdez could be taking orders from someone we don't even know about yet. The fewer people who know what we're up to, the better I'll sleep at night."

Gallagher relented. "You're right, of course. But be reasonable, I could hardly have sent you on such a dangerous assignment without approval from higher up."

"Sounds like you're the one who wants to be higher up."

Gallagher stiffened defensively. "If you're referring

to Stanton's offer of a promotion, I would think you'd be all for it. The higher my rank the more authority I'll have in treaty negotiations with the Indians."

"I've never exactly pegged you as a champion of the red man, Keith." Caleb spoke without censure, his tone matter-of-fact.

"Maybe not. But I don't want them slaughtered like hogs either. I have great respect for men like Eagle Dancer. You've taught me that."

Caleb straightened. "Just what aren't you telling me, Keith?"

Gallagher's cheeks reddened slightly.

Caleb waited.

The major's embarrassment deepened. He spoke quickly, as though if he rushed the words he could somehow avoid Caleb's reaction to them. "It's Marian. That is, it's me. Dammit, when I asked her to marry me, she said the women in her family only marry men who wind up generals."

His friend's obvious discomfiture kept Caleb's initial sarcastic thought forever unsaid. "Marian loves you. She couldn't have been serious."

"But I am. I want an appointment to Washington. Putting an end to Valdez and his gang can help me get it. And get you what you want too. An end to the killing."

Caleb wasn't certain Gallagher's logic was altogether sound, but he didn't press it. They continued down the stairs.

Outside, the cloudless summer sky wrapped the nation's capitol in a cerulean blanket as carriages whisked past along Pennsylvania Avenue. Gallagher tugged on his uniform gloves. "Right now nothing else matters but those Spencers. Bascom needs those guns."

Caleb had no argument with that. Since the end of the war soldiers out West had had to make do with a catch-all arsenal. He'd seen men fashioning breech loaders out of muzzle loaders. The resulting weapons were hardly first-rate. With their .52-caliber rimfire cartridges, the Boston-made Spencers were accurate up to seventeen hundred yards, much better than any current armament at the fort. That was why it was imperative that they get the guns through.

That very evening Caleb and Gallagher had boarded a train heading west. In the baggage car rode ten crates of Spencers. Accompanying the carbines were six soldiers, newly assigned to Gallagher and Fort Bascom.

The journey to rails' end in Council Bluffs, Nebraska, had been strictly routine. In Council Bluffs the Spencers were off-loaded to a wagon, and the trek to Council Grove had proved incident-free as well. From Council Grove to Santa Fe, however, everything changed.

From Council Grove to Santa Fe was Comanche territory.

And *comanchero* territory.

Somehow they had to get the guns through undetected.

Toward that end Caleb and Gallagher had left the soldiers and the wagon bivouacked some ten miles out of town that morning, then ridden ahead to see what arrangements could be made. A six-man military detail would be suicide on the Santa Fe Trail. Nor could they expect help from Bascom itself. The two dozen soldiers who'd accompanied Marian Gallagher three weeks ago had been barely enough to bring the fort up to staff. To have them ride out again would leave Bascom itself vulnerable.

Even after the guns reached the fort, Caleb knew, the problem would hardly be solved. More goods, more guns, more settlers were coming west all the time. The Comanche would dig in, make a last stand. And if they had the firepower with which to fight, there could indeed be an endless sea of dead bodies on both sides.

Somewhere the bloodletting had to stop. And if Caleb could play some small part in stopping it, he would.

Even if it meant infiltrating the *comancheros*.

It was what Stanton wanted, what Gallagher wanted. That his life would be in danger was not a question. He would risk it gladly. What bothered him always was the line he was forced to walk, a line even Gallagher didn't understand.

Couldn't.

Caleb shoved himself up, water sloshing out of the tub onto the pine-planked floor, running in rivulets down the hard, lean planes of his body. He climbed out of the tub and padded across the small room to a square table piled high with clean towels. He dried himself off, his hand lingering on the eight-inch-long scar that jagged from his left nipple to the top of his left shoulder. With an oath he reached for the amulet and settled it about his neck, then jerked open his saddlebags and pulled out a fresh blue chambray shirt and dark trousers. Quickly he dressed, finishing off by tying a red bandanna around his throat.

Peering into a cracked mirror above a tin basin, he ran a brush through his still wet hair, staring at the lean, angular face looking back at him—with its sun-bronzed flesh and dark, slashing brows above eyes the color of gunmetal. Abruptly he turned away, fighting down an almost overwhelming surge of bitterness.

Swearing, he shrugged into his buckskin jacket and settled his Stetson atop his head. It was time to divert his attention. He was hungry. He'd heard they served good food at Hays Tavern. He decided to find out if they were right.

3

Jenna blanched, the hand that held her fork trembling just a little. If Bart Jacobs recounted one more tale of Comanche torture, she was certain she was going to make a most unladylike spectacle of herself and lose what meager bit of the Hays Tavern lunch special she'd been able to choke down.

But Jacobs went on, oblivious.

"I heard tell they flayed the feet of one captive," the sutler said, speaking around a mouthful of fried potatoes, "then made 'im run naked over a bed of hot coals. When they finished with him, he had enough arrows in him to be mistook for a porcupine."

Jenna's stomach lurched. The red checked tablecloth in front of her blurred into a solid crimson mass. She tried shifting her gaze to her plate. It didn't help. On it rested a heaping portion of stewed tomatoes piled high beside a too-rare steak.

She closed her eyes.

Five more minutes, she thought, drawing in a deep,

unsteady breath. Five more minutes and she would politely excuse herself.

A hand touched her arm. She opened her eyes to the solicitous gaze of her other luncheon companion. "Are you all right, Miss Riordan?" Elliot Langston inquired earnestly.

"Fine," she managed.

The dapper, fiftyish Indian agent was not fooled. He glared at Jacobs. "You're upsetting the lady," he said. "Don't you have any sense at all, Jacobs?"

Jenna gave Langston a grateful smile. Though she'd only just met the man, it was already patently obvious Elliot Langston was as well mannered as Bart Jacobs was crude.

Jacobs blinked, bewildered. Langston's admonition had totally dumbfounded him, but he managed to mumble an apology as he stuffed another forkful of potatoes into his mouth. "I just think folks should know the truth, Mr. Langston, about them savages you keep callin' children."

"They are children," Langston said patiently. "Simple children who need to be guided by the more intelligent white man."

"And just how exactly do you guide them, Mr. Langston?" Jenna asked, glad for any conversation about Indians that didn't include mayhem and murder. "Mr. Jacobs makes it sound as if all Indian encounters are at the risk of life and limb."

Langston chuckled. "I assure you, my dear, I am not a brave man. You'd be surprised how many Indian tribes are actually quite eager to have us as friends, not enemies." His hazel eyes twinkled in his pleasantly handsome face. "And, please, call me Elliot."

Jenna smiled, nodding. She glanced about for the waitress, hoping for a glass of water to further soothe her beleaguered stomach, but the buxom matron had disappeared into the kitchen to fetch another order. Today's noontime crowd was keeping even the efficient Mrs. Thane busier than usual. There wasn't an empty table to be had. The woman's practice of regaling each new patron with the tavern's storied roots—built in 1857 by Seth Hays, great-grandson of Daniel Boone and cousin to Kit Carson—no doubt contributed to the ongoing success of her buffalo-steak specials.

With a sigh Jenna settled for a sip of her now tepid coffee, then returned her attention to Langston. "What precisely does an Indian agent do, Mr . . . ah, Elliot?"

"Well this particular agent oversees the activities of other agents in Kansas, Texas, and the New Mexico Territory. I make certain that my Indian charges get all the goods and gifts promised them in our most recent treaty."

Jacobs snorted. "The only goods 'n' gifts a savage needs is an ounce of lead in the right place."

Jenna's lips thinned. "Mr. Jacobs, I am growing quite weary of your un-Christian attitude."

"Oh, you are, are you?" the sutler returned tightly. "Well, maybe you'd have an un-Christian attitude yourself, Miss Riordan, if your brother's scalp ended up decoratin' a Comanche war lance."

Jenna gasped, feeling the blood drain from her face. "I—I" she stammered. "Oh, Mr. Jacobs, I'm so sorry. I had no idea."

Jacobs seemed to shake himself. "It's all right. You don't know no better." He added ominously, "Just pray you never learn."

Embarrassed, Jenna looked away. Though Langston tried to smooth things over by chatting about his various frontier escapades, Jenna could no longer concentrate. She wished only to escape back to the hotel, see to Bess, find Timmy. Though it was likely her brother had bartered a meal in exchange for doing chores for some townsman, she wanted to make sure—if only to take her mind off Jacobs's horrific tales.

For weeks now she had kept her niggling doubts at bay about her decision to bring her brother and sister west. Bess and Timmy had both been happy, eager to leave war-ravaged Virginia behind. Leave behind also bitter memories of neighbors, once friends, who had come to despise them openly for their "Uncle Tom" views. But thanks to Jacobs, Jenna felt her fears firing anew. What if she'd exchanged a bad situation for one that could prove infinitely worse? What if—

No! she reasoned defensively; she'd made the only choice she could. Staying in Virginia was out of the question.

She forced her thoughts elsewhere, anywhere, surprised to find herself conjuring yet again the pleasant image of the stranger in the buckskin jacket.

When she'd come out of the hotel earlier to meet Jacobs for lunch, she'd caught sight of the stranger standing on the boardwalk in front of the barber shop. She couldn't be sure, but he seemed to have been looking right at her. Despite a conscious effort not to, she couldn't help feeling pleased that she had decided to change clothes. Obviously her favorite emerald-green silk had not gone unnoticed.

She'd been disappointed though, as Jacobs guided her toward Hays Tavern, to glance back and see Mr. Buckskin striding off in the opposite direction. But then what had she expected—the man to fall into step behind her?

". . . Miss Riordan?"

Jenna blinked, disconcerted. Langston was apparently eager for some sort of response from her. She only wished she knew about what. "I'm . . . inclined to agree with you," she managed lamely.

To her great relief Langston grinned. "I knew you

were a woman of rare insight. That Tonkawa chief should have known he couldn't pull off such a ridiculous charade on Elliot Langston."

Heaven only knew what she'd just agreed to, but she wasn't about to find out. Instead she lay her napkin on the table. "I hope you gentlemen will excuse me," she said, "I really do have to get back to—" She paused as a new customer strode into the café. She felt her heart skip a beat. The mustachioed cavalry major. The one who'd ridden in with the dark-haired stranger.

Her heart thudded faster as her gaze slid past him. She could scarcely credit how much she was hoping to see his friend stride in behind him. Nor did she fully acknowledge the disappointment she felt when she realized the cavalry officer was alone.

Flustered, she started to rise, again excusing herself.

Langston was beside her at once, helping her with her chair. The look he sent Jacobs prodded the sutler to get begrudgingly to his feet as well.

"Thank you, Elliot," she murmured.

"I hope you don't mind, Miss Jenna," Jacobs said, stepping close, "but I need to talk to Mr. Langston about a business matter. I won't be able to walk you back to your hotel."

"That's perfectly all right," Jenna quickly assured him. She'd grown weary of breathing through her mouth and was only too happy to leave the offensive-smelling sutler behind. She started toward the door, then stopped, suddenly realizing Jacobs had never once brought up the subject of their much-needed trail guide.

She returned to the table. "Mr. Jacobs," she said, "I do hope your business with Mr. Langston includes your asking him about a scout."

"Like I told you, Miss Jenna," Jacobs said, not quite

hiding his irritation, "Mr. Langston knows the territory, but he ain't no guide. I'll find someone. Don't worry."

"Perhaps you should worry," Langston said, casting her a concerned look. "Jacobs already mentioned this scout business earlier this week, and though I'm loathe to alarm you, I feel a duty to warn you. We've had trouble with renegades along the trail. And . . ."—he leaned toward her, as though fearful of being overheard—*"comancheros."*

At Jenna's blank look Jacobs rushed to explain. "Mexican thieves who trade with the Comanch', trade guns and whiskey for hides and . . ."—his brown eyes tracked along her slender body—"human flesh. A pretty yellow-haired lady like yourself would fetch quite a handsome price in Mexico City."

Jenna shivered. For an instant she had the unsettling feeling that Jacobs was adding up the dollar amount himself. Somehow she managed an unconcerned smile. "I would appreciate any help you could give us, Elliot. Two other families will be accompanying my own, and we'd like to be under way by week's end."

"I'll ask around," Langston said. "But I'm afraid—"

"Excuse me, miss?" a voice interrupted.

Jenna turned to see the sandy-haired major, who'd seated himself at the table just behind theirs. Though the lunch crowd had thinned somewhat, the table had not yet been cleared of the leavings of its previous occupants. The major pushed a used plate toward the center of the table, then tugged off his gloves and placed them in the small open space.

"Permit me, madam." He stood and bowed slightly. "I'm Major Keith Gallagher, and I couldn't help but overhear. You're seeking a guide along the Santa Fe Trail?"

"I am." She smiled hopefully. "Do you know someone?"

"I just might."

"How wonderful! Is he here in town? Could you take me to him?"

"I could arrange a meeting this after—"

"I'm helping the lady, soldier boy," Jacobs cut in. "And I don't need no help from you."

"Now, now," Langston chided. "Don't offend our beneficent boys in blue." He quickly made introductions all around.

Gallagher's brown eyes widened with an interest of his own when he heard Elliot Langston was the territorial Indian agent. "If I could meet with you privately sometime today, Mr. Langston, I'd be in your debt."

"I'd be honored, sir."

Gallagher again looked at Jenna. "Where are you staying, Miss Riordan?"

Jenna told him.

"How about if I bring the man around to meet with you and the other travelers, say, around four this afternoon?"

"I'll have everyone there." Jenna could scarcely contain her excitement. "I'm ever so grateful, Major."

"I haven't talked to the man yet," Gallagher cautioned. "He may prove a bit reluctant." His mouth spread into a generous grin, as though he was enjoying some private joke. "But I'll have him at your hotel at four, you can be sure of that."

"Thank you again, Major." With that Jenna made her good-byes.

In her haste to get to Bess and tell her the good news, Jenna paid little heed to where she was going. She rushed out the café door and collided solidly with a small boy hurtling along the boardwalk.

"Timmy!" she shrieked, even as she felt herself falling. In that frozen instant she was aware of her brother,

aware of strong arms catching her up, aware of the
intoxicating scent of sagebrush and leather.

Aware too that the arms did not release her right
away. She straightened, or rather, tried to. The arms
held her fast. "I—I thank you, sir." She twisted to see
the face of her benefactor and found herself staring
into cold gray eyes.

The cold gray eyes of Mr. Buckskin.

"You should look where you're going," he said.

She swallowed. The voice was deep, rich—and filled
with sarcasm! "I'll thank you to unhand me, sir." She
pushed against his forearms, warning herself to take no
notice of the hard muscles evident under that buckskin
jacket.

"My pleasure."

He let go so abruptly, she had to take a half step to
right herself. Her cheeks burned with humiliation—
and outrage! She longed to give him a piece of her
mind. And yet there was something so blatantly un-
nerving about the man that she couldn't force the
words past her lips.

Instead she whirled on her brother, who had stopped
some three feet from where she stood. "How many
times have I told you to watch where you're going,
young man?"

"I'm sorry, Jenna," the young towhead said, his dark
blue eyes wide, miserable. "I didn't see you."

"You can hardly fault the boy," the gray-eyed
stranger said. "The way you came storming out of the
café, you're lucky I didn't trample you myself."

"I don't recall asking your opinion," she retorted,
hands on her hips. Her earlier imaginings about this
man swirled up to taunt her, mock her. Men! They
were either romantic fantasies or real-life barbarians.

"Timmy is my brother, and I'll thank you to mind
your own business." To Timmy she said, "You march

straight over to the hotel, young man, and see to Bess's lunch."

Her brother's face brightened. "Does that mean the doc says Bessie's not sick anymore?"

"He says she's just fine." Jenna's voice softened, and she decided a little exaggeration wouldn't hurt. Timmy had kept most of his feelings about Bess's illness to himself, but Jenna knew how worried he'd been. "I think she'd love some chicken soup."

"Then I'll make sure she gets some," Timmy said, though he made no move to leave. His gaze had settled with obvious awe on the stranger and the tied-down Colt he wore strapped to his lean hips. "You a gunfighter, mister?"

The man grinned, and Jenna felt her pulses race at how the smile seemed to transform his face. Already much too good-looking, the smile was positively devastating. Disconcerted, she failed to notice the man did not answer her brother's question.

"Get going, Timmy," she said. "Now."

"I just wanted to find you," the boy cajoled. "I needed to show you something."

Jenna recognized the spark of mischief now evident in that impish face and wondered ruefully if she was about to be gifted with a lizard or a bullfrog. Despite her frazzled state, she did not repeat her directive that Timmy get himself over to the hotel. Instead she waited, feeling some of the tension drain out of her. Her brother's boundless enthusiasm had ever proved a ray of sunshine on the bleakest of days.

If only Mr. Buckskin would be on his way, she could actually be enjoying this. But he just stood there, regarding them both with those remarkable gray eyes.

Steeling herself, Jenna determined to ignore him. She gave her full attention to Timmy, who laboriously unbuttoned the bottom two buttons of his shirt. Sticking his hand in the opening, he rummaged about his waistline for several fret-filled seconds before he found what he was looking for. With a triumphant grin he extracted his prize—a foot-long garter snake—and promptly thrust it at her.

Jenna had her hand out, but Mr. Buckskin was faster. He snatched the wriggling creature away from a startled Timmy.

"You shouldn't scare your sister like that, boy," he said. His voice was mild, the disapproval in his words, not his tone.

Jenna stood there, her mouth open, staring at him. The man was looking thoroughly pleased with himself. And it was then it struck her. He was congratulating himself—for rescuing her! She almost burst out laughing.

Almost.

Instead she smiled. A most beguiling smile. She found the notion of this imposing man trying so hard to spare her female sensibilities unaccountably endearing.

To cover her conflicting emotions she focused on her brother, letting out an exasperated sigh. "Timothy Riordan, you already have two rabbits, a lizard, and Veronica. You cannot have any more pets. I simply won't permit it."

"But Veronica's a cow. She's not the same as a real live snake! Please, Jenna . . ."

Jenna could tell she wasn't going to win this one. She wasted no more energy trying. "We'll see," she hedged. Sticking her hand out toward Mr. Buckskin, she took a delicious pleasure in watching his jaw drop. But his gaze was unreadable as he deposited the snake into her outstretched palm.

Jenna studied the wiggling reptile, looking it straight in one of its small yellow eyes. "So, what do you think of traveling to California?"

The snake's only opinion was the flicking of its tiny tongue.

She shook her head, handing it back to Timmy. "All right," she relented, "but that's positively the very last one, you understand?"

Timmy let out a happy whoop, then whirled and raced off toward the hotel.

"Don't you dare show that thing to Bessie," Jenna called after him. Bess had never exhibited the same tolerance for Timmy's precious menagerie.

"I won't," he yelled back.

Jenna was fairly certain he wouldn't be so foolhardy, but nevertheless she would keep her eye on the hotel window when she headed back—to see if a certain garter snake came flying past.

Knowing she had no choice, she returned her attention to the stranger. She would apologize for her brother and be on her way. She was surprised to find a look of grudging respect on his face and a very real puzzlement.

"Please excuse Timmy," Jenna began haltingly. What was it about this man that seemed to tie her tongue in knots?

"I'm the one who should apologize. I . . ."

The café door opened and Bart Jacobs sauntered out. He stopped dead, his gaze shifting from Jenna to the gray-eyed stranger and back again. There was a menace in Jacobs's eyes Jenna had never seen before.

"I'll thank you to keep your distance from the lady, mister," Jacobs snarled, coming over to put a possessive arm around Jenna's waist. To Jenna he said, "I finished up with Langston. Now I can take you back to your hotel."

Jenna swayed. Not because she felt faint but from the overwhelming nearness of Jacobs's unclean body. She wanted nothing more than to slap him for daring to touch her, but she couldn't afford to offend the man. If Major Gallagher didn't come through, she might yet need the sutler's help in securing a guide. Resolutely she straightened, and as unobtrusively as she could manage she extricated herself from the man's grasp.

The stranger's gray eyes were glittering with a new contempt. Her stomach clenched, but she dared not betray her true reaction to Jacobs's insolence.

"Ah, Miss Riordan." Jenna was grateful to see Keith Gallagher coming out of the café. "How fortuitous," he said, "I see you've already met Caleb."

"Who?"

"Caleb Harper. The man I told you about."

Jenna's heart sank to her toes. Surely the fates could not be that unkind. "No . . . he isn't . . ."

"The guide I spoke of." Gallagher nodded.

"I'm what?" Harper stiffened, glaring at the cavalry officer.

"Miss Riordan and her family need a guide to continue their journey to California," Gallagher said amiably. "I told her you'd be interested."

"And why the hell would you tell her a thing like that?"

Jenna took a step back from the anger in that handsome face, but her family's desperate need for a trail scout fired her words. "I really would appreciate your considering it, Mr. Harper."

"No."

She winced.

"I'll talk to him," Gallagher assured her, apparently not in the least put off by his friend's temper. "You go on ahead. He'll be by directly."

"Like hell!" Harper snapped.

"Go on, Miss Riordan," Gallagher said again, shooing her away. "It'll be all right, you'll see."

Uncertain, Jenna nodded. Daring a last glance at the

intimidating Caleb Harper, she allowed Jacobs to escort her toward the hotel.

Caleb watched Jenna Riordan walk away, sickened by the sight of Bart Jacobs hovering at her side. Though she seemed to be doing her best to keep space between herself and the odious sutler, Caleb couldn't help feeling a measure of disgust. Why didn't she just slap the lecherous bastard and send him on his way?

Furious, he wheeled on Gallagher. "What the hell was that all about?"

Quickly and calmly Gallagher explained the Riordans' need for a guide.

Caleb swore explosively. "Three tenderfoot families heading to California, and you want *me* to take them there? Have you lost your mind?"

"Not all the way to California," Keith said reasonably. "Just get them to Bascom. Someone else can take them the rest of the way."

"You have lost your mind."

"Hear me out. It makes perfect sense, you'll see." He gripped Caleb's arm and propelled him toward the nearest alley. Caleb jerked his arm free but followed anyway. He could already tell he wasn't going to like this. Not one bit.

In the cul de sac Gallagher glanced about as though to assure himself they were alone. Even so his voice was barely more than a whisper. "I overheard the Riordan woman talking about needing a guide," he said. "And it came to me all at once. Inspiration straight from the Almighty Himself."

"You sure of your directions?" Caleb gritted. "I'm catching the scent of sulphur and brimstone from over here."

"Just listen," Gallagher said. "We get hold of one of

the pioneer wagons, put in a false bottom, and secrete the guns on board. Who would ever suspect?"

"No one will have to suspect. Three families will make a Comanche target in and of themselves. The Spencers will be a bonus."

"Not with you along."

"And how do you figure that?"

"You're known by the Indians hereabouts. Respected. They wouldn't attack wagons led by you."

Caleb lifted his hat, raking a hand through his shaggy hair. "This is crazy." He resettled the hat with an angry jerk. "Worse than that, you're involving civilians, risking their lives."

"They're risking their lives by being here. Whether you guide them or not, they're going. They'll just get someone else to lead the way. And that someone else may not be a man who can talk peace with the likes of Iron Fist."

"I won't do it."

"You will, Caleb. That's an order."

Caleb bristled. "I'm not in the army."

"You work for the army."

"That can be fixed in a hurry."

Gallagher muttered an exasperated oath. "Can you think of a better idea? One that accomplishes everyone's goal?"

Caleb had no answer to that, but he wasn't ready to give in. Not yet. "There has to be another way. Order up more troops. Get soldiers from Larned, Leavenworth, Union."

"Bascom is my first command, Caleb. I'm not going running to other forts to bail out my behind on this. We get the guns through, then we take care of the *comancheros*, then—"

"Then you're the big hero." Caleb made no attempt

to conceal his disgust. "Just how many lives are you willing to pay for that promotion, Keith?"

Gallagher gripped Caleb's shirtfront, his eyes narrowed to slits as his fury rose to match Caleb's own. For the space of a heartbeat neither man moved. Then Gallagher let his hands drop away. His voice was weary. "I'm not out here to cost lives, Caleb. I'm here to safeguard them. I would have thought you of all people would know that."

Caleb's own fists uncurled at his sides. "I knew it. I just wanted to make sure you knew it." He let out a resigned breath. "I'll talk to the Riordan woman."

"It'll work out. You'll see. For the Riordans, for the army, for everyone."

While Gallagher set about arranging the particulars for the gun switch, Caleb marched toward the hotel. He was not looking forward to this. He just hoped Bart Jacobs had made himself scarce. If he crossed paths with the smelly little varmint one more time today, he wasn't going to hold himself responsible. Especially if he had his dirty hands anywhere near Jenna Riordan.

Unwillingly Caleb pictured her in his mind.

Beautiful.

Unpredictable.

A lethal combination.

He had thought he was doing her a favor to corral the garter snake from her brother. Instead she'd been downright amused by his intervention.

And somehow *pleased*.

She'd smiled at him. A dazzling, bewitching smile that lit up her mountain-lake eyes until they seemed brighter than the sky itself. A man could drown in eyes like that, and gladly. A man could even forget a long-ago vow to never again play fool to any woman.

He swore, forcing his thoughts to the job ahead. What he would be playing was nursemaid—nursemaid to a caravan of tenderfoots that included a woman who would wear hoop skirts and silk at high noon in Council Grove.

Caleb could only pray Gallagher was right. That what he had agreed to wouldn't get them all killed.

4

His eyes had been gray. A dark, brooding gray. Jenna couldn't get them out of her mind as she hurried up the stairs to her hotel room. Cold gray eyes. Angry gray eyes. Bemused gray eyes. Set in a most handsome face.

Her heart thudded, despite her best efforts to slow it. Blast the man! He had intrigued her from a distance; close up he infuriated her. Yet somehow intrigued her all the more.

Caleb Harper.

A good name. A strong name. A no-nonsense name. Caleb Harper and his mesmerizing gray eyes.

She paused outside her room, trembling. What on earth was the matter with her? Thank heaven she had convinced Bart Jacobs to go on ahead, to alert the Holts and Kovels to their having procured a guide. Jacobs had balked at first, reminding her Harper had not yet agreed, but she had been adamant. Whether or not Harper agreed hadn't seemed nearly as important, at that moment, as having Bart Jacobs anywhere but at her side. She needed these minutes alone to collect herself. Bess and Timmy depended on her to be the calm one, the sensible one. She couldn't let them see her so agitated.

Taking a deep breath, Jenna forced a smile, then opened the door. The smile grew genuine. Bess was sitting up in bed, her ash-blond hair tumbled about her shoulders. Timmy was perched beside her atop the bedcovers, dealing out playing cards. It had been a long time since her sister and brother had been able to have fun together. Jenna couldn't help feeling better just looking at them.

"I trust you remembered to see to your sister's lunch, Timmy," she said, crossing to the bed.

He nodded, not taking his eyes from his cards. "It should be up in a couple of minutes."

"And what about that other little matter? The one you showed me out on the boardwalk?"

"I put it in the bottom drawer of the bureau."

Jenna rolled her eyes. At least it wasn't likely to slither across the floor anytime soon. She hoped.

Thankfully Bess paid no attention to their exchange. Her pale eyes danced merrily as she smiled up at Jenna. "And how did you enjoy your lunch with Mr. Jacobs?"

Jenna made a face. "My nose may never recover." She put a hand on her abdomen. "Nor my poor stomach."

Bess giggled.

"Do you think he's ever had a bath in his whole life?" Timmy asked, obviously awed by the very possibility of a bath-free existence. Her brother's affection for cleanliness was on the same scale as a fox's affection for a hound dog.

"I wouldn't even want to hazard a guess," Jenna said. "But I'm afraid just sitting near him for the past hour has made me long for a bath of my own."

"Don't worry," Bess said. "I thought as much." She

gestured toward the wooden tub in the far corner of the room. "I had Timmy tell the maid. She should be up with the hot water shortly."

"Have I ever told you what a truly wonderful sister you are?" Jenna reached over to brush back a lock of hair that had wisped across Bess's forehead. "But we really should be more charitable toward Mr. Jacobs. He's been quite a help to us these past weeks. Besides—" Jenna hesitated, not wanting to get her brother and sister's hopes up, then deciding they deserved to know. "We may be traveling with him again shortly."

"He found a scout?" Bess cried, excited.

Timmy leapt up, cards scattering every which way. "Is it that man in the buckskin jacket? The one with the tied-down gun? Is it, Jenna? Is it?"

"Easy now," Jenna cautioned. "Both of you. I'm not sure yet. But a Major Gallagher thinks he can talk the man into escorting us."

"Yippee!" Timmy yelped. "I'm gonna ask him to show me how to use that gun."

"You'll do no such thing, young man! A gun like that isn't for killing rabbits or deer. It's for killing—" She stopped, appalled by what she had been about to say. How dare she make such a presumption? Practically every man she'd seen since leaving St. Joe wore a sidearm. Why was she judging Caleb Harper so harshly? Irritated—as much with herself as with her brother— she pointed toward the door. "I want you to march downstairs and find out what's keeping your sister's lunch and my bath. Go on now. This minute!"

"Aw, Jenna . . ."

"Go!"

He went.

Jenna sank onto the bed and gave her head a sad shake. "I don't know why I'm being so cross with him."

"Don't fret about it," Bess said, patting the back of Jenna's hand. "He's fine. He told me about the man in buckskin. He couldn't quite decide between comparisons—Jim Bowie or Wild Bill Hickock."

Jenna managed a half smile. "He may not be too far from wrong. Mr. Harper was quite . . . imposing."

"Do you think he'll be our guide?"

"I don't know." Jenna was still annoyed with herself for snapping at Timmy. She supposed she could blame it on her preoccupation with Caleb Harper. But there was more to it than that. She cast a worried frown at her sister. "Tell me the truth, Bessie. Do you think I should be stricter with Timmy? That maybe I give him too much freedom?"

Bess pondered the question for a long minute, then said quietly, "I don't think you give yourself enough."

Jenna frowned. "What does that mean?"

"It means you've done a wonderful job with Timmy. And with me too, I might add. But you've got your own life. You forget that sometimes. Talking about Pa this morning made me realize that."

Jenna marched over to the dressing screen and stepped behind it. "You're talking nonsense."

"Am I? You've had to be mother *and* father to Timmy and me since long before Pa died."

Jenna's heart lurched at the guilt threading her sister's voice. She peered out at her. "Do you think I regret that? Is that what this is all about? Because I don't, you know. Not for one minute."

Bess's blue eyes were wide, serious. "You're not getting any younger."

"Rebecca Riordan, I'm twenty-two!" Jenna stomped from behind the screen, planting her hands on her hips in mock outrage. But the smile she had hoped to coax from her sister failed to appear.

"Most girls your age are married with two babes by now," Bess went on sadly.

Jenna yanked at the emerald silk, tugging it off and tossing it atop the fold-out screen. "How long have you been worrying about such foolishness?"

"Don't tell me you haven't thought of it."

Jenna peeled off her remaining layers of clothing, leaving only her chemise and pantalets, then pulled on her blue satin robe, not bothering to secure the sash. "I'll tell you I haven't, because I haven't. And I don't want to hear another word about it."

But Bess had apparently had this bottled up inside her for a long time. She would not be dissuaded. "It's because of Timmy and me that you're not married. Don't you think I know that? At least some of the beaus who came around back home didn't care about your views on slavery. What sent them running was your being responsible for us."

Jenna turned away, tugging at the pins that bound up her hair. "Whatever gave you such a ridiculous notion?"

"Stephen Farraday asked you to marry him."

Jenna stilled. She hadn't thought of Stephen Farraday in more than two years. "How did you know about him?" she asked softly.

Color rose in Bess's cheeks. "You were sitting on the veranda one night. Papa was at the shop. I came down for a glass of milk and I overheard Stephen propose. And I overheard you say yes."

"I was just . . . swept up in the moment," Jenna said. "When I talked to him further—"

"When you told him he would have to accept Timmy and me into the bargain, he changed his mind." Bess's voice wavered slightly, but she plunged on. "It was especially because of me. 'I can't have my bride giving over her life to an invalid'—that's what he said."

"He was a fool!" Jenna snapped. "An irresponsible boy."

"But you were in love with him."

Jenna paced across the room and back, desperate to ease the pain on her sister's fragile features. She could scarcely bear it when she thought of Bess tormenting herself with this secret for more than two years. "I was in love—" she admitted slowly, "with the man I thought Stephen Farraday to be. When I discovered his true nature, I told him he need not call on me again. Bessie, I can stand here this moment and truthfully tell you I cannot even recollect fully what the man looked like. Please, do not think I've been pining away for him all this time."

"No. I know you haven't. Because you convinced yourself it didn't matter. But what about the next time?"

"The man I marry would have to love you and Timmy."

"But what if he didn't?"

"Then I wouldn't love him. It's that simple."

"Jenna—"

She closed her eyes. "Bessie, don't do this to yourself. I have no plans to marry. Not now or anytime in the foreseeable future." She forced lightness into her tone. "Besides I have yet to find a serious-minded, practical man with sense enough to have me."

Bess had to laugh at that. "Oh, Jenna, you could never marry such a curmudgeon. I see you married to a pirate! Or maybe an outlaw! A dashing brigand, who'd bring you flowers, write you love poems, then sweep you off your feet."

"There, you see!" Jenna pronounced. "Such a romantic rogue would have to love you and Timmy. How could he not?"

Bess started yet another protest, but a knock on the

door interrupted her. Gratefully Jenna hurried to answer it. "We'll finish this conversation later." Over her shoulder she said, "I love you, Rebecca Riordan. Don't you ever forget that."

Bess's eyes were so openly adoring, Jenna had to take a steadying breath before she gripped the doorknob. "So what do you think? My bath or your lunch?" Without waiting for an answer, she swung the door wide.

In the hallway stood Caleb Harper.

Jenna blinked, stunned.

He seemed to collect himself first. He yanked his hat from his head, his dark hair spilling in soft waves to the collar of his buckskin jacket. Then he cleared his throat. But whatever he was going to say remained unspoken as his gaze trailed inexorably downward, past her face to settle on the rise and fall of her breasts.

Jenna gasped, indignant, then froze. Her own gaze followed his. To her horror she could all but see the coral tips of her breasts peeking out from the gaping front of her beribboned chemise. She had forgotten to bind up her robe! Her cheeks burning, Jenna jerked the sides of the satin garment together, desperately working the sash. "I—I thought you were the maid."

"No, ma'am." He looked at the floor, twisting his hat in front of him. Her own embarrassment was so acute that for a moment it hadn't registered. He too was blushing!

Jenna backed into the room, then whirled to dart for the dressing screen. "Come in," she squeaked. "But leave the door open." Quickly she scrambled into the cotton dress she had worn earlier in the day.

Harper's booted footfalls told her he'd come about halfway into the room.

"I'm Rebecca Riordan," her sister said from the bed. "Please excuse my attire, sir. I didn't know we'd be receiving guests."

"I'm not a guest," Caleb said, introducing himself. "And pardon the intrusion. I've come to talk about riding scout for you and your family. I've decided to take the job."

Jenna's brows furrowed at how matter-of-factly he said the words, especially after he had so adamantly opposed the idea earlier in front of the café. She supposed she should be impressed by Major Gallagher's powers of persuasion. Instead she felt unaccountably ill at ease. But then what did she expect? She'd just stood half naked in front of the man! With shaking fingers she finished buttoning the last mother-of-pearl circlet at the base of her throat and hurried from behind the screen.

"I'm so glad to hear you say you'll accompany us, Mr. Harper. The others in our party will be pleased as well." There was no undoing what had happened in the doorway. She would bluff this out, then die of humiliation later.

His expression, which had been cordial when he looked at Bess, grew more distant and discomfited when he faced her. But his tone was all business. "I intend to say this only once. I'm not just your guide. I'm the wagon master. What I say is law. Understood?"

"Of course. That only makes sense. You know the terr—"

"I want to speak to your menfolk," he cut in. "Set things straight from the first."

"Menfolk? You mean Mr. Holt? Mr. Kovel?"

"If that's their names. Your menfolk too. Your father? Older brother? Husband?"

He arched an eyebrow at the last and Jenna unconsciously fidgeted with the top button of her dress, assuring herself it was indeed fastened securely. "There are only the three of us Riordans. Bess, Timmy, and myself." At his look of incredulity, she added, "We were traveling with a very large wagon train until Bess took sick."

His gaze trailed up and down her slender body. "There's a lot of physical work involved in taking a wagon across country. Chopping wood, handling a team, building campfires . . ."

That gaze was suddenly much too intimate. Jenna felt as if she were again attired in her robe, perhaps less than her robe.

"I suppose you had a lot of volunteers," he drawled. There was no mistaking his meaning.

Again Jenna's cheeks burned, but this time she faced him squarely. "Your insinuations are not only unfounded, Mr. Harper, they're highly insulting. I have money to pay you for your scouting services. There will be no other payment," she paused for emphasis, "of any kind."

Their gazes locked for long seconds. Jenna wanted nothing more than to flinch, to look away, to be free of that suddenly intimidating stare. But she didn't back down. In a flash of insight she had the feeling he was testing her. And that she dare not fail. Caleb Harper was not a man to whom one could show weakness and come away unscathed. There was something about this man, something hidden, enigmatic. Dangerous. She sensed a hardness in him that made her almost afraid of him.

But she wasn't afraid.

"Be ready to leave in two days," he said at last.

"Fine."

"I'll still want to meet with the other two families."

"I'm sure that can be arranged."

"And I want to check through all your wagons. Make sure no one is carrying any excess weight, that you have the proper supplies, that sort of thing."

"Whatever you think best, Mr. Harper." Jenna

prayed her expression conveyed more self-assurance than she felt.

"Two days, Miss Riordan." He settled his hat on his head and was gone.

Somehow Jenna convinced her legs to move. She crossed the room and shut the door, then sagged against it.

It would take up to two months to reach California. Two months of hot days and cold nights. Two months of bad food and worse weather.

Two months of the enigmatic and dangerous Caleb Harper.

5

From her perch in the wagon box Jenna stared out at the vast, rolling emptiness of the Kansas plain. It had been a week since they'd left Council Grove, and except for the evidence offered by the wheel-rutted road they followed, she could have believed they were the only people on earth. Never had she experienced such an overwhelming sense of isolation, aloneness.

Sweat trickled beneath the brim of her blue poke bonnet and trailed down her forehead to sting her eyes. It was high noon and hot. She had hoped they would have pulled up for "nooning" by now. But the Holts, driving the lead wagon, had yet to signal it was time to stop.

Jenna clucked at her four-horse team and sighed. All about her, brassy green was giving way to burnt summer brown. High sandy hills were broken up only by the muddy, meandering ribbon of the Arkansas River, along which they traveled. The river's own monotony was hardly better served by the grassy islets that dotted its middle. Even the occasional grove of stunted cottonwoods seemed more an eyesore than a break in the daily sameness. Life for the Riordans and their fellow emigrants had settled into a familiar, even monotonous routine.

Monotonous—Jenna considered with a sudden wry twist of her lips—save for Caleb Harper.

Just thinking his name had the power to change her mood. From melancholy to alert. She stood, holding the reins loosely, and scanned the horizon. Any moment now he would come riding in on his big black gelding, looking for all the world like some grand, mythological centaur—man and beast, one. Her heart thrummed faster just to think of it.

As a wagon master Harper was proving tough, but fair-minded. As a man he was proving impossibly aloof. And Jenna had had just about all of that she could abide. Men had courted her, flattered her, even at times villified her, but never had one so pointedly ignored her.

And to her mounting chagrin, the more he ignored her the more he fascinated her.

She longed to talk to him, ask him questions—personal questions she knew she had no right to ask. What made a man choose the kind of life he led? Had he been born and raised in the West, or did he seek it out when he came of age? How much did he know about Indians? Wild animals? Had he ever used that gun on his hip against another human being?

Jenna's cheeks burned, and it had nothing to do with the day's scorching temperature. She tried, for the thousandth time, to tell herself the man was merely a diversion, a convenient distraction to keep her from thinking overmuch about the ultimate uncertainty of the trail ahead. No matter how routine the days were she knew it could all turn around in an instant. Danger could lie behind the next rock, the next curve in the road. From rattlesnakes to flash floods to the name Elliot Langston had hardly dared whisper—*comancheros*.

Yet for a diversion Caleb Harper was proving a disturbingly intimate one. She had memorized everything about the man. The way he looked, the way he talked, the way he moved. He reminded her of nothing so much as a tiger she'd once seen in a traveling side show when she was a little girl. All lean muscle, fluid grace, and bound-up energy. The tiger had been chained. And, Jenna suspected, so was Caleb Harper—tethered to a group of lowly tenderfoots.

Again she tugged at the reins, convincing the right-side lead bay to stop snatching snippets of buffalo grass as he plodded along the dusty trail. "Caleb Harper," she muttered aloud, "tonight you're going to notice me if it kills us both."

"What did you say, Jenna?"

Jenna jumped slightly, twisting to peer into the dim interior of the canvas-topped wagon. "Nothing, Bessie," she murmured. "Go back to sleep."

"I wasn't sleeping. I was just resting my eyes."

Jenna forced a smile. Though her sister was trying to be brave, Jenna knew Bess had slept only fitfully since leaving Council Grove. That was why Jenna insisted she ride in the wagon during the day rather than walk alongside as Timmy did. Thankfully Bess had shown no evidence of a relapse, but still Jenna worried about her.

"We should be stopping soon," Jenna said, again checking the horizon for any sign of Harper. She supposed Emmet Holt too was awaiting orders from the scout before pulling up. Harper might stop them an hour early at night if they came upon a particularly good grazing area for the livestock, but otherwise he kept them to a strict timetable.

Every morning at four o'clock the lookout on duty would rouse the camp. Jenna and Timmy would clamber up, stow their bedding, harness the team, and get breakfast started—all before the crack of dawn. By seven they were on the trail.

Nooning allowed an hour to feed and rest the team and themselves, but then they were on the move again until dusk. Mending, baking, a little gossiping—and it was time to turn in for the night. The next day the seventeen-hour routine would begin again.

But Jenna did not begrudge the hard work and harsh conditions. Each day brought them fifteen to twenty miles closer to California—to Uncle William and their new life. If only she could get over this peculiar fascination Caleb Harper seemed to have aroused in her, she would have no complaints at all.

"No sign of Mr. Harper?" Bess asked, climbing over the wagon seat to sit beside Jenna.

Jenna shook her head.

"Are you going to be making cow eyes at him again if he rides in for lunch?"

Jenna nearly fell off the wagon. "B-Bess Riordan," she stammered, "I do not make cow eyes at the man!"

"It's not just Timmy who follows the man around like a puppy whenever he's about."

"I've done no such thing!" Jenna pursed her lips indignantly, but inwardly she quailed. Was she that transparent? Lord above, had Harper noticed?

"Oh, Jenna," Bess went on, giving her sister a playful nudge, "I'm happy for you. I think you and Mr. Harper would make a wonderful match."

"Match?" Jenna squeaked, horrified. "Match! I find the man vaguely interesting and you're . . . you're marrying me off to the insufferable oaf!"

Bess laughed. "Admit it, Jenna. He's the most fascinating man you've ever met. And you can't stand the fact that he hasn't accepted a single one of your invitations to dinner."

"I was just being polite. He is the wagon master. He—"

"There he is!" Bess pointed.

Jenna's heart skipped a beat, but she deliberately looked the other way. Whatever was the matter with her? Her earlier challenge, that the man was going to notice her or else, rang hollow. As usual just seeing him was enough to turn her to apple jelly. Still, she managed a covert glance, watching him gallop up, riding first to the Holt wagon, bypassing her own without so much as a nod, then trotting back to the Kovels and Jacobs.

She straightened, pretending not to be hurt by the slight. "You see? He is insufferable. And impossibly rude."

Bess giggled. "I think he likes you."

"And I think we should check the canvas; obviously you're getting too much sun back there!" With a quick jerk Jenna brought the horses to a halt, then wrapped the reins around the brake handle. Climbing down, she reached up to assist Bess in doing the same.

"What's for lunch?" Timmy asked, ambling over to join his sisters.

"Salt pork and beans," Jenna said, her gaze unwillingly following Harper as he tied off his horse to the rear of the Kovel wagon. He didn't so much as glance her way.

"Salt pork!" Timmy howled. "Why can't we have something different? Mrs. Holt baked an apple pie yesterday."

"And, as I recall, you ate two pieces," Jenna reminded him sternly. "One of which she'd given you to bring back to me."

Timmy toed the ground with his boot. "I didn't think you'd mind so much."

Jenna shook her head, once again amazed by the

power Caleb Harper wielded over her temper. "I don't mind. But we're still having salt pork. I'll whip up some honey biscuits though, all right? Now see to the horses and Veronica, while Bess and I see to lunch."

"Yes, ma'am."

The physical activity of preparing their food eased much of the tension coiling in Jenna's stomach. She relaxed a little. Within half an hour she was ladling out a hot, hearty meal to her sister and brother.

"Mind if I join you?"

Jenna looked up, startled to be peering into gray eyes, gray eyes shaded by the black brim of his Stetson, gray eyes that gave no hint about what Caleb Harper might be thinking.

"Please do," she said reflexively, handing him the plate she'd just filled for herself. "I'll get another." She hurried to the back of the wagon, using the time to collect her wits. The man was not going to fluster her again.

"I didn't mean join you for lunch," he said, though he accepted the fork Timmy handed him. "I meant I had something to say to you. I've already told the others."

"Oh." Jenna felt the beginnings of a blush, but she fought it down. She gestured toward one of the crates Timmy had set out in the minimal shade provided by the wagon. "Please sit."

He sat down and dug into his meal. Jenna experienced a brief rush of pleasure at the look of approval he gave her honey biscuits. She ignored how surprised he also looked.

"Until I say different," he said between mouthfuls, "I want you all to stay close to the wagons these next couple of days." He looked at Timmy. "That means you too, son. I'll bring back a rabbit or two for cooking. No hunting. All right?"

"Why not?" Timmy complained, then brightened. "Have you seen some Injuns, Mr. Harper?"

"Not exactly."

"What do you mean?" Jenna took a seat on the crate opposite him, his ability to intimidate her surpassed for the moment by her concern for her family.

He shrugged. "You don't have to see a Comanche to know he's there."

Jenna took a deep breath. "Are we in danger?"

"I don't think so. From the sign I'd guess it's a hunting party. Maybe a dozen braves. But I still don't want anyone straying off alone."

"What about you? You ride off ahead of us every day."

"I can watch out for myself, Miss Riordan. I've been doing it for quite some time."

She winced at his clipped tone, wondering why he reserved it almost exclusively for her. So often she'd watched him talking, even laughing with the others on the train. But for her he seemed to have no patience at all. "I only meant that we'd be lost . . . I mean, in great danger if . . . if anything happened to you, Mr. Harper."

"It didn't occur to me that you meant anything else, Miss Riordan." With that he rose and excused himself, leaving his half-eaten meal on the crate.

"I'm still gonna ask him to show me how to use that gun," Timmy said, staring after him.

Jenna didn't bother to protest. As usual Caleb Harper had left her feeling hurt, strangely rejected. And though she wasn't at all accustomed to feeling that way, she supposed she'd best get used to it. It seemed to come with the territory whenever Harper came near her.

She recalled the day they'd left Council Grove. He'd had to go over every square inch of her wagon before he pronounced it fit. And that came only after the wagon had spent two days being repaired at his orders, for he'd said it would have fallen apart midway to Santa Fe if he hadn't noticed the wheels had begun to separate from the iron rims that banded them.

"You're lucky to have Caleb's expertise," Major Gallagher had told her. "I'd hate to think what could have happened to you and your family if you'd had a wagon breakdown on the trail."

No doubt Harper had thought her an incompetent ninny, taking her siblings cross-country without having the slightest notion of what she was doing.

With a sigh Jenna picked up his plate and scraped the leavings into the embers of the cook fire.

"I was right," Bess said, coming over to help with the clean-up. "He does like you."

"Not now, Bessie. Please." She was in no mood.

"He does. He really does."

Jenna scowled. "The man hates me."

Her sister shook her head. "He's so busy *not* watching you that he doesn't notice me watching *him*. It's the way Mr. Holt watches Mrs. Holt sometimes. You know, at night before they sneak away from the wagons for a little while."

"Bess Riordan!" Jenna cried, scandalized. "You're not supposed to be aware of things like that."

"You just wait and see. Mr. Harper won't be able to hide his feelings much longer."

Jenna rolled her eyes, supremely unconvinced. "All right, let's say you're right—the man likes me. Could you tell me then, please, why he has such a peculiar way of showing it?"

Bess thought a moment. "That's an odd one," she admitted. "Maybe he's bashful."

"Bashful? Caleb Harper?"

"Sure, why not? He's rough and tough on the outside,

but how much experience can he have with women out here in the middle of nowhere?"

"Somehow I can't imagine him being deprived," Jenna scoffed acidly.

"You're not being objective. I think he *is* bashful, at least where you're concerned." Bess let out a dreamy sigh. "And, of course, there's always the chance some wretched woman broke his heart."

Jenna groaned. "Enough, young lady. I thought I was the romantic in the family."

Minutes later Bess was settling herself in the back of the wagon, while Jenna climbed up in the driver's seat. As she gigged the horses forward Jenna tried to dismiss Bess's fanciful musings. Her sister had ever possessed a keen insight into human nature, her fragile health often forcing her to experience life as spectator rather than participant. But surely she couldn't be reading Caleb Harper right. Bashful? A broken heart? Jenna shook her head. About as likely as a snowstorm before nightfall.

Still, as she drove out she couldn't help but glance skyward—into the blazing hot sun. She wouldn't mind a little snow. She wouldn't mind at all.

Caleb tightened the cinch on the gelding's saddle and remounted. Touching his spurs to the animal's sides, he rode away from the wagons at a gallop. He kept the pace steady for several minutes before he eased back on the reins and allowed the horse to slow.

For nearly an hour he rode west, then circled north. He could no longer see the wagons, but he knew just where they were. He could also predict where they would be in an hour, or in any other given space of time. He kept himself far enough away to spot trouble, close enough to sound a warning. What he had told

Timmy Riordan was the truth. You didn't have to see Comanches to know they were there.

But now he was making it his business to find them. He was all but certain it was a hunting party. But an outlaw as cunning as Enrique Valdez could just be making it look that way. For the sake of his pioneer charges Caleb wanted to see these Comanches for himself.

Keeping to cutbanks and dry washes, he found them just before dusk. Moving like a Comanche himself, he ground-tied his horse then kept low, making his way to the rim of the dry creekbed. He counted eleven braves. Quohadi Comanche. He recognized several of them— Two Trees, Lame Deer, and others from Eagle Dancer's tribe. Iron Fist was not among them. Bare-chested, dressed in breechclouts and leggings, but no war paint, they were hunkered down around a small fire, cooking some of the meat cut from the carcasses of two gutted deer hanging from a nearby tree.

Briefly he considered riding up to parley with them but decided against it. This late they would insist he join them to smoke a pipe, then spend the night regaling him with tales of bravery. It would be an unforgivable insult to refuse. And he could hardly explain to them he had to get back to a bunch of emigrants who were unwittingly running guns through their territory.

Scowling, he lifted his hat to rake a callused hand through sweat-damp hair. He'd best be on his way. He'd told the Holts to circle up about six and post sentinels as usual, that he wouldn't be back until after dark. But he didn't want to be gone any longer than absolutely necessary. Jacobs could handle himself in a wilderness emergency, but the Holts and Kovels were out of their element. And the Riordans . . .

Caleb tried to shut off the thought but failed. As always, the Riordans were uppermost in his mind. They had been ever since he'd left Council Grove. Bess with her quiet acceptance. Timmy with his youthful spirit of adventure. And Jenna . . . He couldn't even begin to assess where his thoughts were headed regarding that woman.

"Damn Keith Gallagher to hell," he gritted, spurring his horse into a run when he'd left the Comanches well behind. Why in blazes had he ever let the young fool talk him into going along with this madness?

"I had the guns put aboard the Riordan wagon," Gallagher had told him that last night in Council Grove. "Jacobs might get wind of something if we used his. And the Holts and Kovels are already loaded down with more than their teams can handle."

"In other words," Caleb said through clenched teeth, "since the Riordans are using good sense and traveling light, let's overtax *their* horses. And take full advantage of Jenna Riordan's trust in that uniform you're wearing."

At least Gallagher had had the good grace to flush slightly. "They shouldn't have much trouble until you get to the Cimarron Cutoff."

"The cutoff?" Caleb swore. The cutoff was a favorite of Santa Fe traders. A branch in the trail, it snaked southwestward across the panhandles of Oklahoma and Texas and into northeastern New Mexico Territory. Its advantage was cutting substantial distance off the trip to Santa Fe. Its disadvantage was being dry as dust.

"I'm not chancing the cutoff, Keith. Jackrabbits take three-days' rations and a canteen to get across it. The Riordans would never make it with the extra weight of the Spencers."

"But I've got it all figured out," Gallagher insisted. "I'll ride on ahead with the men. We'll get to Bascom, load up on supplies, and be back to the cutoff before you can even get there. Get the Riordans to the cutoff, and you're home free. It'll all take less than three weeks."

"In less than three weeks those people can be dead."

"That won't happen, Caleb."

Gallagher could make all the promises he liked, but in the end they would be as empty as the Kansas plains if word got out about the guns. Caleb doubted even he could forestall a Comanche raid if the Indians knew they could count one hundred Spencers as their prize.

The sun had been gone over an hour when he topped a small hillock and spotted the wagons circled up around a half dozen blazing campfires. His gaze flicked past the Holts, Kovels, and Jacobs. Somehow the campsite seemed to belong to the Riordans alone.

He couldn't even see her yet, and he knew precisely how she looked—every soft curve of her slender body, every corn-silk hair on her head. And a smile that could light the way for a blind man.

He cursed under his breath. These were not thoughts he welcomed. He had made it a point to stay clear of her. But Jenna Riordan was proving very difficult to ignore. She was like some kind of magnet drawing him in, even when he tried very hard to move in the opposite direction.

"Whoa up there!" a voice called.

Caleb jerked back on the reins, annoyed that thoughts of Jenna Riordan had made him careless. He guided the gelding toward the voice. It had come from behind a cougar-sized boulder some hundred feet in front of the wagons.

"That you, Mr. Harper?"

Caleb grinned at young Sam Holt and dismounted. "You're getting better at this, Sam. I didn't even see you this time."

"Honest?" The too-serious thirteen-year-old smiled

shyly. "I was just tryin' to do like you taught me, Mr. Harper."

"You did real good. Just keep your eyes open."

Caleb led his horse toward the camp. Lem Kovel would relieve the boy at ten. Emmet Holt would take over at midnight, then Bart Jacobs at two. Caleb stood watch himself in the stretch before dawn. One guard wasn't enough, but it was better than none at all.

He gave a perfunctory nod to everyone as he strode through camp. His real purpose was to make certain nothing was amiss. Jenna Riordan was still nowhere to be seen, but her sister was working on a sampler, unconcerned. Timmy was trying to convince a lizard to eat salt pork.

Caleb led his horse over to where the others had been tethered for the night. He brushed down the gelding, his gaze again straying to the Riordan wagon. Where was Jenna? She didn't usually turn in before ten, and when she did she slept under the wagon.

Knowing her habits, he assured himself, was just part of his job as wagon master.

He was starting toward the Riordan wagon when Bart Jacobs intercepted him. " 'Bout time you got back, Harper." The sutler's voice carried its usual sneer.

"You got something to say, Jacobs, say it. I'm busy."

"I'm sayin' there's Injuns around, and we both know it."

"They're a hunting party."

"And they could be huntin' our horses. Injuns steal horses as easy as they breathe."

"That's why we keep a guard posted."

"A boy? And a couple of pilgrims? You call them guards?"

Caleb had no patience for this. "If you don't like it, take your wagon and your horses and get the hell out of here."

"I got a right to your protection. I stood by these people when the rest of the train deserted 'em."

"A fact I've never quite understood, now that you mention it. You don't quite fit my notion of a Good Samaritan, Jacobs. Why did you stay?"

Jacobs's eyes narrowed and Caleb saw a flicker of something he couldn't read. Then Bart Jacobs licked his lips and smiled, a most ugly smile. "Who wouldn't want to help Jenna Riordan, eh, Harper? Don't tell me you haven't thought about givin' her a little help yourself." He made a lewd gesture with his crotch.

In the space of a heartbeat Caleb had his gun in the man's face. "Touch her, and I'll kill you."

Jacobs took a step back, his eyes burning with fear—and hate. "You leave me be," he squeaked. "I'll tell the others you threatened me."

Caleb cocked the Colt.

Jacobs whirled and ran toward his wagon.

Caleb reholstered the six-gun, trying hard to control the rage ripping through him. He told himself he would have been angry had Jacobs made his obscene suggestion about any of the women on the train.

Angry, yes. But this was more than anger. It had been all he could do not to pull the trigger. His lips thinned. He was being a fool. Jenna Riordan was a beautiful woman. But that was all she was. A china doll. Hollow, empty.

Or so he kept trying to tell himself.

And yet four nights earlier he'd stood in the shadows and watched her clean and cook a scrawny jackrabbit Timmy had shot for their supper. He'd spent the rest of the night trying to merge that image with the vision he'd seen in emerald-green silk in Council Grove. Tried and failed.

Somewhere, he was convinced, the strain of the trail would win out. Somewhere she would falter and her true nature would be revealed. She would scream hysterically that she couldn't go on, that she'd had enough of the dust and the heat and the bugs and the danger.

It was not from any clue she had given him. It was his own perception, twisted, he knew, by Laurel McKenzie. Laurel had been beautiful too. Daughter of a master sergeant transferred to Fort Union from Pennsylvania, Laurel had been terrified of the West and everything in it. Yet she had also seemed warm and vulnerable and desperately lonely, just as he had been then, longing for a home, a family.

Caleb swore viciously.

Never again.

Somehow Jenna Riordan's presence had scraped at old and buried scars. That was all. He stalked toward her wagon. As wagon master he would make certain everything was all right; then he would turn in.

Bess was still working her sampler, though her hands seemed strangely nervous. Timmy was spreading out his blanket near the fire. "Evening," Caleb said, tipping his hat toward Bess.

She nodded politely, but her gaze darted toward the river some five hundred yards away.

"Hi, Mr. Harper!" Timmy sauntered over to him, as usual openly admiring the Colt on his hip. Caleb had to smile. Easing the gun from his holster, he broke the cylinder and let the bullets slide into his palm, then handed the gun, butt first, to the boy. He watched with approval as Timmy kept the barrel pointed toward the ground.

"Did you ever kill any outlaws with it, Mr. Harper?"

"When you have to shoot a man, it's never something to be proud of, son." He was watching Bess, who was again looking toward the night-shrouded river.

"It sure is one mighty fine weapon," Timmy said.

"I'll show you how to use it sometime, all right?"

"Would you really?" The boy's eyes were wide as saucers. "That would be swell."

"Where's your sister, Timmy?" Caleb hoped he sounded nonchalant. "I want to be sure everyone sticks close to camp." He didn't take his eyes from Bess. There was something going on here, and he was damned well going to find out what. "I wouldn't want anyone crossing paths with those Comanche."

The girl dropped the sampler and leapt to her feet. "I told her it was a stupid idea. I told her—"

"Where is she?"

"She . . . she went to fetch some water."

Caleb glanced at the river. It didn't take more than ten minutes to get there and back. Yet he had been in camp more than half an hour. He felt suddenly cold. "You're not telling me she went alone?"

"I told her not to," Bess said. "I told her she was being foolish. But she was determined to make—" She stopped, her eyes stricken. "You don't think . . . ?"

Caleb was already reloading his six-gun. "Stay here," he warned. Gun ready, he headed for the river.

6

Jenna sat on the fallen log and shivered. Tugging her shawl more tightly about her shoulders, she looked toward camp and wondered what on earth was taking Caleb Harper so long. She'd been out here now for more than thirty minutes. Hadn't the man yet noticed she was missing?

A slight breeze rustled the leaves of the cottonwoods towering above her, their wide-spreading limbs dark and foreboding on a night with only a quarter moon for light. The gentle shushing of the river some dozen feet behind her seemed less than soothing, its black surface more closely resembling some inky abyss.

Where was he?

Blast! She should have listened to Bess. "He's going to be furious, Jenna. That isn't what you want."

But Jenna had been adamant. She had spent the afternoon mulling over ways she might get Caleb Harper alone. To do so, she realized, meant getting him away from the wagons. Meant also disobeying his direct orders that no one leave camp unescorted, ever.

She'd been behind the wagon when she'd seen him ride in. Immediately she'd called to Bess, told her where she'd be. Bess had made one last attempt to dissuade her, and then Jenna had come out here. To wait.

She coughed slightly, the sound echoing in the darkness. The breeze had ceased, the night around her falling into an eerie silence. Even the crickets stilled. Jenna strained her ears. It was so quiet. Too quiet.

Behind her a twig snapped.

Jenna leapt up, whirling to peer into the blackness. Nothing moved. Nothing. Her scalp prickled, her heart thundering in her chest.

Another twig snapped, this time to her left.

God in heaven, why had she been so foolish? What if Indians were sneaking up on her? What if wolves . . . ?

A hand shot out, closed around her mouth, cutting off the scream that rose in her throat. For an instant she froze. This was what it was like to die. Then her arms flailed out. She kicked, gouged, slapped.

A strong arm pinioned her own to her sides. The hand remained clamped over her mouth. A voice hissed in her ear, harsh, cruel. "If I had been a Comanche, Miss Riordan, you would be dead."

Then Caleb Harper released her.

Jenna staggered, twisting, blood still pounding in her ears. "How dare you?" she choked. "You frightened me nearly to death!"

"That was my intention."

She straightened, gasped. "I beg your pardon?"

"You heard me."

"You're despicable!"

"Keep your voice down," he gritted. "Unless you'd like the entire camp to know what a little fool you are."

Unbidden tears burned her eyes, scalded her cheeks. She swiped them angrily away. She didn't want to cry.

She wanted to slap this arrogant man's self-satisfied face.

He just stood there, arms folded, as though he hadn't a care in the world. "Now, would you mind telling me what you were doing out here, Miss Riordan? Your sister said you were fetching water. I don't see a bucket."

"I-I . . ." She pursed her lips. "You're a beast."

"We've established that. What were you doing out here?"

She turned away, her fists clenched. Blast! This was not the way it was supposed to be. He would come out here. He would chastise her for leaving camp, and then she would somehow work up the courage to talk to him, to ask him about himself, about his life, his family. Instead she looked him right in the face and blurted out, "Why don't you like me, Mr. Harper?"

He stared at her. "What?"

Jenna was already slapping her hand to her mouth. *Why don't you like me, Mr. Harper?* Where had that come from? Dear Lord, the man was looking at her as if she'd lost her mind. Maybe she had. How could she have said such a thing out loud? She could feel the blush sear from the tips of her toes to the top of her head, and she was actually grateful for the darkness.

To her utter horror Caleb Harper continued to stare at her. She had shocked him speechless.

"I-I was speaking in general terms, of course," she stammered. *Think, Jenna,* her mind shrilled. *Think! Get yourself out of this.* "You seem congenial enough toward the others—the Holts, the Kovels—but . . . but I feel perhaps I've done something to offend you. That you're . . . somehow . . . angry with me."

"Miss Riordan, I shouldn't have frightened you like that. I . . ." He started to back away. "Maybe I'd best get back. That is"—he gestured toward the camp— "maybe *we'd* best get back."

It was Jenna's turn to stare. The man was completely flustered, aghast.

"I'm sorry," she murmured hopelessly. "I didn't mean to embarrass you."

"I . . . you didn't."

She had. She could see it, even in the shadows. From his completely cavalier attitude when first he'd scared the wits out of her, he was now thoroughly taken aback.

"I am sorry, Mr. Harper. I've behaved very badly. I just . . . I just wanted to know why you didn't like me."

"That's why you were sitting out here in the dark?" Astonishment still threaded his voice.

"It seemed a grand idea at the time," she said forlornly.

"I, uh, don't dislike you, Miss Riordan. I . . ." He fumbled for the right words, and in that instant Jenna sensed a deep truth about Caleb Harper. He was not a man given to open displays of emotion. His terseness was a defense against such vulnerability. Even so, he stood there obviously struggling to find words extremely difficult for him to say, because he had realized, belatedly, that he had somehow hurt her feelings, though it had never before occurred to him that he had the power to do so.

"It's all right," she said, wanting to spare him. "Again, I apologize. I was being terribly unfair. I could have put the whole camp in danger with your having to traipse out here after me."

"No one's in danger, at least not tonight. The closest Comanches are twenty miles from here. And some of them are friends of mine."

"Oh." She took a small step forward. "Well, I was still being unfair to you. You have your job to do, and I shouldn't have let my personal feelings interfere with that."

"You were right, you know. I haven't treated you the same as the Holts and Kovels."

She didn't say anything. Now that he was talking she felt strangely guilty, as though she'd manipulated him into revealing things about himself he would not otherwise have done.

"I misjudged you," he went on matter-of-factly. "I kept expecting you to fail, to give up, to turn to one of the men for help."

"And why would you expect that, Mr. Harper?"

His voice grew soft but somehow cold. "Because you're a very beautiful woman, Miss Riordan. And in my experience beautiful women don't work very hard for what they want."

Part of her took pleasure in his thinking her beautiful. But another part perceived that, coming from Caleb Harper, being thought beautiful was perhaps not a compliment at all. What struck her most though was the slicing bitterness in the words "in my experience." Could Bess possibly be right? Could this imposing man be shielding a broken heart? Or did his attitude spring from a more distasteful source? "Do you often judge people by their looks, Mr. Harper?"

He stiffened abruptly. A flash of something akin to pain flickered briefly across his features, and then it was gone. "No," he said quietly. "Not often."

Jenna stepped close to him, so close she could actually feel his wanting to bolt away. But he didn't. "Perhaps we could begin again, Mr. Harper."

He frowned, puzzled.

"I believe this is how they do things out here in the West." She stuck out her hand. "I'm Jenna Riordan."

He hesitated, then slid his hand in hers. "Caleb Harper."

"Pleased to meet you." She smiled.

"Same here." He did not smile.

She let go of his hand. "You're right. We'd best get back. Bess will be worried." She turned and started toward the circle of wagons.

"I'll be right behind you."

His voice seemed strained, but she did not look back. She didn't dare. She felt weak, exhausted, yet strangely elated. This was a fresh beginning. One Caleb Harper obviously did not relish, but one she suspected he wanted nonetheless.

She had had her moment with him and somehow avoided disaster. She'd come away knowing precious little more than she had before. And yet she'd discovered volumes. Heaven help her, if she wasn't careful, she could even fall in love with the man.

Caleb stood there for long minutes more, trying to understand what had just happened. But he couldn't. Because he didn't understand. Not at all. He had come out here to find Jenna Riordan, at the very least to teach her a lesson for leaving camp alone. And he had. But then something had happened. The very something he had been trying to avoid.

He had discovered exactly what he did not want to know. That Jenna Riordan was far more than a beautiful woman. She was a woman of spirit and vitality and warmth and humor.

In spite of himself he skated the fingers of his left hand across the palm of his right, the place where Jenna Riordan had linked her hand with his. Such a little thing, such an innocent thing. Then why did the very spot seem to burn? Why did he feel for all the world as though she'd just branded his very soul?

Caleb slept fitfully, bedeviled by dreams of white-gold hair and mountain-lake eyes. Again and again he would approach her—a shimmering vision, angelic, unearthly. Again and again he would stop, leave her just out of reach. If he touched her, if he loved her, she would destroy him.

No. He didn't believe it, couldn't.

She called to him, beckoned him, vowed her undying love for him.

He took another step.

She smiled, radiant.

He took another step.

She had something in her hand. "I love you, Caleb. Love you."

He took one last step. She raised one arm, still smiling.

He saw the knife an instant too late.

With an oath Caleb flung back his blankets. In the chill of the night he sat there trembling, his body drenched with sweat. He cursed himself for an idiot.

Jenna Riordan attacking him with a knife? How in God's name had he conjured such an absurd nightmare?

He climbed to his feet, grateful it was his turn to stand watch. Shrugging into his buckskin jacket, he grabbed up his Spencer and stalked to his post. He found Bart Jacobs snoring noisily, reeking of rotgut whiskey. Resisting the urge to rouse the bastard with a swift kick, Caleb dragged him back to his sutler's wagon and unceremoniously dumped him on the ground beside it. He would deal with the man's dereliction of duty later. If he did it now, he just might kill the fool.

Returning to his guard post, Caleb skirted past the Riordan wagon and the three sleeping figures curled up beneath it. Inexorably his gaze trailed to the slender form nearest the rear wheel. Her blankets had slipped down to her waist and he had to fight off an impulse to go over and tuck them more warmly around her. What dreams was she having, he wondered.

He shook his head, more confused than concerned about his own dream. He had fallen asleep thinking of her, about their encounter by the river. *Why don't you like me, Mr. Harper?* The utter guilelessness of the question had startled him. He'd never known a woman, a white woman at least, to be so direct. That she'd then been embarrassed—for them both—had prompted a strange protectiveness in him. He didn't want her to be embarrassed for speaking frankly. Yet he'd found it difficult to speak frankly in return. That his opinion of her mattered had unexpectedly pleased him. And disconcerted him more.

He knew he should get to his post, but he couldn't take his eyes off her. Her unbound hair cascaded about her face and shoulders in pale golden waves. He imag-

ined what it would be like to bury his face in that curtain of silk, to taste those full, sensual lips, to touch . . .

His loins tightened.

Damn! What did he think he was doing? He had no
right. Jenna Riordan was a lady, a southern-bred lady
no less. Prim and proper to a fault. A virgin. An innocent. In polite society he wouldn't even be permitted
in the same room with her.

Disgusted with himself, he strode to his post where
he hunkered down beside a boulder. In less than two
weeks none of this would matter. Gallagher would rendezvous with them at the cutoff. The major and his
troops would then escort the wagons to Fort Bascom
where arrangements would be made to get the Riordans and the others the rest of the way to California.
By then Caleb would be long gone. He intended to ride
out when they reached the cutoff. He didn't want to see
Jenna Riordan's face when she found out about the
Spencers. No matter what explanation Gallagher might
give her, she would feel duped, used . . . betrayed.
And it was suddenly important to him that he not be
there when she first learned to hate him.

He cast a glance skyward. He couldn't think about
the cutoff now. He had to concentrate on the days
ahead, days in which he could expect no help from
Gallagher or anyone else to get these people through
alive.

It would be dawn in a couple of hours. Today they
would make the Great Bend of the Arkansas. From
there the brassy plains would give way to huge ex-
panses of bunchgrass and prickly pear. But it wasn't the
Great Bend that concerned him. It was where the trail
would take them tomorrow.

Pawnee Rock. A hundred-foot outcropping of red-
dish sandstone, hostiles had used it as a lookout for de-
cades. If there was to be trouble along this trek, it

would likely come at the Rock. So far he had resisted telling the settlers about it. He didn't want them worrying too far in advance. But he would tell them today. He couldn't have them riding unaware into possible trouble.

He tensed. Someone was coming. His hand tightened on the grip of his carbine. Turning, he swallowed an expletive. Jenna. "What are you doing out here?"

"I couldn't sleep," she said. She held her blankets shawllike about her shoulders.

In the full light of the crescent moon her hair shone like spun gold. His earlier lust-filled thoughts rose up to taunt him. He dragged his gaze away, staring out into the night. "You'd best try to get what sleep you can." His voice was gruff.

"I thought we agreed on a fresh start."

"I'm supposed to be on guard, Miss Riordan."

She sighed. "I'm sorry. I didn't think. I . . . good night, Mr. Harper." She started to turn away.

"Wait." The word was out of his mouth before he could stop it. She paused. He stared at her, stared at those luminous blue eyes now watching him so expectantly and couldn't think of a single thing to say. "I . . . uh . . ." Damn. "You and your family are . . ." *Son of a bitch.* "You've done a real fine job, bringing your brother and sister West all by yourself."

"Thank you." She hesitated, obviously uncertain if his comment was a backhanded admission that he wanted her to stay. "It's been difficult at times." She continued to watch him, apparently waiting for some sign that she was dismissed after all.

"I can imagine. I, uh, came West myself on a wagon train when I was thirteen." *You're being a damned fool, Harper,* he told himself. But he suddenly didn't want her to leave, not yet.

She took the hint and knelt beside him. A lock of her

hair brushed past his hand. He'd been right. Pure silk. He inhaled the sweet scent of jasmine.

"You've been in the West since you were thirteen?"

He nodded. It wasn't the precise truth, but it was close enough.

"You must like it out here."

"It's my home."

"But a home is a house, a family."

"Not always." Damn, she was so beautiful, so close. He could feel his blood heat, feel banked desire glow hot. There was a warmth about her, a compassion, an empathy that chipped away at the wall he had built around his heart. And it was scaring the hell out of him.

"Do you have a family, Mr. Harper?"

"No."

"No one?" Her voice was sad, wistful, and it made him hurt.

"I think . . . I think you'd best get back to the wagons now, Miss Riordan." He looked away.

"I've done it again, haven't I?" she murmured, a rueful edge to her voice.

"Done what?"

"I've upset you." She climbed to her feet. "I'm sorry. That's something else I've been learning about the West. People don't ask personal questions."

"It's all right," he said, though it wasn't. Because there were questions he couldn't answer. Wouldn't answer. No matter how much his instincts told him Jenna Riordan would understand. He couldn't take the risk.

She started to leave, then stopped. "I almost forgot. Today is Timmy's birthday. That's why I came out here. Bess and I are going to make him a cake. I . . . he'd like you to come by tonight to share it with us."

"I don't think that would be a good idea."

"Please? He looks up to you. It would mean so much to him."

"All right." He would agree to anything to have her gone.

"Thank you."

He watched her walk away, watched her look back several times before she reached her wagon. He kept his face expressionless. Two weeks, he told himself. Two weeks and he would never see her again. He assured himself that would be best for both of them.

Jenna tried again to sleep, but it was no use. Caleb Harper consumed her thoughts. She had hoped things would change between them. And they had. From bad to worse. She had sensed how uncomfortable he was talking about himself. In fact, the man might well be the first she'd ever met in her life unwilling to discuss himself ad infinitum. She grimaced. Ad nauseam. And yet to this man she would have gladly listened for hours, hungering for every scrap of information, every detail of his life no matter how grudgingly given.

With a sigh she shoved back her blankets and clambered out from under the wagon. It was still dark, still half an hour before Caleb, as last watch, would rouse the camp, but she knew she would get no more sleep this night. Nor would she pay another visit to Harper's guard post. She'd had quite enough embarrassment for one evening.

Still, she couldn't help but smile. The man might be a tight-lipped, short-tempered son of a gun, but she liked him anyway. And, while she allowed for possible wishful thinking on her part, she decided Bess was right. He liked her too. Whether he wanted to or not. She just had to figure out why he didn't want to.

A sobering thought intruded. What would it matter if he did return her feelings? The man was an army scout. Once he led them safely to California, he would return to his life here. He would have no use for a place as civilized and as confining as Sacramento. Nor could Jenna conceive of Bess and Timmy living on a frontier army post.

A stab of guilt slashed through her. She was certainly getting ahead of herself. It wasn't as if she were weighing a marriage proposal from the man!

Enough! Jenna told herself sternly. She cast a loving glance toward the two blanket-wrapped figures still asleep under the wagon. They were her life, her first responsibility. Caleb Harper was an infatuation, a passing fancy, an intriguing fantasy to while away some of the tedium of the trail. There would be no choices made, because there were none to make.

Since it was Timmy's birthday, she decided to let him sleep. She and Bess could take care of his chores this morning.

Lighting a lantern, Jenna went to the back of the wagon and began sifting through their supplies to get what she needed to make breakfast. On impulse she climbed in to make certain the new .22 rifle she and Bess had bought for Timmy in Council Grove was still safely hidden away beneath the flour sacks. She smiled. It was. She could hardly wait to see his face when they gave it to him. His old rifle had been bought used back in Spring Hill and was becoming increasingly unreliable. With the new gun perhaps he could get himself that prairie chicken he said he wanted for his birthday supper. Even Jenna had to admit they were all getting pretty weary of salt pork and beans.

She started to turn away when the lantern light cast an odd shadow in the corner of the wagon. She pulled aside the heavy flour sacks, moved the butter churn, and poked a finger through a knothole in the wood planking that made up the floorboards. Shouldn't she be able to see the ground through that hole? She wiggled into the cramped corner and held the lantern as close to the hole as she dared, with so many combustibles close at hand. It was utterly dark beyond the knothole. She frowned. She had paid good money for the repairs Caleb Harper had insisted they needed before they could leave Council Grove. But those had been wheel repairs. If he'd had the floor shored up, why hadn't he said anything to her? She certainly didn't want the man thinking they needed his charity. She got back to her feet. He was going to hear about this.

But for now Timmy's birthday was her priority. Jenna climbed out of the wagon and leaned over to waken Bess. "C'mon, sleepyhead," she whispered. "We've got a birthday cake to make."

When Bess stirred, Jenna put a finger to her lips, pointing at their blanket-swaddled brother near the front end of the wagon. "We'll let him sleep longer, all right?"

Bess nodded, rising eagerly to join Jenna in getting ready for the day ahead. Dawn was breaking and the rest of the camp was soon bustling to life as well. Cook fires blazed up, the aroma of corn bread mingling with acorn porridge and frying bacon.

After having seen to the team, Jenna and Bess gathered up their carefully hoarded chocolate and other cake ingredients and hurried over to the Holt wagon. Millie Holt had promised them full use of her Dutch oven this morning.

"Morning, girls!" Plain-featured, soft-spoken Millie greeted them with her ever-present smile. "Mary and I have been looking forward to this for days."

Jenna smiled as ten-year-old Mary hurried over to help Bess lay everything out on the small table the Holts used during mealtimes.

"We really appreciate this, Millie," Jenna said.

"Nonsense." Millie wiped her hands on her apron.

"We're happy to do it." She gave Jenna a conspiratorial wink. "Mary's got a quite a little crush on that brother of yours."

Jenna laughed. "If she keeps sneaking him pieces of your apple pie, you may find yourself with another mouth to feed on a permanent basis."

They chatted on while the girls prepared the cake batter. Jenna enjoyed these rare moments she got to spend with Millie Holt. She considered the woman a true pioneer in every sense of the word, traveling west at her husband's side, cheerful, uncomplaining. Though Millie too had lost a son to the war, she had not retreated into the isolated bitterness so evident in the Kovels.

"Poor Nelda," Millie clucked, looking toward the Kovel wagon. "I do wish she wouldn't be so standoffish. I invited her and the mister to supper five nights running, until my Emmet finally told me to stop wasting my breath."

"I know what you mean." Jenna sighed. "I've asked her too. There was a time I even thought she was going to say yes, but it's like she's forgotten how."

"And that husband of hers makes darned certain she doesn't remember either."

Jenna watched as the gaunt, bearded Lem Kovel hobbled about on his crutch, harnessing his team. She doubted she'd said more than three words to the man since they'd left Council Grove. His perpetual scowl made even a simple "Good morning" seem unwelcome. She was only too happy to leave the man to his own company.

When the cake was just about done, Jenna decided it was time to rouse the sleeping Timmy. They would eat the confection tonight after supper, but she wanted him to see it now. And she wanted to give him his new rifle. She'd just started toward the wagon when a shout of alarm came from the rear of the train.

Bart Jacobs was livid. Jenna watched the man storming her way. "Where's Harper?" he snapped to no one in particular.

She turned to see Caleb stride up, apparently alerted by the commotion. He was still carrying his Spencer from his stint on guard duty. "What's wrong?"

"Wrong?" the man roared. "I'll tell you what's wrong. Someone stole one of my horses!"

The whole camp followed Jacobs to the picket line. Sure enough an Appaloosa gelding was missing. Thankfully it was the only horse gone.

"Couldn't it have gotten free?" Jenna offered.

"I had him hobbled," Jacobs said. "As well as tied. Damn! I paid thirty dollars for that animal. Look at this!" He held up the severed end of a lead rope and glared at Caleb. "You know who did this, don't you?"

Caleb hunkered down, studying the ground near the horses. It was obvious to Jenna he did know.

"Tell me," she said in a small voice.

He stood, his eyes grim. "Comanche."

Jenna shivered, her thoughts catapulting at once to her foolhardy vigil last night by the river. She could tell Caleb was thinking the same thing.

"I expect you to do somethin' about this, Harper," Jacobs was saying. "I want that Injun caught. I want my horse back."

"The horse is gone, Jacobs," Caleb said, obviously struggling to keep his temper under control. "We can consider ourselves lucky. Probably a brave counting coup. Likely counted it on you too while you were drunk on guard."

Jacobs bristled. "Don't you try to put this off on me, Harper. You're in charge here. You're supposed to know if there's any Injuns around. We're lucky we still got our hair."

"Please, Mr. Jacobs," Jenna interjected. "Fighting amongst ourselves isn't going to help anything." She turned to Caleb. "Just what does 'count coup' mean, Mr. Harper?"

" 'Coup' is a brave act," Caleb explained, though he didn't take his eyes from Jacobs. "An Indian doesn't have to face an enemy in battle to count coup. Touching a sleeping enemy would count, stealing a horse— any act of bravery."

"Damned savages!" Jacobs snarled, bolting toward his saddle mount. "I'm going after that horse."

Caleb stepped in front of him. "No, you're not. Just leave it be. If they wanted to do us harm, they would have."

Jacobs seethed but backed down, making no further move toward his horse.

To Jenna's surprise Lem Kovel limped forward, his thin features twisted with pain and outrage. "I think Jacobs is right, Harper. I don't think savages should be allowed to get away with stealin' from decent folks."

"As long as I'm wagon master," Caleb said, his patience wearing reed-thin, "you'll do as I say. If you want to be wagon master, Kovel—or you, Jacobs—just say so, and I'll be gone."

The threat hung heavy in the air. Kovel and Jacobs exchanged glances. Jenna held her breath. Would Caleb really desert them if these men continued their mutinous ways? She studied him, the cold-steel look in those gray eyes, and she realized she didn't know the answer to that question.

To her vast relief she didn't have to find out.

"You signed on to lead us to California," Kovel said belligerently. "You'd best finish the job."

Jacobs continued to look sullen but said nothing more.

"I'll ride out a ways, see what I can find." Caleb paid no more attention to the two men as he set about saddling his black gelding.

Jenna tried not to be nervous. "Come on, Bess," she told her sister. "Let's go see what's keeping that birthday boy." She could scarcely believe Timmy had slept through all this.

But when they reached the wagon, there he was, still huddled up underneath his blankets. Jenna shook her head. "That boy. Wait'll he finds out we had a Comanche in camp last night."

She smiled, reaching down to give Timmy's blanket a quick tug. Her smile vanished. Beneath the blanket was a second blanket rolled up lengthwise to resemble a body.

Timmy was gone.

8

Jenna screamed her brother's name as she tore about the camp searching for him. The Holts came running. So did the Kovels. Even Bart Jacobs rushed toward her. But not Timmy. She screamed for him again, calling out to him, pleading with him to come out from wherever he was hiding, desperate to know that the hellish vision in her mind could not possibly be true.

"Them damned Comanches." Jacobs spat, peering knowingly under the Riordan wagon. "They took him. They're gonna make him a savage just like them. I heard tell what they do with young'uns."

"No." Jenna gave her head a fierce shake. Only a glimpse of the hysteria mounting in Bess's pale eyes allowed Jenna to control her own rising terror. She spun about, seeking the face of the one person she knew instinctively could set her world right again.

Caleb.

His attention was focused on the ground near the wagon. As she watched he walked back and forth, seeming to concentrate on every speck of dirt, every blade of grass. He strode out several yards toward the river where he continued to pace, his gaze still locked on the ground. For long minutes he didn't say a word. He gave her no hint of what he was finding, what he was thinking.

When Jenna was certain she couldn't bear his silence one more second, he came back over to her. "There's no sign of a struggle," he said. "No sign of anyone with him. Timmy walked out of this camp on his own."

"But why?" Jenna cried. "That doesn't make any sense. He knows what your orders are about going off alone."

She flushed when he looked away briefly, obviously recalling that she hadn't followed his orders very well herself. Why should her brother be any different?

"The Comanche that was in camp," she asked, her voice shaking, "did . . . was he heading in the same direction?"

"No. At least not when he left here."

His words offered her little comfort. The Indian could have spotted Timmy later. Why else wouldn't her brother be here? He would have known he would be missed at first light. Whatever mischief he had planned for his birthday, he would not have wanted his sisters to worry about him. *If he were all right,* her mind thrummed, *he would've come back.*

"Check his things," Caleb said. "See if anything's missing."

Swiftly she did so. "His rifle." She closed her eyes, her heart sinking. Of course. She looked at Caleb. "He didn't want another night of salt pork. Not for his birthday."

She could tell he was trying not to swear as he stomped toward his gelding. He swung into the saddle. "I'll find him."

Jenna caught the black's reins. "I'm going with you."

"I'll find him faster alone."

She kept her hold on the reins. "I'm going."

He swore, then apologized. "Miss Riordan, I know you're worried about your brother. Just let me do my job."

"I'm coming with you, or I'll follow after you. It's your choice, Mr. Harper." She spun on her heel, not waiting for his reply.

Quickly she scrambled inside her wagon, throwing off her dress and pulling on a white blouse and calf-length brown riding skirt. She hadn't done much saddle riding in recent years, but she wasn't about to let that stop her. Tugging on her only pair of boots, she clambered back out of the wagon, thankful beyond words to see that Caleb was still there. He'd even saddled a horse for her. She could tell he was angry, but it couldn't be helped. There was no way she would be left behind.

Bess was at Jenna's side, sobbing. Jenna gave her a quick hug. "Mr. Harper and I will find him. Don't worry."

Bess shuddered violently. Millie Holt hurried over. "Don't you worry, Jenna," Millie said. "I'll see to it she's all right."

Jenna managed a grateful nod, fearful she couldn't speak past the lump in her throat.

"And don't give a second thought to your wagon. Sam will drive it for you."

"Here, Miss Jenna," young Sam Holt said, handing her his flop-brimmed hat. "You'll be needin' this more than me today."

Jenna accepted the hat, settling it over her tumbled mane of blond hair. She'd had no time to bind it up this morning. She crossed to Caleb, who handed her the reins of a sorrel mare, surprised to find a look of grudging admiration in his gray eyes. But right now it meant nothing. All that mattered was finding Timmy.

She mounted. Together she and Caleb rode out.

They rode slowly, cautiously, Caleb's gaze never leaving the rough ground over which they traveled. To Jenna the undulating sea of buffalo grass looked the same in all directions. Yet Caleb never hesitated. He kept them moving along a path only he could see. She didn't question him. Though gripped by a fear such as she'd never known, she felt a peculiar calm as well, a calm infused in her by the very presence of the man beside her. If anyone could find her brother in this vast emptiness, she was certain it was Caleb Harper.

They rode for more than an hour before he held up a hand, signaling her to stop. He dismounted. Jenna did the same. She watched as he hunkered down to pick up several pebbles. He turned each of them over in his palm, then let them fall back to the ground. He studied the horizon, his face not quite masking the concern she was certain he was trying to hide from her.

"Where is he?" She blinked back tears. "Mr. Harper, please, where's my little brother?"

"We'll find him."

"But there's nothing out there." She waved a hand toward the horizon. "Not even a tree. If he were there, wouldn't we see him?"

"This land looks flat, but it's cut by dry washes, arroyos, old creekbeds. He could be in any one of them."

She let out a watery sigh. "I'm sorry. I'm just so worried about him."

"I know."

She looked into those gray eyes, almost undone by the sympathy she saw reflected there. And for once he didn't shutter his feelings away.

"We'll find him, Jen—Miss Riordan. And he'll be all

right. He's a bright boy. He can handle himself out here. I wouldn't say it if I didn't believe it."

She nodded. "Thank you."

Their eyes locked for long seconds, and she had the strangest feeling that he wanted to pull her close, to hold her, reassure her, but that he didn't dare. Because to touch her—even in comfort—was to cross a line he had drawn long before they'd even met. And then the feeling was gone as he seemed to shake himself, his familiar expressionless mask settling into place once again.

"We'd best get moving," he said.

They remounted and rode on, but Jenna was left with a tantalizing glimpse of another side of this enigmatic man, and she would not forget.

They covered another mile before Caleb reined in again some dozen feet from the edge of one of the arroyos he'd told her about. "I'll take a look. We may not be able to cross here, even if Timmy did. It might be too steep for the horses." He handed her the reins of the black. "Stay here."

He walked to the lip of the cutbank and looked down. "Sweet God."

Jenna was at his side in an instant. She gasped. Some five feet below them in the dry creekbed sat Timmy, his right foot seemingly wedged tight between two badger-sized boulders. He was sitting unnaturally still, almost rigid. "Timmy!" Her gaze raced along the drop-off, looking for a foothold. "We've got to get down there. We—"

Very slowly Caleb drew his six-gun. "Don't move, Timmy," he said softly.

Jenna's heart thundered. What—She followed the line of the Colt. Only then did she see it. On the boulder at Timmy's left, a bare eighteen inches from his face—a four-foot rattlesnake.

Caleb levered back the hammer of the Colt.

Jenna couldn't breathe. Her every instinct told her to knock his arm away.

She didn't move.

The snake coiled, hissed, its rattles sounding. Ominous, deadly.

Caleb fired the gun.

Timmy jerked back.

Jenna screamed. Mindless, heedless, she scrambled down the side of the ravine, oblivious to everything but getting to her brother. He was dead. Caleb had killed him. She cradled him in her arms, sobbing. It took her a minute to hear the muffled sound against her throat.

"Jenna, I can't breathe." Timmy struggled against her, trying to get air into his lungs.

"Timmy! You're alive! Oh, thank God! Where are you hurt?"

"I ain't hurt! You're suffocatin' me!"

Jenna sat back, wiping at her tears. "Oh." A wave of unutterable relief surged through her.

"The gunshot made me jump. I'm sorry, Jenna."

Only then did she see the dead snake. Her stomach lurched. She looked away and found herself staring into Caleb Harper's bemused face.

"You are one peculiar lady, Miss Riordan. Live snakes don't bother you, but dead ones do."

The tension of the morning crackled through her, bubbling over into fury, and to her utter consternation, more tears. She leapt to her feet. "Peculiar? I'm peculiar? You could have killed my brother."

"I didn't."

She yanked off her hat, slapping it against her thigh. She was in no mood for logic. To Timmy she shrilled, "What on earth were you doing out here, young man? Do you have any idea how worried I was? How worried Bess still is? I've never tanned your hide in my life, but by heaven I just may start! Indians and rattlesnakes and God knows what else on these plains and an eleven-year-old boy thinking he's Daniel Boone."

"Twelve."

"What?"

"I'm twelve years old," he stated stubbornly.

"And not likely to reach thirteen. What were you thinking?"

Meekly he pointed to a spot some six feet to his right. Lying on the cracked dirt of what had once been a stream bottom was his new .22 rifle. "I wanted to try it out. I wanted to get a prairie chicken. But I dropped it comin' down the bank. Then I got stuck."

Jenna stared at the rifle in disbelief. "Your new gun? But I saw it in the wagon this morning."

"I found it last night," he admitted sheepishly. "I put my old rifle in its place."

Jenna had to concede she hadn't looked all that closely. She'd just assumed she was seeing the new one. It hadn't occurred to her the little imp would pull a switch.

Meanwhile Caleb had gone to his horse to retrieve a small shovel and was now scraping away at the dirt beneath Timmy's trapped foot.

"I can't believe this," she said. "I just can't believe it. I looked right at that rifle and never noticed." If she had, perhaps she would have discovered her brother missing hours sooner. She shook her head. "Never again, young man. Do you understand?"

"Yes, ma'am," he said, appearing thoroughly chastened.

"And I would think you'd have something to say to Mr. Harper as well."

"Yes, ma'am." Timmy looked at Caleb, his face brightening. "That sure was some shot, Mr. Harper!"

Caleb swallowed a chuckle.

"Timothy Riordan!" Jenna fumed.

Timmy hung his head. "I'm truly grateful, Mr. Harper."

Caleb stuck out his hand, which Timmy eagerly accepted. "My pleasure, Timmy."

"Men!" Jenna paced back and forth, while Caleb continued to work on Timmy's snagged foot. "Speaking of men"—she glared at Caleb—"just what did you do to the floor of my wagon?"

He almost jabbed the shovel into his leg. "I don't know what you mean," he said mildly.

"You must know. You had the repairs done, didn't you? When I was checking for Timmy's rifle this morning, I found a knothole and I couldn't see through it to the ground."

He stopped digging.

"I thought it kind of strange, so I tried to stick my finger through it." She gave little note to how stiffly he was holding himself. Timmy's foot must have been stuck more tightly than she had thought. She made a helpless gesture. "It's just that I don't appreciate your having repairs done without telling me."

"I'm sorry." He didn't look at her. "I meant to tell you. It must have slipped my mind."

"Well, I expect to repay you. We don't need charity, Mr. Harper."

"No, ma'am. You don't." He resumed digging, pausing only to wipe at the sweat that had broken out on his forehead.

Jenna smiled, satisfied. "Thank you. I wasn't angry about the wagon. Not really anyway. I didn't mean to seem ungrateful for what you had done to it."

"Don't be grateful, Miss Riordan." His voice was flat. "Not to me."

She had no time to ponder his shift in mood. He'd worked Timmy's foot free and was helping the boy to his feet. Jenna gave her brother a fierce hug, then scolded him all the way back up to the horses.

Minutes later they were headed back, Timmy riding in front of Caleb on the black gelding. They rode in silence for several minutes. Jenna was grateful when Timmy seemed to relax, finally dozing off, his head lolling back against Caleb's chest.

"I can't thank you enough," she said.

"No thanks necessary."

"He and Bess are all the family I have. I don't know what I would have done if anything had . . ." She shuddered. Now that Timmy was safe she couldn't seem to stop thinking of all that could have happened. The Comanche, the snake, the rifle . . . "What became of your family, Mr. Harper?"

For a moment she thought he wasn't going to answer, then he said, "My mother died when I was four. I don't remember her very well. I spent time with relatives after that."

"I'm sorry. Timmy doesn't remember our mother either. I think that's very sad. She was a wonderful woman."

"She must have been."

The way he looked at her when he'd said that made Jenna feel warm all over. With Timmy safe she could dare imagine that she and Caleb were just out riding together. Almost a family outing. He seemed so at ease with her brother. "Don't forget you promised to stop by for birthday cake tonight."

"I remember."

She smiled, feeling almost giddy. "When's your birthday, Mr. Harper?"

"Don't have one."

She must not have heard him correctly. "When did you say?"

He shrugged. "I never had a birthday."

"But that's not possible, Mr. Harper." She laughed. "Everyone has a birthday."

"I suppose they do," he said evenly. "I just don't happen to know mine."

Jenna was stunned. "Surely your mother's family would have . . ."

"Would have buried me with her if they had their way."

Jenna winced at his sudden bitterness. Thunderation! She'd done it again. The gentle comraderie she'd felt was now shattered. She could tell by the way his fist clenched around the gelding's reins that he regretted his outburst. Not that he hadn't meant it, but that by saying it he'd revealed a part of his life he hadn't meant to share.

"I'm sorry, Mr. Harper." Lord above, how often had she said those two words to this man? How many more times would she have to say them? "I shouldn't have asked."

"Forget it."

"No," she said quietly, "I doubt I'll ever do that."

The wagons came into view, and Caleb spurred his horse forward to meet them. Jenna followed. She felt suddenly bereft. She realized that for a few moments she'd dared delude herself that he was actually becoming more at ease in her company, less distant.

Her mood brightened though when Bess raced out to meet them. As Caleb eased the sleeping Timmy to the ground, Bess flung her arms around the child's neck. When Caleb dismounted, Bess hugged him too.

Caleb stood there looking flustered, then mumbled "You're welcome," before he quickly remounted his horse and rode off.

Jenna and Bess helped a still-tired Timmy into the back of their wagon. "This is certainly a birthday he won't forget," Bess said.

"Nor will any of the rest of us." Jenna secured the tailgate and waved a hand at Sam Holt, who indicated he'd like to keep driving. Jenna was only too happy to let him. After hours on horseback she was looking forward to walking for a while. Bess fell into step beside her.

"A snake." Bess shivered as Jenna told her what had happened. "How dreadful! You were certainly lucky to have Mr. Harper with you."

Jenna couldn't help a wistful sigh but said, "Are you sure you shouldn't be resting too?"

"I'm fine. Don't fuss. I'm just so pleased Timmy is safe." Bess's eyes gleamed happily. "So how did you and Mr. Harper get along all by yourselves?"

Jenna kicked at a small stone. "The man is totally unpredictable. One moment he's pleasant, even kind; the next he's a wall of granite. He absolutely will not talk about himself."

"A broken heart," Bess pronounced. "I knew it."

"He doesn't have a heart," Jenna snapped, then instantly regretted it. She recalled the compassion in those gray eyes when she was still terrified about finding Timmy. And that wasn't annoyance he'd shown her when she'd prodded him about his birthday, it was pain.

"You'll make him forget all about her," Bess was saying. "He won't even remember her name."

Jenna blinked, confused. "Remember whose name? What are you talking about?"

"The woman that broke Mr. Harper's heart."

Jenna felt a pain of her own. She disliked the idea of this other woman's existence. For a woman to have wielded such power over a man like Caleb Harper, he must have loved her very much.

"Have you let him kiss you yet?"

Jenna stopped dead, flabbergasted. "Rebecca Riordan, where are you coming up with this nonsense?"

"Well, have you?"

"Of course not!"

"But you want him to. Admit it. I'll bet he's a good kisser too. Don't you think? He's so handsome!" She sighed dreamily. "Oh, Jenna, don't you see? He's your pirate, your romantic rogue."

"A rogue maybe." Jenna grimaced. "But hardly romantic."

"He can learn."

"Rebecca, enough!" Jenna could feel her cheeks burning.

"You're blushing! Oh, wouldn't it be wonderful? Jenna *Harper*. I love it!"

"Not another word." But Jenna too was dreaming. Bess's enthusiasm was infectious. *Was* Caleb Harper a good kisser? Jenna's heart raced as she imagined finding out. Then she shook her head. She was being absurd. The man would scarcely speak to her—why in the world would he ever kiss her?

She smiled.

She was a woman. He was a man. Surely she could think of something.

Jenna suddenly couldn't wait for darkness, couldn't wait for Timmy's birthday celebration to begin.

Camp that night seemed forever in coming. But finally the sun set and everyone settled in. One by one the other campers stopped by to wish Timmy a happy birthday and share in the cake Bess and Mary had made. Even the Kovels and Bart Jacobs, though they didn't linger.

The only person conspicuously absent was Caleb Harper. He hadn't been in camp all night.

"Where is he?" Timmy asked sadly as he tried valiantly to stifle a yawn. "Do you think he forgot?"

"I'm sure he didn't," Jenna said. "But he may have had to scout ahead farther than usual with Indians about." She said it though she didn't believe it. No, Caleb Harper hadn't forgotten. He was staying away deliberately. Because of her.

On any other night she could've accepted that. But not tonight. Not when his staying away hurt Timmy.

Bess seemed to know what she was thinking. She gave Jenna a sympathetic look. "It's been a long day for all of us. Maybe we'd best turn in." She kissed Timmy on the forehead. "Happy birthday, young man."

"Good night, Bessie."

Bess spread out her blankets under the wagon and lay down. Jenna put her hand on Timmy's shoulder. "She's right. We'd best get to sleep."

"But I wanted to give Mr. Harper our surprise."

"Maybe tomorrow."

"It won't be the same tomorrow."

"It can't be helped, Timmy. Come on now, let's—"

The sound of hoofbeats made them both look up. Jenna didn't know whose smile was broader, hers or Timmy's, as she watched Caleb rein in and dismount in front of their campfire.

"Sorry I'm late." The gaze he sent her was unreadable, but he smiled when he looked at Timmy. "I understand congratulations are in order." He handed the boy a small bundle. "Happy birthday, Timmy."

Almost reverently Timmy unwrapped the folded-over swath of deerskin. "Oh, Jenna, look!" He held up a bone-handled hunting knife, its eight-inch blade glinting in the firelight. "Thanks, Mr. Harper! Thanks a lot!"

"You're welcome."

"That was very kind of you," Jenna said shakily. To cover her feelings she offered him the last piece of cake, the one she'd set aside for him, just in case. She prayed he didn't notice how her hands trembled.

"Thank you." He waved aside a fork and picked up the confection with his fingers. Giving her an awkward grin, he wolfed it down.

"Can we give Mr. Harper our surprise, Jenna?" Timmy asked.

Caleb frowned slightly. "Surprise?"

"Jenna told us you didn't have a birthday."

"Oh, she did, did she?"

Jenna could almost feel the man's defenses rise.

"Anyway, I figured, well, if you want, you could share my birthday. Would you like that, Mr. Harper?"

Caleb was now looking decidedly uncomfortable but managed, "I'd like that just fine, Timmy."

Timmy grinned.

Jenna held out a small package. "Happy birthday, Mr. Harper."

Caleb's hand shook slightly as he accepted the package. "I never had a birthday present." Despite his obvious embarrassment Jenna sensed he was also deeply touched. Her own eyes were burning.

"Open it," Timmy urged.

Caleb undid the brown paper and stared at the gold pocketwatch he found inside.

"It belonged to our father," Jenna said softly.

"I . . . can't take this . . ." He held it out to her.

She folded her own small hands around his large one, enclosing the watch in his palm. "We want you to have it—Bess, Timmy, and I. Our mother gave it to Pa on his first birthday after they were married."

Caleb caressed the exquisite carved surface with his thumb. He looked at her, his gunmetal eyes again unreadable. "I, uh, I'm much obliged. I think I'd . . . I think I'd best see to my horse now." Abruptly he took up the black's reins and was gone.

"What's wrong with Mr. Harper, Jenna?" Timmy asked. "Didn't he like the watch?"

"He liked it fine, Timmy. He liked it just fine."

She found him tossing stones into the Arkansas, the dark water rippling outward in ever-increasing circles. He turned at the sound of her approach. His eyes were alive with raw emotion, emotion she knew he was not at all accustomed to feeling. Her own heart pounded painfully in her chest. She stepped close to him.

"You left before I could share another Riordan birthday tradition," she said softly, praying her courage would not desert her. Her need to be near him was so strong it overcame the butterflies in her stomach.

"What's that?" he asked hoarsely.

"The Riordan birthday kiss." She stood on tiptoe, her lips brushing his beard-stubbled cheek.

He closed his eyes. For the space of a heartbeat he didn't move, and then with a low, throaty groan he turned toward her, sweeping her up into a bone-melting embrace. If he hadn't held her, she was certain she would have dissolved into the earth itself. Her whole body seemed turned to liquid, her flesh flame.

She felt her breasts being crushed against the hard plane of his chest, and she desperately wished she could be closer to him still. Inside him somehow. Never had she felt like this. Never had she known she could feel like this.

He rained kisses across her forehead, her cheeks, her eyes. And then his mouth found hers, his lips velvet-soft yet hard, demanding. She reveled in the taste of him, the scent—all sagebrush and leather. Everything powerful and primitive and achingly masculine.

"Jenna. Sweet God, Jenna."

His hands roamed along her back and upward to bury themselves in her hair. His growl of pleasure sent white heat searing to every tiny part of her. This, she realized wonderingly, was what she'd wanted, needed,

longed for almost from the first moment she had met
Caleb Harper—the joy, the magic of his touch.

"Caleb . . . Caleb, please . . ." She'd had some
wine once, a long time ago. It had produced an odd
warmth, a delicious fuzziness not unlike what she was
feeling now. "Caleb." Just to say his name sent sparks of
pleasure rippling through her. Never had anything felt
more perfect, more right than to be in this man's arms.

"Caleb," she murmured, twining her fingers in his
thick, dark hair, "I think I love you."

He stilled, the words like ice water to the fire in his
blood. "No. Don't say that."

"But it's true."

His hands fell away, and he took a step back. "No."

She pressed a hand against his chest, felt the thunder
of his heart. "You want me too. I know it."

"Wanting and loving aren't the same thing." He
made his voice deliberately harsh. But instead of the
pain or the disillusion he expected to see in those incredible blue eyes, he saw only sympathy, tenderness.
His throat tightened, his eyes burning, the need in him
for this woman so fierce, so overwhelming that it took
every ounce of his will not to give in to the throbbing
demands of his body.

"I love you, Caleb," she said again, her voice firm yet
somehow infinitely warm. "I love you."

She touched his face.

He caught her hand. "Jenna, don't . . ."

She saw it then, the pain in those gray eyes. A soul-
deep agony that almost made her cry out. "Tell me."

She felt him shudder, felt him want to speak, but
then he closed his eyes, shuttering away whatever
ghost it was that had risen up between them. He took a
deep breath. "I'm sorry. This shouldn't have happened."

"I'm not sorry."

"You would be, if . . ." He stopped.

"Tell me."

"I can't." With an anguished oath he turned and stalked away from her into the night.

9

In the darkness Jenna stood alone beside the Arkansas and trembled. What had just happened? Why had Caleb deserted her? One minute they were sharing the most passionate kiss she had ever known, the next he was gone.

She had told him she loved him, and he had reacted as though she'd struck him. He had been willing to accept her passion, her warmth, even her caring. But that she should actually love him was something he had obviously not figured into the bargain. He had claimed not to believe her, but perhaps the truth was, he had. Some aching, vulnerable part of him had even wanted to love her back.

And it had scared him to death.

Why? Why would he turn his back on something he so obviously wanted? Was it the life he led? That he had no room in it for a woman and her ready-made family? The thought hurt, but it was not as though she hadn't encountered it before; and oddly, with Caleb, she felt she could dismiss it out of hand. It was not her or

Timmy or Bess. It was Caleb himself. He was hiding something, something he considered vitally important. Something he was certain would change her opinion of him, if she but knew.

Be careful what you wish for . . . She rubbed her arms, gazing at the star-bright sky. A man with an air of mystery about him . . .

She straightened. Mysteries could be solved. She might be a bit naive where men were concerned, but she was not totally inexperienced. It was a long way to California. Time enough for another stolen kiss or two, time enough to get Caleb to trust her. At least she hoped so, because if she hadn't been certain of it before, there was no doubt about it now—she loved him.

With a tremulous sigh she headed back to the wagons. The darkness that had been a welcome cocoon when she'd been in Caleb's arms seemed less so now, but she wasn't afraid. Somewhere in the shadows she knew Caleb was watching out for her. She managed a half smile, wondering if his sleep this night would be as restless as her own.

The next morning Jenna could almost feel the dark circles under her eyes as she pushed aside her blankets and climbed to her feet. Stretching weary muscles, she glanced about but saw no sign of Caleb. Nor had she expected to. He would likely keep his distance, at least for a while. She was surprised, however, to see young Sam Holt heading her way. The thirteen-year-old touched a hand to his hat brim and gave her a shy smile.

"Good morning, Sam," Jenna said.

"Got a message for you, Miss Jenna. From Mr. Harper."

Jenna's heart skipped a startled beat before Sam continued. "He says he'll meet up with us again just before Pawnee Rock. He wants to make sure there won't be no trouble there. Injun trouble." As Sam said the last his grip tightened on the Henry he carried. There was no fear in his eyes, only the quiet determination of a boy who'd become a man the day his older brother died in the war. It occurred to Jenna that if trouble was to come, she would rather have one Sam Holt on her side than a dozen Bart Jacobses.

"Thank you, Sam."

He started to leave.

"Sam?"

He stopped and looked back at her questioningly.

"Did, um, did Mr. Harper say anything else?"

"Ma'am?"

"Did he . . . did he tell you to say anything else to me?"

Sam frowned, his face screwing up as he went over his conversation with Caleb in his mind. "Well, not *to* you exactly, Miss Jenna. But he did say something about you."

"And what was that?" Jenna's heart thudded. Caleb wouldn't have relayed his feelings through Sam, but he might have said something, even inadvertently, that would give her some small measure of hope.

Sam looked uncomfortable. "I don't think he meant for me to tell you."

Jenna's pulses raced. "Tell me what?"

"He said I was to keep an eye on you."

"To kind of watch out for me? Take care of me?" She smiled.

"Sort of, I guess."

Jenna's smile broadened until Sam continued with Caleb's exact words. "Mr. Harper told me, 'Keep an eye on Miss Riordan, Sam. Make sure she doesn't go anywhere near Bart Jacobs. Leastways not alone.'"

Jenna felt as if she'd been punched. "Bart Jacobs? What does Bart Jacobs have to do with anything? Why would Caleb tell you to make sure I don't go near Bart Jacobs?" Her words rushed together.

Sam backed away. "That's what he said, Miss Jenna. I . . . I'd best go help Pa with the horses." He turned on his heel and fled.

Jenna stood there staring after him, trying to decide which emotion she felt more keenly, anger or hurt. It wasn't that she'd expected any declaration of love from Caleb, but to have the man's only comment be some cryptic warning that she stay clear of Bart Jacobs . . . Why would he say that? Lord above! Did he think he had reason to be *jealous* of Jacobs? The thought made her skin crawl.

Her intention to let Caleb approach her again in his own good time vanished in the face of her rising fury. She hadn't been going to confront him about what happened between them last night. But now last night didn't matter. What mattered was why Caleb thought she would even want to be alone with Bart Jacobs.

"Blast the man!" she grumbled as she roused Bess and Timmy for the day ahead. "Just when I think I might understand him a little, he has to be impossible again."

Bess blinked sleepily. "What did you say, Jenna?"

"Nothing." She stomped to the back of the wagon, pulling out what she needed to prepare breakfast. "Romantic rogue indeed. About as romantic as a mesquite bush."

No amount of cajoling from Bess would get Jenna to talk further, and after a while Bess fell silent.

The day promised to be another hot one. To give the horses every possible advantage Jenna walked alongside the wagon with Timmy. Bess too volunteered to walk, but Jenna wouldn't hear of it. Her sister had been feeling much better of late, but Jenna saw no reason to take chances. Besides, she thought ruefully, this way she would not be pestered with questions about Caleb Harper.

"Did you remember to ask Mr. Holt about our horses, Timmy?" she asked. The team had seemed more tired than usual lately.

Her brother nodded. "He said he can't figure it, but that we should double-check the wagon. See if there's something we can leave behind."

Jenna watched the listless movement of the four horses. She had been certain the animals were sound. The Holts and Kovels both had more belongings, more supplies than she and her siblings, yet neither family was having any trouble.

"Maybe you should ask Mr. Harper," Timmy said. "He'd know what to do, I'll bet."

She thought about the extra repairs Caleb had had to order in Council Grove. Now he would think her a bad caretaker of her animals as well. "I'll ask him." She sighed. She had no choice.

As Timmy walked he was busily sharpening his new knife on a honing stone, first spitting on the stone, then rubbing the knife in small circles as Caleb had shown him. He was quite enamored of the whole process. "It sure was nice of Mr. Harper to give me this knife. Do you really think he liked having a birthday?"

Jenna fidgeted with the bow on her sunbonnet. "I'm sure it meant a lot to him." Maybe she should have had Timmy ride in the wagon. Thankfully, he ambled off to chase butterflies with Mary Holt.

Jenna had her own butterflies when Caleb rode in around noon. Despite her supposed resolve to ask him about Jacobs, and her need to ask about her horses, all she could think of as he walked toward her was that kiss. And how much she wanted another one just like it. She dared not look him in the eye, even as he told her there would be no trouble at Pawnee Rock.

"No Indians?" She kept stirring her pot of beans.

"No hostiles," he corrected. "I spotted a small party of Comanche a couple miles off. They saw me too, but they didn't make any threatening moves."

"Does that mean they won't?" She couldn't help glancing up. When she did, his gaze grew suddenly intense, and she could tell he was not thinking of Comanches.

Then he seemed to shake himself. "You and your family stay close to the wagons, Miss Riordan." With that he touched his hat brim and stalked off.

"Damn Injun lover."

Jenna jumped at the sound of Bart Jacobs's voice. She had not heard his approach. She turned toward the scruffily dressed sutler, noting that he too was carrying his rifle. No man in camp was without one today.

"Mr. Harper seems to know a good deal about Indians, Mr. Jacobs." She automatically began to breathe through her mouth.

"Bet one of them savages was ridin' my horse." Jacobs spat a stream of tobacco juice into the dust. "And I'll tell you this for a fact: If I see that redskin what done it, I'll kill him." He scratched at his beard. Jenna took an unconscious step back as she thought she saw something move in that scraggly growth.

"We'd best be getting ready to head out," she managed. "Maybe you should get back to your wagon, Mr. Jacobs."

He scowled. "That don't sound too neighborly, Miss Jenna. In fact, it sounded a mite uppity. It's that scout, ain't it? I seen you watchin' him. Like he's better'n me."

Sam Holt had wandered over. With seeming nonchalance he struck up a conversation with Bess, but Jenna could tell the boy was keeping a watchful eye on Jacobs. It occurred to her then that Caleb's admonition was not about jealousy at all. Impulsively she excused herself and hurried over to where Caleb was adjusting the saddle on the black gelding, preparing to head out again.

He eyed her warily, obviously thinking she was about to bring up last night.

"Why do you want me to stay away from Bart Jacobs?"

He grimaced. "You mean there's a reason you'd want to go near him?"

"You told Sam Holt to make sure I wasn't alone with him."

"That's right."

"Why?"

"There aren't that many places to bathe out here."

Her lips thinned. "Are you going to tell me the truth, or aren't you? What is it? Do you think I find the man attractive?"

"Only if you've suddenly taken leave of your senses."

"My sense of smell especially, I suppose," she said dryly.

He had to laugh. She could tell he tried not to, but in the end he couldn't help himself. "You are the damnedest woman."

"Coming from you, I'll take that as a high compliment. But why do you want me to stay away from him?"

"Because I'm asking you to. Can that be enough for now?"

"All right. I'll keep my distance. But I need to ask you something else."

"Can it wait?" He finished tightening the cinch.

"It's our horses."

He stilled. "What about them?"

"I'm worried. They seem tired."

"They'll make it to the cutoff." His tone was clipped all at once. She took it as censure.

"I've had Timmy feed them extra grain, give them extra rubdowns . . . I just don't know what else to do."

"They'll make it."

"Mr. Jacobs still has two extras he brought along. Maybe I could ask . . ."

He swore. "You haven't heard a word I've said, have you?"

She stared at him, dumbfounded. "I hardly think asking to borrow a horse is—"

"Stay away from him."

"Then *you* ask him," she said, exasperated. "I don't want to be the cause of any delays for the others."

"I've checked your horses myself, Jenna. I wouldn't abuse an animal. They'll make it. If I didn't think so, I'd trade them off at Fort Larned. We'll be going past there tomorrow."

"Oh. Of course. Thank you." Hurt and confused by his continued irritation, she turned to leave.

"Jenna?"

She looked at him.

"I'm sorry. Don't think I'm angry with you. I'm not."

"We've taken good care of the horses, Caleb. Honestly."

"I know." That haunted look was in his eyes again. That feeling that he wanted to tell her something.

"I meant what I said last night," she said softly, hoping that might encourage him. But he only looked more discomfited. Still, he seemed to reach some kind of decision about something. He took a deep breath.

"About the cutoff, Jenna. I . . . there's something you need to—"

A gunshot split the air.

Jenna whirled toward the sound—somewhere near her wagon—but Caleb was already sprinting ahead of her. They arrived to find Bart Jacobs on the ground, sputtering angrily. He was trying to retrieve his fallen rifle, but Sam Holt had his foot across the barrel.

The Holts and Kovels rushed up, weapons ready, demanding to know what was going on.

Caleb pointed north. He had now seen what Bart Jacobs had seen.

Jenna gasped, her heart catching in her throat. Still a half mile off, but riding hard and coming straight toward them were a half-dozen Indians.

10

Instinctively Jenna urged Bess and Timmy behind her as the Indians thundered closer. She stared at the approaching horsemen, transfixed, unwillingly recalling Bart Jacobs's gruesome tales of arrow-riddled bodies. *Savages, murderers, monsters . . . slayers of women and children.* The epithets she'd heard crossing the plains thrummed through her, and she had to consciously will them away.

She became aware of bare chests and copper skin, jet-black hair and animal-hide leggings. The Indians rode effortlessly, as though they and their mounts were one. The brave in the lead carried a lance, eagle feathers dangling near its tip. Tied near the feathers was a square of white cloth.

"They've come in peace," Caleb said, his voice calm, though she thought she detected a slight edge to it.

"They'll get no peace from me!" Jacobs roared, struggling to his feet. "Damned savages!" He groped for the six-gun on his hip. "One of them bucks is ridin' my Appaloosa."

Caleb backhanded Jacobs across the face, then yanked the Smith & Wesson from the sutler's gun belt. "Any man who raises a gun against these Comanch' will answer to me." He tossed the revolver out of Jacobs's reach, then unbuckled his own gun belt and did the same with it. "Is that understood?"

No one else moved. Like Jenna, everyone but Jacobs seemed to regard Caleb with a kind of awe as the scout marched weaponless toward the advancing Indians. He held up his right hand in a gesture of greeting. The Indians kept coming. For a heart-stopping moment it seemed they would overrun him. Jenna resisted the urge to cry out. Barely six feet from where Caleb stood, the Indians reined in.

Before his paint stallion had even come to a halt, the front-riding Comanche was leaping from the animal's back. Maintaining his grip on his lance, the Indian began to gesture wildly, using both hands and speaking with obvious anger in a low, gutteral tongue. Caleb answered him in the same language, his own tone steel-hard, cold.

Afoot Jenna could see that the Comanche was a short, stocky man with a powerful upper body. On his right hand he wore a metal-and-leather glove that ended halfway up his arm. A Spanish gauntlet. She had seen drawings of such things in a history book about the *conquistadors* of the sixteenth century. All this she took in with no particular alarm.

And then she looked at the man's face. A crescent-shaped scar transected his features from the left side of his forehead to his jawline. The long-ago wound had obviously not been properly cared for. Excess scar tissue pulled the skin tight near his mouth, making already unpleasant features more sinister still. Jenna shivered.

"Iron Fist." Jacobs spat. "The most murderin' savage

that ever sat a horse. And Harper is talkin' to him like they was on a Sunday-go-to-meetin' picnic."

"Hardly, Mr. Jacobs," Jenna said. "In fact, they seem to be having a rather heated argument about something."

Jacobs swore, then spat again. "That Injun lover is gonna get us all killed." His right hand, his gunhand, flexed and unflexed. "Thievin' savages. I tell ya, I ain't gonna stand for it much longer."

"We don't have much choice, Jacobs," Emmet Holt said. "We hired Harper to see us through this country. Let the man do his job."

Jacobs was shaking with rage. Jenna could tell the sutler was trying to decide if it was worth the risk to make a dive for his gun. She had no doubt he would not only shoot Iron Fist, he would shoot Caleb as well. Fortunately Caleb was aware of the danger. He looked first at his own discarded Colt, then at Jacobs. It was a silent challenge, a warning. Jacobs's shoulders sagged. He continued to swear but made no threatening move.

Jenna's attention returned to the six Comanches. Despite her fear she was fascinated. There was something wild and primitive yet strangely compelling about them. Like the land itself. She sensed a fierce pride in them. The youngest of the six—a brave she guessed to be all of fifteen—was sitting astride Jacobs's stolen gelding and was regarding her with an open curiosity of his own. The hostility she saw in the eyes of the others was not in this boy's face. He even smiled a little when he caught her watching him.

Embarrassed, Jenna looked away—only to be embarrassed again. Iron Fist had turned his back, gesturing toward the western horizon. To her utter dismay the flap of cloth that covered his private parts in front did not extend to his backside. His taut brown buttocks were fully exposed, the muscles contracting in time with his agitated movements.

Jenna watched Bess's eyes grow wide as saucers. Little Mary Holt, to her mother's horror, began to giggle and point. Timmy did a pathetic job of stifling a guffaw. Jenna wasted no time. Moving swiftly, she shooed both girls and her brother into the back of the nearest wagon.

Iron Fist chose that instant to glance in her direction. It was obvious he did not want anyone, even children, where he couldn't see them. Gesturing angrily, he started toward Jenna.

She froze.

"Don't show him any fear," Caleb said. "He won't hurt you."

Somehow Jenna stood her ground, though her sensibilities recoiled. If she thought Jacobs smelled bad, the stench coming from Iron Fist reminded her of nothing so much as rotting buffalo meat. Even so, she could have tolerated the smell if she had perceived an ounce of humanity in the man. Unlike the five braves still astride their horses, Iron Fist's black eyes glinted with more than hate. Jenna couldn't help but think it: There was a cruelty about him, a nameless evil, that terrified her.

When the Comanche reached a hand toward her, she nearly bolted.

"Easy," Caleb said, drawing out the word as though he were speaking to a skittish horse. "That's it. Good girl."

Jenna was certain she was going to faint, so rapidly was her heart beating, but she held herself motionless as Iron Fist first jerked off her sunbonnet, then ran rough fingers through her unbound hair. When she dared look into that scarred face, she was all but undone by the unmistakable flare of lust she saw there.

"Caleb," she murmured desperately, "I'm going to scream if he doesn't stop. Please, make him stop."

Caleb was already closing the distance between them. Though he was trying hard not to alarm her, trying even harder to remain at least diplomatic with the Comanche, she could tell by the way he was carrying himself that he was savagely angry. Yet she knew he dared not attack the Indian. To do so would be to put every life in camp in jeopardy.

Iron Fist now gripped her upper arm. Holding his lance above his head, he grunted something to his five companions, then made an obscene gesture with his crotch. The other Indians nodded their assent, muttering and laughing among themselves.

Suddenly more angry than afraid, Jenna jerked her arm free. "Whatever you said," she hissed, "you'd better know I'll scratch your eyes out if you put your hands on me again!"

Iron Fist stood stock-still, and for an instant Jenna was certain she had brought a hideous death down upon them all. The Comanche had no idea what she had said, but he knew full well he had been threatened. To her astonishment a grudging respect came into those soulless eyes, along with a sick amusement.

He ignored her after that, signaling his companions to dismount, then he started toward the back of her wagon. For a moment Jenna feared he meant to go after Bess and Mary, but he rummaged about only long enough to pull out a sack of grain. The other braves were taking what they wanted from the Holt and Kovel wagons.

When Lem Kovel moved to interfere, Caleb restrained him. "They won't take much," he said, speaking loud enough for all of them to hear. "It's a cheap price to pay for your lives."

Bart Jacobs glared daggers at Caleb but allowed Iron

Fist to pilfer his wagon as well. "Lucky I got most of my supplies comin' by freighter," the sutler groused. He even went so far as to reach into the pocket of his disreputable coat and pull out a greasy leather pouch, which he then handed to Iron Fist. "You missed this, savage," he sneered. "My best tobacco. Hope you choke on it."

Iron Fist's mouth curved into a mockery of a smile. He gripped the pouch, then gathered up the rest of his trophies. It took several minutes for the Indians to pack their newly acquired goods onto their horses. Five of them mounted. Iron Fist headed for Jenna.

He spoke rapidly, gesticulating and pounding his chest. All the while he pointed at her.

"What's he saying?" she demanded.

"Just go along with whatever I do," Caleb said, his voice terse. He put his arm possessively about her waist. "Smile . . . then kiss me."

"What?"

"Now." He pulled her against him and kissed her full on the mouth. His lips were bruising, forceful, angry, conjuring none of the warmth, the passion she had shared with him last night. Somehow she knew this was for Iron Fist's benefit, and though she wanted to struggle she didn't.

And then the kiss changed.

When it ended, she continued to lean against him, fearful she would collapse if she let go. He took a step back but not before he feathered a hand ever so softly down the side of her face, as if to assure himself she was real. There was no mistaking the passion in those eyes. The wonder.

"There," he said hoarsely. "Now he should believe me."

"Believe what?"

"That you're my wife."

Without preamble Iron Fist reared back his head and let loose with the most blood-chilling sound Jenna had ever heard issue from a human throat. The hate in those twisted features was terrifying to behold. No matter what Iron Fist had wanted, Jenna knew all of this posturing was not just about her. The hate between the Comanche and Caleb ran old and deep. Trembling, she watched as Iron Fist stomped back to his horse. Vaulting onto the animal's back, he gave his lance two quick jerks in the air, let out another fearsome cry, then, along with his companions, thundered off.

It was over.

"Are we safe now?" Millie Holt asked shakily, gripping a wagon wheel for support. The woman had scarcely dared breathe the entire time the Indians were in camp.

"For the moment," Caleb said. "We'd best get moving. There's still plenty of daylight left."

Bart Jacobs snorted, bending to pick up his six-gun. "What's the hurry, Harper? Make a deal with them redskins to lift our scalps up the trail a ways?"

"Get moving, Jacobs," Caleb snapped, "or I'll damned well lift your scalp myself."

The sutler had no stomach for a one-on-one confrontation with Caleb Harper. Grumbling under his breath, Jacobs did as he was told. But Jenna was still too shaken even to think clearly. Somehow she hustled Bess and Timmy into breaking camp, but she couldn't seem to get herself focused on anything. She needed to talk this through; she needed to talk to Caleb.

She caught up with him just as he was about to ride out. With obvious reluctance he dismounted.

"I need to know what Iron Fist was saying about me."

The look on Caleb's face told her he considered lying, but decided against it. "He'd never seen a woman like you before. Your white-blond hair, your blue eyes. He wanted you. He offered me a half-dozen ponies for you."

"So you told him I was your wife."

He nodded. "It was the only way."

"I understand. I'm sure you saved my life."

His face was red under his sun-dark features. "I didn't want to put you through that . . . in front of everyone. I just didn't see any other choice."

"It's all right. Really. He was ready to take me by force, wasn't he?"

"Don't think about it. It's over. Comanches respect marriage. A man doesn't take another man's wife without her husband's permission."

Her eyes widened. "How gallant!" She hadn't meant to sound quite so facetious. Caleb looked disappointed.

"Comanche ways are different from whites'. Don't condemn something you don't understand."

"Maybe you could teach me. Major Gallagher told me you spent a lot of time with Indians, even lived with them."

"Once or twice." He gathered up the gelding's reins. "I'd best get riding. There's a creek up ahead I think we can make by nightfall. It would probably help your horses."

She wanted to shake him. She was starving for information about this man, and yet he gave up tiny pieces of himself only with the greatest reluctance. Well, she wasn't ready to let him go, not yet. "You're sure Iron Fist won't come back?"

"We have a treaty with the Comanche. Even if Iron Fist had a notion, his father, Eagle Dancer, wouldn't let him break the treaty."

"At least not over another man's 'wife.' " She managed a teasing smile.

He blushed again, but he didn't mount up. Maybe he wasn't in such a hurry to leave either.

"You know, where I come from," she went on, taking full advantage of a sudden surge of confidence, "a man could be honor-bound to make good on a claim like that. Duels have been fought over less."

"Oh?" He surprised her with a teasing grin of his own. "And just who would I be dueling?"

"Why, me, of course. I had a fencing lesson once. A gentleman who escorted me to a party thought a lady should be able to defend herself."

"You're not wearing your weapon."

"During our lesson I'm afraid I nicked him in a most unfortunate place."

Caleb nearly choked, his eyes all but leaping out of his head.

Jenna laughed brightly. She had actually scandalized Caleb Harper! "Anyway, he never invited me to another party, nor saw to any more fencing lessons."

"Lucky man. Heaven knows what the second lesson could have cost him."

"I wonder if I could take up fencing again in California. It was quite limbering, as I recall."

"Timmy told me about your Uncle William. He doesn't sound like the fencing type."

"I think you and Uncle William would get along famously. I can't wait for you to meet him."

He looked away. "I, uh, I really better hit the trail. I've got a lot of riding to do."

"Caleb, what is it?"

"What do you mean?"

She frowned. How could she explain? One moment he'd been open, even happy; the next he was closed off again. "You were going to tell me something before Iron Fist rode in. Something about the cutoff . . ."

He shrugged. "It wasn't important."

"Are you sure?"

"I'm sure." He climbed into the saddle.

She looked up at him. "Would you have supper with us tonight? Timmy and Bess love having you around."

"Maybe."

"I love having you around too."

It was one step more than he could handle. "I'll eat in the saddle. I'll be back late. Tell the others, all right?"

She made sure not to roll her eyes. The man was beyond exasperating. But that was all right. She loved him anyway. And, though she was the first to admit she wasn't the best one to judge, she was almost certain he was beginning to care about her too.

All she needed now was to get him to trust her. Because he didn't. She didn't know why, but he didn't. She was not offended. Bess was probably right. Someone, most likely a woman, had taken the trust out of him a long time ago.

Jenna was merely going to put it back.

II

Caleb was true to his word. He did not show up for supper. Muttering under her breath, Jenna sat on a small boulder beside her waning cook fire and helped herself to a second cup of coffee. His declining her invitation, she could accept, even understand. He was as confused as she was about what was happening between them. But it was nearly dusk. With Comanches in the vicinity, shouldn't he at least be in *camp?*

Jenna sighed. This was not a good time to be alone with her thoughts.

Timmy had taken the horses to the nearby creek. Bess had gone off to have dessert with the Holts. Her sister, it seemed, was growing quite fond of young Sam.

"He's a lot like Mr. Harper in his ways," Bess said, before she went off. "He's steady and kind and a little bashful, but you can depend on him. And he needs to laugh more. I'm going to make him laugh." Her smile full of mischief, Bess held up her sewing basket. From it she extracted an old and badly frayed sampler. "I'm going to show him your needlework."

Jenna groaned. The badly worked embroidery was supposed to read GOD BLESS THIS HOUSE, but actually proclaimed SOD BUILT THIS MOUSE. "Where did you find that thing? I thought I'd burned it."

"Never!" Bess clutched it protectively to her bosom. "You don't know what pleasure this has given me over the years."

"I can imagine! You could embroider us up a new wagon if we needed one."

"I had to be better than you at something." Bess spoke gently, but Jenna did not miss the slight wistfulness. Her sister had then given her a quick hug and hurried off to join the Holts.

Jenna took another sip of her coffee. Even with the war there had been occasional parties and plays and dancing. But not for Bess. It would be different in California, Jenna thought hopefully. Healthy air, mild winters. Bess would surely thrive.

Her brother returned then, leading four still moderately wet horses. Jenna peered at him over the rim of her cup. "Did rubbing down their legs in the water seem to help?" she asked.

"I think Ruby's a little better." He patted the sorrel's neck. "But Jack's awful tired."

"I'll mention it to Mr. Harper," she said. "That is, if the man ever decides to come back to camp."

Timmy blinked, confused. "What do you mean, Jenna? Mr. Harper's down at the creek. He was the one who showed me what to do for the horses."

"What?"

"Yeah, now he's takin' a bath." Timmy led the horses off to bed them down for the night.

Jenna was on her feet. Before common sense could rear its ugly head, she scrambled to the back of the wagon, grabbed up a fresh dress and a towel, and headed for the creek.

He wasn't hard to find. She just homed in on the splashing. She was feeling deliciously wicked as she crept toward the near bank. A thick growth of stunted shrubs and towering cottonwoods blocked her view of the water, and she very nearly took one step too many.

The gently shooshing stream was about eight feet across and maybe four feet deep, at least in the spot where Caleb was standing, his back to her. She hunkered down in the tall grass, knowing she should call out to him. She wasn't being fair at all. But she just couldn't spoil the moment. Not yet.

Behind him in the western sky the horizon ran riot with color—red, orange, purple, gold. He was standing there, taking it all in. But to her he was part of it.

The colors grew muted; twilight drifted in. She was about to clear her throat and announce her presence, when Caleb turned leisurely to face her. "Have you been a Peeping Tom long, Miss Riordan?"

She felt her face go scarlet. Thunderation! How long had he known she was there?

"You wouldn't make a very good Comanche."

"I beg your pardon?" Her heart was pounding, her voice barely more than a squeak.

"Your 'sneaking up on a naked man in a creek' skills need a little practice, I think."

"Oh." She sat up a bit straighter, desperate that he not know how mortified she was. "I'll try to do better next time."

"It's this time I'm concerned about."

Her brow furrowed. "What . . ."

"How long are you going to sit there? I'm getting more of a bath than I bargained for."

She scrambled to her feet. "I'm sorry. I, of course . . ." She turned away, thinking to leave, to run, when she spied his change of clothes lying in the grass just a couple of yards from where she stood.

Some devil's own imp must have taken hold of her then, because surely she wasn't the sort who would scoop up a naked man's clothes, but scoop them up she did.

"What are you doing?" he demanded.

"Holding your clothes for you." She said it innocently enough.

"Why?"

"I wouldn't want them to accidentally fall into the creek or anything." She smiled wickedly.

"Give me my clothes."

"You shouldn't be so grumpy," she scolded primly, standing at the water's edge. "I'm sure we can come to some sort of agreement."

"I want my clothes, and I want you out of here."

Jenna supposed he was trying to sound dictatorial, but the truth was, he wasn't even doing a very good job of sounding cross. The scoundrel! He was having as much fun as she was.

"Now, let me see," she said. "What do you suppose all of these fine clothes are worth? Trousers, shirt, buck-skin jacket . . ."

"I'll tell you what you're going to be worth—" He had moved a couple of steps closer to shore, the water now lapping at his waist.

"Oh, stop fussing and give me a fair price." She was having trouble maintaining her glibness as her gaze locked on to his bare chest. With what light there was coming from behind him, his chest and face were in heavy shadow, but that didn't stop her imagination.

"One kiss," he said.

"What?"

"I'll give you one kiss for my clothes."

"Before or after you get out of the creek?" Were these words really coming from her mouth? In her wildest dreams she had never behaved so . . . so wildly!

"I'll leave that up to you, Miss Riordan." He took another step. "What's it going to be?" The waterline ducked below his navel.

She blanched, spinning an about-face, surrendering to cowardice. The water sloshed louder, closer.

"My clothes, Miss Riordan."

He was standing right behind her! Stark naked! She straightened, though her knees seemed turned to jelly. "Your longjohns first?" she inquired with patently false bravado.

He growled unpleasantly but made no move to grab for his clothes. He obviously wasn't going to take any chances on accidentally startling her into apoplexy. Holding only his longjohns in her right hand, Jenna stuck the hand—quite carefully—behind her. He accepted them without comment.

His socks were next.

Then his pants.

And his boots.

She tossed aside the jacket and hat for the moment. Her full concentration was on his shirt. As long as she was behaving beyond redemption anyway, she intended to have a closer view of his chest. Feigning nonchalance, she turned to face him, her grip on the shirt shifting slightly. She was just about to hand it to him when she felt something solid inside the folds. She shook out the shirt and found herself holding some sort of amulet. She squinted hard but couldn't make out much detail in the dim twilight. Yet she could sense the care and precision that had gone into making the piece. "It's beautiful."

He didn't answer. He just slipped it around his neck, but she knew the mood had shifted. The lightheartedness was gone. He wasn't angry, just a little subdued all at once.

She held out his shirt, no longer eager for the game. He shrugged into it but hadn't yet started to button it, when she noticed the scar—eight inches of marred flesh that arced from his left nipple to the top of his left shoulder. Without thinking she reached out, skimming her fingers along its length. "My God . . ."

Caleb jerked back. The shudder that coursed through him had nothing to do with his memory of the wound. Her hand on his flesh had been flame to dry tinder. Holding his hands rigidly at his sides, he forced himself to take several long strides away from her. "It happened a long time ago."

"How?" She was too caught up in the obvious horror of such a wound to see what she had wrought in him.

"Our Comanche friend," he managed. He would go mad if he didn't get away from her. Now. Either that or he would grab hold of her and never let go.

"No wonder you hate him." She shuddered, imagining the ferocity of the battle the two of them must have fought. Her mind leapt to Iron Fist's twisted features. "That scar on his face . . . ?"

He didn't say anything. He didn't have to.

"I'm sorry. How awful for you both."

"I think it best if we say good night." He grabbed up his jacket and hat and started toward camp without another word.

Jenna didn't protest. She knew he was fighting sudden, bitter memories. He needed to be alone. She let him walk ahead of her. She didn't even remind him that she hadn't gotten her kiss.

Sleep eluded Caleb, but then he had known it would. It had been one helluva day. Seeing Iron Fist again would have been enough. But to see the look in the

Comanche warrior's eyes when he had dared touch Jenna had sent a tearing rage through him such as he'd never known. If Iron Fist so much as came near her again . . .

Caleb shut his mind to the thought. It simply would not happen. He wouldn't allow it to happen.

He wished he had as much control over something else the Comanche had said. Iron Fist had boasted about becoming war chief one day soon, that then no one could stop his killing the white settlers. Not even Eagle Dancer.

Iron Fist had always been more brag than substance, but a war chief would have much power. Caleb just had to hope the Comanche council in Eagle Dancer's band wouldn't support the kind of hate Iron Fist espoused, by selecting the warrior to such an honored position.

For now, if Caleb truly felt the Comanche represented a danger to Jenna and the others, he could always ask for troops from Fort Larned. Gallagher wouldn't like the interference, but Gallagher be damned if Caleb thought the settlers' lives were at stake. Not that Caleb didn't already know what Larned's answer would be. Their commanding officer would never justify enough protection to count, not for such a small caravan. For the questionable difference a soldier or two might make, it was better not to call the extra attention to themselves. Caleb grimaced. No doubt Larned would justify plenty of troops if they knew about the Spencers, but he could say nothing about the carbines to anyone.

He lay there trying hard to keep his thoughts focused elsewhere, but inevitably they returned to Jenna. The more he tried not to think of that woman, the more completely his thoughts were consumed by her.

Damn! How had he managed to keep his hands off her tonight? Her touch had all but driven him insane.

He had wanted nothing more on God's earth than to press her down into that sweet, lush, wet grass and feel her naked beneath him, to feel his very essence buried deep inside her, his body linked to hers on the most primitive of levels and the most exalted.

His loins throbbed, and he cursed. He had learned long ago to endure sexual frustration. Out here the places a man could indulge his appetites were as scarce as summer rain. But what he felt for Jenna Riordan went beyond any lust of the body. He wanted her heart, her soul, her mind. Her spirit.

Son of a bitch. He climbed to his feet, pacing back and forth like a caged panther. He was being a damned fool. He could want Jenna from now until the end of time. It didn't matter. He would never have her. When they reached the cutoff, she would discover his duplicity and hate his guts. Gallagher would retrieve the Spencers, and Jenna would know that they had used her wagon, used her, to transport guns through Indian territory.

Even if she didn't hate him, he was hardly in a position to offer her much of a life anyway. What did he even have? Scout's quarters on an army post? With times when he could be gone for weeks, even months on end? His next assignment—infiltrating the *comancheros*—might even get him killed.

And if all that weren't enough, there was that other little matter, the one that would surely turn Jenna's stomach, if she but knew. It had certainly repelled Laurel McKenzie the day he had been fool enough to tell her. The day he had asked her to be his wife. He had been young then, naive, foolish. He had risked a little of his heart, and more of his pride.

And lost.

What would he be risking to tell Jenna?

He shuddered. All that he was, all that he would ever be.

And that he was not willing to do. He closed his eyes, the choice made. In five days he would ride out of her life forever.

12

Jenna adjusted her sunbonnet, but still had to shield her eyes from the oppressive glare of the afternoon sun as she trudged alongside her four-horse team. The dust disturbed by plodding hooves mingled with the sweat beading on her face and neck. She swiped at the grime with her handkerchief, grateful Caleb was riding ahead of the Holt wagon. Not that he would notice her looks anyway. He had scarcely come near her these past two days—not since their unplanned evening at the creek. Nor had he permitted any opportunity for the episode to be repeated.

She sighed. Why was it for every step she took toward him, Caleb seemed to leap two steps back? Had she misread him so badly? Had her love for him blinded her to his reaction to that love? Was he embarrassed by it? Was he trying to spare her feelings?

No. He cared for her. She was sure of it. Whether he wanted to or not. There was something else holding him back, that same hidden something she had seen in his eyes that night he had first kissed her. Blast the man!

What could have made him so guarded, so closed off about himself?

Heaven knew she wasn't privy to that many facts about the life he had led. What did she really even know about him? That he worked for the army. That his mother had died when he was four years old. That his relatives were so indifferent they hadn't even remembered his birthday. And that he had once been in a battle with Iron Fist, a fight vicious enough to have left both men scarred for life.

And yet it wasn't facts that mattered. She loved Caleb on instinct alone, trusting the intangibles that spoke volumes where he would not. His empathy, his intelligence, his kindness, his passion, even the very wariness that kept him from trusting *her*—all were interlocking pieces of a most fascinating puzzle. She simply could not be wrong about him. She could not be wrong about loving Caleb Harper.

She would just have to be patient. If he cared about her as much as she hoped he did, he couldn't continue to shy away from her indefinitely. It was still a long way to California. She smiled. The man would have to be made of stone to ignore her over so many days—and nights—to come. Especially if she put her mind to it.

Unless—

She stopped dead.

Unless he wasn't here. The thought jolted through her in a rush. In three days they were to rendezvous with Major Gallagher. After that Caleb wouldn't have to manufacture excuses to stay away from her. He could get Gallagher to do it for him.

Or worse. Gallagher to take his place! Gallagher to guide the wagons!

Jenna trembled. He wouldn't. Would he? Her heart sank. Of course he would. The emotional risks were too high for a man as closed in as Caleb Harper. Given the chance, why wouldn't he take the easy way out? Never resolve his feelings about her one way or the other?

Her gaze shot toward him, her eyes boring into his back, as though staring at him could somehow get him to turn around, to ride back and face her. Now. But he rode on.

The wagons were approaching a narrow corridor between two forty-foot bluffs. Caleb disappeared from her line of sight as the passage curved in a wide arc to the left.

"You're not going to get away with this," she murmured. "You're not." Tonight she would find a way to be alone with him, to force his hand, even if she had to interrupt his stint of guard duty.

She was so intent on her plan that, at first, the movement on the ridgetop didn't register. Only Timmy's sudden shout made her look up.

"Indians, Jenna!"

She gasped, startled to see a lone Indian horseman ride up to the rim of the left bluff. She squinted, shading her eyes. It was the boy, the one who'd been riding with Iron Fist. The young brave, it seemed, had not yet fully satisfied his curiosity about them.

Jenna raised her hand to wave, smiling when the youth raised a hand in return. In that instant the crack of a rifle sounded, echoing off the craggy cliffs on either side of her. For a heartbeat nothing changed, and then the boy seemed to rise up slightly on the Appaloosa's back. Before Jenna's horrified gaze the youth crumpled forward, his body tumbling over the gelding's withers. His shoulder hit the ground hard, but for the rest of his body there was only the air at the bluff's edge. He landed with a sickening thud on the rutted trail some thirty feet from where Jenna stood.

"Got 'im!" Bart Jacobs sprinted up from the rear of

the last wagon. "I finally got that savage son of a bitch that stole my horse!"

Jenna bolted toward the Indian, even as Millie Holt hustled Bess and Mary away from the horrible scene. Jenna reached the broken body at the same time Sam and Timmy did. The Holt boy's face was gray, but his too-serious eyes were filled with disgust.

"You had no call to do that, Mr. Jacobs," Sam said.

Jacobs was paying no attention. He was already seeking a purchase on the craggy cliff face, ready to scramble up to reclaim his horse. He'd just discovered a game trail when Caleb thundered up. Jenna watched Caleb's eyes as he looked first at the Indian boy's body, then at Jacobs, then at her. He must have read everything in her face. With a roar of undiluted rage he spurred the black toward Jacobs.

The sutler had time only to let out a thin shriek of terror before Caleb dove at him from the gelding's back. The two men rolled and twisted on the hard earth, Jacobs's fear no match for Caleb's fury. Caleb pinned the sutler on his back, straddling his midsection. With one hand he manacled Jacobs's wrists above his head; with the other he hammered his fist into Jacobs's face.

No one moved.

Caleb hit him again.

No one interfered.

And again.

"He's going to kill him," Jenna whispered as much to herself as anyone else. The sutler's head lolled to one side, his eyes glazing dully. She couldn't move, couldn't think, couldn't seem to do anything but watch. But her words must have had some effect on Lem Kovel and Emmet Holt. Suddenly they were moving, each man grabbing at one of Caleb's arms, pulling, yanking him away from Jacobs's inert body.

Caleb wrenched free, sending both men sprawling, then dragged his Colt from the holster on his hip. He leveled the barrel at the unconscious Jacobs and thumbed back the hammer.

"No!" Jenna didn't even know she'd said the word aloud, until Caleb turned to look at her. The savagery in him was a terrible thing to see. But as she watched he closed his eyes and sucked in deep lungfuls of air. When he again opened his eyes, he was still furious, but the killing light was gone.

He shoved his gun back into its holster. "I won't have to kill him," he said. "The Comanches will do it for me."

The full meaning of his words didn't register as Jenna turned her concentration to the Indian boy. He was dead. Whether from Jacobs's bullet, or the fall, or both, she didn't know. All she knew was how young, how fragile, he looked lying there.

Without thinking, she smoothed his thick, dark hair away from his face, surprised at how soft it was. Jacobs had once told her Indians put bear grease in their hair. This boy had apparently not bothered, or perhaps hadn't had any with him.

"I wonder if he's got a ma and pa," Timmy said, his voice hushed, sad.

"His father is Two Trees."

Jenna looked up to see Caleb had moved near, his face grim but his eyes now edged with sorrow. "One Wolf was his only son."

"What are we going to do about this, Harper?" Lem Kovel demanded. "What if the Comanches find out?"

"Do you think the others are close by?" Emmet Holt asked, upending a bucket of water over Bart Jacobs's head.

"If they were close, we'd be dead," Caleb said. "As

for them finding out—I'm going to tell them, when I hand this murdering bastard over to Iron Fist."

The sutler moaned, struggling to a sitting position. Caleb's words hadn't penetrated at first, but then suddenly Jacobs lurched to his feet, swaying drunkenly. "You ain't turnin' me over to no Comanch'," he slurred through bloodied lips. "Ain't nobody turnin' me over to no Injuns for bringin' that buck to justice." He waved a hand toward One Wolf's body.

"Maybe Iron Fist will understand," Caleb sneered, stalking toward the sutler. "Maybe he'll make you a member of the tribe for being such a brave warrior." He gripped Jacobs by the back of the shirt and propelled him toward the black gelding.

Jacobs's wild-eyed gaze swung toward Holt and Kovel. "You can't let him do this."

Kovel stepped in front of Caleb. "It was only an Injun, Harper. We ain't turnin' Jacobs over to no redskins for that."

"Jacobs done murder," Emmet Holt put in. "But I got to go along with Kovel. We can't turn over one of our own."

The look on Caleb's face told Jenna he didn't much care what either one of them thought. But in front of her he paused. "And what do you think, Miss Riordan?"

There was a challenge in those words, though she couldn't for the life of her fathom a reason for it. A little unsteadily she rose to face him. Her heart hammered painfully because she knew she was about to disappoint him.

"The Comanches would torture Jacobs, wouldn't they?" It wasn't really a question.

"Slow and hard." Caleb spoke as though he relished the idea.

She looked at Jacobs, his clothes torn, his face covered with blood, his right eye swelling shut, and felt only loathing and disgust. She thought about how he must have trained his rifle on the boy, how he must have smiled when he pulled the trigger. And she thought about a man named Two Trees, who now had no son.

"This has to go against the treaty you've spoken about," she offered. "Give Jacobs to Major Gallagher. The army will know how to deal with him."

Caleb snorted derisively. "A month in the guardhouse. Maybe."

"Or maybe hang him," Emmet Holt put in, obviously seizing on any chance to discourage Caleb's particular brand of justice.

"Hang for killing an Indian? You ever hear of that being done, Holt?"

Emmet shook his head. "But I'd testify. So would we all. He wouldn't get off with no month in the guardhouse."

Caleb's gaze again centered on Jenna. "That your verdict, Miss Riordan? Army justice?"

Why was he so angry with *her?* Why was she being singled out as some sort of villain? "I can't condone your handing him over to be tortured," she managed, her hands twisting in front of her. "I'm sorry you wish that I could, but I can't. No matter what he's done."

Bitter, coldly furious, he turned away from her. Slamming Jacobs against the gelding, Caleb pulled free the lariat tied to his saddle, then roughly hog-tied and gagged the man.

"You two are in charge of him." He pointed to Kovel and Holt. "If I see him loose, I'll kill him."

"We may need his gun," Kovel complained. "Where could he go anyway?"

"If I see him loose," Caleb repeated, "I'll kill him. So I guess it's up to you."

While Kovel and Holt half carried, half dragged Jacobs back toward his wagon, Caleb returned his attention to One Wolf. Gently, as though cradling a sleeping babe, he lifted the lifeless body.

"Are you going to bury him?" Jenna asked timidly, still undone by the odd sense that she had somehow betrayed Caleb just now.

"It's not the Comanche way to bury their dead."

"Then what are you going to do?"

His lips thinned. "I'm going to bury him."

She shuddered, somehow knowing what such a sacrilege would cost him. His voice went on, relentless, ominous. "Then you'd best start praying the Comanche don't find him. If they even think we had anything to do with this, God help us."

13

Everyone was on edge. For the first time since they left Council Grove, Caleb ordered camp made long before nightfall. He circled up the wagons in a spot some two hundred yards from a narrow creek—close enough to make use of the water after a sweltering day, far enough away to provide ample warning should anyone dare approach. He then made three terse announcements. One, that the Comanche's body would not be found; two, that Emmet Holt and Lem Kovel were to divide up Jacobs's turn at night watch; and three, that Jacobs was to be kept tied to the rear wheel of his wagon until Caleb said otherwise. He then turned and stalked toward the creek, leaving no doubt he wanted nothing more to do with any of them—at least until dark.

Jenna stared after him, feeling for all the world as if he'd just closed a door between them. What broke her heart was that she had no idea why. Surely he couldn't hold it against her that she didn't want a man tortured to death, even a man as vile as Bart Jacobs.

"Mr. Harper sure is mad, isn't he, Jenna?" Timmy sighed.

"I'm afraid he is, Timmy."

"Do you think he won't be our friend anymore?"

"I don't know." Her voice shook.

"Maybe you should talk to him," Bess said softly.

"He doesn't want to talk."

"He doesn't want to," Bess agreed, "but he needs to, and so do you. Go on." She inclined her head toward the creek. "Timmy and I will make supper."

Jenna bit her lip. "I'm afraid. What if he won't speak to me?"

"Then it's the same as if you stayed here." Bess gave her a reassuring hug. "If he'll talk to anyone, he'll talk to you. And if you really love him, it won't matter what he says, only that you listen."

Jenna blew out a long, shuddery breath. "You're right." She had to try. If she let Caleb keep that door closed tonight, she had no doubt he would keep it closed forever.

But rather than follow on the man's heels, she decided to let him be alone for a while, hoping the shade and the relative coolness of the creek would take the edge off his anger before she sought him out.

Forcing herself to stay busy, Jenna helped Bess and Timmy get a pot of antelope stew going and tried not to dwell on how different the camp felt tonight. Even Millie seemed fretful, nervous, as she prepared her cook fire. Little Mary clung to her skirts like a shadow.

Bart Jacobs's well deserved predicament wasn't helping anyone's mood. The sutler was trussed up like a Thanksgiving turkey, half his face swollen and discolored from the beating Caleb had given him. The labored sounds of his breathing carried throughout the camp, but Caleb had been adamant that the man remain gagged. When Caleb had removed the gag earlier, Jacobs had spewed out a string of obscenities the likes of which Jenna hoped never to hear again, all the while he'd entreated Lem Kovel to cut him loose.

She dared a glance at the sutler, wondering how a man beaten so badly could still exude such hate. Involuntarily she shivered, turning back to her stew. It occurred to her that Jacobs must be getting hungry, but she wasn't about to volunteer to feed him. She sprinkled a little more salt into the simmering pot.

Bess came up to take a turn stirring. "I thought you were going to talk to Mr. Harper," she prodded, not ungently.

"I wanted to give him some time to himself."

Bess made a face. "Coward."

Jenna straightened. "I am not!"

"Are."

Jenna turned and strode over to the back of her wagon. She sighed heavily. "Am."

Bess followed. "You know, I think our water barrels need refilling." She picked up the bucket and handed it to Jenna.

Jenna frowned. "The barrels don't—" She caught on to Bess's meaning. "Maybe they do at that." She looked toward the creek, then set the bucket down. "No. No excuses." She gave Bess a hug. "Thank you." Stiffening her spine, Jenna headed toward the tree-lined watercourse.

It took her nearly half an hour to find him. He was sitting beneath a huge cottonwood, a full half mile upstream from camp. His long legs were stretched out in front of him, his hands locked together above his belt. His black Stetson was angled low, covering his face, and he had shed his buckskin jacket and blue chambray shirt, evidently to take advantage of any stray breeze that might waft by.

Jenna swallowed hard, staring at that broad expanse

of bare chest. The moonlight of the other night had not done him justice. He was beautiful. Like the statue of a Greek god she had seen in some long-forgotten book. All lean, hard muscle. The jagged scar that interrupted the dusting of dark hair only served to enhance how appealing he looked. He was wearing the deerskin amulet, and for the first time she saw the soaring eagle painted on its surface. She experienced a brief flush of jealousy, sensing suddenly that he had been given the amulet by a woman. But the feeling did not persist, and she was able to attribute it to her own wild nervousness.

She tried to look elsewhere, anywhere, only to have her gaze return again and again to that masculine chest. She watched its steady rise and fall for long minutes, startled to realize finally that he was asleep.

She plucked at the leaves of the shrub in front of her. He looked so peaceful after such a tense afternoon. It didn't seem fair that she disturb him.

Coward, Bess's voice echoed.

Jenna mustered her courage and stepped close.

Forever after she would never be certain of the exact sequence of events, but in a flash of movement she found herself pinned to the ground, Caleb's six-gun at her throat.

She didn't move, didn't even blink.

Caleb's eyes were wide with disbelief, then horror. With an oath he sagged back against the tree. "I could've killed you."

Jenna had to remind herself to breathe.

"Don't you know better than to sneak up on a man like that?"

"I . . . I'm sorry." She struggled to sit up, picking distractedly at the leaves tangled in her hair.

"What the hell are you doing out here anyway?" He shoved the Colt back into its holster.

"I-I wanted to talk to you." Her heart was still pounding painfully.

"Forget it. Go back to camp." His voice was curt, clipped.

Jenna dug her fingernails into her palms to keep her tears at bay. If she let him send her away now, he would win. And he would lose. They would both lose. Somehow she kept her voice steady. "I'm not leaving."

"Then I'll go." He grabbed his shirt.

Jenna stayed his hand. "Give me five minutes. Please."

His eyes reflected his indecision and more than that —the wariness she had come to know too well. He didn't want to stay, didn't want to talk to her for fear of saying more than he dared. But he did stay, and Jenna took heart from that.

She began slowly. "I think what Bart Jacobs did was monstrous." She twisted her hands together on her lap. "I want you to know how sorry I am that it happened."

Caleb said nothing, his face now unreadable. Fearful that she might be making things worse, Jenna continued uncertainly. "That day Iron Fist was in camp, I remember looking at him—at the boy I mean, at One Wolf, and he seemed different. I mean he wasn't . . . he didn't . . ."

The words seemed lodged in her throat. It was as though some part of her knew where this was leading, and she suddenly didn't want to get there. She had to force herself to go on. "One Wolf didn't seem to hate us —my family, the Holts, the others. He even . . . he even smiled at me."

Caleb looked away but still said nothing.

"I . . . know how difficult it must have been to . . . to go against his beliefs. To bury him, I mean." Damn the man! Couldn't he at least grunt, nod, do *something?* Finally she could bear his silence no longer. "All right, just say it!" she blurted out. "Say it! You hate me, don't you? You hate me for stopping you from killing Jacobs."

Another full minute ticked by before he said quietly, "I could never hate you, Jenna."

She trembled with relief, as much for the fact that he had spoken as for the words themselves. "Then why do you seem almost to want to sometimes?"

"Go back to the wagons." His voice was weary, tired, as though he'd been fighting a losing battle for a very long time. "Your five minutes are up." He shrugged into his shirt and levered himself to his feet, brushing at bits of leaves and grass that clung to his trousers. He started to button his shirt.

Jenna rose beside him. He'd worked only two of the buttons when she caught his hands, cocooning them in her own.

"Jenna, don't . . ."

"I asked you once why you didn't like me. Do you remember that?" She could feel his heartbeat. "I embarrassed you nearly to death."

He looked away.

"I didn't mean to. I didn't understand how difficult talking about . . . about feelings is for you. I don't want to hurt you, Caleb."

"Jenna, please . . ."

"I'm doing it right now, aren't I?" She let go of him, turning to gaze into the murky waters of the creek. "I'm sorry. I came out here only because I care about you, because I was sorry that Indian boy's death hurt you, and because, I don't know, I just keep thinking that, in spite of what you say or do, you want me to care. You want me to love you."

She was pushing him and she knew it. He was either going to jam that door shut for good, or maybe, just maybe, he would step aside and let her in. "I'll say it again, and I'll keep saying it until you believe me." She turned around. "I love you."

He raked a hand through his dark, tousled hair, his eyes despairing. "And I'll say it again—you don't even know me."

"Yes, I do. In more ways than you know."

"You think so?" He let out a cynical laugh. "Here's how much you know me, Jenna. In three days you'll never see me again. When we reach the cutoff, I'm riding out. I'm leaving you and the others to Gallagher."

"No, you're not." It was not a plea but a statement of fact. "You might want to leave, you might even think you can, but you won't. Because you can't leave me. I'm in your blood, Caleb. Just like you're in mine."

"No."

She lay a hand alongside his face, trailing her fingers along his stubble-roughened jaw. "Liar."

His eyes burned her, seared her, the torment in their gray depths an agony to see. He was still afraid to love her, afraid to trust her. She longed to know why but couldn't find the words to ask. But then she didn't want answers anymore. All she wanted or needed in the world right now was to touch him, to be touched by him. Seemingly of their own volition her fingers shifted, feathering across his lips, his cheek, his temple to weave lightly through his hair. She curled a stray lock behind his ear, then stood on tiptoe to brush his mouth with a kiss.

He was holding himself rigidly still, and though she knew little of the full range of a man's passion, she sensed in Caleb Harper the power of a whirlwind held in check by a rapidly fraying thread. She had but to cut him free.

She kissed him again.

With an oath he pulled her to him, crushing her

against him, burying his face in the silken curtain of her hair. Reckless, heedless, he bore her down onto the cool, damp grass, his hands roving hungrily across her shoulders and down. "You're so beautiful, Jenna, so beautiful. I want you. God help me, I want you so much." He bit back a groan as he tugged at the buttons of her dress, roughly pushing the material aside to capture a firm breast still hidden beneath the gauzy softness of her chemise.

Abruptly Jenna stiffened, feeling suddenly shy, afraid. What was she doing? What was she letting him do? Instantly she regretted her timidity as Caleb jerked away, levering himself into a sitting position, his breathing harsh, irregular. He was not looking at her.

"I'm sorry," he muttered. "I thought you wanted . . ." He swore.

She curved a hand over his shoulder, wincing when he pulled away. She had loosed the whirlwind without counting the cost. "It is what I wanted. I mean . . ." Her cheeks were on fire. "Oh, Caleb, I'm the one who's sorry. I don't . . . I'm not sure what I'm supposed to do. I . . . I've never been with a man. Not . . . not like this." She had proved one thing today at least. A person could not die of embarrassment. Otherwise she would no longer be breathing.

Caleb brought his knees up, supporting his head with his hands. Of course she'd never been with a man. She was an innocent. A lady. He cursed himself for an idiot, jamming his hands through his hair. "Go back to camp, Jenna. We'll both forget this ever happened."

"No." She sat up and circled her arms around him from behind, pressing her face against the warm flesh of his back. "I'll never forget. I don't want to forget. I want to learn. Please. Teach me, Caleb. Teach me how to make your body burn the way mine does when you touch me."

He arched his head back, certain he was about to lose his mind. "Jenna, for the love of God, get away from me!"

"No." On instinct alone she began to feather kisses across his back, bringing her hands up to touch his nipples, as she had felt him touch hers.

He twisted around, capturing her face in his hands. "Do you know what you're doing? Jenna, do you really know?"

"I know I love you."

He stared into those mountain-lake eyes and for the first time he believed her. This woman loved him.

Just as he loved her.

The realization struck him like a thunderbolt.

He loved her. He wanted to marry her. He wanted to have children with her. He wanted to spend the rest of his life with her.

And he could never have any of it.

Tell her, a voice inside him thrummed. *Tell her the truth. She'll understand. She will.*

No. He was too aroused, too desperate to be honest now. He couldn't take the chance. He would have this time with her, and in three days he would ride out as planned. This one time, this one night he would love and be loved—and no one would take it from him. No one.

They were lying side by side. He kissed her cheeks, her chin, her neck. His loins tormented him to take her quickly, but he kept his movements patient, unhurried. He didn't want to alarm her again. He made no further move to undress her, contenting himself with caressing her through the frustrating barrier of her clothes. He concentrated on her breasts, kneading the pliant mounds, daring to suckle them through the layers of spun cotton. Her nipples grew taut beneath the subtle magic of his mouth, his fingers. He heard her breath catch, felt her body tremble. She cried his name, lacing her fingers in his hair.

Hard, ready, he unfastened his fly, sliding his pants down, taking care to shield his nakedness from her. He lifted her skirts and petticoats, eased down her pantalets, all the while he murmured sweet, gentle words, words he hadn't even known he knew, and his hand slid up to caress that most intimate part of her.

She gasped.

He withdrew his hand.

Jenna bit her lip, hiding her disappointment. She had not meant any disapproval, but she hardly knew how to ask him to continue. His touch had sent waves—erotic, sensual—rippling to the very core of her. She wanted more.

But then he was rising above her, staking his arms on either side of her. She felt something hard, rigid, against her thigh.

"Open yourself to me, Jenna," he said hoarsely. "I need to be inside you. I need to be part of you."

Her body throbbing, she did as he asked.

He drove himself forward, his mouth smothering her cry of pain. He held himself still, soothing her, petting her, reassuring her, until he could bear the thunder in his loins no longer.

And then he was moving, stroking, faster, faster.

Jenna felt herself respond, felt her own body seek to match his rhythm, his fire. This was what she wanted. This was what she needed . . .

And then there was something wrong. Still atop her, he withdrew. She felt him shudder, heard him curse, then felt something warm, wet on her thigh. Before she even fully realized what was happening, he had tugged on his pants, grabbed his bandanna, and was awkwardly helping her clean up as best he could.

His face was almost as red as the kerchief. He

wouldn't meet her eyes. "I didn't want to chance your being with child. I should have thought of it sooner. I should never . . . damn . . ."

She lay her palm against his cheek, forcing him to look at her. "Thank you."

"For what? For taking your virginity, your innocence? For being completely irresponsible?"

"For loving me."

He closed his eyes, feeling raw, exposed, terrified. *Three days,* his mind taunted. *Three days, and he would never see her again.* "Jenna . . ." Her name was a croaking whisper. He dragged in a deep lungful of air. "There's something I need to tell you. Something . . ."

She pressed her fingers to his lips. "Later." He was in enough pain. If sharing this secret would bring him more, she didn't want to hear it. Not now.

"No. I should . . ."

She kissed him.

"Jenna, let me . . ."

She kissed him again.

He tried once more to say something, but the words disappeared when Jenna's hand skated across his belly. He sucked in his breath, his pulses quickening yet again.

"I was afraid before, Caleb," she whispered. "I was afraid because I didn't know what to expect. I do now." She slipped his shirt off his shoulders, daring to glance down at the tautening bulge beneath his denims. She reached a tentative hand toward the opening of his fly. "I want to see . . ."

He gripped her arms, and she was forced to look up. His eyes were twin flames of awe, disbelief. "You're a lady," he said, bewildered.

"I'm a woman. I want to see the man I love." She bit her lip, suddenly unsure. "Is that wrong?"

"Wrong?" he repeated, dumbfounded. He had been

with a saloon woman or two, but it was their job to please a man. Laurel had suffered the onerous needs of his body only once—and that was in the dark, with her clothes on. Considering how much she had loathed the experience, he later suspected that it had been her way of precipitating his proposal. *A woman does her wifely duty. A man is like an animal, he can't help himself.*

"I-I" he stammered, "I thought you wouldn't want . . . I didn't want to frighten you any more than you already were."

"Then it's all right? For me to see you, all of you?"

He managed to nod, his blood turning to fire. He touched one hand to her breasts.

Jenna understood. Her fingers trembling, not with fear but with anticipation, she unbuttoned her dress front, shrugging off the bodice, letting it fall to her waist. Then she was undoing the ribbons of her chemise. Her breath was coming in short, tiny gasps. With her fingertips she took hold of either side of the delicate fabric. Never taking her eyes from Caleb's face, she parted the filmy cotton, laying open her breasts to his heated gaze.

He sat there, his arms locked at his sides, seeming not to trust that he could touch what his eyes already caressed.

Jenna lifted his right hand and brought it to her left breast. She couldn't tell whose hand trembled more, hers or his, when she cupped his rough palm against her tender flesh. Her breast seemed to swell to fill his hand, a gasp of exquisite pleasure tearing from her throat.

Her cry broke the last bonds of restraint in him.

Clothes flew everywhere, anywhere. He undressed her; she undressed him. They gloried in each other's nakedness, delighting in each other's pleasure.

He taught. She learned.

She taught. He learned.

With his hands he opened for her the awesome wonders of her own body. She clung to him as wave after wave of unutterable ecstasy crashed over her, until in the lee of one crest she saw how desperately he needed his own release. She opened herself to him, urging him to take her, take her now.

He slid into the wet, welcoming softness, drunk with lust, love. Coherent thought was distant memory. He was all instinct, all raw animal power. He was a man. She was a woman. His woman. With a sated groan he spilled his essence inside her.

For long minutes afterward they lay twined together, unmoving. Though she was loathe to do so, Jenna was the first to stir. If she was gone from camp much longer, someone might come looking for her. She pushed to a sitting position, Caleb's arm sliding free of her back. She kissed the tips of his fingers, then let the hand fall onto the grass. She smiled. He wasn't asleep. But the man was most definitely exhausted.

"Do you think we could do it again?" she teased.

He moaned. "Have mercy, woman."

She giggled.

He levered himself onto one elbow, remaining so as she dressed. She didn't feel even remotely shy with him anymore. She could prance around naked in front of him all day. She said as much.

He chuckled. "Then you may as well dig the grave now. I wouldn't last a week."

She leaned over to give him a playful swat on his bare behind. "You'd better get dressed yourself, Mr. Harper. There's a lady present."

He pretended to look around. "Where?"

She took his clothes, which she had gathered up for him, and dropped them on his head. He muttered something she couldn't hear and decided it was just as well. At least he started getting dressed.

When he finished, he came over to her, his manner now earnest, concerned. "We'd best not go back together. I don't want anyone . . ." He didn't finish.

"You don't want anyone thinking I came out here to ravish you?" She was trying to cajole him back into his good humor, but he remained serious.

"If anyone says anything, makes some kind of remark . . ." He shifted, twisting the brim of his Stetson in his hands. "I don't want you hurt."

"Nothing can hurt me with you around, don't you know that?"

His gaze dropped to the ground. All that he was, all that he stood for would eventually bring her nothing but hurt. In three days she would know about the guns. Even if she could forgive him that, there was still the little matter of his infiltrating the *comancheros.* Not exactly the kind of life a man could ask a woman to share.

But how could he not ask? He loved her.

On impulse he tossed his hat aside and slipped his amulet from around his neck. He settled it over Jenna's head.

"Oh, Caleb, I couldn't."

"It's the only thing I have that means anything to me. I want you to have it."

She touched the soft doeskin, her eyes brimming with unshed tears. "You wore it next to your heart. Now I'll wear it next to mine."

He couldn't speak for a minute, and when he did he couldn't find the right words. "I just wish things could be different."

"Different how?"

"The day's still coming when you'll despise me."

"No. That can never happen." But she could see plainly that he was in no mood to argue the point. At least not now. She wasn't worried. She still had three days.

"You'd better go," he said. "I'll follow in a few minutes."

"All right." She brushed his cheek with a kiss, then started toward the wagons alone. "I love you. Remember that."

Caleb watched her leave, feeling for all the world as if he'd already lost her. And it was his own blind, stupid fault. He blew out a disgusted breath. For what? For Gallagher? For an outlaw named Enrique Valdez? For his own blasted pride? Well, the hell with it. The hell with all of it. Jenna had a right to make up her own mind. No matter what the cost, he would tell her the truth in the morning.

14

Caleb took his turn on watch, rifle ready, listening to the sounds of the night. He perched himself on the stump of a cottonwood felled years past by pioneers already long settled in California dreams. Or perhaps broken by them. To his left some twenty feet distant was an open area on the banks of the narrow creek. The half moon far above gave him a good view of the treeless expanse and beyond. Thirty yards to his right were the wagons. Nothing seemed out of place, yet he couldn't shake a feeling of unease.

He grimaced. Or maybe it was guilt. He shouldn't have let his passion get out of hand with Jenna. She deserved better. A self-conscious smile tugged at one corner of his mouth. But apparently she didn't want better. She loved him. Him. Caleb Harper, army scout.

Yes, but if she knew . . .

No. She would understand. Thinking she wouldn't was just a knee-jerk defense he'd gotten used to after his experience with Laurel. To even think Jenna would

judge him the way Laurel had was not only unfair to
Jenna, it was absurd.

Jenna was like no other woman he'd ever known.
She'd stirred feelings inside him he hadn't even known
he had, feelings he wasn't even sure he wanted to have.
Feelings of tenderness, gentleness, softness that
seemed alien to his very nature. And yet when he was
with her they seemed as natural as breathing.

Her passion had astonished him. Once past her initial
nervousness she had been as free, as abandoned as his
wildest dreams could have hoped. And because she had
been, so had he. For the first time in his life sex had
been more than a physical release. He had felt warm
and safe and cherished. And he had tried hard to make
Jenna feel the same.

He wanted nothing more than to go to her this minute, take her in his arms, assure himself it had not been
all just some wondrous dream.

Instead he stood and paced. He couldn't indulge his
own wants right now. His responsibility was to the
camp. With a resigned oath he forced his thoughts
away from Jenna.

He reflected on the upcoming rendezvous, wondering if Gallagher was going to be at the cutoff as scheduled. If not, it would be up to Caleb to decide whether
or not to proceed without him. So far, the journey had
proved safe enough for his pioneer charges, but that
didn't mean it was going to stay that way. After the
cutoff the land grew harsher, more unforgiving, the
points of civilization fewer and farther between. And
there was always the unpredictability of Iron Fist. . . .

Caleb wanted that troop escort. For Jenna's sake, and
for the sake of the others.

And, he thought bitterly, he wanted justice for One
Wolf.

More to the point, he wanted justice from Keith Gallagher. Gallagher was a good man, a good soldier. But sometimes the two didn't mix. The major's private sympathy for the plight of the Indian didn't always translate into public condemnation of white treaty violations.

But would that include cold-blooded murder?

Standard army procedure would be to look the other way, even offer tacit approval for one less Comanche in the world. But Caleb had no tolerance for standard army procedure. Not in this case. And not from Keith Gallagher.

The major's recent preoccupation with a promotion did nothing to bolster Caleb's confidence. Dealing harshly with a white man for killing an Indian wouldn't sit well with a civilian population already awash in bigotry, nor would it strengthen Keith's image with his equally bigoted superiors back East. But if Gallagher expected Caleb's help ferreting out *comancheros,* the major had damned well better prove himself colorblind with Bart Jacobs.

For now, Caleb would give Gallagher the benefit of the doubt. He would wait and see.

Even if Gallagher failed, Caleb doubted his own conscience would let him renege on his agreement to bring Enrique Valdez and his *comanchero* killers to ground.

An unwelcome thought intruded. Where would that leave him with Jenna? It could take weeks, months to expose the full range of *comanchero* activities along the Santa Fe Trail. Jenna would be in Sacramento by then. Would she wait for him? Would she want to? California was filled with eligible bachelors with big ranches, big gold strikes, big bank accounts. Not that money would matter to her. But such men would have an air of power, success, and sheer civilization about them that Caleb could never hope to match.

He grimaced, not liking the direction of his thoughts but unable to come up with any argument that held sufficient sway against them. Going after Valdez could well cost him—

A twig snapped. Caleb's gaze jerked toward the creek in time to see a white-tailed deer bounding away into the night. Startled by a coyote? Or something more sinister?

His every sense alert, Caleb scanned the creekbank. Though he saw nothing out of the ordinary, his feeling of unease returned. Deepened. It was almost as though he was being watched. He trod closer to the creek.

A half-hour's search proved fruitless.

He headed toward the wagons.

Squared off and separated from one another by several feet, the four wagons didn't make much of a defense fortress, but that had never been Caleb's intention anyway. With such a small company he'd long since decided it was better to look harmless than entrenched. Besides, according to Gallagher, Caleb's very presence was supposed to keep trouble at arm's length.

Then why did he feel so damned edgy?

He paused first at the Riordan wagon. Jenna and her brother and sister lay curled up underneath it, asleep, Jenna near the front wheels, Timmy in the middle, Bess near the rear. He had to smile. Jenna and Bess had taken to corraling Timmy as best they could ever since his birthday hunting expedition.

His smile softened as his gaze flicked back to Jenna. It was all he could do not to touch her, to kiss her awake and tell her he loved her. It seemed so easy to admit it now. He wished he'd said the words aloud just once earlier tonight. But he would make up for it in the morning. He'd damn well announce it to the whole camp.

Somehow he would talk her out of going to California, at least for now. She could stay at Bascom with Marian Gallagher. After Valdez was in jail Caleb could take Jenna and her family to Sacramento himself. He'd never thought much about settling down before, but then he'd never found the right woman to settle down with. Maybe they could start a ranch, raise horses, kids. . . .

The thought filled him with such an unexpected rush of pleasure he had to force himself to move on, to not wake Jenna immediately and tell her all about it.

He stopped next at the Kovel wagon, then the Holts, finding nothing amiss.

At the Holt wagon young Sam stirred slightly and opened his eyes. "Something wrong, Mr. Harper?" The boy's fingers closed reflexively on the rifle lying next to him.

"Nothing, Sam. Go back to sleep."

The boy closed his eyes. Caleb waited for him to drift off again, thinking of how one day Sam Holt was going to make one helluva man.

Though loathe to do so, Caleb headed toward the last wagon and Bart Jacobs. In the distance a coyote howled, the mournful cry sending an unexpected chill through him.

He tried unsuccessfully to shake it off as he spied Jacobs's shadowy outline. Tied in a sitting position to the rear wheel of his wagon, the sutler snored loudly at his approach. Caleb's mouth twisted in disgust. He was certain the bastard was only feigning sleep to avoid a confrontation. Not that it mattered. Caleb wouldn't go within six feet of him. If he did, he was liable to kick the son of a bitch's teeth in.

But even that wouldn't have eased the tension in him. Damn! Something was going to happen. And soon. He just wished to hell he knew what.

It was still a half hour until dawn, but he decided he

needed to talk to Jenna. Maybe all he was feeling was an attack of nerves. After all, he'd never been in love before.

He frowned, tightening his grip on his rifle. That wasn't it and he knew it. Nevertheless, he headed toward Jenna's wagon. He wanted to see her, assure himself she was all right.

Hunkering down beside her, he watched her sleep for a long minute, struck by the sudden realization that his life was no longer his own. It was now and forever inextricably linked with this angel-haired woman and her mountain-lake eyes. The thought at once terrified him, yet exhilarated him more.

He reached to wake her, then stayed his hand. A noise out of sync with the night drifted toward him. He turned his head toward the creek. Rage lashed through him. Bart Jacobs. Leading an unsaddled horse. How in the hell had that bastard gotten loose? Caleb almost brought up his rifle and shot Jacobs where he stood. But there was something so furtive about the way the sutler was moving that Caleb's scalp prickled.

Soundlessly he rose and followed.

Jacobs continued toward the creek, not once looking back. Caleb caught up with him just as he entered the thicket of trees. "Going somewhere, Jacobs?"

Oddly the sutler seemed unperturbed. "Ain't none of your business, Harper. I ain't takin' no more orders from you."

Caleb jerked the barrel of his rifle toward camp. "Get moving."

"Only if I get a turn with that little slut of yours."

Caleb backhanded the sutler across the face. Too late he realized he had played into Jacobs's hands. From behind something hard cracked viciously across his skull, sending him to his knees.

"Good work, *amigo*." Jacobs grabbed up Caleb's rifle

and six-gun. "Now it'll be even easier than we planned."

"*Si,*" came the unfamiliar voice. "You wait here, *Señor* Jacobs, I will signal the others." The English words were heavily accented.

Terror sliced through Caleb. Terror for Jenna. He struggled to rise. A savage boot to the ribs sent a shaft of agony knifing through him. He couldn't breathe. Jacobs's voice seemed very far away.

"Them Spencers'll bring one helluva price."

His companion chuckled malevolently. "So will the woman."

Get up! Caleb's world was a swirling, black haze. *Get up. Get to Jenna.*

The gun barrel again crashed across his skull, drowning him in a sea of blackness.

Jenna was dreaming. She was standing on a sun-drenched hillock knee-deep in a rainbow of wild-flowers. Caleb was off in the distance, but he was coming toward her, and he was smiling. The haunted look was gone from his gray eyes.

He came close, reached for her.

The sun, the hill, the flowers disappeared. In their place was a vast and empty desert.

And she was all alone.

Jenna awoke, her heart thudding. What kind of a nonsense dream was that to have in the aftermath of Caleb's lovemaking? She felt almost disloyal, even though she could hardly be held accountable for a dream.

Yet now she was wide-awake, and she was still having a hard time shaking the feeling of abandonment.

She was about to throw off her blankets and get up, thinking perhaps that moving about would calm her a little, when she caught the sound of nearby footfalls.

She would know that stride anywhere. Caleb was coming toward her wagon. Quickly she closed her eyes. It would be better if he thought her asleep. She wasn't certain she could hide how unnerved she had been by the dream.

She sensed him bend close, and she almost opened her eyes. What better way to set her foolish fears to rest than to just have him hold her? She wouldn't have to say why. But then she heard him rise, walk away.

Jenna eased up onto one elbow, peering past Caleb in the murky predawn light.

She gasped.

Bart Jacobs.

Somehow the man had gotten loose, and now Caleb was following him. She swallowed. *Stalking* him?

Suddenly frightened, she pushed back her blankets and got to her feet, careful not to awaken Bess or Timmy. She resisted the urge to run after Caleb. The noise would alert Jacobs. If the man could free himself, he could also arm himself. If he started shooting, she didn't want Caleb distracted by her being in the line of fire.

Neither did she want Caleb shooting Jacobs. No matter what the circumstances, she would be left to wonder forever if Caleb had done to the sutler exactly what Jacobs had done to One Wolf.

Murder was murder.

Her heart pounding she hurried to waken Emmet Holt and Lem Kovel. They would know what to do.

Quickly she told both men what she had seen. Sam too had awakened and joined them. They all looked toward the creek. Neither Caleb nor Jacobs was anywhere in sight.

"Please," Jenna said, "we have to do something. They could kill each other."

"One of us should go after 'em," Emmet agreed, but he made no move to do so.

"Harper had no cause to truss up Jacobs like he did," Kovel grumbled. "I don't blame him for takin' off."

Holt's eyes narrowed. "Don't tell me you're the reason he's loose."

"Hell, no, but I don't see no point in—"

"Gentlemen, please," Jenna interrupted desperately. "We have to—"

"Look!" Young Sam pointed toward the creek.

Jenna's mouth dropped open in utter bewilderment. A rider was holding a torch aloft at the edge of the treeless break. There was no mistaking the torch bearer's black hat and buckskin jacket.

"What the hell is Harper doing?" Emmet demanded. "And where the hell is Jacobs?"

Emmet Holt would never know. A bullet screamed out of the breaking dawn and took him square in the chest. He was dead before he hit the ground.

"Pa!" Sam screamed, dropping beside his father's body. "Pa, no!"

For an instant Jenna froze, her mind recoiling from the reality of Emmet Holt's lifeless body, and then Lem Kovel was shoving her, shouting at her to move, *run!*

"Indians!" he bellowed. "Shoot at anything that moves!" He had to half push, half drag young Sam away from Emmet's body.

Fear for Bess and Timmy drove Jenna past her own terror. Racing back to her wagon, she found Timmy scrambling out of his blankets, grabbing up his rifle. Bess held his old rifle, loading it with shaking fingers. Jenna joined them under the wagon. It struck her as a pathetic place to die.

"Don't worry, Bessie," Timmy assured her. "Mr. Harper won't let them hurt us."

Jenna shot a glance toward the creek, saying a desperate prayer that Timmy was right, only to see the buckskin-clad rider slam his heels into his horse's sides and send the animal bolting across the creek and into the clearing beyond.

"Caleb!" She cried out to him, even as he vanished from her line of sight. In his place were a dozen horsemen pouring across the creek on heavily lathered mounts. Eight Mexicans, four Indians, all shouting, cursing, all bringing weapons to bear on the tiny camp.

Jenna wanted to scream, run. Death rode those horses. Death for herself, Bess, Timmy. Death for them all.

And Caleb was gone. Caleb had run. Why? *Why?*

"Get ready!" She heard Lem Kovel shout. "Make every bullet count."

The riders were almost on top of them.

Jenna dared a quick glance around—split-second images forever frozen in her mind. Lem Kovel shielding his wife's body with his own as they scrambled beneath their wagon, rifles ready. Millie Holt, ashen-faced, clutching a sobbing Mary. Sam trying desperately to get Millie to take Emmet's old six-gun. And failing. Sam's gaze flitting toward Bess, then skittering away when Bess looked up to give him a brave smile. Jenna's own heart turning over as she saw in Sam's eyes a reflection of her own despair.

Then, grim-faced, deliberate, Sam Holt turned away, sighted down the barrel of his rifle and fired.

Jenna watched the first rider fall, feeling a sudden, wild exhilaration that appalled her. But she didn't have time to dwell on it. An arrow thunked into the wagon bed above her head.

Jenna took aim with her own rifle, fired, missed.

Timmy fired. A rider tumbled from his horse.

Bess reloaded as fast as she could.

The attackers circled tighter, ever tighter about the

wagons. A bullet zinged off the iron rim of the wheel next to Jenna, a metal shard stinging her cheek. She swiped at the blood but otherwise gave it no notice.

A Comanche astride a paint stallion thundered past, howling maniacally, firing arrows from a quiver on his back faster than Jenna could fire her rifle.

Recognition ripped through her, her blood turning to ice.

Iron Fist.

He saw her at the same time. Sawing back on the reins of his mount, he nearly set the paint on its haunches. In one motion he leapt from the animal's back and settled another arrow into his bow. His black eyes twin pits of hate, he advanced on Jenna, the scar that twisted his features now a slash of crimson warpaint that gave Jenna a grotesque vision of how it must have looked when Caleb first laid open his face.

The Comanche leveled the arrow and drew back the bowstring. He was less than eight feet away.

Behind her, Jenna heard Bess working frantically to reload Timmy's weapon.

"Hurry, Bessie!" Timmy shrilled. "Hurry!"

Terror clawed through Jenna, making her movements rushed, clumsy. She fumbled with the rifle, firing into the dirt just inches from the Comanche's moccasined feet.

He bared his teeth in a hideous mockery of a smile.

Jenna felt his arrow hiss past her head. A soft cry sounded behind her, so soft Jenna wasn't even certain she'd heard it. She turned to see an image that would haunt her to her grave.

The feather-tipped arrow was imbedded in Bess's chest, a small circle of blood staining the yellow gingham she wore. Her blue eyes were wide, frightened, her hands reflexively curled around the arrow shaft. She looked at Jenna with a mixture of hurt and confusion, as though she couldn't believe anyone could do something so cruel. Her lips moved, but she made no sound. With a tiny, forlorn sigh she crumpled forward and lay still.

An anguished scream tore from Jenna's throat. On her hands and knees she crawled toward Bess, but before she could reach her a hand twisted in her hair, yanking her savagely back. The hand then hauled her to her feet. Jenna found herself face-to-face with her sister's killer.

For a heartbeat she didn't move. Then like a wild animal she sprang at Iron Fist, tearing at his face, his chest, his hair, scratching, clawing, gouging, sobbing with grief and fury.

A wild-eyed Timmy hurtled up behind the Comanche, wielding his empty rifle like a club. But before he could land a blow another painted Indian thundered past, scooping Timmy onto his horse.

Jenna made a futile lunge toward her brother, before Iron Fist slammed his gauntleted fist into the side of her head. Her knees buckled, her mind reeling, the horror of the last few minutes stunning her far more than the Comanche's blow.

Bess was dead.

Timmy was gone.

She couldn't summon the strength to see what might have become of the others.

She only knew the battle was over.

The remaining attackers swarmed over her wagon, upending it, ripping at its undercarriage like maddened wolves rending their prey. Ten crates of U.S. army rifles spilled out onto the blood-spattered dirt.

. . . *the day will come when you despise me.*

Jenna felt the last spark of life go out of her. She barely noticed as Iron Fist dragged her over to his paint stallion. She offered only the feeblest protest as he lashed her belly-down across its back.

   . . . *the day will come when you despise me.*

Screams and more screams echoed throughout the camp, followed by an eerie, chilling silence.

The whole attack couldn't have lasted more than five minutes.

Jenna stared at her bound wrists dangling limply toward the ground, a shred of sensibility returning. Timmy. She had to help Timmy. Surely they wouldn't kill a little boy.

Awkwardly she arched her head up and forever wished she hadn't. Iron Fist stood over the lifeless body of Millie Holt, his arms spread wide, exultant. In one hand he held a bloody knife. In the other . . . Jenna didn't hear her own scream as her world spun away into madness.

15

Pain. Deep, throbbing pain seared through every part of her. For a long time Jenna had no awareness of anything else. She tried to think, tried to remember, but her whole world was reduced to ceaseless, mind-numbing pain. She could scarcely breathe. She couldn't even seem to open her eyes.

A nightmare. She must be having some horrible nightmare. She recalled snatches of it and nearly sobbed out loud. Bess murdered, Timmy in the hands of savages, and Caleb . . .

God in heaven, how could she have conjured such a vision? She would put an end to it at once. She would wake up. She would see Bess and Timmy asleep beside her. See Caleb bend close, his gray eyes brimming with love for her.

Jenna forced her eyes open. Nothing was as it should have been. The ground moved beneath her, dry bunch-grass passing by with blurring speed. The pressure on her chest and stomach was unbearable. Thunder racketed about her head, driving needle-sharp knives into her skull. A storm? She tried to raise her head, see the sky, but found she had neither the strength nor the will.

The thunder wasn't thunder at all, but horses' hooves. She was belly-down across the back of a running horse, surrounded by more running horses.

The nightmare was real.

Bess, Timmy, blood, gunfire. All real.

And Caleb. Caleb riding away. Caleb leaving them to the mercy of savages.

Awareness receded. Jenna welcomed the descending curtain of blackness.

When she again awoke, it was to the feel of rough hands dragging her from the stallion's back. When the hands let loose she collapsed to the hard-packed earth. Reflexively she curled her knees to her chest and for long minutes lay there, unmoving. Part of her never wanted to move again.

Part of her wanted to die.

"Bessie. Oh, God, Bessie." Her sister couldn't be dead. Couldn't be.

Memories tumbled over her. Fragile, trusting Bess. At seven bringing her a fistful of dandelions. At thirteen gifting her with a sampler that read DEAREST SISTER, DEAREST FRIEND. At fifteen teasing her about making cow eyes at Caleb Harper. Bess loving, laughing.

Bess never to love or laugh again.

"Let me die," Jenna whispered. "Please, God, let me die too."

Timmy.

Her brother's name was like a splash of cold water. Jenna could almost hear Bess's voice, gentle but chiding. Now was not the time to mourn the dead. Now was the time to help the living.

But what if Timmy was dead too? What if . . . ? No. Jenna struggled to a sitting position, ignoring the ache in her abdomen, the cruel burn of the rope that still bound her wrists. Timmy was alive. He had to be. Frantically she looked around, her gaze skittering past everything, anything, until she spied her brother. He was tied hand and foot but apparently unhurt beside a grazing roan.

Despite the horror of their circumstances, a shudder of relief coursed through her. Timmy even tried to give her a brave smile, though his chin trembled.

"Are you hurt, Timmy?" she called.

His eyes widened anxiously, his gaze flicking behind her. Jenna turned to see Iron Fist striding toward her, his painted face a mask of fury.

"No talk," he snarled.

Jenna had no time to wonder at the Comanche's use of English. His hand lashed out. She cringed, but not far enough. The blow landed with stinging force along the side of her head.

Her eyes burned, her mind reeling, but she fought off a new wave of unconsciousness. She couldn't black out. Not again. Her brother needed her. Though inwardly she quailed, she sat up straight and glared at the Comanche, all but daring him to strike her again. To her surprise he only sneered contemptuously and walked away.

Forcing herself to be calm, Jenna slowly took in her surroundings. She guessed by the position of the sun that it was late afternoon, but she had no idea how far or in what direction they had traveled from the wagons. A head count of their captors told her there were ten left—four Indians, five Mexicans, and one man she could now see was white, though he dressed like his Mexican compatriots, right down to his sombrero and serape. All were heavily armed, and most seemed to be taking orders from one of the Mexicans, a burly man with a thick mustache and cruel black eyes. Over and over Jenna heard the name Valdez.

The encampment itself looked temporary. No horses were tethered, no cook fires started. They seemed to have stopped only to rest the animals and to check more thoroughly the contents of the crates that had been hidden in the bottom of her wagon. The crates, strapped to three separate travois, served as damning reminders of Caleb. Just thinking his name was a knife to her heart. How could he have left them to this? How could he have left *her?*

Desperately her mind groped for answers. Perhaps he'd seen the riders coming and had ridden out to head them off. Perhaps he'd seen Iron Fist and tried to parley. Perhaps he'd even been killed . . . No. She had watched him signal these men with her own eyes, watched him ride past them without a shot having been fired, watched these men tear into the underside of her wagon, no one else's. With bitter irony she recalled Caleb telling her not to thank him for the extra repairs he'd had done in Council Grove. Only now did she know why.

She bit her lip until she tasted blood. She had to keep her tears at bay. If she started crying, she feared she would never stop.

Deliberately she returned her attention to the camp. The ugly reality of Caleb's betrayal only exacerbated the ugly reality that surrounded her. She and Timmy were not the only prisoners, but they were guests of honor in comparison to the others.

Innumerable scratches and bruises and tattered clothes told her Lem and Nelda Kovel had been dragged at least part of the way behind galloping horses. Nelda appeared unconscious, lying facedown in the dirt some three feet from her husband. Lem's face was twisted in agony, his bad leg turned at a grotesque angle beneath him. Jenna's stomach lurched, and she had to turn quickly away.

Sam Holt sat stoically beside one of the Mexican bandits. Like Timmy, the boy was bound hand and foot, but Sam had not escaped this morning's battle unscathed. His left eye was swollen shut, his face bruised and bloodied. What struck Jenna the most was the utter coldness, the emptiness she sensed in him. His expression did not change, even when he felt her watching him and glanced up briefly with his good eye. In his face Jenna saw the fate of his mother and sister. Millie and Mary Holt were as dead as Emmet and Bess.

Bleakly Jenna wondered if perhaps they weren't the lucky ones after all. Their deaths had been mercifully swift. As for herself and the others . . . Jenna shuddered. The way their captors circled like jackals about the battered Kovels, mercy was the farthest thing from their minds. Two men ripped and tore at what was left of Nelda Kovel's clothing, until the woman was stripped naked. Nelda Kovel didn't move. Jenna found herself hoping Nelda was dead.

Whether she was or not didn't seem to make much difference to the men bending over her. They pinioned her on her back and dropped their trousers. Jenna retched into the dirt. Only a shouted curse from Valdez kept them from their vile intent.

Jenna looked over to see the burly Mexican ripping through the crates of rifles. He would load first one, then another, then another. Each time the Spencers failed to shoot. Finally, in frustration, he slammed the stock of one of the guns against a boulder, shattering it to bits. Jenna didn't have to understand Spanish to know that he was cursing savagely as he did so.

Iron Fist rushed over, shouting in Comanche.

Valdez shouted back.

More of the men tried the weapons. The Spencers would not fire.

Iron Fist's face twisted with rage. Without warning he pulled a knife, waggling the glinting blade at Valdez. In that same instant Valdez's men leveled their six-guns at Iron Fist. No one moved. Valdez raised a hand, as if to tell his men not to interfere. He spoke in angry, clipped tones that suggested he was as furious about the guns as Iron Fist.

For her part, as Jenna watched the deadly standoff unfold, she could scarcely credit how fervently she just wished these two men would kill each other.

Instead Iron Fist seemed to relent, his thirst for blood cooling, though it did not entirely disappear. With an angry jerk he resheathed his knife. Whatever was wrong with the Spencers he did not blame Valdez.

But the fury over the guns had to be spent somewhere. Like rabid dogs the men turned on the Kovels.

Jenna thought nothing more could shock her.

She was wrong.

Over the hours that followed Jenna prayed for the mercy of unconsciousness, anything to blot out what these animals were doing to the Kovels. For the Kovels themselves she prayed for death.

Her prayers went unanswered.

Her memory flashed briefly to Bart Jacobs's brutal tales of Comanche horror back in Council Grove. She would not need his tales now. She had her own. She felt her hold on reality begin to slip away.

Timmy.

She gave herself a violent shake. She had to stay alive, stay sane for Timmy. Her brother was huddled on the ground next to a stocky Comanche. This Indian was the only man who had not taken his turn with Nelda Kovel. Not that he had shown her any sympathy either. But at least he had stepped aside, come over to Timmy, seeming to be doing his best to distract the boy from the horrors around him. And for that Jenna was grateful.

But there was no way to spare him what happened next.

Valdez was beside her. He gripped her arm and hauled her to her feet. Nelda Kovel's sightless eyes stared into the setting sun. Now it was Jenna's turn. She heard Timmy scream her name as Valdez pawed at her, attempted to kiss her, his stinking breath blowing hot across her face. Her bound wrists made it impossible to fight back.

She wished for a knife, a gun. She would use it on her brother first, then herself. She would spare them what these savages had done to the Kovels.

But she had no weapon.

Valdez tore at her dress, ripping the bodice, exposing her breasts to his leering gaze. Instinctively Jenna shrank away, but not before the amulet Caleb had given her spilled free.

"No!"

The voice was Iron Fist's. Jenna almost dissolved into a fit of hysterical laughter. Evidently he had decided he would be first, as if she could tell one pig from another. Valdez released her. She struggled to stay on her feet, though her knees threatened to buckle. She would not give these animals the satisfaction of hearing her beg.

To her astonishment Iron Fist gestured to the amulet, gripping it in his fist and speaking harshly to Valdez. The rawhide thong dug into the back of her neck, but Jenna held her ground.

Valdez glared furiously, then backed away.

That quickly, it was over. Jenna blinked uncomprehendingly as Iron Fist shoved her toward his paint stallion. The Comanche had won, and for no reason she could fathom, he was letting her live. For now.

In a frenzy of motion the outlaws broke camp. Sam

Holt was hefted onto the back of a bay horse being ridden by one of the Indians. This brave and one other broke off from the group and started north. Sam managed a sad smile, as though to tell her good-bye. Jenna knew with a sudden, strange certainty she would never see Sam Holt again. She found herself unable to even say a proper prayer for him. God had stopped listening to her at dawn this morning.

The Mexicans and the white man headed south, taking the malfunctioning guns with them.

That left two Indians. Iron Fist slung Jenna across the back of his horse. His companion settled Timmy in front of him.

Iron Fist was starting to mount when Lem Kovel let out a rasping moan. Until then Jenna had been certain he was dead. No body so brutalized could hold a spark of life. With obvious annoyance the Comanche stalked over to what was left of the settler. He drew his knife and summarily slit Kovel's throat, then scalped him.

Jenna only stared dully.

The Kovels' tortured bodies were the final blow, the final mockery to the trust, the love she had invested in Caleb Harper. She raised aching eyes to the vast emptiness of the plains and saw in them no hope for rescue, no chance for escape. She discovered she had one prayer left in her after all—that if there was a hell, Caleb Harper was in it.

Caleb sputtered, coming groggily awake as a bucket of water was upended over his head. He tried to move, tried to rise, but couldn't. His hands were tied behind his back. He shook his head in a vain attempt to clear it, only to nearly pass out again from the ensuing agony. But the physical pain was nothing compared to the jagged memory that tore at him.

Jenna!

Comancheros.

"I'm not sure this was a very good idea, boss." Bart Jacobs's voice.

Raw fury coursed through Caleb. Raw fury coupled with blind terror, terror for Jenna. He peered through the straggling strands of dark hair that had fallen in front of his eyes. Two figures stood silhouetted before him, neither man recognizable against the glaring light of the setting sun. Caleb squinted, able then to discern Jacobs as the figure to the right. The other man would have been unidentifiable, in any case. He wore a hood over his head, two slits cut in the flour sack enabling him to see.

"Where's Jenna?" Caleb demanded. "Damn you, Jacobs, where is she?"

"All in good time, Mr. Harper," the hooded man said, his voice low, rasping, obviously disguised. "All in good time."

Caleb's brow furrowed in a desperate attempt to search his memory. But to his befuddled senses nothing about the man seemed familiar. Caleb pushed himself to his knees, then awkwardly gained his feet. He swayed drunkenly and cursed his body's weakness as he again almost blacked out. "If anything's happened to Jenna, to her family . . . I'll kill you. My hand to God, I'll kill you both."

"Now, now, Mr. Harper," the hooded man tsked-tsked. "This is not what I had expected from you. After all, I know your background. I think you and I could work very well together on several projects I have in mind."

Caleb was only vaguely listening. He was nearly out of his mind with worry about Jenna. He struggled to get his bearings, figure out where he was. From the sound and the scent he guessed they weren't far from the creek. That meant the wagons should be . . . He tromped out of the timber and collapsed to his knees, feeling for all the world as though he'd just been poleaxed. Grotesque charred hulks were all that remained of the wagons.

His head slumped to his chest. "You're dead, Jacobs," he swore softly to himself. "Dead." Then he lurched to his feet and headed toward the wagons.

The two men followed.

Caleb stood amidst the carnage, his eyes burning as he stared at the crumpled bodies of Bess Riordan and Millie and Mary Holt. Behind him the hooded man's voice remained maddeningly even. "The army's going to wonder why you're alive, why these people are dead, the Spencers gone."

"Where's Jenna?" he hissed again.

This time the hooded man couldn't hide his irritation, but it was directed at Jacobs. "You didn't tell me the woman meant that much to him."

"I didn't know," Jacobs whined defensively.

The hooded man leaned close to Caleb, apparently not wanting Jacobs to hear what he said next. "Mr. Jacobs is not important in this matter, Mr. Harper. You can help me with Valdez and his friends, as no one else could. You can convince Eagle Dancer to join in my dream for war."

"Who the hell are you?" Caleb snapped.

The man went on as though Caleb hadn't spoken. "Maybe I'll even let you have Miss Riordan back, relatively unharmed. It can be arranged, you know. I want war, Mr. Harper. I want war between the white man and the red, because I stand to gain a great deal of money and power from both sides."

Caleb strained at the ropes that bound him. All he heard, all he knew was that Jenna was alive. Jenna was alive and in the hands of monsters.

"I can see you're a little too upset to consider all of

this rationally right now," the hooded man observed blandly. "I'll tell you what, we'll talk again soon." He pulled a watch from inside his shirt pocket. "But for now I'm afraid I have to rush off. I still have to rendezvous with some of my men."

Caleb felt a new pain as he stared at the watch. It was the one Jenna had given him for his "birthday." "Touch Jenna," Caleb snarled, "and your *comancheros* will look like altar boys by the time I'm finished with you."

The man was unfazed. "Your threats mean nothing to me, Mr. Harper. Only your cooperation matters. Only your cooperation will gain you what you want. Oh, and I wouldn't mention anything about our little talk to anyone. That is, if you want to see Miss Riordan alive again. If you do, I'll know. You won't know how I'll know, but I'll know." The hooded man turned to Bart Jacobs. "You may do the honors, Mr. Jacobs."

With a wicked smile Jacobs drove the butt of his rifle into the side of Caleb's head.

Caleb again awoke to the sound of voices. This time he wasn't sure if it was dark or he was blind.

"He's coming to, sir!"

Caleb sat up, surprised to find he was no longer tied. His head ached abominably, but he fought off the pain. Jenna. He had to find Jenna.

"Are you all right?" a voice asked, a voice at once familiar but somehow altered, strained.

Gallagher.

Caleb kept his eyelids half closed. It made the pain more tolerable somehow. "Keith . . ."

"How do you feel?"

"Jenna . . . I have to find . . ." He tried to rise, but Gallagher laid a firm hand on his arm.

"You'd better take it damned slow, old friend. The first soldier that checked on you told me you were dead."

"He might have been right." Caleb winced, his head throbbing with every beat of his heart. He looked at Keith, a new kind of pain lancing through him. "You've seen Millie Holt? The girls?"

Keith nodded, his brown eyes clouded with misery.

"I figure they've taken the others hostage. If we start after them now . . ." Again Caleb started to get up. Again Gallagher stopped him.

"You're in no shape to go anywhere. Besides, even you can't ride trail in the dark. It won't be dawn for another half hour. And," he added somberly, "we've got to give these folks a decent burial. I've got a detail working on it."

Caleb sagged back, only now hearing the sound of shovels scraping into hard earth. A half-dozen campfires gave light to the troopers' grisly task. Blessedly the bodies had been covered by a tarp. Caleb didn't think he could bear the guilt of seeing them again. "What are you doing here anyway, Keith? This isn't the rendezvous point."

"I drove the troops like a madman. We went past the cutoff and came on through." He shook his head. "I can't believe this. I just can't believe it. Dead settlers. No Spencers. Do you have any idea how this is going to make me look in Washington?"

Caleb stiffened, and Gallagher rushed to amend his words. "You know what I mean. I feel horrible about what happened to these people. But how many more settlers are going to die with those guns in the hands of Comanches?"

Caleb rubbed a hand across the back of his throbbing head. "None, thank God."

"What?" Gallagher demanded. "What are you—"

"I pulled the firing pins. I boxed them up myself in Council Grove to come later by freight hauler."

Gallagher let out a relieved sigh. "That's some consolation at least."

"Maybe now you won't be in quite so much trouble back East, eh?" Caleb hadn't meant to sound quite so bitter.

Gallagher's lips thinned. "I don't think I like what you're inferring, my friend."

"Well, *friend*," Caleb snapped, his temper slipping, "I don't much like any of this. These people are dead because of your harebrained scheme to—"

"Now just a damned minute!" Keith gritted. "You can't put this on me. I thought the Comanche were your friends."

"This wasn't Comanche. It was *comancheros.* "

Gallagher's jaw dropped. "Damn. They probably saw the women! Of all the blind rotten luck . . ."

"There was no luck to it, Keith. They knew exactly what they were after, and they were after the guns."

"That's impossible. No one knew about those Spencers but me and . . ." he hesitated.

"And?" Caleb prodded acidly.

Gallagher cursed and kicked at a clod of dirt. "Ah, hell, Caleb, I don't know what's the matter with me. I know none of this was your doing. I just . . . God, these bastards murder children. I've been in battles before, seen soldiers killed. But this . . ." He gestured helplessly at the scene around him. "This is straight from hell." He let out a long, slow breath. "What happened?"

In a bone-weary voice Caleb related everything he could remember—from having been blindsided by a man with a Spanish accent to Bart Jacobs's treachery, leaving out only the part about the hooded stranger. At this point he wasn't even certain he hadn't hallucinated the entire episode. In any event the man had threatened Jenna's life. Caleb couldn't take the risk.

Gallagher listened in silence, his gaze shifting from sympathy to confusion to outright disbelief by the time Caleb had finished. Caleb felt a strange stirring of foreboding.

"You're telling me Bart Jacobs knew about the Spencers? That he somehow relayed that information to the *comancheros*? That this attack was premeditated, even orchestrated by Jacobs?"

"That's exactly what I'm telling you."

Gallagher rose and stalked some ten feet away to the tarp that shrouded the dead. He raised up one end.

Caleb stared at Bart Jacobs's body, a bullet hole placed neatly between the sutler's eyes.

"Care to explain this?"

Caleb sat there, stunned, confused. "They must have double-crossed him."

"Somebody's double-crossing somebody."

Caleb lurched to his feet, his temper gone. "Don't dance around it, Keith. If you've got something to say, say it."

"Fine," the major snapped. "For starters, why the hell are you alive and these people dead? Not only that, but since when do *comancheros* leave behind good horseflesh?" He pointed toward Caleb's own black gelding. "Pretty charitable of them, don't you think? And your only explanation is to put the blame on a dead man?"

"Jacobs wasn't their leader. He took orders."

"From whom?"

"I don't know."

"Dammit, Caleb, none of this makes any sense." He paced back and forth in front of Jacobs's body. "And now I have only your word that the Spencers are inoperative."

"That's right, Keith. My word."

Gallagher drew in a deep lungful of air and let it out.

"I can't believe you're involved. I don't believe it. But this . . ."

"Makes for a very nice frame."

"Who would go to so much trouble? And why?"

"I wish I knew." Caleb remembered the hooded man's words *I know your background*. But to Keith he said only, "Maybe we can take advantage of it."

"What do you mean?"

"I was going to find a way to get the *comancheros* to trust me. Now it looks like I've got an open invitation to join."

Gallagher chewed his lower lip. "It would seem you do."

"Right after I find Jen—Miss Riordan and the others."

"My troopers can do that. You go after Valdez."

"They'd spot you a half day away. They might even kill the hostages. One man has a better chance."

Gallagher relented. "All right. But when you ride out of here, you'd best consider yourself a fugitive."

"What?"

"When I get back to Bascom, I'll issue a warrant for your arrest. That should further your cause with Valdez."

Caleb had to agree.

"And Caleb . . ." Gallagher went on.

"Yeah, Keith?"

"You'd best watch your back."

Caleb's gaze met Gallagher's. "I'll do that."

Caleb crossed to his horse, frowning to find his buckskin jacket and hat draped over the saddle. Things were making less sense by the minute. He shrugged into the jacket, then gingerly settled the Stetson over the lump on the side of his head. He took a deep breath and mounted, the action almost causing him to black out.

Gallagher hurried over. "Dammit, Caleb, this can wait a day or two. You're not going to last five miles."

"Jenna Riordan's out there with a gang of madmen. I'll last to hell if I have to."

He spurred the horse away from the camp, urging the horse into a gallop. His head throbbed unmercifully, but he didn't ease up. His thoughts were consumed by Jenna and what they must be doing to her. How she might even be dead by now, or wishing she were.

16

Timmy was all that kept Jenna alive. If not for her brother, she would have done something, anything to provoke Iron Fist into killing her. The agony was simply beyond bearing. She stumbled, fell for the hundredth time, the rope that tethered her behind the Comanche's stallion all but wrenching her shoulders from their sockets. The coarse hemp tore at her already savaged wrists, her bloodied knees scraping against dirt, scrub, brush.

Iron Fist didn't even glance back. He just kept the horse at a plodding pace, talking in conversational tones to his companion. Somehow Jenna struggled to her feet. Her only comfort was that Timmy was not being treated the same way. Her brother still rode in relative comfort in front of the other Indian.

It had been four days since the two Comanches had split off from Valdez. At first Iron Fist had been content to sling her over the back of his stallion like a sack of grain. But their first night on the trail had changed all that. In the light of their waning campfire, he'd come to her, leering, manipulating his breechclout to display his rigid sex. Though tied, Jenna had screamed, kicked, fought with a strength borne of hell-spawned terror. Timmy too had tried to attack the scar-faced Indian.

"You leave my sister alone!" His hands tied behind his back, Timmy booted Iron Fist in the shin with bone-cracking force.

Iron Fist grunted in pain, backhanding the boy across the face, sending him sprawling into the dirt. When he bent to hit him again, the other Indian caught his arm.

Quickly Timmy scrambled toward Jenna. "Are you all right?" he whispered as the two braves squared off, arguing heatedly.

"I think so," she managed shakily. "Are you?"

He nodded. "Two Trees likes me, I think. He isn't mad all the time like Iron Fist."

"Two Trees?"

"He pointed at himself today and said Two Trees. So I guess that's his name."

"Does he know any more English?"

"He never answered, if he does."

"They could have picked up a few words here and there, or they could just be trying to fool us. We'll have to be careful what we say."

"Do you think we're going to die, Jenna?"

"Of course not." She said it, though she didn't believe it. Timmy might have a chance. Jacobs had mentioned young captives raised to be "murderin' savages," but she had no such illusions for herself. She just prayed Timmy wouldn't have to watch.

"Do you think Mr. Harper is coming after us? I didn't see him at the camp yesterday morning. Maybe he got away."

Jenna thought about lying but decided false hope was worse than no hope at all. "If Caleb were tracking us, he would have found us by now. Remember your birth-day?"

"He saved my life."

Jenna had meant to remind Timmy of Caleb's incredible tracking abilities. Now she herself was forced to recall Caleb's saving Timmy from the rattlesnake. She felt a rush of pain, bittersweet. How could he have protected them one day only to lead them to their doom another? It didn't make any sense. Was there something in all this madness she was missing? Something that would exonerate Caleb from the damning evidence of her own eyes?

She let out a shuddery sigh. There was nothing.

Bashful, Bess had called him. Jenna choked on the bile rising in her throat. Cunning monster was closer to the truth.

I don't have a birthday.

There's something I need to tell you . . .

It's the only thing I have that means anything to me.

The day will come when you despise me.

Tears scalded her cheeks. She couldn't have been that wrong. She couldn't.

Madness. It was all madness.

Caleb would come. Caleb would rescue her and Timmy, tell them it was all some dreadful mistake, that Bess was still alive, that Millie and Mary were fine, that the Kovels . . .

Jenna gripped her stomach, her hand flying to her mouth, stark images of the Kovels ripping through her mind.

And Caleb . . . Caleb riding away . . . *running . . .*

"Jenna . . . Jenna don't cry. Please don't cry."

Jenna shook herself, focusing on her brother's distraught young face. "I'm . . . I'm fine, Timmy.

I'm . . ." More tears fell, and she bit her lip until she
tasted blood. Only then did the tears stop.

"Don't be scared, Jenna," Timmy said. "I don't want
you to be scared." His lower lip quivered, and Jenna
forced herself to take several steadying breaths.

"We'll be all right, Timmy," she said. "Just don't do
anything to make Two Trees angry with you. Promise?"

"I'm not going to let them hurt you." The defiance in
his voice gave Jenna new courage when she had none
left.

"Major Gallagher will find out what happened," she
said. "He'll come for us. What we have to do is stay
alive."

"Maybe I could get Two Trees's knife . . ."

"Don't you dare! I mean it, Timmy. I don't want—"

The Comanches stopped arguing. Two Trees stalked
toward her. Jenna tried not to flinch, fearful he had
merely decided to join Iron Fist in raping her. Instead
he pointed at her amulet, just as Iron Fist himself had
done when speaking to Valdez. To her astonishment
Iron Fist glowered at Two Trees, but made no further
move to attack her.

She and Timmy were allowed to get what sleep they
could. The next morning she discovered that whatever
words had prevented her rape did not prevent torture.
Iron Fist tethered her behind his horse and took off at a
gallop.

She'd heard Timmy scream, but then her senses
seemed to go numb. She'd felt little pain, her body
bouncing limply along the hard ground. Her only real
awareness was an oddly detached certainty that the
Comanche had decided to kill her. Her searing regret
had been for Timmy, that he would have to watch her
die. But just that suddenly Iron Fist pulled up, staring
at her as she gained her feet. Jenna stared back. With-

out tears, without curses, without pleas. Just stone-cold loathing. After that he'd kept the horse at a walk.

But she'd hardly felt grateful.

The sun's merciless rays burned her face, her scalp. Her tattered dress offered little protection to the rest of her body. Day after day dawned into a repeat of the one before it, until Jenna worried she actually had lost her mind, her scattered senses dooming her to relive Iron Fist's torment for the rest of her life.

Noon of the sixth day told her different. They topped a shallow rise, and Jenna found herself looking down into a surprisingly lush valley. Nestled in that valley were as many as three hundred conical structures, many with smoke drifting from openings at the top of the cones. North of the encampment she could see a large herd of horses. Even in her exhausted state Jenna couldn't suppress a spark of curiosity as she limped into her first Comanche village. Sights, sounds, smells assailed her senses. Barking dogs, laughing children, cooking meat, tanning hides . . .

Ebony-haired, copper-hued men and women dressed in buckskin and beads emerged from tepees to regard her with a curiosity of their own and an open contempt. Jenna's hope that someone would object to Iron Fist's horrific treatment of her was dashed in an instant. People flocked around the two braves, treating them like conquering heroes, pounding them on the back, smiling, gleeful.

Iron Fist stalked back to her and summarily sliced through her bonds with his knife. Gripping her hair, he said something to his people, his mouth twisted in an angry sneer; then he released her to accept more hearty congratulations.

Two Trees, meanwhile, was trying to lead Timmy away, but the boy balked, lunging toward Jenna. "I'm not leaving you," he said.

Jenna looked into Two Trees's eyes and knew her brother would be safe. "Go with him, Timmy. I want you to go with him."

"No. I want to stay with you."

"I'll be all right. I'm sure we'll be allowed to see each other later." She kept her voice steady, her eyes calm. "Go on now."

Reluctantly Timmy did as she asked, though he looked back over his shoulder time and again as Two Trees escorted him toward a much decorated lodge in the center of the village.

Jenna let out a shaky sigh. Timmy was safe, but she wasn't so sure about herself. Yet for the moment she couldn't muster the strength to care. She sagged to the ground. A dog came up to sniff at her heels, growling nervously. She didn't move.

A small boy poked her with a stick. She didn't move.

Several women crowded close. Jenna was aware of a circle of moccasined feet surrounding her. Surely one of these women would take pity on her, help her. Though her every muscle throbbed painfully, Jenna pushed to her feet. She gazed hopefully at the woman nearest her.

The woman spit in her face.

Jenna felt something snap inside her. Without thinking, she drew back her fist and socked the woman square in the jaw. The woman tumbled backward, landing on her rump in the dirt. Jenna turned on the others like a cornered badger. They could damned well kill her, but she would take no more abuse from anyone.

To her surprise many of them started laughing, their mirth directed at the woman Jenna had hit. No one else made any hostile move toward her. In fact, a couple of the women were watching her with something akin to amazement. The woman she had hit climbed to her feet. Jenna braced herself, studying a square face now suffused with fury. But there was a wariness there too.

The woman shouted something in Comanche and gestured contemptuously at Jenna, as though Jenna was now beneath her notice. But even Jenna was not fooled. This woman had just suffered a stinging setback to whatever reputation for toughness she might have had. The jeering laughter continued. The woman stalked away, grumbling angrily.

Another woman stepped out of the crowd. Jenna kept her fists ready.

"Not hurt you," the woman said. She was young, pretty, garbed in a doeskin dress that fell to midcalf, though it had a fringed slit on one side to expose a shapely thigh. Her long black hair hung in twin braids with intricate beadwork twined through the plaits.

"Change clothes," the woman said.

Jenna read kindness in those dark eyes. It seemed so very long since anyone had looked at her with kindness. She could have wept, except she knew it would be seen as weakness. She maintained a rigid posture, even as she allowed the young woman to lead her to a nearby tepee.

The girl gestured toward the entry flap.

Swallowing her fear, Jenna ducked inside. She stood there, sidestepping a little to allow the girl to enter behind her. Jenna was surprised at how cozy, how pleasant it was inside the odd structure. About fifteen feet high at its apex, the tepee exuded a more homey atmosphere than some houses she'd been in. Sunlight filtered dimly through its animal-hide walls.

The floor was mostly dirt, though bits of grass still clung to life here and there, not yet completely worn away by the tepee's occupants. To her left and right were piles of furs and buffalo robes, no doubt used as beds. Arranged neatly against one part of the curved

wall were things Jenna guessed to be cooking utensils—
a buffalo rib for stirring, turtle-shell bowls, among other
things.

What caught and held her attention though was the
cook fire, built into the ground in line with the opening
at the tepee's top. Several pieces of meat were hanging
from sharpened sticks positioned around the fire. The
flames hissed, popped as the meat cooked, bits of fat
occasionally dropping into the pit.

Jenna unconsciously licked her lips. She had been fed
poorly and only with great reluctance by Iron Fist this
past week. She almost fainted at how wondrous the
cooking meat smelled. She looked questioningly at her
newfound benefactor. The girl smiled.

Jenna bolted for the meat, dropping to her battered
knees in front of the fire. She burned her fingers as she
tore what she guessed to be venison from the sticks and
wolfed it down. She didn't want to give the girl a
chance to change her mind.

But the girl knelt beside Jenna, studying her anxiously. "Slow," she said, pointing to the meat.

Jenna nodded, forcing herself not to gobble the food.
She felt nauseated enough after Iron Fist's brutal treatment. She didn't need to make herself sicker. She sa-
vored the next piece of meat, all the while glancing
furtively at the entryway. Any second she feared Iron
Fist would storm in and drag her back outside. The
Comanche couldn't be aware of how kindly she was
being treated, or she was certain he would put a stop to
it. Jenna herself wasn't sure why this girl was doing
what no one else in her tribe had yet done. Treating her
like a human being.

When Jenna finished eating, the girl smiled, pointing
to herself. "Painted Sky."

Jenna returned the introduction, saying her own
name.

"Jen-nah." The girl nodded. "Jen-nah."

Painted Sky's eyes were so warm, so understanding, Jenna could almost have believed the girl knew everything Jenna had been through. The thought sparked a tiny flare of hope. "Painted Sky, can you . . . would you help me? Would you help my brother and me get away? Escape?"

The girl frowned, partly, Jenna guessed, because she hadn't quite been able to follow Jenna's hurried English. Somewhere Painted Sky had been taught the language, but Jenna doubted she had much opportunity to keep that knowledge fresh. Jenna repeated her request more slowly, adding a makeshift sign language when she couldn't make particular words understood.

Now Painted Sky was frowning in earnest. She shook her head. "Jen-nah stay. Not go. Iron Fist kill."

The Comanche girl said the words so matter-of-factly Jenna shuddered. "But he'll kill me if I stay."

"Not kill. Beat maybe, not kill."

Jenna blinked back tears. "I can't stay here. Please understand. Timmy and I have to get away. We're not Comanche. We don't belong here."

"Stay."

Jenna could see it was no use. Who was she trying to fool anyway? Even with a horse and a week's supply of food she couldn't risk escape. Where would she go? In which direction? What kind of terrain would she be facing? Her shoulders sagged along with her spirits.

"Jen-nah take bath," Painted Sky said, gathering some things together from around the tepee. "Come."

The thought of a bath buoyed her a little. She accepted the blanket Painted Sky gave her to carry. "Iron Fist?" She wanted to avoid the Comanche as long as she could.

"He smoke pipe with Eagle Dancer."

Jenna recalled the name. Iron Fist's father, Caleb had

told her. A man of peace, he'd said also, if that wasn't just another lie. Perhaps if she could somehow meet with Eagle Dancer, talk to him . . .

"Iron Fist not return tepee long time."

Jenna's heart turned over, the words jolting thoughts of Eagle Dancer from her mind. "Return? This tepee is—"

The flap snapped open and Jenna cringed, then straightened. The Indian woman who had spit in her face ducked inside. The woman's eyes blazed hate. She raised her fist to Jenna, but a firm command from Painted Sky stopped her. The other woman began to speak rapidly in Comanche, her tone shifting from belligerent to whining.

But Painted Sky obviously won her point. The woman stomped back outside.

Painted Sky then turned and gave Jenna a sympathetic look. "Do not turn your back on Talks Too Much," she said simply. "It will not be safe."

"Why does she hate me? She doesn't even know me."

"She is wife to Iron Fist."

Jenna blanched. "Surely she doesn't think I want anything to do with him."

"You . . ." Painted Sky groped for the right words, "you property Iron Fist. Slave. Talks Too Much not like share lodge with white woman."

"Share?" Jenna's knees threatened to buckle. "This is where I will stay? With Iron Fist and Talks Too Much?" Her earlier illusion of the tepee's coziness was suddenly replaced with one of crushing confinement, terrifying intimacy.

"Me stay too."

"You?"

"Iron Fist husband."

Jenna felt her head spin. "Iron Fist has two wives? You . . . ?"

Painted Sky smiled. "Him not beat me. Beat Talks Too Much."

"But how could you be married to that—" She swallowed the rest. She dare not risk the tenuous bond between herself and Painted Sky. More questions whirled through her mind. About what it would mean to be Iron Fist's slave. About her brother. About life in the village. But Painted Sky would answer none of them. At least not now. Jenna's thoughts flashed painfully back to the antislavery essays she had once written, how her idealistic moralizing hadn't even come close to the savage reality of being the "property" of another human being.

"Take bath," Painted Sky urged again. "Feel good."

The lure of the bath kept Jenna from succumbing to new visions of horror. She even managed to ignore the venomous look she encountered from Talks Too Much outside the tepee. The woman was on her knees, vigorously scraping the hair from a massive buffalo hide with a sharp-edged stone. Jenna could tell the woman would be just as content to use that stone on her.

Limping painfully, Jenna continued after Painted Sky. The creek was about five hundred yards away, but to feel clean again Jenna would have crawled. Without any encouragement from the Indian woman, Jenna stripped out of her filthy clothes, leaving them in a ragged pile on the bank. As an afterthought she tugged off Caleb's amulet as well.

With a sigh of unutterable relief Jenna stumbled into the burbling water. It was like dying and going to heaven. She slogged to midstream, lowering herself to her knees, reveling in the feel of the cool mud on the creek's bottom, the tepid water reaching to her chin. For long minutes she simply let the blessed wetness seep into her aching bones.

Jenna huddled there, trying to block all thought, to

merely be, exist, to find some small pleasure in living again. Though cruel reality surrounded her, for this tiny space of time she found peace.

Painted Sky seemed to sense Jenna's need to be alone. The Comanche woman entered the creek several yards downstream.

An hour passed, maybe two, before Jenna finally sloshed her way back to the grassy bank. The bruises and scrapes that covered nearly every square inch of her body throbbed dully, but she felt better than she had at any time since this nightmarish week had begun.

Painted Sky was already dressed and sitting on the bank, busily tending to the repair of some garment that resembled the one she was wearing.

Jenna watched curiously, settling the Comanche woman's coarse-spun blanket around her shoulders. A wayward breeze stirred the still-wet strands of her hair.

Minutes later Painted Sky handed Jenna the repaired dress, along with a pair of moccasins.

Jenna gasped. "For me?"

The woman nodded.

Genuinely thrilled Jenna stood and pulled the soft doeskin dress over her head. She was nearly the same build as Painted Sky and the fit was perfect. Jenna ran her fingers over the finely worked shells and beads ornamenting the bodice. "It's beautiful."

Painted Sky beamed.

They were about to start back to the village, when Jenna remembered Caleb's amulet. She considered leaving it, the memories of its giver too painful, but twice the amulet had kept her from suffering serious harm. In a perverse way Caleb was protecting her, even though she wouldn't be here in the first place if not for his treachery. She retrieved the talisman and settled it about her neck.

A cry from Painted Sky made Jenna look up sharply.

"Iron Fist not tell me." The Comanche woman showed the first trace of anger Jenna had seen in her. "Him not tell me you belong—" She didn't finish.

Belong? Jenna stiffened. The amulet wasn't protection. It was proof of ownership! The amulet told the world she *belonged* to Caleb Harper. And Caleb Harper was friend to the Comanche. That was why she had not suffered Bess's fate or Millie's or Mary's . . . or Nelda Kovel's.

Hadn't Caleb told Iron Fist she was his wife? *A Comanche doesn't take another man's wife without his permission.*

That Iron Fist had honored that code, no matter how grudgingly, only proved beyond doubt how closely tied Caleb was with these people.

Had he given her the amulet the night before the attack with the express purpose of keeping her alive? Was he going to ride into this village one day to reclaim his property?

A searing rage ripped through her, deeper than any she had ever known, deeper even than the hate she felt for Iron Fist. The Comanche made no pretense about who or what he was—a cold-blooded killer, a man who murdered whites because he hated them as virulently as Bart Jacobs hated Indians. But Caleb had been nothing of what he presented himself to be. His warmth, his caring, his compassion even, she was convinced, his supposed bashfulness had all been part of a carefully woven fabric of lies.

Damn him. Damn him to hell. Why had he kept her alive, when he must have known she would never forgive him for what had happened to Bess?

Nothing made any sense anymore. She had too many questions and no answers. Unless . . .

"I must see Eagle Dancer," she said.

Painted Sky shook her head. "Eagle Dancer not well. See only Iron Fist."

"But I belong to Caleb Harper." Jenna all but strangled on the words. "I am . . . his wife. Eagle Dancer is friend to my husband."

An unreadable look came into Painted Sky's dark eyes, but she said only, "Not see. Eagle Dancer not strong."

Jenna decided not to press her, following meekly behind the Comanche woman as they returned to the village. But when Painted Sky headed for Iron Fist's tepee, Jenna veered toward the most decorated lodge, the one in the middle of the village where Two Trees had led Timmy.

Before Painted Sky could stop her Jenna ducked inside Eagle Dancer's tepee. She immediately wondered if she'd made a terrible mistake. Iron Fist glowered furiously from across the fire, gesturing fiercely with his gauntleted fist that she get out. The gray-haired Indian sitting cross-legged beside him, however, seemed unperturbed by the disturbance.

The lodge, she noted, was much like Iron Fist's own, smelling of tallow and leather and woodsmoke. But Eagle Dancer was not at all what she would have expected of the man who was Iron Fist's father. Three eagle feathers dangled from his scalp lock, while metal cones sewn into the outer seams of his leggings jingled as he shifted forward to get a better look at her. She was barely five feet away from him, but the way he squinted strongly suggested failing eyesight.

His age she couldn't have guessed, his features careworn but somehow timeless. Bare-chested, he had muscles that rippled with the kind of strength normally seen in much younger men, but his skin was sallow beneath its copper hue and Jenna recalled Painted Sky having told her the chief was not well. The look in his eyes was what surprised her most. There was none of the cruelty in this man that was so much a part of Iron Fist.

"Where is my brother?" she demanded, deciding if she was already in trouble for intruding, she might as well make the most of it.

Iron Fist again waved his gauntleted fist at her.

Jenna repeated her question.

Eagle Dancer said something in Comanche to Iron Fist. With obvious reluctance the warrior rose and peered out of the lodge, summoning Painted Sky to join them. The Comanche woman would serve as interpreter. Jenna could tell this was all highly unusual. As before, she had the palpable sense that she was being treated differently because of the amulet. She had been unconsciously clutching at it when she'd entered the tepee. Even with his poor eyesight Eagle Dancer had seemed to recognize it, something indefinable flitting across his otherwise inscrutable features.

Jenna again asked about Timmy.

"Your brother with Two Trees," Painted Sky said, after talking with Eagle Dancer. "Two Trees's son gone." A sadness crept into her dark eyes. "Not know—" She struggled to find the right words. "Not know where—" She shook her head.

Jenna hid the horror that swept through her. Two Trees! Now she remembered. Two Trees was father to One Wolf, the young brave Bart Jacobs had so ruthlessly murdered. She thought about telling Painted Sky the truth. Perhaps Two Trees would be better off knowing his son was dead than forever wondering what had become of him. But fear kept her silent. What if she and Timmy were somehow found guilty by association? Painted Sky's next words swept any notions of sympathy from her mind.

"Tim-my Two Trees's son now. Make Comanche. Call Wolf Cub."

Jenna recoiled in revulsion. These people were going to turn her brother into the kind of savage who had killed their sister? Over Jenna's dead body! She started to say as much but instantly drew rein on her temper. She had no power here. No say in anything these people did. To react with fury was to invite fury. Her only hope, no matter how distasteful, was to continue to foster the Comanches' mistaken belief that she belonged to Caleb Harper. Her stomach churning, she again said the loathsome words, "I am Caleb Harper's wife."

Iron Fist looked uncomfortable as Painted Sky translated. Jenna got the feeling the Comanche had not as yet informed the chief of his new prisoner's status. Still, if Eagle Dancer was in any way annoyed at his son, he made no show of it in front of Jenna.

Words flowed rapidly between Eagle Dancer and Painted Sky. Apparently the chief had much to say to the wife of Caleb Harper.

"Eagle Dancer tell you Ca-leb Har-per Comanche name Restless as Night Wind," Painted Sky said.

Jenna thought she should have been surprised to discover Caleb had a Comanche name. But she was not.

"One day Night Wind come back for his woman," Painted Sky went on. "Iron Fist make you Comanche. Make Night Wind proud. Eagle Dancer name you Captures the Sky With Your Eyes."

It was too much. Jenna could conceal her emotions no longer. "I don't want a Comanche name," she gritted. "I don't want to live with Comanches. I don't want to be a Comanche. Comanches killed my sister." Her voice grew shrill. "Iron Fist killed my sister. I want to be gone from here. I want my brother gone from here. And I never ever want to see Caleb Harper again."

Painted Sky's eyes went wide with shock and not a

little hurt. Though Eagle Dancer and Iron Fist waited expectantly for her translation of Jenna's words, the Comanche woman said nothing.

"Tell them," Jenna snapped. "Tell them both."

Painted Sky shook her head.

"Tell them!"

Eagle Dancer said something. Painted Sky began to speak, but Jenna could tell from the expression on the men's faces that Painted Sky was conveying nothing of what Jenna had actually said. In a hissed aside the Comanche woman made it clear that to do so would be very dangerous, not only to Jenna but perhaps to Timmy as well.

Jenna tried another tack. "We can't stay here. Please, Painted Sky. Can't you at least ask Eagle Dancer to take us back to our own people?"

Painted Sky's lips compressed in a grim line.

Jenna knew she was beaten. She didn't ask again.

Throughout their conversation Eagle Dancer had grown obviously more tired, until even Iron Fist looked worried. But protocol apparently did not allow an end to the talk until Eagle Dancer dismissed them. At last the chief did so. But before Jenna followed Painted Sky and Iron Fist out of the tepee, Eagle Dancer rose to grasp her hand. He didn't say anything, but Jenna could almost have sworn she saw tears in the old man's eyes.

Back at Iron Fist's lodge Talks Too Much was still hunched over the same buffalo hide. Iron Fist kicked her as he walked by. The woman worked faster, even as she cast another hate-filled look toward Jenna.

Inside the tepee Iron Fist ranted for several minutes.

"Iron Fist say Night Wind's woman weak," Painted Sky said. "Poor choice for wife. But Eagle Dancer tell him make you Comanche, Iron Fist make. Iron Fist not beat." Jenna was sure Painted Sky had added the last on her own.

But even assurances she would not be beaten did not make Jenna feel better. Nothing could make her feel better.

Make Timmy a Comanche. Make her a Comanche.

She shuddered, hopelessness settling over her, a cloying despair that seeped into her very soul. She was going to die here. She was going to grow old and die, sharing a home with the man who had killed her sister. Jenna sank onto a buffalo robe, and for the first time in days, she wept.

Iron Fist stalked out of the tepee. A yelp from Talks Too Much told Jenna he'd again taken out his annoyance on her.

Jenna literally cried herself to sleep. When she awoke, it was pitch-dark. Strange, grunting noises sounded from across the tepee. It was all Jenna could do not to run screaming into the night. Iron Fist was having sex with one of his wives. Jenna burrowed her head into the leathery softness of a deerskin pillow and tried not to vomit.

In the darkness of the lodge she saw her future—bleak, empty for endless days and nights to come.

The next morning she discovered just how right she was. It was soon obvious that Iron Fist had charged Painted Sky with the personal responsibility of teaching Jenna the ways of the Comanche. The Indian woman took to the task cheerfully, even eagerly. If Jenna's own heart hadn't been so desolate, so burdened by Bess's death and by Caleb's betrayal, she might have taken more pleasure in the lessons Painted Sky taught her.

Over the days and weeks that followed, Jenna learned to scrape a hide, to make tallow, to soften doeskin to supple perfection by chewing on it, to make pemmican with dried meat and pecans. The hard work actually proved a blessing—it filled her days and by night let her collapse into an exhausted, dreamless sleep. Because no matter how much she had come to care for Painted Sky and a few other women about the camp, the fact remained she was a prisoner—without freedom, without rights.

Her position as Caleb Harper's wife gave her only as much privilege as Iron Fist would allow, which so far meant only he would not beat her. Even that tiny concession, she was certain, had more to do with her being Caleb's supposed wife than with any mercy on Iron Fist's part.

The times that were worst were those rare occasions she caught glimpses of Timmy.

She was watching one late afternoon as the boy scampered happily behind Two Trees, dressed in a breechclout, his once pale skin tanned to a deep brown. If not for his blond hair and blue eyes, he could have been mistaken for any boy in the village.

"Don't look so sad, Jenna," he said, pausing as he passed her.

"These people killed Bess," she said, unable to hide her hurt. "Have you forgotten that already?"

"Iron Fist killed Bess." Timmy's chin jutted out stubbornly, his hand resting on the bone handle of the knife Caleb had given him for his birthday. She'd almost choked the day Two Trees had given it back to him. "One day I'll challenge him for that."

"You will not!"

"I will. And I'll kill him." He rushed off then, responding to a shout from Two Trees.

Raw agony sliced through her. Two months ago she had lost Bess. Now it seemed she was losing her brother as well.

All because of Caleb Harper.

That night she lay awake atop her buffalo robes, recalling what Painted Sky had said that first day in Eagle

Dancer's tepee. *One day Night Wind come back for his woman . . .*

Hatred, cold and deadly, closed around her heart. Jenna prayed most fervently that Painted Sky was right.

Caleb couldn't remember the last time he'd shaved or taken a bath, had a full night's sleep or a hot meal. Weeks? Months? He didn't know. He didn't care. Only one thing drove him on.

Jenna.

He reined in the black and took a swig from his canteen, using his shirtsleeve to wipe at the sweat and grime of his brow. All around him the southern New Mexico landscape was as barren and desolate as his soul. Here and there a few mesquite bushes clung to life, some prickly pear and agave, but in the early days of September twisted branches and spiny leaves more closely resembled the skeletal claws of death.

Jabbing the cork back into his canteen, he nudged the black wearily northward. The clues he'd followed into Mexico had brought him full circle. He still couldn't believe all that he had found out. Couldn't, or wouldn't.

How long had it been? Six weeks? Seven? It was the best guess he could make.

He recalled the first few hours after he'd left Gallagher. It had been all he could do to stay in the saddle. But somehow he'd gotten used to the throbbing in his skull.

He'd ridden first to where he'd buried One Wolf. The grave was on the same path the killers had taken. Caleb had said nothing of One Wolf to Gallagher, convinced the attack on the Riordans was solely the work of *comancheros.* But neither he nor Gallagher had missed the Comanche arrow in young Bess Riordan. For now, both men were willing to believe the *comancheros* were deliberately trying to deflect the blame to renegades. And yet, Caleb thought grimly, if Iron Fist had discovered One Wolf's death . . .

He was grateful to find the grave undisturbed. The thought that Iron Fist might be involved in any of this had sickened him more than he cared to acknowledge. He and the Comanche had had their differences, but Caleb wanted to think even Iron Fist would not disgrace Eagle Dancer by riding with *comancheros.*

From the site of One Wolf's grave the killers' path proved surprisingly easy to follow, but then they had likely expected no pursuit. They were dragging three travois for the Spencers, but they had not yet stopped to discover the weapons useless.

It was late afternoon when Caleb saw the buzzards circling. He spurred the black into a gallop. Even before he reached the scene he counted two bodies. His heart twisted. He wasn't proud of the relief that coursed through him to find Lem and Nelda Kovel, but he was desperately grateful the two mutilated corpses did not belong to Jenna and her brother.

He chafed at the time it cost him, but he felt compelled to construct some sort of marker for the Kovels, piling rocks atop their remains, because he had neither the strength nor the means to dig a grave. Jenna would have wanted him to do that much.

The work gave him the chance to think, to consider. He had checked the sign. From here the *comancheros* had split up. Two riders headed north, two west, and a half dozen south. Three trails. One hellish choice. Which group had taken Jenna?

He sagged to the ground, his head in his hands, overwhelmed by an aching despair. If he made the wrong choice, the other trails would be blown to dust, vanished by the time he discovered his mistake.

He thought of her then, her mountain-lake eyes brimming with love and laughter, her corn-silk hair tumbled about her lovely face, her honey-sweet voice whispering, "I love you."

With a savage oath he pushed to his feet. To think of her as she was, was to think of her as she must be; grieving, terrified, betrayed. He had to keep such imaginings at bay, or he would go mad.

He forced his attention to the task at hand. It was obvious now that the outlaws had discovered the worthlessness of the Spencers, though they had still taken the weapons with them. The weapons and perhaps three live hostages—Jenna, Timmy, and Sam Holt. Young white captives could bring a premium price in certain parts of Mexico. Rich, perverted men who wanted new playthings.

Logic sent Caleb south.

He rode as far as Matamoros, just across the border in Mexico. Valdez had been there all right, but there had been no white captives with him. Caleb had paid a high-enough bribe to the lieutenant in charge of a troop of *soldatos* to be assured the information given him was correct. Caleb also let it be known that he was available to aid the *comanchero* cause once his woman was returned.

It was that last bit of information that had netted him an unexpected bonus—a clandestine meeting with the hooded stranger. Caleb had allowed himself to be disarmed, then, flanked by four armed *banditos,* he was led into the windowless back room of a dilapidated *hacienda*. The hooded man sat with his feet up on a spur-scarred desk.

"So we meet again, Mr. Harper."

"Where's Jenna?"

"Please. Your manners. Would you like a drink?"

"No. Thank you." Caleb held his temper under rigid

control. He would say and do nothing that would jeopardize getting news of Jenna out of this man.

"That's better. Please . . ." He gestured toward a cane-back chair with most of its cane missing. "Sit."

Caleb sat down. "Business must be kind of slow," he drawled, casting a contemptuous glance around the room.

The mystery man chuckled. "Believe me, Mr. Harper, my normal quarters are much more . . . sumptuous, shall we say."

"Who are you? Why the mask?"

"No, no, Mr. Harper," the man waggled a finger at Caleb. "I ask the questions."

"You can ask whatever the hell you want, but you won't get any answers until I know where Jenna Riordan is."

The hooded man dragged his feet from the desk and leaned forward, shaking his head. "One woman should never wield so much power over a man, Mr. Harper. It isn't . . . healthy."

Caleb stood so abruptly that three of the banditos drew their weapons. The hooded man held up a staying hand. The outlaws remained alert but did not fire. "Listen to me," Caleb hissed. "I'll tell you what isn't healthy. Knowing where Jenna Riordan is and not telling me—that's not healthy. If anyone has harmed her in any way . . ."

"Your threats bore me, Mr. Harper. I had hoped we could do business."

"Like you did business with Bart Jacobs?"

"Mr. Jacobs's personal vendetta against One Wolf could have cost me much more than money. That kind of insubordination I cannot tolerate."

"What the hell do you want from me? Why did you arrange this meeting?"

"As I told you before, Mr. Harper, I know your background. All of it. It could prove quite useful to me. As could your fondness for our Indian brothers and sisters."

"Just say what you want. Say what it would take to get Jenna back."

"For starters—the firing pins of those Spencers."

Caleb felt a helpless rage. He couldn't trade the firing pins for information about Jenna. To do so would be to put a hundred more guns into the hands of men like Valdez and Iron Fist. "They're safe" was all he said.

"Tell me where they are, and I'll tell you where you can find Miss Riordan."

"I tell you where they are, and I'm a dead man. Besides, you're lying. If you knew where she was, you'd have her here. We could make a trade, straight up."

"Maybe, maybe not."

"And maybe Jacobs wasn't the only one of your people guilty of 'insubordination.' Maybe somebody else got a little greedy."

Caleb couldn't know for certain, but he would have sworn the jaw of the man under that hood was now clenched in cold fury. Caleb turned toward the door. "When I find Jenna, we'll talk."

"When you find her, I'll listen."

"How will I know where to get in touch with you?"

"We'll find each other, Mr. Harper. Never fear."

With that, Caleb left. He thought about waiting around, trying to discover the identity of the hooded bastard, but the man was so well protected, Caleb conceded he had no chance. Nor could he be certain he'd done the right thing in not pushing harder for some clue to Jenna's whereabouts. Obviously even if the man knew where she was, he had no power to retrieve her, or he would have done so. He would have done anything to get those firing pins. It was an ace in the hole Caleb would save for another day.

For now, he had no choice. He had to backtrack.

The pace he set was relentless, insane, as he cut back into New Mexico. It was as though if he kept moving, somewhere, anywhere, he would eventually have to find Jenna. He'd ridden day and night for nearly a week, when he finally had to bow to the folly of his actions. The black was exhausted. The animal would die if he continued to push it so hard. A dead horse would do him no good in his search.

After that he took to riding mostly at night, resting the gelding during the heat of the day. The times he stopped were the worst, the times just before he'd fall into a fitful sleep. It was then he couldn't fight them anymore, when memories of Jenna would overwhelm his every defense. He would remember what it had been like to kiss her, touch her, make love to her, to see the unquestioning trust and love in her eyes.

What must she be thinking of him now? She wouldn't know where he had been the morning of the attack. She wouldn't know what Jacobs had done. She would know only that when she had needed him most, Caleb was gone.

With no leads left, without even vague rumors, he knew he should head for Fort Bascom, check in with Gallagher. But the major would expect action with Valdez, expect Caleb to abandon his futile hunt for Jenna. Within a day of the fort Caleb veered east.

He would ride first to Eagle Dancer's village. He would take the time to play a distasteful hunch. Iron Fist might not ride with *comancheros*, but Caleb had little doubt the Comanche had had past dealings with the thieving cutthroats. He hated the thought of bringing Eagle Dancer into this, but there was no help for it. He would do whatever it took to find Jenna.

Caleb honored Eagle Dancer too much though to ride into the village looking and smelling like a grizzly bear. He waded into a creek about two miles downstream from where he'd found the band to be camped. There he shaved his beard, then scrubbed two months of filth from his clothes, his body. Both would dry quickly in the midday sun.

Bathing in the creek roused more cruel memories. He could look toward the bank and almost see Jenna as she had been the night she had grabbed up his clothes, offering them back to him for the price of a kiss.

His eyes burned. He would give his soul for that kiss.

With a sigh he slogged his way to the grassy bank. His midnight hair now trailed past his shoulders, and he caught it back in a rawhide thong to keep it out of his face. When his clothes were dry, he shrugged into them, then pulled on his buckskin jacket and settled the black Stetson atop his head. Mounting the tired gelding, he headed toward the village.

It had been a year since he'd last seen Eagle Dancer. His reception by the band ranged from warm and enthusiastic to cool and aloof, from the various warriors he saw as he rode in. The squaws and children, however, seemed universally pleased. He smiled at several he knew by name as he guided the black through the maze of lodges. He wanted to make it to Eagle Dancer's lodge before he ran into Iron Fist.

But it was not to be.

Iron Fist stepped from his tepee directly into Caleb's path, arms folded across his chest, eyes dark with challenge, hate.

Caleb dismounted. He should speak first of this to Eagle Dancer, and he knew it, but old animosities died hard. Besides, if there was the remotest chance Iron Fist had heard anything about Jenna, Caleb wanted to know now. He spoke rapidly in Comanche. "You remember the woman I claimed as my wife?"

Iron Fist nodded, an odd smugness coming into his black eyes.

"She was stolen from me by *comancheros*. Have you heard of this?"

To Caleb's astonishment Iron Fist smiled, a thoroughly unpleasant smile. "I have heard of it," Iron Fist said. "I have done it." He gestured toward his lodge.

Caleb's insides froze. God in heaven, no. He couldn't move, couldn't speak as the deerhide opening was pushed aside from within. Not all this time. No.

Incongruously he noted first her deerskin dress and moccasins, her angel hair done up in two long braids. But it was her eyes that stunned him, slammed the breath from him. In all respects this was Jenna, the woman he loved. In all respects save one. The look in those mountain-lake eyes. His every instinct told him to go to her, take her in his arms, hold her, and never let go. But the look in those eyes stopped him. Her words staggered him.

"If I had a gun, I would kill you."

17

Jenna heard the commotion outside the lodge and cautiously peered through one edge of the entry flap to see what was happening. Her heart almost stopped.

Caleb.

Despite all the pain, all the mistrust, all the heartbreak he had caused her, she felt a sudden tiny flare of hope. Hope that she had been dreadfully wrong, that he was here looking for her, had come to rescue her and Timmy. And then Caleb dismounted to talk to Iron Fist, to pass the time of day with the murderer of her sister. Hate roiled up inside her, hate so intense she thought she might choke on it.

She stepped out of the lodge.

She tried to keep her expression neutral, indifferent but knew she failed. The hate was simply too deep. She meant every word of her threat to kill him.

"Jenna, I . . ." He took a step toward her, and unconsciously she took a step back. "We need to talk," he said. "You need to understand—"

"Understand what? That you're a lying bastard?" He

flinched, the reaction disconcerting her a little. But she kept her guard up. She would not be fooled by this man again.

"We need to talk," he repeated, the words absurdly rational, restrained.

It was all Jenna could do not to laugh in his face. "I have nothing to say to you, except that I hate you. Will always hate you for what you've done to me and my family."

"I can explain. I—"

"I don't want your explanations, Mr. Harper. Or should I say your lies?" Now she did laugh. Cold. Cruel. "How many lies have you told me since we left Council Grove? How many? Have you kept track? Twenty? A hundred? How many more would you like to tell me now?"

He held her gaze, saying nothing, his eyes sad but maddeningly steady, until it was she who was forced to look away.

"I will talk with Eagle Dancer," he said then. "It will be expected; then I will come back to talk to you."

He turned toward Iron Fist, speaking rapidly in Comanche. Jenna had learned a little of the language these past two months but not enough to keep up with such a quick exchange. Still, it was enough to know that she was their chief topic of discussion. With obvious reluctance Iron Fist led Caleb toward Eagle Dancer's dwelling. The other Comanches who had thronged about for Caleb's arrival trailed away to be about their own business.

All except Two Trees and Timmy. Her brother made his way toward her from the back of the crowd.

Jenna ignored him. She stared after Caleb, seething. *I will come back to talk to you.*

Come back and I'll kill you, she thought fiercely,

turning toward Iron Fist's lodge. She would find no gun in there, but there was a skinning knife . . .

"Why were you so angry with Mr. Harper, Jenna?"

Jenna whirled on her brother, her frustration, her rage at Caleb still simmering hotly. The edgings of confusion, betrayal, in Timmy's wide blue eyes broke the last vestiges of her control. "Why was I so angry?" she shrilled. "Why was I so angry with Caleb Harper? Only because he hid guns in our wagon. Only because he turned us over to Iron Fist. Only because he might as well have struck Bess down with his own hand."

She went on to spare Timmy none of what she had seen the morning of the attack.

"That can't be true!" Timmy protested. "Mr. Harper wouldn't signal Iron Fist. You said he followed Bart Jacobs. Maybe Mr. Jacobs got the drop on him. Maybe—"

"Stop it!" Jenna hissed. "Stop it, Timmy! I don't want to hear it. Did you see him?" She gestured furiously in the direction Caleb had gone. "Did you see him at all just now? Did you? He looked like he just stepped out of a damned bath house."

Timmy's mouth twisted angrily, but his eyes reflected the stinging hurt he felt at being the butt of her fury. "You'd wash my mouth out with soap if I ever talked like that!" he yelled. "And I don't care what you say. You're wrong about Mr. Harper. He'd never hurt Bessie, or me, or anybody. He's our friend. He gave me a birthday present. And we gave him a birthday. He never had one, and we made him happy. We did! You just take it back, Jenna. You just take it back what you said about him!"

"I will not." She gripped his bare arm, giving him a fierce shake. "And I'm sick and tired of your looking like a savage. You're a Riordan, Timmy. Do you hear me? *Timmy*. Not Wolf Cub."

He jerked his arm free. "Two Trees treats me better

than you do!" With that he backed toward the Indian, who reflexively put a hand on the boy's trembling shoulder.

Jenna went rigid, crushed by Timmy's words, yet unwilling to take back anything she had said. She glared at the stoic Comanche. "He's not your son. He's my brother! You'll not have him. One day we'll be free of this place, free of you and your people!"

Two Trees just stared. He hadn't understood a word she'd said, a fact that only made her more furious. He even looked a little sorry for her. Timmy continued to look hurt.

Tears of rage rimming her eyes, Jenna ducked into the lodge. She needed to get away from them both. She needed to be alone.

Inside the tepee she sank to her knees and tried not to give in to hysteria. This was Caleb Harper's fault. All of it. Everything. From the day she had met him in Council Grove to this very moment.

Why don't you like me, Mr. Harper?

Oh, God, why did she have to remember that? Her cheeks burned. How could she have been such a fool? How could she not have seen him for what he was?

She trembled. But what was he?

She had seen him angry, sad, embarrassed, hurt, happy, frustrated, aroused, withdrawn, irritated, compassionate, even . . .

In love?

No! No, it was lies. All lies. All of it. What was the matter with her? What was she thinking? Any minute now he would be coming in here to lie to her again. She had to be strong. She had to be ready.

She sat there trying to gather her wits. She was glad Painted Sky had ridden off this morning in search of wild honey, even gladder that Talks Too Much was visiting another lodge. The woman's brother, a surpris-

ingly amiable warrior named Tall Bear, had asked Iron
Fist that his sister be present to help his wife, Quiet
One, deliver their second child. Iron Fist had gladly
assented. He too had grown impatient with Talks Too
Much's constant bickering about Jenna's presence in
the tepee.

But none of that mattered now.

Jenna's fists knotted in the skirt of her doeskin dress.
She regretted her harsh words to Timmy. She should
not have let her temper get the better of her. Timmy
was only making the best of a terrible situation. She had
come to a vague acceptance of her lot here of late herself. Though she hoped always for rescue, she genuinely liked Painted Sky and some of the others.

And, of course, Timmy had not known of Caleb's
treachery. She supposed it was only natural that he balk
at believing it. Heaven only knew how many times she
had wanted not to believe it herself.

But somehow seeing Caleb today had loosed all the
ugly memories—Bess, the Holts, the Kovels, the guns—
like a lance to a festering wound. No matter what lies
he might conjure to excuse what he had done, she
would never forgive him.

Never.

Behind her the entry flap opened briefly, allowing a
shaft of sunlight to blanket her back. Then the light was
gone. She didn't have to turn to know.

Caleb had kept his promise.

Though he didn't speak, didn't move from in front of
the entryway, his presence seemed to fill the lodge. She
could feel his eyes boring into her back.

The silence grew unbearable, but Jenna was determined not to be the one to break it.

Finally he cleared his throat and spoke haltingly.
"I'm not sure where to begin—"

"I hate you."

"The guns, you know about the guns—"

"I hate you."

"Gallagher and I . . . we—"

"I hate you."

"I'm sorry . . . about Bess . . . about . . ." He sighed heavily. "I'm sorry."

Jenna knew he was holding his hat in his hands, knew he was twisting the brim, knew how achingly vulnerable he looked, how lost. With a violent oath she sprang to her feet, whirling to face him.

Exactly. She had pictured him exactly.

"No!" She screamed it, sobbed it, launching herself at him, fists flailing. "Don't you dare look guilty! Don't you dare look sad!" She pounded on his chest, slapped his face, not stopping even when he offered no defense. She hit him until she had no strength left, and then it was his hands that caught her, steadied her as they sank to the ground together. She sagged against him, sobbing, felt his arms go around her and hated herself for wanting only to stay there, to have him hold her, protect her, make all the weeks of madness go away.

He held her close, his chin resting atop her head. He spoke quietly, almost wearily. She didn't want to listen, didn't want to hear, but she couldn't seem to help herself. He told her of working for Gallagher, of loading the Spencers in Council Grove, of Bart Jacobs and the sutler's involvement with the *comancheros*. All the while his voice was laced with a soul-crushing guilt. Her mind whirled. He was doing it all over again. Making her believe. Making her care.

"You're lying," she managed desperately, not lifting her face from his chest. "I saw you on that horse. I saw you ride away."

"It wasn't me."

"Then who was it?"

He shook his head. "I don't know. Jacobs. Valdez. Does it matter?"

Tears trailed down her cheeks. She knew she should push away from him, knew she was being twice the fool, but she couldn't yet seem to bring herself to move. "Why?" she murmured. "Why did you let Gallagher put guns in my wagon?"

"Because I was there . . ." His voice was broken, bitter. "I was there to protect you."

For long minutes she huddled against him, too exhausted even to cry anymore. At last, eyes aching, she pushed away from him. Something wasn't right. She had to think. And to think clearly she couldn't stay in Caleb's arms. She climbed to her feet.

He rose to face her. "I'd give my life to change what happened."

"I don't want your life. I want Bess. I want Timmy home and safe."

He closed his eyes. "I can't say anything to make it different. I can't do anything to fix it."

"You could take Timmy and me out of here."

He paced across the dirt floor, stopping on the opposite side of the tepee. "I could take you to Bascom," he said, not looking at her. "But . . ." He stopped.

"But what?" Her heart hammered. He was offering her rescue. He was here to save her after all. Then why did she know he was about to take it all back? "But what?" she pressed, not really wanting to hear.

He turned. "I could take you, but not Timmy. He—"

"Are you out of your mind?" she cut in. "Leave my brother here? Leave him to savages?"

He winced but said only, "I have no say over what happens to Timmy. He doesn't belong to me."

She staggered. "Belong?" That was it. Belong. She touched the amulet dangling about her neck. "When you gave this to me, I thought it was because it meant something to you." Her voice cracked. "That *I* meant something to you. I didn't realize it was your brand, your proof of ownership." She yanked off the talisman and threw it at his feet. "Your bill of sale."

He stooped to retrieve it, the look in his eyes unreadable. He ran a thumb across the soaring eagle on its surface. "Has Iron Fist . . . has he . . . did he hurt you?"

"You mean did he rape me? No. He only beat me senseless. He only tortured Mr. Kovel. He only raped Mrs. Kovel. He only killed my sister."

"I swear to God I never knew Iron Fist was involved. I thought it was *comancheros*. I went to Mexico. I only came here because I thought Iron Fist might know of a link to Valdez."

She stepped close to him, knotting her fingers in his shirtfront. A sudden terrible hope seized her. "You want me to believe you, Caleb? You want me to believe you're innocent? Then kill him. Kill Iron Fist. For what he did to Bess and Millie and Mary and the Kovels. You kill him, and then I'll believe you." He could avenge Bess. He could make everything right again. She would believe him. She would love him. She would trust him. "Kill him, Caleb."

"I love you, Jenna." His eyes were anguished, despairing. "I'd do anything for you. Anything."

"Then kill him."

"I can't." He twisted away, looking for all the world like a man about to carry out his own execution.

"Why?"

His next words rocked her to her soul.

"Iron Fist is my brother."

18

For a full minute Jenna couldn't breathe. She stared at Caleb as though she'd never seen him before in her life. His gunmetal eyes, his midnight hair pulled back at the nape of his neck, his sun-dark skin. "Iron Fist is a Comanche."

"A Comanche whose father is Eagle Dancer."

"You can't . . ." She felt hollow, light-headed, as if she were about to faint. "You're not . . ."

"Eagle Dancer is my father."

Her knees buckled, and she would have collapsed if Caleb hadn't moved swiftly, catching her up in his strong arms. She made no protest as he carried her over to the mound of buffalo robes that served as her bed. He went to one knee, easing her back, his gray eyes alight with concern, but there was another emotion there as well, a darker one she couldn't quite read before he shuttered it away.

"You're lying," she managed. He'd told her countless other lies, hadn't he? This was just one more. "You're lying," she said again, this time with a whimper. Her

whole body trembled. "Please tell me you're lying."
Caleb Harper could not be brother to her sister's murderer.

"It's true," he said simply.

Jenna choked back a sob, her stomach churning. It
was all she could do not to be sick. She dared a glance at
Caleb, expecting more of his feigned sympathy. Instead, to her astonishment, his features had grown
stoic, almost impassive.

Almost.

The man was a master at masking true feelings, that
much she'd granted him. How else could he be such an
accomplished liar? But something about admitting his
relationship to Iron Fist had tipped the scales out of
balance. Whether he wanted her to or not, she saw in
that face what he had tried so hard to conceal just seconds before.

Bitterness. Bitterness edged with betrayal.

The realization jolted her because it made no sense.
Why would Caleb Harper feel betrayed? And by
whom? Hadn't everything gone exactly the way he'd
planned it? He and Iron Fist.

His brother.

Hatred, cold and dark, blocked the light of reason. "A
Comanche," she whispered aloud, more to herself than
to him. "You're a Comanche."

"A half-breed, to be precise."

She shook her head, understanding neither the
epithet nor the pain with which he said the words. "So
many lies," she said. "So many lies." She ticked them off
from memory, swallowed up now by a bitterness of her
own. "You told me your mother died when you were
four. That you came West when you were thirteen.
That you had no family, no birthday, no one." She could
feel the shaky hold she had on her control slipping,
collapsing, but she could do nothing to stop it. "And

now you tell me you have a brother and a father and
. . . what? Two wives? Five children?"

He didn't answer. In fact, he had the temerity to
seem stung by her sarcasm.

Furious, she pushed to a sitting position. "How dare
you? How dare you look hurt, angry? My sister is dead.
My brother is being raised by a savage. And you sit
there looking as though *I* am supposed to feel sorry for
you."

"I don't expect you to feel anything for me, Jenna.
Not anything at all."

Oh, but you do, Jenna thought fiercely. It was there
in the way he looked at her—in the tone of his voice, if
not in his words. He did expect her sympathy. Or at
least some kind of understanding. Well, she would show
him sympathy. She would show him understanding.
Like hell, she would!

Like a bursting dam, she spewed forth weeks of pent-
up rage, sobbing out in hideous detail the terror of the
attack on the wagons, Bess's death, the utter savagery
of what had been done to the Kovels. And for each
separate act of horror she laid the blame squarely at
Caleb's feet.

He didn't flinch, nor did he interrupt. He allowed her
verbal assault to go on, just as he had allowed her to
attack him physically when first he'd entered the lodge.

Finally, out of sheer exhaustion, she stopped. Her
head was pounding; her ribs were aching from the
power of the sobs that had racked her. Caleb reached
into the pocket of his buckskin jacket and extracted a
clean kerchief, handing it to her without comment. She
swiped at her tears, blew her nose, and stared, bleary-
eyed, at this man with whom she had once made magi-
cal love. "God damn you to hell," she murmured.

"Where do you think I've been these past two
months?" he asked softly.

Without conscious thought she arced her hand back and brought it down with stinging force across his face. Her palm burned, and she couldn't help but cringe at the darkening imprint of her hand on his cheek. It was all she could do not to touch it, to soothe the pain in those gray eyes, pain that seemed all at once to have nothing to do with her having struck him. Instead she forced a contemptuous laugh. "From the looks of you, hell must include a bath house and a barber."

"I haven't seen my father in nearly a year. I decided I shouldn't look like a pig."

"Why not? You are one."

He muttered an oath, and she watched him visibly suppress his temper. Why? What was the point of continuing his charade, when she so obviously didn't believe a word he said?

"You planned everything with Iron Fist, didn't you?" she prodded. "Everything."

He started to reply, then stopped. "Believe what you want, Jenna. It doesn't matter anymore."

"It matters a hell of a lot," she snapped. "You played your part very well, Caleb Harper. Or should I say Night Wind?"

He looked away.

"I loved you. Damn you, I loved you. Was that part of the plan? Or was that just a little bonus for you? Like our night by the creek. Were you laughing inside, Caleb? Were you? When you held me, when you touched me, when you—"

He caught her wrists, his grip fierce, his voice hard. "No. You won't mock that night. I won't let you."

"That night makes me sick. You make me sick."

His eyes were wild and for a chilling moment she thought he might harm her. Then just that suddenly he released her, his hands dropping away, his features weary, haggard with defeat. "I'll saddle a horse. I'll take you to Bascom, to Gallagher."

"You'll take Timmy too."

"No."

She drew her hand back, ready to slap him again; then her own shoulders slumped. What was the point? She hadn't the power to force this man to do anything. "I won't go without my brother."

"Then you won't go."

Tears slid down her cheeks. "I'll kill you for this. My hand to God, someday I'll kill you."

"Maybe you will." His voice had a strange emptiness to it. "But a piece of advice—don't do it here. My father's people might not understand."

"Oh, they'll understand," she said. "If there's one thing a Comanche understands—it's killing."

He stiffened. "That's enough."

"Enough? I don't think so. In fact, I don't think I've even begun."

"Jenna, don't."

His tone was more plea than warning, but she paid it no heed. "Don't what? Don't besmirch the reputation of these murdering savages? These people are animals!" She said the words even though she didn't believe them. She said the words, because she suddenly realized their power to hurt him. And she wanted to hurt him. She wanted to hurt him as badly as he had hurt her.

And she succeeded. Only too well.

The empathy, the compassion, the concern that had shaded his every action, his every word since he'd entered the lodge—even when he'd been angry—vanished. The caring she had believed to be only a facade was gone.

Except that it had been no facade. She saw that now. Now that it was too late.

He was still sorry about what had happened. But it wasn't the same.

Now she knew by whom he had felt betrayed.

She could apologize. She could take the words back. At least try to explain why she'd said them.

She could. But she didn't.

Because Caleb Harper was Iron Fist's brother.

Because Caleb Harper was a half-breed.

That was the secret he'd kept from her. That was the part of his past he couldn't share.

Because he had feared her reaction.

And she had reacted exactly as he had feared.

Not because he was a half-breed.

But because Iron Fist was his brother.

Had he told her the truth before the attack on the wagons, his Comanche blood wouldn't have mattered. She knew that. In the deepest, most honest reaches of her soul, she knew that. But he hadn't. And because he hadn't, his deception was forever tangled with the death of her sister, and she didn't know how to separate the two.

She no longer trusted Caleb. He no longer trusted her.

They glared at each other, the silence between them growing uncomfortable, tense. Jenna could tell Caleb wanted nothing more than to bolt from the tepee and not look back. But his conscience kept him there, his sense of obligation. After all, the man still had to feel guilty about the Spencers being in her wagon. And she knew he felt guilty about Bess. Though not exactly proud of herself, it occurred to her that she could play on that guilt, use it to her advantage. Perhaps she could yet persuade him to rescue her *and* her brother. It might be their only chance.

Jenna took a deep breath. "I believe you," she said

slowly, tentatively. "I believe what you said about the raid on the wagons, about Bart Jacobs and Valdez."

He said nothing.

"But I don't know what to think about Iron Fist, about his being your brother."

"Think whatever you like."

"No. I want you to tell me." If she could understand Caleb's past—his true past—maybe she could find a way to get through to him about Timmy. When he didn't respond, she added, "Don't you think you owe it to me?"

The look he drilled her suggested he didn't much give a damn what she thought he owed her. He stood and paced to the opposite side of the tepee, obviously at war with himself. But the need to clear the slate between them won out. His face grim, his voice cold, he began to speak.

"My mother's name was Jo Ellen Harper." Each word was like drawing blood. "She and her family were among the first whites to settle in east Texas back in the early thirties." He jammed his hands into the pockets of his trousers. "She lived on a small dirt farm with her parents, two brothers, a sister, and a cousin named Thad. My mother was the youngest. She was twelve."

He began to pace, rarely looking at her. "It seems Cousin Thad had been a handful for his parents back in Maryland. He was seventeen when he was caught setting fire to a neighbor's house. Just the day before, the neighbor had let Thad off with a lecture for trying to steal money from him. This time the neighbor wanted Thad jailed. To spare him his mother begged my mother's parents to take him out West with them. I guess they hoped hard work would set him straight."

Caleb paused to rake a hand through his dark hair, the gesture pulling several strands free of the leather thong that bound them. "Well, Cousin Thad didn't take to hard work. He didn't take to much of anything. Except trouble.

"I remember coming on a jackrabbit hole once. I couldn't have been much more than three."

Jenna wondered at the digression, but the reason for it became all too clear as he continued, "Somehow I got my hands on a baby rabbit and brought it back to my mother. She started to cry. I'd never seen her cry before. Years later my father told me of a time on the farm when she'd heard unholy screams coming from a grove of trees. She ran toward them in time to find Thad laughing. He'd poured kerosene on a mother rabbit and her babies and set fire to them."

Jenna shuddered. She was suddenly certain she didn't want to hear any more of this, but she was just as certain that she had no choice. For Timmy's sake. And, she acknowledged reluctantly, for Caleb's. His words were coming more quickly now, as though the faster he said them the faster he could again lock them away.

"The Harpers and two other families had been working their farms for about six months. They'd managed to reach an understanding with the Comanche in the area, a bartering kind of arrangement that was almost friendly.

"Except for Thad. He'd been in a scrape or two with a couple of bucks and was lucky to escape with his hair. My mother's father tried talking sense to him. Thad swore the Comanche were at fault.

"One day Thad and a friend were out hunting deer. They were on foot, when they came across a Comanche brave and his young wife out riding. It was the first time the two lovers had been alone together since the birth of their son three months before."

Caleb's eyes grew dark, almost black. "Thad decided no Indians should be riding when he had to walk. He shot the brave in the back; then he and his friend spent the night taking turns raping the brave's wife."

Jenna gasped but did not interrupt. She doubted Caleb would have heard her if she had tried.

"In the morning they killed her and took the Comanche ponies back to the farm. Thad bragged about his courageous battle with two bloodthirsty savages."

Jenna felt sick.

"Unfortunately for Thad his friend broke down a few days later and told the truth. My mother's father beat Thad half to death. But there was no law to answer to, not for killing Comanches.

"Everyone was scared, afraid of retaliation, but Thad assured them no one would know who did it. Except that the brave he had shot wasn't dead. He came to and found his wife. Over her naked, battered body he swore vengeance. He dragged himself to a creek, tended his own wounds, and kept himself alive with hate. After a week he managed to half walk, half crawl the forty miles back to his village.

"The white settlers paid for what Thad had done. The brave mounted a war party and swept down on all three farms, killing anything that moved. Except on the Harper farm. The brave didn't want Thad dead.

"During the battle the Comanche noticed a young girl who had fought like a mountain lion to save her family. He admired her courage. She and Thad were the only ones taken alive."

A glint of satisfaction shone in those dark eyes. "It took Thad Harper four days to die."

Unwillingly Jenna thought of Lem Kovel. His cruel death now seemed merciful in comparison. "You consider that justice, don't you?" she asked, already knowing his answer.

"Thad Harper was a murderer."

"He killed one person. Perhaps his life should have

been forfeit. But how many innocent lives did that Comanche brave take? Lives as innocent as his own wife's?"

"You don't understand the way of the Comanche." A shading of defensiveness had come into his voice.

"And you do?" Jenna climbed to her feet. She was angry now. She had felt compassion for the Comanche brave whose wife had been so brutally murdered. But nothing could justify the price the man had exacted for her death. Nothing. And if Caleb saw it any other way, then maybe she was getting her first true look at him after all. "Caleb," she asked softly, not urgently, "do you really think that Indian brave had the right to kill all those people? Your mother's whole family?"

"That Indian brave was Eagle Dancer."

Jenna let out a long breath. She had guessed as much. "The question still stands."

Caleb ignored it, saying instead, "He took Jo Ellen into his lodge. He taught her the ways of the Comanche. She became mother to his infant son. Eagle Dancer named her She Who Fights Like a Lion. Three years later he took her as his wife. A year after that I was born."

"Your mother submitted willingly to your father?" The question was out before Jenna could stop it.

Caleb went rigid. "My mother loved my father. The only memories I have of her smile and her laughter are the time we spent with the Comanche. After she was taken from here, there were only tears."

"Taken? She had to be taken from the Comanche?" After all that had happened to her? Jenna found the thought incomprehensible, surely just wishful thinking on Caleb's part.

"When I was four, a trapper came through the village. Always before my mother had been careful not to be seen by any white men." A new anguish threaded his voice. "I remember I wanted so badly to see what kind of presents the man had brought to trade. I ran out of the lodge before my mother could stop me. The man cuffed me away, and my mother stormed out to berate him. Comanches don't hit their children.

"Later the man must have passed on what he had seen. Soldiers came, but because there was a treaty they waited until my father and most of the other braves were out with a hunting party. Then they rode into the village. The troop's commander threatened violence if my mother and I didn't come with them."

He dragged in an unsteady breath. "This woman . . . this woman who had faced up to a Comanche war party got down on her knees. She got down on her knees and begged the soldiers to let us stay. They spit on her, spit on us both. They called her a whore, called me a half-breed. But they said even a white whore couldn't stay with the Comanche." His mouth twisted bitterly. "After all, they said, 'these people are animals.' "

Jenna closed her eyes. She felt a biting shame she could hardly bear, made worse because there was no way to set things right. She had said the words to hurt Caleb. Now she wished for a way to explain that she had hurt herself far more. In those few ill-advised words she had flown in the face of the very bigotry she had spoken out against her whole life. And she had done it for the most scurrilous of motives—vengeance.

"Caleb, I—"

"Eagle Dancer searched for us, but we'd already been sent East. My father and mother never saw each other again."

"Caleb, stop. Please."

He paid her no mind, determined, it seemed, to give her precisely what she had asked for: the truth, all of it.

"Back in Baltimore my mother's family looked on her

like she was trash." He gave a sick laugh. "They wouldn't look at me at all. I was their 'little savage'— my mother's sin to be paraded out and shamed before anyone who would listen.

"I remember her spending a lot of time in a room with no windows. She wouldn't light the lamp; she would just sit on the floor, rocking back and forth, crooning a Comanche song for the dead. I would curl up on her lap, hoping my being there would give her some comfort at least." He shuddered, shaking off memories too painful for any words. "She grew weaker by the day. In six months she was dead."

Jenna crossed over to him and placed a trembling hand on his sleeve. "I'm so sorry." She no longer knew what her feelings were for this man, but her heart ached for the little boy he had been.

"I don't want your pity."

"It's not—" She stopped. What was the use? He wouldn't believe her, any more than she had earlier believed him.

Caleb pulled the amulet from his pocket. "My mother made this for my father. It was all she had left of him. It was all I had left of her."

Jenna's eyes burned as she recalled the night Caleb had settled the rawhide talisman about her neck. *It's the only thing I have that means anything to me.*

"I was shunted from relative to relative, all of them doing their 'Christian duty' and making damned sure I knew it. When I was thirteen, I ran away and never looked back. I made my way to St. Joe, where I hooked up with a wagon train.

"The train's leader was a man named Josiah Burke. He took me under his wing, taught me a helluva lot about living off the land, and maybe proved to me for the first time that all white people weren't bastards. He encouraged me to find my father's people. Though he'd never met Eagle Dancer, Burke had heard of him and knew him to be an honorable man. He even had a general idea where I might find him."

"So you came home," Jenna said softly.

"Home." Caleb's tone was bittersweet. "I rode in bold as brass. I didn't know there'd been some recent raiding by renegades. The raiders turned out to be Kiowa. But at the time the army was on the alert and so were the Comanche. I was lucky I didn't have twenty arrows in me before I made it to Eagle Dancer's lodge. He took one look at me and knew. He didn't have to see the amulet. He welcomed me. But his first son, the son of his murdered first wife, offered no words of welcome. In the white world I was hated for my Comanche blood. Iron Fist hated me for my white blood."

Jenna bit her lip, recalling the brutal scars on both men and realized there were more scars she couldn't see.

"I did my best to fit in. I stayed for two years. I went through my vision to become a warrior and took the name Restless as Night Wind. I felt like I belonged. I wanted to belong. The tribe accepted me, but Iron Fist never did. One day he challenged me. I had to accept or lose face. I never really thought he would try to kill me."

"But he did." It wasn't a question.

"I left when I was certain Iron Fist would live. I didn't want my father to have to choose between his sons. I drifted, found work here and there. For stage lines, freighters, the army."

"You told no one of your Indian blood?"

"I learned not to. It was easier that way."

"Does Major Gallagher know?"

Caleb let out a cynical snort. "Do you think I'd be his trusted scout if he did?"

"But he's your friend."

"He's Caleb Harper's friend. Caleb Harper is a white man."

"That's not fair."

He gave her a mocking smile. "Since when has life been fair, Miss Riordan?"

His addressing her so stiffly hurt, though she couldn't have said why. Part of her welcomed the formality. It put distance between them, however illusory. And she needed that distance. Listening to the painful account of his past had roused unexpected sympathy in her. After the past two months she would have thought herself immune to the pull this man could have on her emotions. But she was wrong. Despite his aggressive posturing, she knew he was only covering up an agonizing vulnerability. And, against her will, she felt herself drawn to him yet again.

Shaken to the core, she turned on him. "You have to take my brother and me out of here. Now."

"We've been through all that. Timmy stays."

She tried to read an ulterior motive in those gray eyes, but he gave no hint of what he was thinking. "You can't be that cruel. You can't be."

"Cruelty is second nature to the Comanche."

"Stop it."

He sighed. "You'll be safer here."

"What do you mean? Safer?"

"I still have to find out who Jacobs was working for." He told her about the man in the mask. "He's likely a white man, educated. If you stayed at Bascom, you could be at risk."

She worried her lower lip. "There was a white man with Valdez, but he took orders, he didn't give them."

"Did you hear a name?"

Jenna shook her head.

"It doesn't matter. I'll find him. I'll find Valdez. Those are the two who have to be stopped."

"How?"

"By making them think I'm one of them." His gaze again grew cynical. "That shouldn't be all that difficult, wouldn't you say, Miss Riordan?"

Jenna felt her cheeks heat, but she faced him squarely. "I can't undo what's happened, any more than you can."

He picked up his hat and settled it on his head. "I'd best get back to Eagle Dancer. He isn't well." He started toward the entryway, then stopped. "Of course, I'll speak to him about moving you out of Iron Fist's lodge."

Her heart thudded, her skin prickling with a sudden wariness. "What are you talking about?"

"Eagle Dancer thinks you're my wife." The words were cold, sarcastic.

Jenna swallowed hard, any protest she might have made clogging in her throat. There wasn't a hint of compassion or caring in those gray eyes as he spoke his next words. "The buffalo robes you share tonight will be mine."

19

The midafternoon sun was high and hot, but Jenna sat on the dirt floor of Iron Fist's tepee and shivered. What had Caleb meant by his cryptic pronouncement that tonight she would share his robes? Surely not the obvious. There hadn't been even a glimmer of desire in those gray eyes. If anything, he'd been as anxious to get away from her as she'd been to see him go.

Then why the barely veiled threat? Why a threat at all? Hadn't he hurt her enough? Or was this a payback for her own cruel words?

Damn him. She didn't know what to think, what to feel anymore, where Caleb Harper was concerned. She couldn't even trust her own judgment. He'd proven that well enough.

She shuddered, clamping a hand over her mouth and tried hard not to be sick. Her head throbbed and her stomach ached. What she wanted most was to lie down and give herself up to the oblivion of sleep. But she didn't dare. Caleb could be back any minute. What if his threat didn't stop with words?

Though her knees threatened to buckle, Jenna climbed to her feet and made her way over to the badger-pelt pouch in which Talks Too Much kept her hide-cleaning tools. With trembling fingers Jenna reached inside and extracted the Comanche woman's eight-inch skinning knife. She jerked it from its sheath, her gaze fixed on the wicked blade glinting in the translucent light of the lodge. Her heart pounding, she resheathed the weapon, found a rawhide thong, then fumbled with her skirt. Giving herself no time to think, she quickly secured the knife to her right thigh.

Behind her the entry flap snapped open. Guiltily Jenna yanked down her skirt and whirled. A shudder of relief coursed through her. Painted Sky. Jenna forced a smile, though her voice was shaky. "Welcome home, Painted Sky. Your search for honey was successful?"

The Indian woman's huge grin faded. "How can you talk of honey, Sky Eyes?" she asked in near-perfect English. She had become so enamored with relearning the language that Jenna's own Comanche lessons had suffered in comparison. "Everyone in the village speak of Night Wind. He come for you."

"Not for me," Jenna said. "Caleb came to see Eagle Dancer. He didn't know I was here."

"He know now. This good day. Your husband home."

"He's not my husband." Jenna instantly regretted the words, uncertain how wise it was to admit that her relationship with Caleb had never been formal or legal under white law.

Painted Sky only shrugged. "Not matter. He take ponies to Eagle Dancer. Today marry you Comanche way."

Jenna swayed, sinking to her knees. "What? He's doing what?"

"He have Talks Too Much and others put up his

lodge." Painted Sky giggled merrily. "Tonight you share his robes."

Jenna felt the blood drain from her face. Only the utter guilelessness with which Painted Sky spoke kept Jenna from fainting. "He can't do this . . . he can't. . . ."

Painted Sky frowned, coming over to kneel beside Jenna. "Night Wind strong warrior. Him do. You see."

The blood rushed back to Jenna's face. "That isn't what I meant," she choked out. "I mean I don't want . . . I . . ." Tears slid from her eyes.

Painted Sky stared at her, aghast. "Not want Night Wind? Why you not want Night Wind?" The woman actually seemed offended.

"I've told you . . . I've told you what happened to my sister." Jenna stiffened, feeling suddenly offended herself. "You knew, didn't you? You knew Iron Fist was Caleb's brother. You knew Caleb was half Comanche. Why didn't you tell me?"

"Night Wind's place to tell you."

"I thought you were my friend."

"Painted Sky Night Wind's friend first." A quiet pride shone in the Comanche woman's eyes. "I listen to your talk of Ca-leb Har-per. I know your hate. Your hate is wrong, Sky Eyes."

"You weren't there. You can't know how it was."

"I know Night Wind's heart is good." Her voice grew soft, wistful. "And gentle." She squeezed Jenna's hand. "Same heart beats in Ca-leb Har-per. Him not kill."

"Painted Sky, please . . . I—" The sound of many hoofbeats distracted her. Jenna rose and hurried to the tepee entrance. Peering out, she spied Caleb astride his black gelding, leading a string of a dozen ponies toward Eagle Dancer's lodge.

Her heart thundered. No, not Caleb, not Caleb at all, but Restless as Night Wind.

His midnight hair hung loose, brushing his shoulders, two eagle feathers twined in his scalplock. He was naked from the waist up, his broad chest glistening with sweat, his sinewy thighs, encased in deerskin leggings, hugging the gelding's back. He looked at her as he rode past, his gray eyes revealing nothing. As for Jenna, she couldn't take her eyes off him, whether out of wonder or fear she couldn't have said.

When he reached Eagle Dancer's lodge, he dismounted. Jenna had to step away from Iron Fist's tepee to see around the dozens of Comanche who were now watching Night Wind with a curiosity of their own. Though his back was to her, she could picture clearly the respect in his gray eyes as he handed the reins of the lead pony to the Comanche chief. Eagle Dancer, though looking increasingly frail of late, nodded gravely as he accepted his son's gift.

"If the horses are gone in the morning," Painted Sky said, "that mean Eagle Dancer accept you as Night Wind's wife."

Jenna hugged her arms tight against her roiling stomach. "But what if *I* don't accept? What if—"

Painted Sky touched Jenna's arm in sudden warning. Jenna started, only now noticing Iron Fist stalking toward her, glowering, furious. He snarled at her in Comanche. Jenna caught words that meant Night Wind and truth, but couldn't sort out their connection to her.

She stood her ground. She had yet to win a battle of wills with the vile-tempered Indian, but she no longer lost them either. Usually he would settle for raising his gauntleted fist at her, then turn and stamp away in disgust. Jenna's own fists curled reflexively at her sides. If not for Timmy, she would have driven Talks Too Much's skinning knife into Iron Fist's heart weeks ago.

To her surprise the Comanche gripped her arm and propelled her toward Eagle Dancer's lodge. She tried to dig in her heels, but his hold on her was too painful. He released her only when they reached Caleb's side.

Jenna didn't know whose eyes reflected more anger —Eagle Dancer's or Caleb's; but Iron Fist faced them undaunted. Launching into a lengthy tirade, he gesticulated wildly, pointing from Caleb to Jenna and back again.

Jenna's heart froze. She understood just enough. Iron Fist had overheard her talking to Painted Sky. He knew she and Caleb had never been married.

"She is a slave," Iron Fist spat in Comanche. "Nothing more. The amulet meant nothing. I took her. She belongs to me. I will have what is mine. I will use what is mine." He manipulated his sex beneath his breechclout, proud, leering.

With an explosive curse, Caleb backhanded Iron Fist across the face, sending the Comanche buck sprawling into the dirt. In the next heartbeat Iron Fist went for his knife. Caleb had already drawn his.

Only a sharp command from Eagle Dancer kept the two men apart.

Caleb held himself still, his knuckles showing white where he gripped his knife.

Jenna trembled, terrified, doing her best not to show it. Painted Sky had joined her and was discreetly translating, but Jenna didn't have to speak any language at all to know that her life depended on the outcome of this confrontation.

"One of my sons dishonors the People with lies," Eagle Dancer said, his mouth twisting with distaste. "I will know which one." He turned to Night Wind. "Is this woman your wife in the white man's eyes, my son?"

Caleb hesitated ever so slightly, then answered in a level, measured tone, "We have been together as man and wife."

Jenna did not permit herself the luxury of embarrass-

ment. She was too busy studying Caleb. She had seen
this outer coolness before and knew it to be false. Inside, he was a man at war with himself. He was
sidestepping Eagle Dancer's question, and both men
knew it. She knew also how much the Comanche val-
ued the truth. To a Comanche a lie was as abhorrent as
cowardice in battle.

Eagle Dancer waited.

Iron Fist sneered.

Jenna's terror mounted. If Iron Fist prevailed, he
would kill her, but only after she was longing for death.
She remembered Nelda Kovel and shuddered.

Caleb started to speak. She gave him no chance to
finish. She couldn't take the risk. She didn't really believe he would hand her over to Iron Fist, but neither
did she believe he was prepared to lie for her. Not even
to save her life.

"Night Wind is my husband," she blurted in Comanche, the words reckless, heedless, without thought to
consequences. "It is as he said: We have been together
as man and wife." Her mind raced wildly, desperately.
She had to say something, anything to get them to believe her, to keep them from handing her over to Iron
Fist. "I-I carry his child."

Caleb's jaw dropped, his features stunned, disbeliev-
ing. Iron Fist cursed. Eagle Dancer's gaze held hers,
searching, steady. Jenna didn't flinch. It was an outra-
geous, foolish lie, and she knew it. Why couldn't she
have thought of something else? She expected any moment that one of the Comanche women would name
her the liar she was. But surprisingly none did. Some of
them even seemed to believe her. After all, she'd only
been here two months. Surely it was possible for a
woman to conceal a pregnancy at least that long. Right
now all Jenna wanted to do was make it through this
day. She would deal with tomorrow when it got here.

Eagle Dancer still gripped the lead rein of the string of horses Caleb had brought him. "Your woman has much courage, Night Wind. You have chosen well. As chief I have had but two sorrows—the first, that my sons do not accept each other as brothers. And the second, that I might not live to look upon the face of my first grandchild. Now you and Sky Eyes have given me one of those gifts."

Caleb only nodded, his gaze riveted on Jenna. He obviously didn't trust himself to speak, because he didn't say a word. Did he believe her? She couldn't tell. She bit her lip, recalling his threat about tonight. Had she only traded one corner of hell for another?

"There will be great feasting in the village this night," Eagle Dancer was saying. "We will celebrate Night Wind's return to the People. And we will thank the Great Spirit for our new daughter, Sky Eyes, and the child she brings us."

Iron Fist grunted contemptuously. "My father has become blind as well as sick to believe lies from a white slave."

"Enough," Eagle Dancer said.

"No! It is not enough!" His voice rose in a shout to any who would listen, "Believe my words: Night Wind will betray us, betray our chief, betray the People. He and his sky-eyed woman will bring death to us all!"

Tension crackled in the warm, still air. In a very real way Iron Fist had just challenged his father for leadership of the band. A quiet muttering could be heard among the gathered throng of braves.

Despite the ravages of his illness, Eagle Dancer straightened and stepped toward his eldest son with an air of quiet dignity that the scar-faced Comanche could never hope to match. And yet in this particular time and place Jenna sensed brutality had the edge over dignity. "Enough," Eagle Dancer said again.

A long minute passed. Even Caleb offered no interference. This was between Eagle Dancer and Iron Fist.
To Jenna's astonishment it was Iron Fist who backed
down. Even through the virulence of his hatred for his
brother and for her, Jenna saw something in Iron Fist's
eyes she had never seen before.

Respect. Respect and love for his father.

Iron Fist shot one last hate-filled look at Jenna; then,
ordering Painted Sky to come with him, he turned and
stalked away.

Jenna had no time to feel relief. Caleb's strong hand
locked about her wrist. "It seems you and I have more
to talk about."

"No . . . I mean, I . . . we . . ." His gray eyes
were twin slivers of ice. She gave up any attempt at
protest, allowing him to lead her toward the herd of
horses at the north end of the village.

He didn't say a word as he wrangled out a paint gelding, slipped a bridle on it, then swung up onto its bare
back. In spite of herself Jenna's pulses raced at how
wild, how primitive he looked, every inch a Comanche.

He held out his hand.

She hesitated, then realized she was only postponing
the inevitable. Catching his wrist, she allowed him to
haul her up behind him. The action hiked up the skirt
of her doeskin dress, exposing nearly the full length of
her thighs. Too late she realized she had also exposed
Talks Too Much's skinning knife. He slanted a glance at
the knife, one corner of his mouth ticking upward in a
mocking smile. She stiffened defiantly.

With a wild whoop he kicked the gelding in the sides,
setting the beast into a hard gallop. Jenna nearly rocked
backward over the horse's rump. In self-defense she
flung her arms around Caleb's waist, cringing at the
feel of his naked, sweating flesh. She clung tight, her
cheek pressed against the broad expanse of his back.

They rode that way for miles, until Jenna was finally forced to relax, to sit back a little, to allow the wind to rush against her face, her braided hair to slap lightly against her back.

Caleb—she couldn't yet completely give herself over to thinking of him as Night Wind—guided the paint toward a weather-ravaged oak, standing as lone sentinel on an otherwise treeless expanse of plain. He reined to a halt beneath the tree and perfunctorily eased her to the ground, then joined her. His moccasined feet made no sound as he crossed to the massive trunk and slid to the hard-packed earth in front of it.

He hadn't said one word since they'd left the village, but she expected him to speak to her now, if only to give her a piece of his mind for being so foolish as to claim she was carrying his child. Instead he folded his arms across his chest and stared at her, just stared, saying nothing.

Jenna swallowed. Fine. She could wait him out. Why borrow trouble? Heaven above, maybe the man had actually believed her! If he thought her pregnant, perhaps he would acquiesce to her demand that he take her and her brother away from here, to the safety of Fort Bascom. Dare she try and draw out the charade?

She took a deep breath. "About the baby . . ."

"There is no baby," he snapped. "And we both know it. Damn it, Jenna. What the hell were you thinking?"

For an instant she was unsettled by his sudden flare of temper; then her own temper fired. "As a matter of fact, I was thinking of Nelda Kovel! I was thinking I didn't want your damn brother to do to me what he had done to her!"

A muscle in his jaw worked. "Why did you say anything at all? My father was talking to me."

"Maybe because I had no idea what you would tell him."

"Do you honestly think I would have let Iron Fist take you?"

She didn't answer right away, and to her surprise she saw a flicker of pain in those flint-hard eyes. She let out a resigned sigh. "I didn't want you to have to lie to your father. You might have tried, but I doubt you would have been very good at it. He wouldn't have believed you."

"Well, that leaves us with a rather monumental problem, don't you think?"

"What do you mean?"

"You're not pregnant. Maybe you can pass that off now, but what about a month from now. Or two? Or three?"

"I-I'll just say I had a miscarriage." She couldn't believe she was having such an intimate conversation with a man who so clearly despised her. "Besides, if you'd take Timmy and me to Bascom, we wouldn't have to worry about a month or two, would we?"

"I'm not going through all that again."

"Damn you! You've got no right—"

"On the contrary," he drawled with just a trace of menace, "I have every right. Now. You're my wife."

She blanched. "I most certainly am not!"

"Oh, but you are, Jenna. Today you married me under Comanche law."

"I don't recognize Comanche law."

His voice was silky-soft, yet somehow cold. "I do." He rose to his feet with the grace of a stalking panther and padded toward her, all sinewy muscle and male heat. "You shouldn't have told my father you were carrying my child."

Jenna took a step back. "Don't . . ."

"Don't what?"

"Don't frighten me." Her voice quivered. "Please."

He stopped, still some five feet away from her, his

eyes unreadable. "My father is dying. Earlier today I doubted he would last the month; then I watched his face when you told him about the baby, about his grandchild. You gave him a reason to live, Jenna." His own voice shook. "Except that you gave him a lie."

"I didn't mean to hurt him, Caleb. I like your father. I just wanted—"

"I know what you wanted. You wanted to be free of the Comanche, free of me."

"Can't you understand that?"

"I suppose I can. Maybe I can even arrange it for you."

A warning bell sounded in her head, but she ignored it. "And for Timmy?"

"I could try. I could talk to Two Trees."

Jenna experienced a relief so profound it was all she could do not to throw herself into Caleb's arms out of sheer gratitude. But she knew better. "When?"

"You already know the answer to that, Jenna."

The bell sounded again. "What are you talking about?"

His voice—warm silk, edged in ice. "You can leave the day you give me a son."

20

Caleb turned away from the terror in Jenna's eyes and stalked back toward the twisted oak. He was being a bastard and he knew it. But he couldn't seem to help himself, stop himself. For an instant this morning the sun had shone bright in his world again. Jenna was alive, and he'd found her. And then the light had gone out, ripped away by Jenna herself.

She hated him.

Yet he could have endured her hate, even considered it his due, for his part in secreting the Spencers aboard her wagon. What he couldn't endure or accept—or forgive—was the hate she bore him for his Comanche blood.

These people are animals.

The words had slashed him, gutted him, left him bleeding, raw. And he'd despised himself for it. Despised her for making him vulnerable again, making him care. How could he have been such a fool? How could he ever have believed she would be different? How could—

"Are you going to rape me, Caleb?"

He spun around at the sound of her voice so close behind him. He'd been too absorbed in his own misery to hear her approach. Fear still hovered about the edges of her blue eyes, but she'd summoned up a quiet courage as well, which unaccountably annoyed him. He stiffened, forcing a cynical smirk. "Rape, Miss Riordan? Is that what you're now calling our night by the creek?"

Her cheeks darkened beneath her tanned flesh and Caleb felt a stab of remorse, but he did not take back his cruel words.

"No," she said evenly. "I'm calling that one of the biggest mistakes of my life."

His jaw tightened. "Yes, I suppose you would consider it a mistake—now that you know you slept with a half-breed."

To his astonishment she swore. "I've had just about enough of this half-breed business. Your Indian blood has nothing to do with this."

"It has everything to do with it," he snarled, "and you know it. Or maybe your comment about Comanches being animals was just another *mistake.*"

She let out a weary sigh. "No," she said quietly. "That was deliberate. Very deliberate and very much a lie. I said it to hurt you."

"You did a damned fine job." The words were out before he could stop them. He regretted them at once as he watched her brows furrow, her gaze grow thoughtful. It was as though she were trying to see inside him somehow, see through him. And she did.

"Is that why now you have to hurt me?" she asked softly.

He stiffened, a swift and angry denial rising in his throat. But he never said the words. He turned his back on her, felt his cheeks grow hot. *The buffalo robes you share tonight will be mine . . . You can leave the day you give me a son.* . . . "Sweet Christ," he murmured, raking a hand through the midnight hair that brushed his shoulders, "I did all but threaten to rape you, didn't I?"

She reached for him, her fingers skimming his arm, tentative, uncertain, before they dropped away. "It's all right. I understand."

"No, it isn't all right." He kept his back to her. His flesh, where she had touched it, quivered, throbbed, ached to be touched again. He swallowed hard. "Dammit, Jenna, I'm sorry. I am sorry."

He heard her expel an unsteady breath. Her voice was just as unsteady when she spoke. "I'll forgive you, if you forgive me." He could feel her trying to smile, knew she hadn't quite succeeded.

"Deal," he managed hoarsely. He was holding himself rigidly still. He knew she wasn't talking about forgiving him for the Spencers or for Bess's death or for Iron Fist. She was talking only about the wounds inflicted by their war of words. But just to hear the softness, the gentleness in her voice again was to hear the rain after a searing drought. And in that instant he wanted her, wanted her as badly as he had ever wanted anything in his life.

He curled his fingers into his palms. "We . . . we'd best head back to the village." He made no move toward the gelding. She was so close, so damned close.

"What will you tell Eagle Dancer about the baby?"

He sucked in a deep breath, grateful for a change of subject, even one as painful as this. "I'll tell him you were mistaken. He'll understand."

"But his health . . . you thought a baby might . . ." She let her voice trail off. Caleb guessed she didn't want to examine too closely any notions that her having a baby might prolong Eagle Dancer's life.

"It'll be all right," he assured her. The thought of

Jenna having his baby wasn't one he dared dwell on himself. "We'd better go." He forced himself to walk toward the gelding.

Jenna followed. "I never meant any harm to your father, Caleb. Please know that. He's been very kind to me."

"It's all right." Against his better judgment he turned, catching up her hand in his, meaning it as gesture of reassurance, comfort.

Their gazes locked. For a heartbeat neither one of them moved. Then slowly, almost reverently, Jenna raised his hand to her face, cupping its callused roughness against the softness of her cheek. He stared, mesmerized, as she turned her face into his palm, then brushed her lips, warm, moist, along the length of his rein-scarred fingers. Her mountain-lake eyes were wide, questioning, and just a little afraid.

Caleb groaned. The fearsome hold he'd maintained on his self-control wavered. She slipped the tip of one of his fingers into her mouth. His hold buckled, collapsed. He made one last, desperate grasp at sanity. "I don't want you to be sorry this time, Jenna. I don't want you to be sorry. Tell me to end it, and I will."

Her answer was to bring his free hand to her breast.

With an oath he gathered her to him, his lips crashing down on hers, his mouth hungry, fevered. "Jenna, sweet God, Jenna, I've missed you, wanted you . . . so much, so much . . ." He drove his tongue into the wet, welcoming recesses of her mouth.

Jenna gasped, momentarily overwhelmed by the intensity of his need—and her own. But she made no attempt to run from the feeling. She wanted this, wanted it badly. It felt good to be held again, to be touched, to be desired.

All the misery, the grief, the pain of the past two

months receded, fell away. It would be back, she knew. But for this time, this moment, it was gone.

Yesterday didn't matter.

Tomorrow didn't exist.

She clung to him, her legs no longer willing to support her, and when he eased her down to the hard earth, she moaned beneath him, her breath coming in short, tiny gasps. "Caleb," she murmured, "Caleb, please . . ."

She closed her eyes as he undressed her, reveling, writhing in the erotic ministrations of his hands, his mouth. When he suckled her breasts, she felt the very core of her grow hot, wet, ready.

His hands stilled. Jenna opened her eyes to the passion-dark visage of a Comanche warrior. Her heart turned over, fierce, proud.

With deft fingers she freed him of his moccasins, his leggings, his breechclout, then she slid a hand across his flat belly and down. "Show me your fire, Night Wind. Make me your Comanche wife."

His eyes burned with wonder, joy. She had spoken the words in Comanche.

Primal, savage, he pressed her down, then drove himself inside her, his need greater than any he had ever known, his pleasure as wild and untamed as the land that surrounded them. And when he was ready, more than ready to spill his seed inside her, he cried out, the words an incoherent mix of Comanche and English, but their meaning as old as Adam and Eve. He took her with him as he gave himself up to the shuddering power of his release.

Later, much later, when Jenna lay nestled, content, in the arms of her lover, she made the disconcerting discovery that she no longer knew his name. Was he Caleb or Night Wind? Was he both, or was he neither?

She didn't know. If pressed, she doubted he would have been able to answer the question himself.

To the west she watched the sunset, the brilliant ball of light brushing the sky in broad strokes of red and purple. She wished fervently she could believe her own world could be made beautiful again. But then she had learned not to believe in wishes. Wishes were dreams, and dreams did not come true. Reality would intrude again, and soon.

After all, she was still a Comanche prisoner, and so was Timmy. Her only chance at freedom lay in the hands of Caleb Harper. And yet in a strange way Caleb was as much a prisoner here as she was. A prisoner caught in the crossfire of his own heritage.

Caleb Harper. Restless as Night Wind.

One day he would have to make an impossible choice, where to win was to lose. And Jenna couldn't shake the odd foreboding that she too would be forced to choose, and that the choice she made would break her heart.

Caleb awakened from his pleasure-sated nap in no mood for introspection. On their ride back to the village Jenna tried several times to engage him in conversation but received only ambiguous grunts and shrugs for her efforts. She made no secret of her frustration, but if it bothered him, he didn't show it. What drove her wild was that, for once, if she could have gotten him to talk about what he was feeling, she was certain she could have learned volumes about this enigmatic man. But, for whatever reason, he had chosen to shut her out.

He remained just as uncommunicative once they reached the village. It was full dark by then, but scores of conical tents lit by the light of their interior cook fires glowed like oddly shaped lanterns. Caleb guided the gelding toward the center of the village, where from the sights and sounds and smells that surrounded them, it was obvious their wedding feast had gotten merrily under way without them.

Arcing one leg over the paint's head, Caleb slid to the ground, then reached up to help her do the same. "Try and act like you're having a good time," he said. "For my father's sake, if nothing else."

Jenna swallowed a sarcastic remark. It was as if this afternoon had never happened. "Are you ever going to tell me what's wrong?" she asked as they headed toward Eagle Dancer.

He hesitated, then said, "Sorry. I'm just tired."

She had no time to press him for the truth. He left her to take his place beside his father. The leader of the Comanche band was one of several men sitting cross-legged in a circle around a crackling campfire. The braves were each taking a puff on a long-stemmed pipe, then passing it on to the next man. Jenna recognized the ritual. The pipe was brought out for any momentous occasion—good or bad.

Fighting off an odd feeling of abandonment, Jenna smiled and nodded her way through a gathering of Comanche women and children. Within minutes she was feeling better, genuinely touched by many of the well-wishers. From a toothless old squaw named Laughing Eyes, Jenna received a fine ermine pelt. From a wise and wonderful young mother of four she received a wooden bowl and spoon. "Feed husband good, him keep wife happy." Jenna had to laugh. Her mother had long ago gifted her with similar way-to-a-man's-heart advice. Some things, it seemed, were universal.

"You are happy, Sky Eyes?" Painted Sky asked, coming up to give Jenna a heartfelt embrace.

"Everyone's being very kind," Jenna said, deliberately misunderstanding the Indian woman's question.

Painted Sky was not about to be put off. "I will miss you in my lodge. But you will be happy with Night Wind, yes?"

"Have you seen Timmy? We had a quarrel this morning and—"

Painted Sky caught Jenna's arm. "What wrong?"

"Not a thing," Jenna said with feigned innocence. "I just need to see my brother." She really did want to talk to him, make certain he knew that her marriage to Caleb was a sham, at least as far as she was concerned. This afternoon she might have been persuaded to feel otherwise, but Caleb's true colors were emerging once again. The man obviously didn't trust her. And she definitely didn't trust him. Hardly a solid basis for a lasting relationship.

"Not know where Wolf Cub is," Painted Sky said, her feelings very obviously hurt. "I help you look?"

Jenna caught Painted Sky's hand. "I'm sorry. I just can't talk about Ca—about Night Wind right now. Maybe some other time."

"You worry he not love you?"

"Of course not. I mean, I'm not worried, because I don't care if he loves me or not."

"Not good to start marriage with lie, Sky Eyes."

"I'm not the one who's lying. He—" Her lips thinned. "I'm sorry. This isn't fair. It's not just that I can't talk about Night Wind, Painted Sky—I shouldn't." Caleb's investigation of Valdez, if it really existed, would eventually lead to Iron Fist. Though she loathed the Comanche warrior with all her heart, she couldn't ask Painted Sky to choose between their friendship and loyalty to her husband. "I really do have to find Timmy." This time she hurried off in search of her brother before Painted Sky could voice any new objections.

She found Timmy with Caleb. They were standing outside of Caleb's newly erected lodge, talking in hushed, earnest tones. Seeing Caleb so open, so animated with her brother made Jenna instantly, irrationally furious.

"What are you saying to him?" she demanded, striding up to Caleb.

Caleb straightened, his jaw tight, apparently not taking kindly to being spoken to in such a tone, at least not in front of her brother.

Jenna did not back down. "I asked you a question."

With boyish insistence Timmy wedged himself between the two adults. "Let me tell you, Jenna. Let me tell you what he said."

Jenna scarcely heard him. She was too busy imagining Caleb's attention to her brother as a ploy to preempt her position in Timmy's life, to further erode any desire he might have to ever leave Two Trees. That way, when Jenna insisted Timmy accompany her to Fort Bascom, Caleb could honestly tell her that Timmy didn't want to go.

"Night Wind said he's my uncle now," Timmy cried. "Isn't that great, Jenna? He and I are related."

Jenna ground her teeth together so hard her jaws hurt. "Yes, Timmy, that's great."

"He says he's going to take real good care of you too. You should see—"

Caleb put a hand on Timmy's shoulder. "Careful, pardner. Us men don't tell our womenfolk all our secrets."

"Secrets?" Jenna snapped.

Timmy grinned. "I almost forgot, Night Wind. Sorry."

"It's all right."

Jenna less than subtly pulled Timmy out of Caleb's reach. "I want to know everything *Mister Harper* told you, you understand me?"

Timmy squirmed and Jenna fumed. She had just put

her brother in the same untenable situation she had tried to avoid for Painted Sky. She was asking Timmy to divide his loyalty. "Never mind, Timmy. You go on along to Two Trees. We'll talk tomorrow."

Timmy looked dubious as he cast a mournful gaze back at Caleb.

"We won't talk about what Mister Harper said," Jenna assured him.

Timmy heaved a relieved sigh. He threw his arms around her and gave her a wet kiss on the cheek, something he hadn't done in a very long time. Jenna's eyes stung with unshed tears. "Happy wedding, Jenna!" he cried.

"Thank you, Timmy. Good night."

He started to race off, then skidded to a halt, coming back to give Caleb a quick hug as well. "Happy wedding, Night Wind."

"Thanks, Wolf Cub."

"Hope you're not 'specting a kiss though."

Caleb grinned. "The hug was just fine."

Jenna watched her brother disappear down the path between tepees that led to Two Trees's lodge. She tried and failed to suppress the bitterness she still felt about how at home he seemed here. She knew he hadn't forgotten Bess, that he grieved for her in his own way, and yet his very acceptance of his Comanche life seemed a slap in the face to Bess's memory.

Hurting, angry, she stiffened her spine. It was time to face her husband. "Don't you ever try to turn my brother against me again. Do you hear me? Ever."

He gripped her arm and pointed toward the lodge. "We'll have our wedding night inside, if you don't mind. Not out here for every old woman in the tribe to gossip about tomorrow."

She jerked her arm free. "Don't touch me."

"That isn't what you said this afternoon."

She swore.

"Tsk-tsk. The West has not served your genteel southern manners very well."

Jenna slapped at the tepee's entry flap and ducked inside. He was right. They should have this out in private.

Inside the lodge she straightened, stunned. She had been in many tepees throughout the village, but none would compare with this one. A thick, luxurious bearskin rug covered almost the full area of the tepee's right side. Many of the cooking utensils stacked inside an old steamer trunk were products of the white man's world, not the Comanche.

And to her unabashed delight just to the left of the unfortunate grizzly's head was a small wooden washtub!

Jenna was around the firepit and on her knees in front of the tub as fast as she could move. It was filled to the brim with hot water!

She spun around, staring at Caleb. "When did you— How could you possibly—Who—"

He shrugged. "I left instructions with Painted Sky. She was happy to do it."

"It's wonderful! Thank—" She stopped, abashed. She had completely forgotten how furious she was with him just minutes ago over his secret little talk with her brother.

"Secrets." She blanched. "This was the secret you and Timmy . . . ?" She gestured helplessly toward the tub.

He nodded, his face unreadable.

"Oh, dear!"

"Apology accepted."

"But I didn't . . ." She looked at him. "I'm sorry."

"I know you worry about Timmy," he conceded gently. "Don't. Two Trees loves him very much. No harm will ever come to your brother at the hands of a Comanche."

She no longer had the will to argue the point. At least not tonight. "Thank you for the bath."

"You're welcome." His voice was husky, whiskey-warm.

She swirled her hand in the heated water.

"Aren't you going to get in?"

She climbed to her feet, so thrilled at the prospect of a real bath that she almost started to pull off her dress.

Almost.

She glanced self-consciously at Caleb. He was standing in heavy shadow; the darkness outside, coupled with the barely glowing embers of the fire, gave him the appearance of some mythic beast come to ravish her in the night. "Aren't you going to leave?"

He quirked an eyebrow at her. "On our wedding night?"

She frowned, uncertain. "Are you teasing me?"

"I'm trying to, but I guess I'm not doing a very good job of it, am I?"

She crossed over to him. "Why wouldn't you talk to me on our way back to the village today?"

"I had a lot of things to sort through in my mind."

"And I don't?"

He pulled her to him. "Dammit, Jenna, when I'm around you, sometimes I don't have the sense God gave a rabbit."

She trembled, leaned close, drawn as ever to the magic of being in this man's arms.

"Are you afraid of me?"

She shook her head. "Not that you'll hurt me, no. I mean, physically hurt me."

"Well, I'm afraid of you."

"What?"

"I'm scared to death. Jenna, sometimes I want you so

much it makes me crazy. And then I think of how different we are, our lives, what we want, what we need. I just . . . damn . . . I'm sorry. I'm so sorry I ever got you messed up in my life."

She touched a finger to his lips. "No. No more apologies. No more words. Not tonight." She gave him a tender smile. "Even the bath can wait."

She kissed him.

He kissed her back.

The water was cold when Jenna finally took her bath.

Jenna did not question the nightly surcease they found in each other's body. Nor did she worry that never, not even in the most fevered moments of their passion, did either one of them again say the words "I love you."

Only during the day, when Caleb was gone on a hunt with other braves, and Jenna was about her daily tasks taking care of the lodge, did the niggling doubts intrude. Was he only just trying to get her pregnant after all? It had been two weeks, and yet she knew he had not told Eagle Dancer of her "mistake" about the baby. Nor did he make any mention of when, or if, he would take her and Timmy to Fort Bascom.

Still, when she didn't let herself think about it too much, she found herself growing accustomed to the rhythm of their lives here. Other times she would worry that the day might come when she'd have grown to like it too well. At least she was getting used to the way the Comanche did things.

Like their custom of moving every three to four weeks. When the current site became unpleasant, the whole village pulled up stakes and traveled twenty to thirty miles to a fresh location.

On this bright October day Jenna was making ready for just such a move. It was the first time striking the lodge would be solely her responsibility. When she had lived with Iron Fist, his other wives had done their share of the work. Since moving was primarily a task left to Comanche women, she could expect no help from Caleb. Besides, he was out taking care of their horses.

She was surprised then to hear him duck into the lodge behind her.

"Don't tell me you're here to help me with the bear-skin?" She smiled, turning to face him. The smile vanished.

He was gripping his rifle, his face cold, determined. "Stay inside," he ordered gruffly. "Don't come out, no matter what you hear."

"What is it? What's wrong?"

"Do what I say." With that he was gone.

Jenna bristled but did not follow. Cautiously she crossed to the entry flap and peered out.

She gasped. Dismounting from a chestnut gelding in front of Eagle Dancer's lodge was Major Keith Gallagher. Her heart pounded. Freedom! Surely he had come to rescue her and Timmy, take them with him to Fort Bascom.

Then why had Caleb ordered her to stay out of sight?

It was then she realized that Gallagher was alone. Blast! Why didn't Caleb want Gallagher to see her? What was he up to?

She considered bolting outside, presenting herself to the army officer and demanding his help. But she didn't dare. Such foolhardiness could get Gallagher killed.

She waited an interminable hour for the men to emerge from Eagle Dancer's lodge, then held her breath as Caleb and Gallagher headed in her direction. Had Caleb at last told Keith about her? Was the major coming to take her and Timmy back to civilization? And what would she think about it, if he did?

It was a decision she didn't have to make. As the men came closer she realized, to her astonishment, that they were involved in a heated argument. She strained to overhear, hoping desperately for some kind of confirmation that Caleb was indeed still working for the army, as he had claimed.

"I don't give a damn what you think, Keith," Caleb snapped. "Just ride the hell out of here." He paused, then added, "While you still can."

"Is that a threat?"

"It's whatever you want it to be."

Gallagher jammed a finger into Caleb's chest. "I risked my life riding in here, but I did it hoping you would listen to reason. I can see I was wrong. Mark my words, old friend, if you even think about dealing those missing firing pins to *comancheros,* I'll see you at the end of a rope."

"Good-bye, Keith."

Gallagher cursed. "If I'd known for one minute that you were a damned half-breed—"

Caleb slammed a fist into Gallagher's face, driving the major back, landing him butt-first in the dirt.

Jenna closed her eyes. *Keith Gallagher is Caleb Harper's friend. Caleb Harper is a white man.*

Gallagher rubbed his jaw and climbed back to his feet, but he made no move to retaliate. No doubt he was taking his surroundings into consideration. "Don't think this is the end of it, Harper. I'm not forgetting that I put you in charge of a bunch of tenderfoots, and they ended up slaughtered. You're going to pay for that one too. You're going to pay for it all."

Caleb touched the knife sheathed at his side. "I suggest you leave while you still have a full head of hair, Keith."

Livid, Gallagher stomped over to his horse and

mounted. With a final look of disgust at Caleb, he jammed his heels into the horse's sides and rode out.

Caleb stormed into the tepee, his face a mask of fury. He stopped cold when he saw Jenna. She could have sworn he looked as though he'd forgotten she was there. As for herself, she imagined she looked as sick as she felt.

"You heard?"

She nodded.

He let out a low, hissing breath. "You weren't supposed to."

"Obviously not."

He took a step toward her but stopped when she shrank away from him. He kept his voice low as he spoke. "Jenna, I swear to you, our little performance out there was for Iron Fist's benefit, not yours."

"I didn't see Iron Fist anywhere."

"He was out there."

Had he been? She didn't know. "You want Iron Fist to think you're finished with the army?"

"It's part of the plan. I've told you before that I intend to get myself into the *comancheros*. I want those men, Jenna. All of them. And I want their leader, the man in the mask, the one who pulled the strings."

"But it's so dangerous. What if Iron Fist suspects something . . . ? What if—"

"I'll be all right."

How could he be so certain? "Iron Fist hates you."

"If he thinks there's any chance I'm willing to make a deal for those firing pins, he'll lead me to our hooded friend." He chucked a hand under her chin. "That man has your father's watch, Jenna. I want it back."

She turned away. This was all so confusing, terrifying. "When are you leaving?"

His answer was to begin changing from his Comanche garb into his white man's clothes.

"How . . . how long will you be gone?"

"A month, maybe two. No more than that. Don't worry, when I come back I'll personally escort you to Fort Bascom. And I promise I'll do everything I can to convince Two Trees to let Timmy go as well. You can both be on your way to your uncle in California."

She wanted to ask him why he seemed suddenly so anxious to be rid of her, but she didn't. "Why can't you just take us now? Why couldn't you have let us leave with Keith?"

"Keith was alone," he said too quickly, not meeting her gaze. "One man wouldn't be any protection, especially not with that uniform of his. He's lucky he got in and out of here alive."

Why did his answer sound rehearsed? Jenna tried to tell herself she was imagining things. She stepped close to him, the thought of his not being there in the night suddenly, crushingly real. "Don't go."

"I have to. It's time to stop Valdez."

"I want him stopped too, Caleb. More than anything. But I'm afraid."

He pulled her to him, held her close. "You're a woman with more courage than a battalion of soldiers. You'll be fine. I've arranged for you to stay with Eagle Dancer, not Iron Fist. Besides, I fully expect Iron Fist to be on my trail ten minutes after I'm gone."

"Caleb, I—"

"I can't answer your questions, Jenna. It wouldn't be safe for you to know too much. All I can ask is that you trust me. Just trust me. Can you do that?"

She didn't answer.

He gave her a self-mocking smile. "I doubt I'd trust me either."

"It isn't that . . ." She stopped. It was exactly that, and they both knew it.

He ducked out of the lodge. Reluctantly Jenna followed. He readied his black gelding, then hesitated before mounting. From the pocket of his trousers he extracted his mother's amulet. Without preliminaries he slipped it over Jenna's neck. "It's still the only thing I have that means anything to me." He paused, then added, barely audibly, "Except you."

He mounted then and rode out, not once looking back. She knew he didn't look back, because she didn't take her eyes from the path he rode until he was long out of sight. *Trust.* Such a fragile thing. Such a desperately important thing.

I'll be back soon.

With one hand Jenna fingered the amulet; with the other she touched her abdomen. She'd been aware of the changes in her body for several days now but had chosen to ignore them, deny them. Now that it was too late she didn't deny them any longer. She should have stopped Caleb, told him. She hadn't been lying to Eagle Dancer after all.

She was carrying Caleb's child.

21

Caleb didn't come back. Not in one month, nor in two. Winter came and, behind it, spring; and still Caleb had not come. The winter months were the hardest, when Jenna huddled beneath her buffalo robes in the dark and cold of night, longing for Caleb's warmth and protection, even as she grew heavy with his child.

And even when she did manage to sleep, it brought no surcease. Nightmares tormented her, nightmares that came in two forms, both equally devastating. In one, Caleb lay dead, tortured to death by the butchers he was trying to bring to justice. In the other, Caleb himself was the butcher, garbed in full Comanche regalia, replete with warpaint, murdering all who despised his Indian blood.

Jenna woke from these dreams, trembling, terrified, desperate to talk about them, exorcise them, but she dared share them with no one. Eagle Dancer would not understand. And in the light of day Jenna could never bring herself to burden Painted Sky with the hideous visions. Instead Jenna did the best she could to block them from her mind, going about her daily tasks with a vengeance, driving herself to exhaustion because she had learned it was the only way she might sleep free of dreams.

Exhaustion wasn't too hard to come by, now that part of her daily routine included caring for Eagle Dancer. Despite her best efforts though, and those of the band's medicine man, his condition continued to deteriorate. There were days when she had to feed him because he was too weak to feed himself. She didn't mind. She had come to care about him deeply, to respect his wisdom and his unexpectedly gentle ways. And, when he wasn't too tired, she loved to hear him speak. The old man was filled with stories about the two years Caleb had spent with the People. Jenna never tired of hearing the chief talk about his son.

"There was the day he tracked his first wolf," Eagle Dancer told her one snowy evening as Jenna prepared their meal by the fire. "Without food, without horse, without weapon."

He spoke in Comanche, and Jenna responded in kind. "Tell me about it, Father." He had asked her to call him that many weeks before, and though at first awkward about it, Jenna had grown more and more accepting, until she could imagine addressing him no other way.

"He followed it into the Sangre de Cristos."

Jenna had heard of the New Mexican mountain range. But now she could see it in her mind's eye, smell it, taste it as the chief described the rugged terrain with its undulating green peaks of juniper and spruce, a pine scent so strong it seemed to permeate even the rocks. Caleb would easily be at home in such a place.

"The wolf was a lobo. No mate. No pack. Night Wind followed him for eight days and eight nights. When the wolf slept, he slept. When the wolf moved, he moved.

Before Night Wind returned to the village, the wolf had eaten out of his hand."

Jenna felt a strange, vicarious exhilaration at the thought of Caleb gaining the trust of a wild animal. Her eyes misted as Eagle Dancer continued.

"Night Wind is like that wolf, Sky Eyes. For too many years he has been alone. Now he is alone no more." The old man smiled. "Remember, the wolf mates for life."

Jenna blushed.

"Do not be modest, Sky Eyes." He chuckled. "You have tamed your wolf. He will eat out of your hand."

He closed his eyes, drifting off to sleep. Jenna tucked his robes under his chin, her throat tight. Eagle Dancer made it sound so easy. He couldn't know that the trust between her and Caleb had already been broken once and then mended with the most fragile of threads. Only time would tell if the threads would hold. And the more time that passed that Caleb didn't return, the more fragile those threads became.

For the village itself the winter had proved a good one. Usually February was known as the month the children cry for food, but this year the band's subsistence diet of jerked meat and pemmican had been supplemented occasionally by fresh game. Such rare feasts were cause for celebration and sharing. The only deaths came from illness or old age. All in all, the People considered it a good sign.

Jenna wished she could share in their optimism. Instead she went on brooding about when, or if, Caleb would return. Her melancholy was hardly lightened by the fact that Timmy had gone off with Two Trees early in December to join up with another band of Comanche. She hadn't seen or heard from her brother in months. Nor could she completely suppress her suspicion that Timmy's leave-taking hadn't been the result of another one of Caleb's "secrets."

She probably would have given herself over completely to her depression if it hadn't been for Painted Sky. The Indian woman frequently stopped by to fuss over her, humor her, and otherwise help her forget her absent husband and brother. At times Jenna felt Painted Sky was more involved in her pregnancy than Jenna herself.

When spring brought the buffalo, every man, woman, and child in the village had a job to do, but Painted Sky still made time to be with Jenna. "Your man-child come very soon now," Painted Sky said, helping Jenna scrape the coarse hair from the hide of a massive male buffalo Iron Fist had killed two days before. "He be strong and brave like Night Wind."

Jenna didn't even ask anymore how Painted Sky could be so certain she was carrying a boy. Jenna simply accepted it as fact. "He'll be strong all right," she said, smoothing a hand over her distended belly. "He already kicks like a mule."

Painted Sky laughed, then set aside her scraping stone. "Come," she said, climbing to her feet. "We have worked long enough today. Let us walk."

Jenna didn't argue. Though her legs had been bothering her lately, she preferred a slight cramp to the back-breaking work of cleaning a hide. Besides, Eagle Dancer had had an especially difficult night last night. He was resting comfortably now, but Jenna knew this might be the only time she could get away from the village for a while. It would be nice to wade in the creek.

Though Painted Sky walked slowly, it was all Jenna could do to keep up with her. "Just make sure we don't head where any of the braves are out hunting," Jenna told her.

"Why is that, Sky Eyes?"

"I don't want to be mistaken for a buffalo."

Painted Sky giggled. "I am glad to hear life in your voice again, dear one."

Jenna sighed. "I haven't been very good company lately, have I? How ever do you put up with me?"

"I love you," she said simply. "Your sister is dead. Now I am your sister."

Jenna blinked back tears. When had it happened, she wondered. When had it happened that she had come to feel so at peace, so at home with these people? "I feel the same for you, Painted Sky," she said, knowing deep in her heart that Bess would have approved.

They continued in comfortable silence the remainder of the quarter mile to the creek. April had brought rain and wildflowers to the land, and Jenna and Painted Sky made frequent stops to pluck daisies and twine them in the braids of each other's hair. Despite the slow pace and the short distance, Jenna was exhausted by the time they reached the creek.

"I'm sorry," Jenna said. "Walking has become more of a task than listening to Talks Too Much tell me what a poor Comanche I make."

"You make good Comanche. Night Wind be proud when he come back."

Jenna felt a familiar ache just to hear his name. The nightmares had been especially vivid last night. "Do you really think he'll be back, Painted Sky?"

"Of course, Sky Eyes. He must see his son. And," she smiled, "he loves you."

Jenna sank down in front of a willow tree laden with spring buds. "Then why has it been so long? Why hasn't he come back?" She let out a watery sigh. "Any day now I'm going to have his baby. If he loves me so much, why isn't he here?" Her voice broke, and she swallowed hard. She wasn't going to cry, not in front of Painted Sky.

The Indian woman gave Jenna's hand a reassuring squeeze.

It was suddenly more sympathy than Jenna could bear. Like a bursting dam, she began to sob, aching, racking sobs that shook her whole body.

Painted Sky pulled her close, holding her, stroking her hair as Jenna cried brokenly, telling her friend of the horrid dreams that had tormented her for months. "He's dead. I know he's dead. That's why he hasn't come back."

"No, dear one," Painted Sky said softly. "Night Wind is not dead. Iron Fist would have told me if it were so." The Comanche warrior had returned only the week before after having been gone for months himself. He had been in his usual belligerent mood, stirring up talk of war throughout the village. Thankfully Eagle Dancer still commanded the respect of his people, and Iron Fist was largely ignored.

"Iron Fist said something about Night Wind, didn't he?"

Painted Sky nodded. "I did not speak of it because I did not wish to frighten you. But now I see you are more frightened by not knowing."

Jenna sat up. "Tell me."

Painted Sky kept hold of Jenna's hand. "He say Night Wind shot—"

At Jenna's gasp, Painted Sky rushed to continue, "Not dead. Not dead, I promise. But Night Wind . . . Night Wind in jail."

"Jail?" Jenna's free hand unconsciously touched her abdomen. "What jail? Where? When? How badly was he shot? Is he all right?" She started to get up. "I have to talk to Iron Fist."

"No. He must not know I speak to you of this. If he did, he would say no more."

Jenna sagged back. "Tell me everything, Painted Sky."

"Night Wind in place called Juarez. Long time now."

"What did he do? Why is he in jail?"

Painted Sky shook her head. "Not sure. Iron Fist say something about guns. Firing pins for guns. And shipment for new guns."

Jenna's heart thundered. She recalled Caleb's saying he would use the firing pins as bait against the *comancheros*. Then why was he in jail? Where was Gallagher? Why hadn't the *comancheros* been captured if some sort of deal had been arranged? Had there been a double cross? And if so by whom? Unbidden thoughts intruded. Had Caleb been caught actually delivering the firing pins? Had he duped someone else into transporting more guns?

No. No. Something had gone wrong. Maybe Gallagher didn't even know Caleb was in jail. Maybe—"I need to get to Fort Bascom. I need to talk to Major Gallagher."

Painted Sky's gaze trailed to Jenna's midsection. "You cannot make such a journey, even if you knew the way."

"I have to do something. I can't leave him there."

"Iron Fist will help."

Jenna was unable to mask her skepticism, but Painted Sky was adamant. "He go soon. It is why he came back. Make plan to free Night Wind."

Free him, Jenna wondered fearfully. Or kill him? "Why would Iron Fist ride all the way back here to make plans if Night Wind is in Juarez?"

"Not know."

A new horror struck through Jenna. "Because he's planning something else too, isn't he?"

Painted Sky looked away.

Jenna's blood ran cold. It was spring. It was time for

white settlers to once again be crossing the plains. "Eagle Dancer is dying. Iron Fist wants to be war chief. Last year he rode with *comancheros*. Last year he killed my sister. This year he wants all-out war, doesn't he? Doesn't he?"

Painted Sky didn't say anything for a long minute. Finally she spoke again, her voice resolute, filled with a quiet pride. "White men kill my first husband, because he was Comanche. No reason, just because he was Comanche.

"One spring white men slaughter a thousand buffalo and take only the hides. They leave the meat to spoil in the sun. Laugh at Comanche. One hunter sick with red spots. Comes to village. Make many of the People sick. Talks Too Much sick. White doctor will not help."

"Measles?" Jenna had heard the disease was deadly to Indians.

Painted Sky nodded. "Talks Too Much with child. Lose child. No babies for Iron Fist."

"I'm sorry."

"You are my sister. I pray my people and your people one day live in peace. But do not ask me to speak of this again. Not even to you, Sky Eyes."

Jenna felt Painted Sky's pain. It was a moral dilemma where rights and wrongs were decided by point of view. Jenna would have her own crisis of conscience to deal with soon. If Caleb had told the truth about infiltrating the *comancheros*, he could one day be the cause Iron Fist's downfall, even his death. Yet she could say nothing of this to Painted Sky.

Loyalty. Trust. Kinship. For the first time she understood the terrible choice Caleb was being forced to make between the white world and the Comanche.

Jenna embraced her friend. "I really am sorry."

Painted Sky hugged her back. "I know."

Jenna picked up a stone and arced it into the creek. A

change of subject was in order. "You know," she began timidly, uncertain if Painted Sky was still in the mood to talk, "Night Wind and I first made love in a place like this. Of course, I didn't know he was Night Wind then. He kept his Comanche blood a secret."

Painted Sky bore no grudge. She once again spoke openly. "He scared. Not want you to be like the other."

"What other?"

Painted Sky blushed. "Should not have said."

"Another woman? A white woman?" Bittersweet, Jenna recalled Bess's starry-eyed assertion that Caleb had had his heart broken, that that was what had made him gun-shy with Jenna. "Did you know this woman, Painted Sky?"

"Never see her. You angry with Night Wind?"

"Not at all. In fact, it might help me understand him a little better. Please tell me."

"Her name Laura or Lorelei or . . ." Painted Sky pressed her fingers to her temples to try and rouse her memory.

"Her name doesn't matter," Jenna said. "I just want to know what she did to hurt Night Wind."

"He love this woman, want to marry her in white man's church."

Jenna looked away, fighting off an unexpected surge of jealousy. "What happened?"

Anger threaded Painted Sky's voice. "He told her he was half Comanche."

Jenna closed her eyes. Of course.

"He come for a visit soon after. Pretend he not care. But I can see. He hurt by stupid woman."

Jenna warmed to Painted Sky's obvious indignation in Night Wind's behalf. "She was very stupid," Jenna agreed, more than a little surprised that Caleb would have shared such a humiliating episode with anyone, even Painted Sky. Her friend's next words solved that mystery.

"He only tell me because he drink too much firewater."

Jenna tried to imagine Caleb drunk but couldn't. He was a man who held his feelings and emotions in tight check, yet under all that control was a caring, deeply vulnerable man. Or so she wanted desperately to believe. She had known she had hurt him with her own cruel words all those months ago, but only now did she fully comprehend the scope of that hurt. "No wonder he doesn't trust anyone."

"What you say, Sky Eyes?"

Jenna looked up at her friend. "Nothing. It doesn't matter." She shuddered. "Oh, Painted Sky, I miss him so much."

"Iron Fist get him out. He come home."

"His home is with the Comanche, isn't it?"

Painted Sky shook her head. "His home is with you. Night Wind walks in two worlds, Sky Eyes, but he is at home in neither. You have given him a home."

"I hope so."

"Believe. You see." She stood. "Rest now. I go find berries for pemmican."

Jenna leaned back and closed her eyes. She stroked her abdomen, talking in soft, lilting tones to her unborn son. "Home. Your father is coming home, little one. Soon now. He has to be." Tears slid down her cheeks. "So I can tell him how very much I love him."

Jenna woke to Painted Sky's gentle nudge on her shoulder.

"Night coming. We go back to village."

Jenna groaned, stretching muscles stiff from having dozed off on the damp ground. "I don't know if I—"

She gasped, a sudden sharp pain rippling through the lower half of her body.

Painted Sky knelt beside her. "The baby comes?"

Jenna panted hard, trying to catch her breath. Her heart was pounding. She had known it would be soon, but now that it was happening she wasn't ready for it at all. "Oh, Painted Sky, I'm afraid. I'm afraid. I don't know anything about having babies."

Painted Sky smoothed a hand over Jenna's face. "I know plenty. You be fine."

The pain eased, and Jenna peered up into Painted Sky's calm dark eyes. The fear left her.

While the contractions were still several minutes apart, Painted Sky hurried back to the village for anything she could think of that would make Jenna more comfortable. She also brought several soft pelts to swaddle the baby in after he was born.

Jenna's labor took most of the rest of the night, but with Painted Sky's gentle reassurances and wise counsel, Jenna made it through with only one regret. As her baby entered the world what she wanted most to see was the face of her husband as she gifted him with his son.

"He is a fine boy," Painted Sky said, lifting the baby into Jenna's outstretched arms. "Night Wind will be proud."

Painted Sky let her rest for another hour; then amazingly Jenna was able to get to her feet and walk slowly back to the village, while Painted Sky carried the baby. At Eagle Dancer's lodge the Comanche woman reluctantly relinquished the child. "You will let me care for him sometimes?"

"You have to ask? You will be his favorite aunt. But now I must introduce him to his grandfather."

A look of profound sadness crossed Painted Sky's

lovely features. "The child will not remember the great Comanche chief who was his grandfather."

"He'll remember, Painted Sky. I promise you." With that Jenna ducked into the heavily shadowed lodge. This morning she had laid extra skins across the tepee's sloping sides to shield Eagle Dancer from even the dimmest light. Though his eyesight had all but failed him, even the vaguest sunlight now seemed to cause him pain.

Jenna stepped quietly over to the pallet on which Eagle Dancer lay. After his restless night she didn't want to disturb him.

To her surprise his eyes were open, and he was looking more alert and content than she had seen him in some time. "You have brought my grandson, Sky Eyes."

"How did you know, Father?"

"He is Night Wind's son." No more needed to be said.

Jenna helped Eagle Dancer sit up, then lay the sleeping baby in his arms. The chief's gnarled fingers moved with infinite tenderness across the child's tiny features, seeing with his hands what he could no longer see with his eyes.

"His grandmother's name was Jo Ellen," Jenna said softly, knowing it was acceptable to mention Fights Like a Lion's white name. "His white name will be Joel."

"Is good. But Night Wind's son needs Comanche name."

"And he will have one." She paused, her mind filling with thoughts of what Painted Sky had said earlier. "I have named him Walks With Pride in Two Worlds."

Eagle Dancer's clouded eyes grew misty. "Is good."

"I love you, Father." She needed to say the words.

"You bring honor to my people and your own, Sky Eyes. You are a fine daughter. You will help Night Wind learn to walk in both worlds like his son."

"I will try."

Eagle Dancer handed her the baby and lay back. "Just one sorrow now."

"The anger between your sons?"

He nodded.

Jenna took his once strong hand in her own. "I will ask them to be brothers."

"Is good." He would say no more.

Jenna let out a low, keening sound as she sang the Comanche death song.

The next few days were a blur of grief over the death of Eagle Dancer, joy over her thriving son, and pain because Caleb was not there to share in either emotion. She also had to accept the humiliating reality of returning to Iron Fist's lodge. At least Painted Sky's comforting presence made the transition less traumatic. It was all Jenna could do not to ask the Comanche about Night Wind.

For Iron Fist's part, he seemed almost to deliberately arrange things so that Painted Sky and Jenna were never alone. Not that it mattered. When the Comanche left camp a week later, Jenna immediately cornered Painted Sky, speaking in English so that Talks Too Much would not understand. "Do you think he's gone to get Night Wind?"

Painted Sky grinned. It was the only answer Jenna needed. The two women danced around the tepee until Talks Too Much came after them with a stick. Then they danced around the village.

Two months went by. Jenna's soaring hopes dipped low again. She was certain something had gone dreadfully wrong. Maybe both men had been killed by prison guards.

Or maybe they've just gotten sidetracked attacking wagon trains, a mocking voice taunted.

To take her mind off one horrific scenario after an-

other, Jenna immersed herself in caring for her son.
Every morning she would put Joel on his cradleboard,
strap him to her back and go off walking or riding for
hours. A couple of times she even imagined pointing
the horse in the direction she believed Fort Bascom to
be and making a run for it. If she could talk to Major
Gallagher, find out what was going on with Caleb . . .
But common sense won out. She wasn't sure where the
fort was. She couldn't risk the baby's life.

Caleb would be back. And then everything would be
all right. They would find Timmy. They would go to
California . . .

She reined in, frowning, realizing with a start that
the thought of living in California was now as foreign to
her as the idea of living in a Comanche village had once
been. Well, she supposed she would get over it once she
got there.

She pushed the thoughts away as she started back
toward the village. She didn't want Painted Sky to
guess what she'd been thinking. Whenever Jenna even
brought up the subject of leaving, Painted Sky became
inconsolable.

She was a hundred yards from the lodge, when she
spied Iron Fist's gelding ground-tied beside it. Jenna
kicked her mount into a run. She was off the horse and
into the tepee in one motion. For the first time in her
life she was glad to see Iron Fist. "Where is Night
Wind?" she demanded breathlessly, unhitching the
cradleboard from her back.

Iron Fist said nothing, but the look on his face was so
chillingly self-satisfied that Jenna experienced a searing
rush of foreboding. Fighting it off, Jenna turned to
Painted Sky. "What is it? Where is he?"

"He come."

Jenna's heart leapt, but the smile that sprang to her

lips vanished as she realized there had been no joy in Painted Sky's voice, only a terrifying sorrow.

"Tell me," Jenna said, clutching the baby close. "Please. What's wrong?"

"Nothing wrong," Iron Fist said. "Everything right. Night Wind come."

Jenna felt a cloying dread. Painted Sky's tortured expression did not change.

"Tell me!" Jenna screamed.

Iron Fist smiled, a most unpleasant smile. "Night Wind no longer white man. Night Wind renegade. Night Wind ride with *comancheros.* "

Jenna's heart turned over. No. Caleb wouldn't— Like a thunderbolt it hit her. Of course! She should have thought of it before. How else would he return but as a full fledged *comanchero*? It was the very role he had sought in the dangerous game he was playing. And apparently he was playing it very well. She started to let out a sigh of relief, but at Iron Fist's curious look Jenna realized it would do better if she seemed upset. "You're lying!" she snapped.

"Army want Night Wind," Iron Fist said.

"Want him for what?"

"Want him to hang."

Jenna didn't have to feign the shock that slammed through her, but she had no time to dwell on it. Riders were coming in.

Scooping the baby into her arms, she peered outside.

A dozen horsemen thundered through the village. Armed, brutish-looking. Jenna cringed and shrank back. Terror pulsed through her, as she recognized the man in the lead.

Enrique Valdez.

And to his right . . .

Jenna stared in abject horror.

Caleb.

He hadn't yet seen her, but she couldn't take her eyes off him. His face painted, his bronzed body glistening with sweat, he looked every inch a savage. But what nearly sent her to her knees was what he carried in his left hand. He held it aloft—letting loose with a blood-chilling Comanche war cry. It was a lance, a war lance, a war lance laden with human scalps.

22

Clutching the baby to her breast, Jenna walked woodenly toward where Caleb sat astride a roan gelding. Her heart thundered; her legs barely obeyed her. This could not be the man whose return she had hoped for, prayed for, for nearly a year. When she reached the roan, Caleb swung one bare leg over the gelding's head and slid to the ground in front of her. When he looked at her, his features were hard, implacable. When he looked at the baby, he showed no reaction at all.

None.

She reminded herself it was an act, assured herself it had to be this way. To ride with *comancheros*, Caleb would have to behave like a *comanchero*. But would even these men expect him to be so cold toward his own wife, toward a child he had never seen?

She pulled the blanket back from the baby's face. "This is your son, Caleb," she said, hating the nervousness threading her voice. "His name is Joel, for your mother. His Comanche name is—"

With an oath Caleb drove his war lance into the dirt at her feet. "Iron Fist's gift to me is my gift to my son."

Jenna swallowed the bile that rose in her throat. Terrified, she dared step close to him, whispering urgently so that only he could hear. "You're scaring me. Caleb, please, even these butchers can't expect you to treat your wife this way."

"These butchers don't condemn me for my mixed blood." He spoke evenly, normally, making no attempt to keep their conversation private.

Jenna again felt an icy chill of foreboding. Her eyes flicked to the lance. She suppressed a shudder at the half-dozen scalps dangling from it. Just how far would Caleb go to convince these men of his allegiance? How blurred would he let the line between hunter and quarry become?

Trust me, Jenna, he had said. *It wouldn't be safe for you to know too much.*

Safe? Was he just trying to keep her safe? But what could be wrong with a gesture, a sign, a touch? Anything to quash her mounting dread. He had to know she wouldn't do anything to jeopardize his charade.

A glance behind her told her Iron Fist had come out of the lodge, along with Painted Sky. The look on her friend's face only added to Jenna's distress. Painted Sky had known Caleb for years longer than Jenna had. And it was patently obvious Painted Sky was sickened by what she was seeing, sickened by what her eyes told her Night Wind had become.

If this was an act, it was a very good one.

Jenna held on to one last glimmer of hope. Perhaps he was just not taking any chances; perhaps he was just waiting until they could be alone. "Are you . . . are you staying?" she asked.

"I came for my son."

"To see him?" Her heart pounded.

He did not expand on what he had said.

"Why don't we talk in the lodge?" She started to back away but found her path blocked by a barrel-chested man who had lumbered up behind her. Dressed in trail-stained buckskins and an equally stained sombrero the man grinned leeringly at her, displaying a row of blackened, decaying teeth.

"I bet ya don't remember me, do ya, missy? Ike Gravshaw's the name. I was there with Valdez last summer. If it hadn't been for that little necklace yer wearin', we woulda had us a good time." He caught hold of one of her braids, toying with the strands of hair at its tip. "A real good time."

"Don't touch me!" She shot a despairing glance at Caleb, but he made no move to interfere.

Gravshaw laughed. "You expect help from the 'breed? It ain't gonna happen, missy. You see, he don't want you no more. Somebody shoulda warned ya about 'breeds. They got no loyalty."

"Leave her be, Ike." Caleb's voice was thick with menace.

Finally! Jenna almost sobbed with relief, until he added, "Our buyer isn't going to want damaged goods."

"Buyer?" she repeated numbly. What in God's name was going on?

"My escape from Juarez didn't come cheap, I'm afraid."

"What are you talking about?"

"I couldn't face another twenty years in that hellhole. Not when I had a ticket out. But don't worry, Jenna. It won't be so bad. In fact, you should be relieved. You'll be free of me. Free of the Comanche." His voice was acid. "After all, these people are animals."

"Caleb, please, what are—"

Without warning he scooped the baby away from her.

Jenna screamed, lunging after him. She had a vague awareness of Painted Sky rushing toward her, being held back by Iron Fist. Everything else was blotted out by Caleb's next words.

"I said you could leave the Comanche the day you gave me a son." He chuckled malevolently. "I just didn't say where you would go."

She screamed again as Ike Gravshaw grabbed her; then blessedly her world went dark.

Caleb felt the walls of hell closing in on him. He had known since he'd left Juarez two weeks ago that his reunion with Jenna would have to be this way. But that hadn't made it any easier. He wished to heaven there had been some way he could have warned her, let her know what was going to happen, but to do so could have cost her her life. And he wasn't about to take that risk.

He held his son close, telling himself over and over that he would find a way to get to her, find a way to make it right.

It had taken every ounce of will he possessed to let Ike Gravshaw touch her, to let the hulking brute bind and gag her. His only consolation was that she had fainted.

"Why are you doing this?" Painted Sky demanded, jerking free of Iron Fist's hold on her. "How can you treat Sky Eyes like Tonkawa slave? She is your woman. She is mother to your son."

"Stay out of this, Painted Sky," Caleb warned. "It doesn't concern you."

"She is my sister. I will not let you harm her."

"I said stay out of it!" He gave no hint of the pain it cost him to have this woman he had long considered a

friend look on him with such contempt. Nor did he
object when she took the baby. He felt somehow unclean to hold his son under such circumstances.

"The baby will need to be fed," Painted Sky said. "He
will need his mother."

The image of Jenna nursing their child was an agony
beyond bearing.

"I think I'll watch," Gravshaw smirked, his hand
moving toward where Jenna's full breasts curved beneath the doeskin of her dress.

Caleb's gun was in Gravshaw's ear. "Touch her, and
I'll kill you." He could feel Iron Fist's eyes on him, but
he didn't care. He drilled a look at the Comanche warrior. "I made a bargain. It didn't include this pig having
any rights to the woman."

Valdez had come over to watch. "Night Wind is right,
Iron Fist. The woman is worth nothing to us if she kills
herself, which she would do when Ike is done with
her."

Gravshaw chortled, taking no insult. "Guess that has
happened a time or two." He stood and wandered off,
looking for some of the whiskey the *comancheros* had
brought to share with the Comanche.

Caleb knelt beside Jenna. He would take her into
Iron Fist's lodge, where she could have some privacy at
least. Her bonds made it awkward to lift her, but he
managed. She was still unconscious. Cradling her
against his naked chest, he carried her to the tepee,
then ducked inside. In the one instant they were alone
he dared press his lips against her hair. "I'll get you out
of this, I swear," he whispered, even though he knew
she couldn't hear him.

Iron Fist joined them then, keeping a watchful eye
on Caleb as he lay Jenna gently atop her buffalo robes.

Painted Sky followed with the baby. Settling the infant on his cradleboard, the Comanche woman imme-

diately hurried to Jenna's side. When she began to work the ropes, Iron Fist barked out a series of orders, chief among them that Jenna was not to be untied. Painted Sky was to help the baby nurse, then take the child and leave the lodge. Guards would be posted outside to see that he was obeyed. If Painted Sky resisted, a wet nurse would be found, and Jenna would not be allowed to see the baby at all. Nor would Painted Sky.

To Caleb he said, "You will not come in here again."

A muscle in Caleb's jaw jumped, but he held his temper. Iron Fist had never completely believed Caleb's conversion to being a renegade. He didn't want to fuel that suspicion now. "I have no reason to come to this lodge. Not anymore. She is no longer my woman."

Iron Fist gave no indication whether or not he believed Caleb. But he made no move to leave the lodge until Caleb went out ahead of him.

"I find Valdez," the Comanche said. "We talk."

Caleb agreed. He might as well. There was nothing more he could do for Jenna right now. "I'll meet you in five minutes. I'm going to change into my white clothes."

At Iron Fist's frown Caleb said, "I need to get used to them again. I'll be meeting with Gallagher in a few days, remember? That's when I find out where we intercept that shipment of gold Valdez and our mysterious hooded boss are so anxious to get their hands on."

"Gold to buy guns for Comanche."

Caleb headed for his horse, needing to get away from the bloodlust in Iron Fist's eyes. This whole plan had become so twisted, so convoluted, there were times Caleb wasn't sure who was working for whom. And right now, with Jenna in such desperate danger, he wasn't sure he cared.

It could have been so simple. He thought about the plan he and Keith had come up with last year, the one that included the fight he and Keith had staged in front of Iron Fist, the one unfortunately witnessed by Jenna.

As expected, Iron Fist had followed Caleb out of the village that day. And soon after, a meeting had been arranged with "Mr. Hood." Caleb would bring the Spencer firing pins out of hiding in exchange for a considerable amount of "Mr. Hood's" gold, gold that Iron Fist would use to buy even more guns. "Mr. Hood" would be told when the next army payroll was being shipped, thus gaining in the bargain himself.

Caleb would get all of this information to Keith, who would then set a trap designed to snare all parties at once.

Except that again, as with the Riordans, something had gone dreadfully wrong.

A staged ambush had gone awry. Though six *comancheros* were killed and the firing pins destroyed, Caleb wound up with a bullet in his back and a twenty-year prison sentence south of the border. The army payroll had disappeared. Valdez and Iron Fist had gotten away. And no word had been heard from "Mr. Hood" for months.

As Caleb had slowly recovered in Juarez he waited for some word, some sign from Gallagher. Though out of his jurisdiction, Caleb had been certain the major was doing everything he could to set Caleb free, even if it meant blowing Caleb's cover.

Days passed, then weeks, then months.

Caleb had lain awake night after night on a stinking pallet on a stone-cold floor, his thoughts consumed by Jenna. He would dream of her, hot and passionate in his arms, then wake to an endless emptiness. He thought he would go mad.

Then one day a Mexican bandito named Ricardo Quinones was assigned to share his cell. It turned out to be no accident. The man was an emissary from "Mr.

Hood." If Caleb agreed to certain terms, an escape could be arranged.

The terms had made Caleb's blood run cold.

"You must give up your beautiful blond wife, *señor*," Ricardo told him. "A collector in Mexico City has offered a fortune for her. He was to have gotten her last year, but something went wrong. He has doubled his offer."

Caleb told Ricardo to tell "Mr. Hood" to go to hell.

Ricardo cautioned that might not be the best course. "If I tell him you said no, you are to meet with an unfortunate "accident" in the prison yard, *señor*. Your Comanche brother has said if that happens, he will no longer protect the white woman."

Caleb was grateful Iron Fist wasn't in the cell with him. He would have broken the promise he once made to his father. He would have killed his Comanche brother.

"Tell your boss I agree to his terms," Caleb said.

Ricardo had had two more bits of news. It was in that fetid cell in Juarez that Caleb learned of the death of Eagle Dancer. The pain from that blow had scarcely begun to register, when Ricardo dealt him another. Caleb had again not been there for Jenna when she had needed him the most. "Your wife has borne you a son. You are a father, *señor*."

Caleb had let out a roar of unholy rage, bloodying his fists against the unyielding stone walls, begging Jenna to forgive him.

The next day his cellmate had been released as mysteriously as he'd arrived. Two days later Caleb's guard had handed Caleb the key to his cell. Caleb was free and heading north. He was intercepted almost at once by Valdez, Iron Fist, and the others. He would have no chance to warn Jenna.

And so today he had hurt her—scared the hell out of

her—rather than risk further rousing Iron Fist's suspicions. In the months Caleb had spent in that jail cell, he'd become convinced of one other thing—it had been Iron Fist's bullet buried in his back.

Tomorrow he would get a chance to tell Jenna the truth. He and three others were to head south with her, take her to the perverted creature in Mexico who thought enough money gave him the right to own another human being.

Caleb reached his roan and flipped open his saddlebags, pulling out his denims and a chambray shirt. He dressed quickly, then added a tied-down Colt to his hip. Tomorrow three *comancheros* would be dead.

Jenna struggled against the ropes that bound her. Outside the lodge it had grown dark, and she could hear the whoops of the Comanche mingled with the slurred Spanish obscenities of their outlaw guests. Both *comanchero* and Comanche had been drinking for hours. She prayed the bastards would stay clear of Iron Fist's lodge. Any second she expected to see Ike Gravshaw's brutish form loom above her to make good his vile threat.

The image spurred her to redouble her efforts to free herself.

Her wrists were already bloody and raw, the coarse hemp savaging her tender flesh. To add to her burden her milk-engorged breasts were swollen, throbbing. It had been five hours since Painted Sky had last brought the baby in to nurse. Not having Joel with her only added to Jenna's terror. Painted Sky would protect the baby with her life, but she would be no match for a band of rabid beasts.

How could Caleb have done this? Damn it to hell! How could she once again have been such a fool?

Behind her she heard the sound of leather ripping.

She twisted to see the blade of a knife being worked through the tepee wall. Even against the gag, Jenna started to scream, certain it was Gravshaw.

"Hush, Sky Eyes," Painted Sky said as she wiggled inside the tear. "It is only me." She was carrying Joel.

Jenna sobbed with relief, grabbing her baby the instant Painted Sky had cut through the ropes that bound her.

"Oh, Painted Sky . . ."

"Walks With Pride need mother."

"Night Wind . . . he . . . he . . . how could he?" Jenna trembled. The baby began to fuss. Quickly Jenna bared her breast, letting him nurse, lest the guards hear him and investigate. "So many lies," Jenna said, sobbing. "So many lies."

Painted Sky's dark eyes reflected Jenna's own torment. "Not know this Night Wind. Maybe jail change his spirit. He is cruel. Hard. I am sorry for my sister."

As Jenna fed the baby, Painted Sky scurried about the tepee gathering up supplies. "You must go. You must run, Sky Eyes. I have left a horse for you tied by the creek."

"I can't. Oh, Painted Sky, where would I go?" Jenna thought guiltily of all the times she had thought about running away since the day she'd first been brought here. Even without a gang of *comancheros* to track her down, she had never had the courage to tackle the wilderness alone.

"There is a fort. We have spoken of it. It is west and then north." Painted Sky gave her what directions she could. "Take you six days, maybe seven."

"I can't." Jenna sobbed brokenly.

Painted Sky gripped Jenna's shoulders. "You can. You must." She took a deep breath. "They will kill you."

Jenna swiped at her tears. "I could hide by the creek."

"No, they would find you."

Jenna climbed unsteadily to her feet. "All right, but I can't take the baby. I can't risk his life. Caleb would never let them hurt his son."

"To hurt you," Painted Sky reasoned slowly, "they would hurt Walks With Pride. Or they would use him to make you come back."

Jenna was not convinced. "If I get lost, Joel will die. I can't . . ."

"Must. You know land now. You move with the People many times. You Comanche. More Comanche than Night Wind." Her expression grew dark with loathing. "Night Wind not deserve his son."

"What about Iron Fist? He'll know you helped me."

Painted Sky tried to smile, failed. "Only beat Talks Too Much."

Tears slid from Jenna's eyes. "One day Walks With Pride will know the woman who saved his life. I will see you again, Painted Sky. I swear it."

"Great Spirit watch over my sister."

"And mine," Jenna said, giving the Comanche woman a fierce hug.

Settling the now sleeping Joel to his cradleboard, Jenna then secured the cradleboard to her back. Fighting back more tears, she accepted the bag of supplies Painted Sky handed her. Flashing her what she hoped was a courageous smile, Jenna slipped out the gash in the rear of the lodge.

She moved quickly, stealthily away from the village, heading toward the creek, grateful to see there was virtually no moon. She took advantage of every shadow. Her prospects of eluding pursuit were slim. She was all too aware of that. But her chances of survival if she stayed were none at all.

She found the dun gelding Painted Sky had left for her, walking the horse a half mile clear of the camp before she dared mount. As she rode away, alone with her infant son, into the vast and empty wilderness, she thought about the threat she had once made to kill Caleb Harper. She wished to heaven she had done so when she'd had the chance.

"What do you mean, there's been a change of plans?" Caleb snapped, glaring at Enrique Valdez.

"Do not worry, *señor,*" Valdez said cajolingly. "It will save you a long, wearying trip. You do not have to accompany the white woman to Mexico City."

Caleb let no reaction show on his face.

"Our *compadres* will see to it that the beautiful *gringa* is delivered as planned. You must attend to another duty. There is to be a meeting with our leader tomorrow."

Caleb knew he had no choice but to give in. "All right. I just don't like surprises. Next time let me know sooner." Inwardly his thoughts were racing like a runaway locomotive. Not Ike Gravshaw, not anyone, was taking Jenna anywhere.

Leaving Valdez to his tequila, Caleb stopped first at the medicine man's lodge, then tracked down a full bottle of whiskey. Adding the right herbs to the amber liquid, he then continued on to Iron Fist's lodge. He had to free Jenna, give her and the baby a chance to run. He would give her directions to a place she could hide until all this was over and he had a chance to come for her. If she balked, he would make it clear what the *comancheros* had in mind for her.

Ruffling his long, dark hair and swaying slightly, Caleb approached the two *comanchero* guards sitting in front of Iron Fist's tepee. "You boys look thirsty," he slurred, holding up the bottle. "Join me in a drink?"

Before long the two outlaws were out cold.

Caleb was about to duck inside, when he heard Ike Gravshaw call his name. Caleb cursed.

"Valdez sent me to fetch her."

Caleb stiffened warily. "For what?"

"He thinks she should be at the party. A little entertainment." Gravshaw glanced contemptuously at the two unconscious guards. "Never could hold their liquor." He started into the tepee.

Caleb caught his shoulder and jerked him back. "Valdez knows this isn't what I agreed to."

Gravshaw snorted. "I don't think he much gives a damn what you agreed to. Besides, you don't have to worry about the money—we'll be careful. We won't leave no marks on her."

"I said no."

"Maybe Valdez won't like hearing you say that."

"So why don't we let him settle it?"

Gravshaw started to turn away, then whirled and swiftly ducked inside the tepee. Caleb gripped his knife and dove after him. He would kill the bastard if he had to, and make up a story afterward.

But inside the lodge they found only Painted Sky. Jenna was gone.

Gravshaw swore, then scrambled back outside, shouting, bellowing at the top of his lungs for Valdez.

The *comanchero* leader came running, or rather stumbling, to Iron Fist's tepee. Others followed.

Caleb had to fight to hide his relief about Jenna as the *comancheros* began to spill into the lodge. He also had to pretend to be angry with Painted Sky. "Where is my son?"

Her eyes shining with quiet defiance, Painted Sky said, "He with his mother, where he belongs."

"Find her!" Valdez shrieked. "She must not get away. *Stupido!*"

Gravshaw and three of the more sober *comancheros* headed for their horses.

Caleb started to follow.

"You stay here, *amigo*," Valdez said. "It is not your fault the woman is gone. You will meet with *el jefe* tomorrow as planned."

It was there. On a silver platter. Valdez, Iron Fist, and their hooded leader in the same place. A year's work, a year in hell that would finally pay off.

Caleb threw it all away.

"The woman has my son. I'll be back when I find her."

Valdez tried to protest but stopped, apparently seeing the futility in it. Iron Fist was too busy with preparations to be made war chief. For the first and only time, Caleb was grateful the Comanche council had so honored his half brother. The ceremony would last several days.

Caleb readied his horse, then checked the Spencer carbine in his saddle boot. The irony of its being a Spencer was not lost on him. His face grim, he settled his black Stetson on his head, then mounted and headed out, grateful they had only a sliver of a crescent moon to guide their path.

Caleb led the way for the others—Ike Gravshaw, Hank Mitchell, Rafael Rodriquez and Carlos Mendoza. Considering the amount of whiskey they'd consumed, it was amazing any one of them could sit a horse. The night, so far, had favored Jenna. Caleb prayed it would continue.

He found her trail almost at once but made sure the others didn't. Taking care not to be too obvious, he led them off in the opposite direction. He was inordinately pleased though to discover that once Jenna had put some distance between herself and the village, she had done a pretty fair job of disguising her trail.

As he rode, the night breeze drifted cool air across his face. Bittersweet memories assailed him of another search, the day he and Jenna had ridden off to find her straying brother. He remembered how she had looked —innocent, stubborn, strong. Her innocence was gone now, stolen by him. And even her stubbornness and strength might not be enough to see her through this.

When the crescent moon disappeared behind a bank of clouds, Caleb convinced the others that they had to hole up until daylight. He knew Jenna had kept moving. It would give her an extra eight hours on them, at least.

The next morning he spent two hours casting for signs amid the grumbling of his compatriots.

"I thought you was supposed to be such a great tracker, Harper," Gravshaw said. "A blind man'd track better'n what I see here."

Caleb ignored him, moving off into the mouth of a wide canyon. He was certain Jenna had gone farther south. He could waste several hours today crisscrossing the canyon floor. He was stunned, then, to see a fresh hoofprint. He recognized it at once as being from the animal Jenna had been riding. Caleb scuffed at the print with his boot.

"What the hell you doin', Harper?" Rafael Rodriquez demanded, scowling darkly at the spot where Caleb's foot rested. A sudden awareness dawned in his eyes. "You're letting her get away!" he shouted, spinning to alert the others, even as he clawed for the six-gun on his hip.

Caleb was faster. The man was dead before he hit the ground.

Gravshaw cursed, grabbing for his rifle. Mitchell and Mendoza did likewise. Caleb's gaze swept the treeless expanse surrounding them. For miles in any direction he could see nothing that offered the slightest bit of cover.

He took a last, desperate gamble. Maybe, just maybe, he could outrun them. Vaulting onto the roan's back, he spurred it into a gallop, in a race for his life across the canyon floor. He would find a place to make a stand. These men would kill him, but he would do his best to take them with him. On his life, he vowed, these men would not find Jenna.

23

Jenna stared at the bloodied, battered body of Caleb Harper. Three bullets. Why wasn't he dead? It wasn't fair that she should have to finish the job. She gripped the knife, poised it over his chest, and fought an overwhelming urge to drive the blade into his heart.

Her palm sweated, her head throbbed. *Do it.* She let out a low, keening moan, every muscle in her body bowstring-tight. *Do it.*

With a savage curse she arced the knife downward.

At the last instant she drove the blade into the dirt.

She sat there, sobbing, exhausted, furious with her own cowardice. How could she let this monster live? Her face twisted with self-disgust. Well, she might not have the courage to kill him, but that didn't mean she had to do anything to save his life. Pushing to her feet, Jenna went back about the business of making ready to leave.

Damn him, her mind thrummed. *Damn him to hell.*

He groaned. She ignored him, making a last check of

the dead men's possessions. She didn't want to overlook anything that might help her and the baby survive.

He groaned again.

Shaking out a lariat, Jenna tethered the stray horse she'd caught to her dun; then she settled the cradleboard over her shoulders. She would ride out. She would not look back. Gathering up the dun's reins, she prepared to mount.

Joel let out a piercing wail.

Jenna turned her head, trying to hush him with the sound of her voice. It didn't work; he cried louder. With a sigh Jenna shrugged out of the cradleboard and tried to nurse him. He wouldn't eat; he cried louder.

She sang to him, rocked him.

He cried louder still.

"Hush, Joel," she murmured. "Hush." She was getting desperate. How far did sound carry in this place? "We can't stay here. We can't." The buzzards circling overhead had attracted her attention. They could just as easily attract someone else's.

Like Valdez's. Or Iron Fist's.

They had to leave. Now. She mounted the dun. The baby wailed, sobbing as she had never heard him sob before.

"Your father's a murderer, a butcher," she said, her voice breaking. "You're better off if you never even know his name."

The baby cried.

Jenna cried.

Then she dismounted.

Setting the cradleboard on the ground, Jenna crossed to Caleb and pressed her fingers against his throat, disappointed to discover again that his heart still pumped life through his veins. Bitterly she accepted the fact that killing him was not her choice to make. She would do what she could to keep him alive.

Maybe it would work out for the best, she thought viciously. Maybe she could spring the trapdoor on the gallows herself.

She glanced at her son. He had stopped crying the minute she'd gotten off the horse. She experienced a thoroughly unpleasant stab of guilt. "All right," she muttered, "I'll do what I can. But that's all."

She nursed Joel for a few minutes as she tried to decide how best to transport Caleb out of here. The unsullied innocence of her child relaxed her, took the edge off the killing rage that had almost overwhelmed her. Never had she felt such fury. Not even when Bess had died. If someone had put a knife in her hand that day, she doubted she would have been able to kill Iron Fist.

The Comanche warrior was twisted. He couldn't help what he was. But Caleb? Caleb had had her love. She had had his child. And still he had gone off to become a savage. Not the savage that people called him because of his mixed blood. But a savage beast akin to a rabid dog.

It took half an hour of pulling, pushing, and cursing, but finally she got Caleb belly-down over the bay horse's back. She didn't worry about his wounds. Not yet. She had to find shelter, a place to hide. If she tended to him here, she might as well send up smoke signals to her pursuers.

Settling herself on the dun, she took one last look around. Dead horses, dead men, swarming insects, feasting buzzards. It was a sight straight from the bowels of hell. A few of the more audacious buzzards no longer cared if she was there or not. They would not be denied their dinner. Jenna realized it was the tender ministrations of their beaks and talons that had kept her from recognizing what was left of Ike Gravshaw, when first she'd arrived on the unholy scene. If she had, she would have known instantly that one of these men was Caleb.

Her heart thudded as she recalled her earlier conclusion that the wounded man had taken the others with him, that the wounded man had been fighting the other three.

Caleb fighting Ike Gravshaw and the others?

No. She wasn't going to start that again.

Maybe soldiers had killed them.

But soldiers, logic reasoned, would have buried them.

Perhaps they just turned on each other, killed each other because that's what rabid dogs did.

She gigged the dun forward, tugging on the lead rope of the bay. Whatever happened, happened. Right now all she cared about was getting as far away from these bodies as she could before nightfall.

It was dusk when she found a shallow cave some twenty feet above the canyon floor. She wouldn't even have known it was there if it hadn't been for a diving hawk, spearing a diamondback that had been basking on the ledge in the warmth of the setting sun. A short search led her to a nearly invisible switchback. Quickly she guided the two horses up the twisting trail. A few strategically aimed rocks convinced the cave's current resident to relocate, and Jenna declared the place home, at least for the night.

Jenna got the baby settled first, then eased Caleb from the bay. She left him where he fell. It took her half an hour to find a hidden patch of ground with enough grass for the horses. She tethered them and returned to the cave.

Caleb hadn't moved. She should check his wounds, she knew. But the sun was gone and it was getting cold. She made certain Joel was warm, then built a small fire near where Caleb had collapsed. She would need the light to see.

Suddenly, furiously, she stamped the fire out. What was she thinking? The light, the scent could carry for miles. Besides, if there were bullets still in him, she could never get them out by firelight anyway. She would have to wait for the sun. Caleb would live through the night, or he wouldn't. It was out of her hands.

Settling a buffalo robe about her shoulders, she snuggled Walks With Pride close. She chewed on a little of the jerked meat Painted Sky had packed for her.

Caleb shifted, moaning feebly. His body twitched. He showed no signs of consciousness, but Jenna could tell he was shivering. She watched him for several minutes, wrapping her robe more tightly about herself and the baby. His shivering grew more violent, his breathing more ragged. The movement was aggravating his wounds.

Angrily Jenna climbed to her feet and tossed her robe on top of him. She retrieved a smaller pelt for the baby, but she had nothing but a threadbare blanket from Caleb's own bedroll for herself.

She shivered but stayed where she was.

She waited for the robe to warm Caleb. It didn't. He seemed to shiver even more violently as the night progressed and the temperature dropped. Resigned, Jenna crossed over to him and climbed beneath the robe. When he continued to tremble, she spooned herself in behind him, pressing her breasts against his back, allowing the heat from her own body to warm him.

She woke with a start in the middle of the night, wondering briefly if she'd heard the baby. But when she rose to check him, he was sleeping peacefully. Then she realized it was not noise that had awakened her, but silence.

Caleb's ragged breathing had ceased.

Not even thinking, she scrambled back over to him, throwing off the buffalo robe and pressing her palm to his chest. It was cold. She shook him. His head lolled to one side, but he made no sound. Desperate, she pressed her hand to the wound in his shoulder.

He gasped.

Jenna let out a shuddering sigh of relief. Then she got angry. "Damn you!" she gritted. "You're not going to make me care. You're not!" She tucked the robe around him once again, but did not lie down. Not caring how cold she got, she spent the rest of the night beside Walks With Pride.

She woke to the first rays of dawn. She rose quickly, quietly, not wanting to disturb the baby. She was out of excuses. It was time to check Caleb's wounds.

If possible, it was worse than she had thought. She peeled off his clothes, the cloth sticking where the blood had dried. She used some of their precious water supply to pry the fabric loose as best she could. He was drenched with sweat by the time she'd finished undressing him.

She checked the wound in his leg first. The bullet had gone through, but she could tell it was beginning to fester. The wound in his side was ugly, but it involved mostly flesh. That bullet too had gone through. The one in his shoulder was the deepest, the rawest. She didn't have to be a doctor to know the bullet was still in there. There was no exit wound. She would have to use her knife to get it out.

And she would have to have a fire.

Using dry tinder, she built a small, smokeless flame, then lay the knife blade across it. As the steel glowed hot, Jenna shuddered. What was she thinking? She didn't know anything about digging bullets out of bodies.

Caleb groaned, restless, stirring a little, as if he sensed what was coming. Jenna reached for the knife, then hesitated when she saw how badly her hand was shaking.

She touched Caleb's forehead. He was burning up.

His breathing grew more labored.

Damn, damn, damn. She didn't want his life in her hands. It wasn't fair. It wasn't right. Hadn't he caused her enough grief?

"What happened back there, Caleb?" she murmured. "What happened back there with Gravshaw and the others?"

His face contorted as a spasm of agony rocked him. She wouldn't have to probe for the bullet. He was going to die. Right here, right now. He had to die. No one could live with that much pain.

But he kept right on breathing.

She thought she heard him say her name, then decided she'd just imagined it as he seemed to sink further into unconsciousness once again. If she was going to get the bullet out, she had best get it out now.

She wedged a small stick between his teeth, just in case.

Gripping the knife by the hilt, she brought the reddened blade to his inflamed flesh. She touched the wound. He cried out, his body twisting instinctively away from this new agony. Jenna tried too late to hold him down with her other hand. The blade slashed an angry six-inch gash across his chest.

Jenna gasped, horrified. She dropped the knife, pressing her hand to her mouth, certain she was going to be sick. It took her several minutes to compose herself.

Then once again she picked up the knife, praying as she'd never prayed before. Taking a deep, steadying breath, she hovered over him, bringing the knife to his torn flesh. This time he didn't move.

Sweat broke out, glistening across his chest. Still, he didn't move. Despite her best efforts not to notice, she sensed the strain in him, the awful agony. She continued to pray.

From somewhere far away Caleb could feel this new invasion of his flesh. At first it meant nothing. Just more of the same. He'd been shot—he remembered that. Twice? Three times? Did it matter? The new pain intruded again. Deeper.

He was lying in a dark, dark place. And he was very cold. But he couldn't seem to move, to get away from either the darkness or the cold. Or the pain. And yet somehow he knew if he wished it, he could be free of it all. The choice was his.

He could go more deeply into the blackness, or he could go toward the light that shimmered far away. The deeper the blackness, the more vicious the pain. And yet he recognized, strangely, that the pain was life. And the light . . . the light was death. He could feel the choice, like a presence beside him.

With the pain came a voice. "Don't move." The voice repeated the command over and over. "Don't move."

But he wanted to move—he had to. He had to get away from the pain.

"Caleb, for God's sake, don't move."

Jenna's voice. Jenna. She was here.

In the light?

No. No. Jenna was at the edge of the darkness, the pain.

The light grew brighter, closer.

Not yet. Not yet.

I need to see my son. I need to tell Jenna I love her. Let me. Please let me . . .

"Don't move."

His brow furrowed. The pain increased.

He was going to be conscious. *Don't let me be conscious.*

His whole body began to shake. *Don't move.*

Fire. Fire in the light. Fire in his body. He was on fire. He had to put it out.

The command came again. "Don't move!"

Why? Why did she want him to lie still when he was on fire? Didn't she see the flames?

His breathing came in ragged gasps.

Hurry! His mind screamed it. *Jenna, hurry!*

A strangled sound, an inhuman sound born in the base of his throat tore through his clenched teeth. His whole body trembled, but still he did not move.

The bullet. She'd found the bullet. He sensed it, knew it. She was using the knife. The knife . . .

Sweet God, she was going to kill him!

She pulled the knife free as his body twisted violently, desperate to get away.

The darkness was back.

Gently, gently it bore him down into the abyss.

Jenna huddled beside Caleb, staring at the small misshapen chunk of lead that lay so innocuously in the center of her palm. She shuddered at the terrible power of it. The power to hurt, to maim, to kill. The bullet was still coated with Caleb's blood.

"It's done, Caleb," she said. "It's done. You can sleep now."

He didn't hear her, she knew. He was deeply unconscious again. But she felt better saying the words. Her feelings for this man were still conflicted, ambiguous, unsettled, but that didn't stop the awe she felt for what he had just done.

He had just done, not she. Somehow he had kept his

body still during the awful assault of the knife. If he hadn't, she shuddered to think what might have happened.

He looked so pale lying there, so helpless. In spite of herself, she reached for him, her hand tentative, uncertain—

The baby began to fuss. Jenna shook herself. There was no recapturing lost dreams. "In a minute, little one. In a minute."

She tore up one of two clean shirts she had plundered from the dead men, rolling the strips of fabric into crude but effective bandages. Quickly she bound up Caleb's shoulder, then tended his other two wounds as well.

When she'd finished, she saw to the baby, then went to check on the horses. She deliberately took her time walking back. She tidied up the camp and invented new ways to keep herself busy. Still, time and again, she found herself at Caleb's side. She couldn't seem to help herself. She would sit there for hours and just watch him breathe.

Somehow, she knew, he was aware of her being there. Somehow, she knew, it made a difference. The haggard lines of pain etched deep in those disturbingly handsome features seemed to ease just a little. The ragged breaths slowed, became more measured, even. She smoothed a damp cloth across his brow, squeezed water between his parched lips.

Toward dusk his gray eyes fluttered open, and it seemed for just an instant he recognized her. He smiled, a long-ago smile from a night on a creekbank when she had brazenly stolen his clothes. Then he drifted off to sleep again.

Unbidden tears trailed down her cheeks. Furious, Jenna wiped them away. This wasn't going to happen. She wasn't going to be lulled into feeling sorry for him.

She wasn't going to be lulled into feeling anything at all.

For the next three days she had no difficulty keeping that vow. Between attending to Caleb's almost constant needs and the needs of her two-month-old son, she was too exhausted to feel. Except at night, just before she would drift to sleep. Then the memories would come, the memories of the other Caleb, the one who had made such wondrous love to her. And the other Night Wind, the one who had been torn to the heart by her own cruel words: *These people are animals.*

Trust me, Jenna. I need you to trust me.

She had. One time too many.

Or maybe not enough.

She touched the amulet between her breasts. *It's the only thing I have that means anything to me.*

She buried her face in her hands and wept.

It was the fourth morning after she'd removed the bullet that she woke to find him watching her. For a minute she thought she was dreaming, and then when she realized she was not, she flung back the buffalo robe and scrambled to the other side of the cave. "Y-you were . . . uh," she stammered. "You were cold."

"Actually," he said, his words slow but blessedly coherent, "I was quite warm. Thank you."

"That isn't what I . . . that isn't . . ." Damn! "How long have you been awake?" She glanced at Joel, hoping for a distraction, but the baby was still contentedly asleep.

"Half hour maybe." Talking was an obvious effort.

Self-consciously she touched her hair. She knew it was a sight. She hadn't dared use any of their precious water supply for anything so frivolous as bathing. Then she was furious with herself for even thinking about her appearance. What did it matter what she looked like to this man?

"I . . . you've been sick. The bullet was . . . the bullet . . . I . . . we need . . . we need water." Blast! What was the matter with her? He was supposed to be the incoherent one!

She watched him struggle to sit up and fail, the effort leaving him sweating, exhausted. She stayed where she was.

"Describe where we are," he said, sinking back. "And I can tell you where to find water."

He gave her directions to a brackish pool that turned out to be about fifteen minutes away on horseback. The water tasted nasty, but it was wet. Jenna filled all her canteens and hurried back to the cave.

They said nothing to each other as she went about the routine she'd established of playing with Joel, feeding him, then preparing something for herself to eat.

Stiffly, perfunctorily she fed Caleb some of the broth she had made from a jackrabbit she'd managed to snare. Her hand shook every time she brought the spoon to his mouth. For his part, he remained silent, only watching her with a curious sadness in those gunmetal eyes.

The next day he was able to sit up for short periods of time. Jenna left him with the baby when she went to check on the horses. She returned to find Caleb holding Joel on his lap, his large hand trailing with obvious wonder over the tiny face of his child. Her heart twisted with a bittersweet joy, but she kept her features carefully indifferent as she approached him.

"You said you had given him a Comanche name," Caleb said. "I didn't give you a chance to tell me what it is."

Jenna knelt beside them, taking the baby's small hand in her own. She said the words in Comanche. "He is Walks With Pride in Two Worlds."

Caleb's eyes grew overbright. For a minute he couldn't speak. Then he managed a quiet "Thank you."

"I didn't do it for you," she lied, terrified of the sudden, aching longing she had to be in his arms. "I did it for him."

He nodded. "It's a good name."

Jenna busied herself tidying the camp. "You should probably sleep."

"I've slept enough to last me a year." He sighed. "I want to thank you for saving my life."

She straightened.

Caleb held up a hand. "I know. You didn't do it for me. You did for him." He nestled the baby in the crook of his good arm.

Jenna thought to deny what he said, but she didn't. It was the truth.

"You picked a good place to hide, Jenna."

"They must not be looking anymore, or they would have found us. I'm not that good a Comanche."

"I suppose they think that a white woman and a baby wouldn't last very long out here." Caleb gave her a wan smile. "They don't know you very well."

She ignored the compliment. "What will they think of Gravshaw and his friends not coming back?"

"They'll probably think I killed them."

"Why would they think that?"

"Because Iron Fist never did trust me to give you up."

"Why?"

His mouth tightened. "I can't imagine, can you?"

Her heart skipped a beat. "No. No, I can't." To cover the odd pain his words had caused she asked, "Why *did* you kill those men?"

Bitterness flared in those gray eyes. "I guess I had nothing else to do that day. You know how untrustworthy we 'breeds can be."

"Stop it! That's not fair. You threatened to take my baby, Caleb. Don't twist this back on me. If you really were just pretending, you could've given me some kind of sign, something."

"*If?*" The bitterness changed to ice.

"Yes, *if!*" she hissed. "Give yourself a little credit, Caleb. You are one hell of a liar!"

He lay the baby on the cradleboard beside him, his voice raw with anger. "If they'd suspected for one minute that I wasn't what I seemed to be, they would have killed me where I stood. And that, my dear wife, would have left you and Walks With Pride to their tender mercy."

"Don't you call me your wife! You rode out of my life for a year! A year! Whether you were playing *comanchero* or not, you had no right to do that to me." Her voice quivered, broke. "No right."

The fury went out of him. He sagged against the rock wall at his back. "There's nothing I can do to change what happened."

"You said the same thing about Bess dying."

He closed his eyes. "You were going to kill me, weren't you? When you found me out here?" It wasn't really a question.

She looked at the ground.

His voice achingly weary, he said, "I wish you had."

Tears blinding her, Jenna stormed from the cave. She had to get away, be alone. She ran to where the horses were tethered, sinking down in front of a massive boulder. She cried until she had no tears left.

Hours later when she returned, it was to find Caleb asleep, Joel still curled in the crook of his arm. She took the baby, hugging him close. "I was wrong, little one," she whispered. "You should know your father's name. His name is Caleb Harper. And his name is Restless as

Night Wind." She kissed his soft, chubby cheek. "And I was wrong about something else too. So very, very wrong. I don't hate your father." She glanced at the dozing Caleb. "I don't hate him at all."

24

It was another four days before Caleb had healed enough to sit a horse. During that time he and Jenna spoke to each other with a kind of stilted politeness that drove her mad. When she did try to start a more personal conversation with him, he would immediately beg off, using pain or fatigue as an excuse to feign sleep. Finally she gave up, hoping that if she allowed him the company of his own thoughts, perhaps he would be beset by some of the same images that haunted her—their first kiss, the night they'd first made love, the day he had made her his Comanche wife.

But he was still brooding and withdrawn the morning they headed out for Fort Bascom.

It took another six days of strained companionship to reach the fort. The sun was setting when they topped the rise that overlooked the rolling plain on which Bascom had been built. To ground her in her new surroundings, Caleb gave her a brusque geography lesson. The fort was bordered on the north by the Canadian River, to the west by Mesa Rica, and to the south and east by level plains, gentle hills, and rock-stewn cedar brakes. They had already crossed several small, mostly dry creekbeds to get this far.

Jenna reined her horse to a halt. Fort Bascom had, in a very real way, been her destination for over a year. Yet now that it was within reach she had to resist the urge to turn and ride as hard and fast as she could in the opposite direction.

Caleb halted his mount beside hers. "Do you need to feed the baby?"

"He's fine. He's sleeping."

"Then what is it?"

"Iron Fist told me the army wants to hang you."

"So I've heard."

"Then maybe you'd best not ride in with Joel and me."

"I'll be all right."

"More game-playing?"

"It's not a game, Jenna," he said evenly. "It's never been a game. I'm trying to stop a war. Iron Fist, Valdez, and whoever the hell pulls their strings are trying their damnedest to start one."

"Does Major Gallagher know that you . . . ?" She hesitated.

Caleb's mouth tightened. "Do you mean does he know whose side I'm really on?"

She felt her cheeks heat. "I didn't mean it that way."

"It doesn't matter. In any event, Keith and I need to talk. What better way than for him to arrest me?"

"You think that's what he'll do?"

"I would in his place."

"But what if . . . what if something goes wrong?"

"You mean what if they hang me?"

She swallowed hard.

He shrugged, wincing slightly from a twinge in his still-sore shoulder. "I don't think that'll happen."

"I won't let it happen!"

He gave her a curious look but said only, "We'd better go. We've already attracted the attention of the sentry."

Jenna nudged her mount into motion, but she made no pretense about being as cavalier as he seemed to be. At least, she reasoned a little desperately, if he were in the guardhouse, he wouldn't be able to ride out of her life, something he would otherwise have every opportunity to do. She wasn't ready for that to happen. Not yet. Not until they had settled some things between them.

The realization had been growing for days. It had started in the pain of believing that if not for Joel, she might have left Caleb to die. But gradually the truth won out. She could never have left him. Because she loved him. She had never stopped loving him. That was why his apparent betrayal had been so excruciatingly painful.

But she wasn't the naive young woman of twelve months ago. She knew love wasn't enough. The pain had run too long, too deep. Only time would tell how willing either of them would be to build a bridge to cross it.

She kept the dun close to the bay as they rode through the main gate of Fort Bascom. Evidently the fort's occupants weren't accustomed to too many visitors. Officers and enlisted men alike, along with a handful of women she guessed to be officers' wives, rushed out of various adobe buildings to watch their arrival. Jenna's tentative smile was quashed by the open hostility in many of their faces.

Even the look on Major Keith Gallagher's face was a less than welcome one. The officer was striding across the parade grounds, shouting orders as he went. His brown eyes were riveted on Caleb.

"Sergeant Gibson," Gallagher barked, "I want that man placed under arrest at once!"

A burly sergeant snapped off a quick salute. "Yes, sir." He drew his gun and leveled it at Caleb.

Caleb dismounted, offering no resistance, but that didn't stop the sergeant from giving him a violent shove. "Been after you for a long time, 'breed. We might hang you before nightfall on your reputation alone."

Jenna had been watching all of this with growing alarm. "Major Gallagher, please! Caleb is still recovering from serious wounds. Ask your sergeant to show a little human decency."

"Human decency?" Gibson snorted. "To this murderin' half-breed? About as likely as a snowball in—"

"Sergeant!" Gallagher cut in. "Escort the prisoner to the guardhouse. Now."

"Yes, sir."

Jenna watched as the sergeant continued to prod Caleb in the back with his pistol. She was glad for the distraction when a pleasant-looking, slightly plump young woman bustled up to her. "I'm Marian Gallagher, dear. The major's wife. You look positively exhausted. I insist you come with me at once. You'll stay in our quarters. We have a spare room for you and the baby."

"Thank you, I—"

"Whore!"

Jenna gasped, whirling to face the disapproving glare of a thin, pinch-faced woman dressed in blue calico. "What did you say?"

"Whore," the woman repeated, bold as you please. "Or maybe you prefer 'slut.' Or 'Injun lover.' Take your pick."

"That's enough, Nettie!" Marian Gallagher took Jenna's arm. "Come, dear. Pay no attention."

But it was hard not to pay attention as Marian led her across the parade grounds. Jenna didn't miss the eloquent shudders of disdain and disgust from the other women. Snippets of their conversations, deliberately loud enough for her to overhear, drifted toward her. "Squaw woman . . . slept with some Injun . . . Look at that little heathen she's carrying . . . Makes you sick, doesn't it . . . ?"

Jenna felt a flush of rage mingled with a fierce protectiveness. This was the kind of prejudice Caleb had endured all his life. It was the kind of cruelty her child would one day face.

She was glad when Marian led her into a one-story adobe structure set apart from the others. It was good to be out of the range of those horrid women. She found the Gallaghers' quarters to be surprisingly roomy as well as pleasantly furnished.

"You make yourself right at home, dear," Marian told her, "while I get us something to eat."

"Please don't go to any trouble."

"No trouble at all. Do you know how rare it is to get visitors?" She ducked into the kitchen, calling over her shoulder. "You'll find a crib in the spare room there on the left. I keep it around to give Keith inspiration."

Jenna smiled. She found herself liking Marian Gallagher very much. She settled the baby in the crib, giving him a gourd rattle to amuse himself, then found her way to the kitchen. "Can I help?"

"All done."

Jenna's eyes widened at the silver tray Marian was holding. It was brimming with tea and cakes. "I take my civilization where I can get it," the woman said. "Now, back to the sitting room."

Jenna took a seat on a worn, but finely made Queen

Anne's chair. She smiled gaily as Marian made a big fuss about serving her, insisting she take an ample supply of cakes.

"Heaven knows, I don't need to eat them all myself. Though Keith keeps telling me he likes a woman with some meat on her bones. I suppose that's why I always make double batches."

Marian then poured her own tea, but before she sat down she took a quick detour into the spare room. "I just wanted a peek at the baby," she gushed, coming back to join Jenna. "He's so precious. Handsome too. Like his papa."

Jenna bit her lip, wondering if she dared press this woman's kindness just a little further. She decided she had no choice. "Marian, just how much do you know about Caleb and me?"

Marian didn't hesitate. "Keith and I don't have any secrets, Jenna."

Jenna leaned forward. "Then you know Caleb is innocent."

"I know he's risking his life for very little personal gain."

Jenna was so grateful to discover Caleb had another champion that at first she didn't notice the shadow of concern that had come over Marian's features. When she did, she prompted gently, "What is it?"

"Nothing. Nothing really. Heavenly days, after what you've been through, you don't need to hear any of my petty little problems."

"Please tell me." She liked this woman. Maybe listening would help.

"Sometimes I worry about Keith. He's so fixated on getting his promotion. There are a lot of generals in my family, and he thinks . . ." Marian sighed. "He doesn't believe I love him just for who is he."

"I know what you mean," Jenna said softly. "I feel the same way about Caleb."

"Oh, listen to us, will you? You're here. You're safe. Everything will work out for the best. You'll see." Marian rose. "You go in and lie down. And while you're resting, I'm going to get your bath ready."

A brief nap and a steaming hot bath did wonders. Jenna felt better than she had in weeks. She also felt just a trifle strange wearing something other than her doeskin dress. She looked at her image in Marian Gallagher's mirror, hardly recognizing the sun-bronzed face that she saw there. The yellow taffeta dress she was wearing only accented the darkness of her skin. She was surprised at the garment's near perfect fit, until Marian explained it was her "wishful thinking" dress.

Jenna had just finished brushing out her hair when the post surgeon stopped by to examine her and Walks With Pride. He pronounced them both remarkably fit. He was going to leave, when Jenna asked him about Caleb.

"His body is mending," Dr. Virgil Anderson said, speaking over the wire-rimmed spectacles perched low on his nose. "You did a remarkable job caring for his wounds, Miss Riordan. I couldn't have done better myself. But . . ."

"But what?"

The physician took off his glasses, rubbing his nose where they'd left a red mark. "There are wounds of the body and wounds of the spirit. I've heard what they're saying around the post, but I first met Caleb Harper at Fort Union eight years ago. He's a man I'd ride the river with anytime. None of this *comanchero* business makes any sense to me. But then, I'm only a doctor, not a miracle worker." Anderson studied her with gentle brown eyes. "Where Caleb Harper is concerned, I think I'm looking at the miracle worker."

Jenna flushed. "I appreciate your concern, Doctor. Caleb and I do have a lot of things to talk about."

"Sometimes it isn't talking that helps. Sometimes it's listening."

Jenna nodded. "I'll remember that."

After the doctor had gone, Jenna decided it was time to see Caleb for herself, make certain he was all right. She hadn't forgotten Sergeant Gibson. Before she'd reached the door Keith Gallagher intercepted her.

He flashed her a winning smile. "I know you must be tired, Miss Riordan, but Marian and I would be honored to have your company for dinner."

"Thank you, but . . ."

"Please? We're having another guest who's most anxious to see you again."

Jenna frowned. She didn't know anyone else at the fort. Her hopes flared. "Caleb . . . ?" Had Keith manufactured some excuse to free him from the guardhouse?

Gallagher quickly shook his head. "I'm sorry. I didn't mean to give you that impression. This is a gentleman you might remember from Council Grove. A Mr. Elliot Langston."

Jenna did remember. "An Indian agent, I believe. He was very gracious to me over lunch." Jenna straightened suddenly. A lunch that had included the despicable Bart Jacobs. "I would be most interested in renewing my acquaintance with Mr. Langston," she said. "And, Major," she put her hand on Gallagher's sleeve, "I also need to talk to you privately about Caleb."

"Of course. I've been expecting that you would. Will tomorrow be all right?"

Jenna sighed. She supposed it would have to be.

Elliot Langston rose from his seat at the table the minute Keith escorted her into the room. "Miss Jenna, I was so delighted to hear you'd been rescued. I've only just arrived at the fort within the hour."

Jenna paused, momentarily taken aback. It was only then that she realized she didn't think of it as being rescued anymore. She felt a pang of loneliness and thought of Painted Sky, wondering what her dear friend might be doing at just this very minute. She had worried often that Painted Sky might have put her own life in danger by helping her escape. But then Jenna had to smile. Painted Sky would have gotten the better of Iron Fist. She always did.

Jenna's smile faded as she noticed Langston's own smile had become a brazenly intimate one. The man must have thought she was looking at him when she was thinking about Painted Sky! Of all the conceited— Jenna took her seat. "Are you still an Indian agent, Mr. Langston?" she asked evenly.

"Please, it's Elliot, remember? And I most certainly am, my dear. In fact, my job is more important than ever." He passed her a heaping bowl of mashed potatoes, somehow making that gesture irritatingly personal. "I can't tell you how sorry I am about your tragedy. Believe me, this country would be better off without the likes of that half-breed vermin over in the guardhouse."

"Caleb's Indian blood has nothing to do with this," Jenna said, setting the bowl down with a decided thump. "I would think you of all people would know that."

"I meant no disrespect to his bloodlines, Miss Jenna, I assure you. I meant only to refer to his criminal behavior."

"If you want to talk about vermin," she said bitterly, "then talk about Bart Jacobs. Weren't you a friend of his?"

Langston had the good grace to look affronted by

such a notion. "Actually, we were only marginally acquainted. But I understand he met a fitting end."

"Indeed he did, *Mr.* Langston." She rose. Gallagher and Langston did the same. "Excuse me. I suddenly have the most dreadful headache."

"Oh, you poor dear," Marian fussed. "You go in and lie down at once. And don't give little Joel another worry. I intend to entertain the little darling all night."

"Thank you, Marian. Thank you very much."

Jenna was only too glad to seek the refuge of her room. But not to stay. Quickly she crossed to the window. As quietly as she could she opened it, then climbed out and headed toward the guardhouse.

A towheaded corporal who couldn't have been more than nineteen was standing watch in front of the thick iron door. For once Jenna was glad men found her looks agreeable. A little harmless flirtation and the boy was only too eager to open Caleb's cell.

Jenna found Caleb lying on a pallet on the dirt floor. He rose to his feet, his movements stiff, pained. Though it was barely dusk, his features were in heavy shadow. The only light in the tiny, cramped room came through the twelve-inch-square barred window in one adobe wall.

"You didn't have to get up."

"What the hell are you doing here?"

She flinched. "I-I wanted to make sure you were all right. That bully of a sergeant had no right to—"

"I'm fine. This is no place for you. Please go."

"I didn't come here to upset you."

"Then why did you come?" He stood against the wall opposite her. It was the greatest distance he could put between them in the small room.

"I want . . . I need to know if things are all right between you and Major Gallagher."

"Keep your voice down!" he snapped.

"I-I'm sorry." She took a deep breath, feeling herself on the verge of tears.

Caleb blew out a long breath. "I didn't mean to bite your head off. I don't much like being in this damned cage." He raked a hand through his shoulder-length dark hair. "I'm not the only one getting rough treatment around here. I have a pretty fair idea what you've been going through."

"Don't think about it. The Gallaghers have been wonderful."

"I'm not talking about the Gallaghers, and you know it." He crossed the room, stopping just inches away from her. It was all she could do not to touch him. For just an instant she could have sworn he was resisting a similar impulse of his own. Even in the shadows his breathing seemed deep, aroused.

Jenna's pulses raced. *Kiss me, Caleb,* her mind pleaded. *Kiss me and everything will be all right again. Just kiss me.* But she said none of this out loud, and the next minute whatever spell it was that had bound them up was gone.

He began to pace. "I've been doing some thinking." His voice seemed strained, maddeningly distant. "I don't want you to have to put up with the kind of vicious gossip I know people are capable of. I don't want Walks With Pride to go through what I've been through."

She waited, not certain where he was leading.

"I want you to know that you're welcome to my protection."

"Protection?"

"It might help to give the child a name, a white name." His face was grim. "You could marry me."

"Marry you?"

"Under the white man's law."

Jenna's heart raced madly. She was overjoyed and

terrified all at the same time. They still had so much that needed to be said. But if he loved her, maybe they really did have a chance. His next words dashed her budding hope.

"This would all be for the baby's sake, of course."

"Of course," she echoed numbly. He didn't love her. He just wanted to do the honorable thing—for Joel's sake. Well, she had a little pride left. "I'm sorry, Caleb, I can't marry you."

He nodded. "I understand."

No, Jenna thought bleakly, *you don't. You don't understand at all.* But she couldn't say the words, couldn't explain. There had been too much heartbreak already, for both of them. Perhaps this was for the best.

"Good-bye, Caleb."

He did not look up, so she could not see what was in his eyes as she silently let herself out of his cell.

Jenna woke to the sound of Caleb's voice. *All I can ask is that you trust me. Just trust me. Can you do that?*

"Yes," she said the word aloud, even as she realized that his voice had been a dream and that she had been asleep. Caleb was not there.

With a sigh she rose from her bed and padded across the plank floor of the spare room in Major Gallagher's quarters. It had been so real, so real. She opened the window. The night air drifted in cool, almost cold. Familiar scents teased her nostrils—woodsmoke, leather, sage, and horses. Scents that reminded her all too intimately of Caleb.

She peered behind her through the shadows toward the baby's cradle, resisting the urge to pick Joel up, hold him, knowing if she did so she would start crying again.

The pain twisted, deep and hard. How could a marriage proposal from Caleb hurt so much?

Maybe she should have said yes. At least then she would have him. She shook her head, hugging her arms tight against her. She would have him fully, completely. His love. His trust. Or she wouldn't have him at all.

Her quiet good-bye had been exactly that. He didn't love her. There was no point in tormenting either one of them with lost dreams, lost hope. But as she stared into the moonless night she couldn't help but worry about him; she couldn't help but love him.

How much longer would he be in that awful guardhouse? How much longer would he have to bear the brunt of the army's investigation of Valdez and his *comanchero* cohorts? No matter how Caleb might reassure her, there was no way for him to be certain how they would react to his having killed Gravshaw and the others. To take such a chance was all but suicidal. And yet she knew Caleb would take that chance, take any chance, to prevent more bloodshed between whites and Comanche.

She stood there in the night chill and felt her palms begin to sweat. The more she thought about the danger Caleb was in, the more panicked she became. She checked the clock on her dressing table. It was well past midnight. But she suddenly didn't care. She had to talk to Major Gallagher.

She crept out of her room, wondering how best to wake him. She was surprised to find him in the sitting room, talking to Langston.

Jenna wasted no time. "Forgive me, Major. I must speak to you."

Langston looked up at her, his hazel eyes narrowing with a lazy intimacy that in one night had become supremely annoying. Jenna unconsciously gripped Marian's nightgown tighter around her. The cotton gown was quite voluminous, and though comfortable for sleep, Jenna realized belatedly it was not something she should be wearing in mixed company. Her lips thinned with determination. It was too late for modesty now.

"Just what exactly is so urgent, Miss Riordan?" Keith asked, his voice straining to hide the irritation he felt. "Mr. Langston and I have serious business to discuss."

"I would think the well-being of your friends would be considered urgent, Major. Caleb is your friend, isn't he?" Distastefully she recalled Gallagher's half-breed epithet back in Eagle Dancer's village. She suddenly had to assure herself the comment had been part of the charade.

"As a matter of fact, Caleb is my best friend," Keith said, some of the irritation seeming to leave his voice. Perhaps he was as edgy about the danger Caleb was in as she was.

"Then you must be very worried about all the trouble he's in." She glanced meaningfully at Langston.

"It's all right," Keith assured her. "Mr. Langston is my liaison to Washington. I've just been filling him in."

"You told him about Caleb?" Jenna was not at all sure that was a wise idea, but she could hardly criticize him for it in front of Langston.

As for Langston, the Indian agent was looking highly impressed by what he'd been hearing. "Harper's working for the army from within the *comancheros* is ingenious, Major. But tell me, how is your plan going to proceed from the guardhouse?"

"With an escape, of course."

Jenna stepped close to Gallagher. "When? When is he going to escape? And how do you know the sentry won't shoot him?"

A sudden impatience colored Gallagher's handsome face. He reached into his pocket, pulling out his watch. "It really is quite late, Miss Riordan. I think you should—"

Jenna was no longer listening. She stared at the ex-

quisitely detailed watch, feeling for all the world as
though the air were being squeezed from her lungs.
*The man in the mask . . . has your father's watch,
Jenna. I want it back.* The man in the mask . . .

Her fingers curled around the terrifyingly familiar
casing. "Where did you get this?" She took a step back
from the strange light in Keith Gallagher's eyes.

Caleb paced the confines of his cell like a caged wolf.
It had been a helluva night. First, Jenna. God, he
couldn't even think about Jenna. And then, five minutes after she'd gone, Keith had come waltzing in to
announce plans of Caleb's imminent escape.

"Why so soon?" Caleb had gritted. "I don't like admitting this, but I'm not exactly a hundred percent.
Three bullet holes can do that to a man."

"It can't be helped. We have to move on this now."

"Why? You have some new information?"

Keith nodded. "You remember that abandoned hacienda about ten miles from here?"

"The one back in the hills?" Legend had it the place
had been built nearly two hundred years earlier by a
Spanish nobleman who believed Spain would one day
reclaim the New World.

"Well, it's not abandoned anymore. A couple of pa-
trols have reported recent activity out there."

"So? Some settler maybe."

"No." Keith's voice rose with excitement. "That's
what it's supposed to look like. But what's really happening is that *comancheros* are using it for a headquar-
ters."

"Ten miles from this fort? That's ridiculous! Where
did you hear of anything so idiotic?"

Keith flushed. "From Elliot Langston. And you'd best
believe it too, old friend. Because it's the truth."

"Who the hell is Elliot Langston?"

"You'll meet him later."

Caleb studied Gallagher with a sudden cold suspicion. "Dammit, Keith, what did I tell you about letting anyone else know what we're up to?"

"He doesn't know your role in this, I swear. In fact, he thinks I'm quite clever. I'm going to let you escape, then double-cross you and follow you to your cutthroat friends."

"How does he know about this hacienda?"

"He's territorial Indian agent. He's gotten word from some Comanche bucks he slips whiskey to that there's been a lot of odd activity out that way. For example, Iron Fist has been seen going in and out of the place. Don't you see? It has to be where they're getting their orders. Our friend in the mask may even be there."

Caleb hunkered down. He raised the cuff of his right pant leg, securing the sheathed knife Keith had brought him to his ankle. "They may not welcome me with open arms, you know. I killed Gravshaw."

"Blame it on lust. They'll understand. In fact, they may approve."

"Careful, Keith," Caleb warned.

"I didn't mean any offense. Jenna Riordan is a very special woman. She has to be, to survive what she did. And I'm sure the two of you will get everything ironed out. But you can't think about that now. We're so close to the end of all this, Caleb. So close. I can feel it."

"Close to your promotion?" Caleb suddenly wasn't liking the desperate enthusiasm in his friend's voice. He had an unpleasant premonition that Keith Gallagher wasn't telling him everything.

Keith's hackles rose. "I thought we'd been through all that."

"Have we?"

"It's all arranged. You tell Valdez and his *patron* about a new shipment of Spencers expected day after tomorrow. To the *comancheros* it'll look like the wagons are being driven by freighters, but those freighters will be my soldiers. We'll have them, Caleb. We'll have them all."

Caleb wished he believed that. But the odd foreboding he'd felt earlier was getting stronger. He said nothing of it though as Keith left.

That had been four hours ago.

Fours hours of waiting for the bolt of his cell to be drawn back. Worse, he thought grimly, four hours of trying not to think about Jenna.

He'd handled his proposal all wrong. He knew it the minute the words were out of his mouth. But he couldn't call them back. And somehow he couldn't force himself to amend them either. His pride had suddenly gotten in the way. He'd remembered too vividly the brittle rejection of Laurel McKenzie.

Not that he expected bigotry from Jenna. He didn't. But neither could he guess what her response might be. To tell her the truth, to tell her how desperately he loved her had become too much of a risk to take. Better to be turned down for what amounted to a business arrangement than to link his proposal to where it really belonged—his heart.

The finality of the way she'd said good-bye still echoed with agonizing clarity. But he told himself she would be better off. He would see to it she had money, of course. He would provide what he could for his son. But he would not be part of either of their lives.

To see Jenna and not have her was simply too painful to bear.

He started pacing again. He had to stop thinking about—

The bolt of the cell rasped against its hinge. Caleb moved stealthily to the deepest shadows of the small room.

The door creaked open ever so slightly, but no one entered the room. Caleb felt the hair on the back of his neck rise. Something wasn't right about this. Keith should have looked in, given him the all-clear. With the wariness of a stalking panther Caleb padded to the cell door.

He peered through the narrow slit made by the barely open portal. Nothing moved. In fact, the night seemed too still, with an almost palpable menace to the silence. What the hell was going on? Was this some kind of trap? By Keith? It didn't make any sense.

Caleb pulled the knife from the sheath at his ankle and nudged open the door a little farther. He straightened. On the ground, four feet away from where he stood, lay the lifeless body of the young guard. His throat had been slashed.

A knife wound. Caleb knew instantly who would be blamed.

He stepped out into the darkness and sensed rather than heard a *whoosh* behind him. A hand slashing downward with a knife.

Caleb whirled, bringing his hand up, catching the arm of his attacker and stopping the deadly plunge of the blade.

Valdez.

"I forgot, your Comanche blood gives you eyes in the back of your head, Night Wind. But no matter. It will still be my pleasure to kill you."

"I don't think so," Caleb said, his voice whisper-soft, deadly. "The pleasure is going to be mine."

The two men circled each other, feinting, slashing like mountain cats. Caleb wanted nothing more than to make Valdez's death long and painful. But he didn't dare. They could not battle for long undetected.

Besides, Caleb had to get away, find Gallagher. The

major had some serious explaining to do. At the point of a gun, Caleb thought fiercely.

"Halt!" came a shout from across the parade grounds. "Who goes there?" A bullet zinged through the night.

Instinctively Caleb ducked. The movement saved his life. Valdez's blade ripped the air just where Caleb's throat had been. The lunge drove the outlaw off-balance. In a heartbeat Caleb brought his own knife arcing upward, burying it to the hilt in the gut of the *comanchero*.

Valdez let loose a string of obscenities, but Caleb was already gone. Valdez roared like a maddened beast. For his trouble he got two bullets in the chest from an advancing soldier. He dropped like a poleaxed steer, dead.

Caleb had not stopped moving. He kept to the shadows behind the adobe buildings. He should leave the fort, he knew. Instead he made his way to Gallagher's. He intended to find out what the hell had gone wrong.

"Sound the alarm!" came a shout from back near the guardhouse. "That damned half-breed has escaped! And he killed Wilson!" More soldiers poured out of the barracks. "Shoot Harper on sight!"

Jenna struggled against the ropes binding her wrists, barely able to think past the terror that pulsed through her. She cast a fearful glance around the finely appointed master bedroom of a Spanish-style ranch house. She hadn't known evil could have such exquisite taste.

Across the room, scorning a dainty French provincial chair to his left, sitting cross-legged on the floor was Iron Fist, his scarred face revealing nothing of what he might be thinking. Jenna's heart thundered. "Iron Fist, please," she said, speaking in Comanche, "you can't be party to this. Your father . . . your father would be ashamed. He was a man who wanted peace for his people."

Iron Fist didn't even blink.

Jenna forced herself to take deep gulps of air. She had to calm herself, had to make herself think clearly. If she didn't, she would die here tonight. She knew that as she had never known anything else.

Thoughts of her death sent her mind careening to her son back at the fort. Her baby would have no mother.

She swallowed grief-choked tears. He might already have no father.

God in heaven, why had she said anything about that damned watch? The instant she'd seen it, she had realized its deadly significance. Why then had she been fool enough to let on that she knew?

She could still remember the look in Keith Gallagher's eyes. Flustered, confused, taken aback, he had stammered something, and then Elliot Langston—

Jenna stared at the crumpled form to her left. Keith hadn't moved since Iron Fist had dragged him in here. Not that he could. He was bound hand and foot, just as she was.

Wake up, her mind pleaded. *Wake up.* They would have a better chance to get out of this together.

The unconscious figure moaned, stirred.

"Are you all right?" Jenna whispered, casting a wary look at Iron Fist. He made no move to interfere.

Keith groaned again, pushing awkwardly to a sitting position. "What happened?"

"Don't you remember?" Jenna asked.

"The watch." He winced, obviously suffering from the huge welt on the side of his head. "After that . . ."

"After that . . ." came a malevolent chuckle, "you made the mistake of mentioning who had given you that watch . . . Major Gallagher."

Jenna glared at Elliot Langston as the bastard rose from the brocaded chair that fronted a stylish dressing table. "A most generous gift too, don't you think? But, as it turned out, a rather foolish one."

Langston's studied veneer of civility was gone. In its place was the face of a man more monstrous than Iron Fist could ever have been. Because Elliot Langston was a chameleon, capable of mimicking whatever emotions might be called for in a particular situation, but capable of feeling none of them. All that mattered to Elliot Langston was what he wanted, when he wanted it.

Faster than Keith had been able to react, Langston had drawn a hidden derringer from his vest pocket. He had held Keith and Jenna at bay, then gone to the door of Keith's quarters. He'd opened it and allowed a waiting Enrique Valdez to come inside.

"You know what to do about Harper," Langston had said.

"I do, *el jefe*. With pleasure."

It had been all Jenna could do not to scream. But Langston made it clear that to do so would cost her son his life. "Keep your mouth shut, and your heathen brat can stay here. Open it, and I'll bring him along. You won't like what I do to him. Understand?"

Jenna could only nod. She was too terrified to speak.

"All right, we're going out the back. And we're all going to be very quiet."

"You'll never make it, Langston," Gallagher said. "I might have been fool enough to fall for your act. But this . . . you'll never get away with this."

"On the contrary, I've been getting away with quite a bit for over a year now."

"Please, Elliot," Jenna put in fearfully. "I . . . it's cold. May I get my clothes?" She was still wearing Marian's nightdress.

He acquiesced with a leer. Jenna forced herself to

ignore his watchful gaze as she pulled on her yellow
dress. Her modesty didn't matter nearly as much as the
one desperate chance Langston had unwittingly given
her. As she passed Joel's crib she slipped her father's
watch under the baby's blanket.

She nearly collapsed with relief when Langston
failed to notice. The Indian agent then ushered them
out into the night. They'd ridden to the hacienda. Keith
made a lunge for Langston's gun. It earned him a blow
to the head.

Jenna cast a contemptuous glance around the room.
"This is all bought and paid for with your blood money,
isn't it?"

"Quite tasteful, don't you think? Quite lovely. Like
you, Miss Riordan."

Jenna shivered. "Why?"

"For money, of course. And power. You see, the Indians really are like children. I shall point them toward
war, and they will think it's all their own idea." He gave
a self-satisfied smirk. "Ultimately the whites will win, of
course. And I'll make even more money from all the
new settlers. Jacobs was right: The Indian really is an
inferior species."

Jenna stared at Iron Fist. How could he work for this
man?

Langston went on gloating. "Tonight actually turned
out rather well, all in all. I didn't like having to alter my
plans at the last minute. Too many things can go wrong
when one does that. But now . . ." He smiled, rubbing
his derringer along his jaw.

"Now instead of having Mr. Harper kill you, Major
Gallagher, Iron Fist will kill you both. Mr. Harper will,
of course, get the blame."

He looked toward the door. "Valdez should be here
any moment with Harper, or with his body. I wasn't
very specific. Sometimes I like to give my hirelings a

little latitude. But just a little. Bart Jacobs should have remembered that."

"You're despicable," Jenna hissed.

"You wound me, Miss Riordan. And after all the trouble I've gone through for you. But that was my fault, I suppose. I did allow my baser instincts to get the better of me. Most uncharacteristic. But when I saw you in Council Grove, I knew I had to have you. I pretended to offer Harper a trade, because I needed him to find you. I didn't know Iron Fist had helped himself. And then Iron Fist threw Comanche law at me. I couldn't get you back because it seems you were actually fornicating with his half-breed brother.

"But no more. No more." He smiled, a chilling smile that didn't reach his eyes. "If either of you doesn't believe in hell, I promise you, you will before the night is over."

Caleb leaned against the adobe walls of the hacienda and tried to regain a small measure of his waning strength. He couldn't be certain, but he thought the wound in his shoulder had broken open. It was either blood or sweat trailing down the inside of his shirt. Right now he didn't much give a damn which.

He flexed his fingers around the walnut grip of his Colt and edged along the outer wall, listening. Jenna was in there with a madman. He would have to be careful; he would have to be very careful.

He had cased the perimeter of the house and knew exactly where each of three guards was posted. He was, in fact, surprised to find only the three. Langston was an arrogant ass, on top of everything else. Caleb supposed the bastard had sent most of his men off after the new shipment of Spencers that Keith had so obligingly told him about.

"Dammit, Keith, how could you trust a snake?" he

muttered aloud, then grimaced. Maybe it was more a question of balance. Caleb didn't trust enough. Keith trusted too much.

He reholstered the Colt and pulled out his knife. It was time to take out the guards. Calling on every instinct he had as a Comanche, he made his way toward the first of the three sentries. The man was sitting on a stone fence, smoking a cigar. It would be his last.

Swiftly, stealthily, Caleb dispatched the other two guards in turn, then made his way to the back door of the house. He listened for a long minute but heard nothing on the other side. Cautiously he lifted the latch. It was unbolted.

Inside, he found himself in a huge kitchen, a myriad of aromas assailing his nostrils. His nerves on edge, the smell of so much food was almost nauseating. Quickly he made his way out of the kitchen and into a long, dark hallway.

As he moved he thought back to what had happened earlier that night when he'd escaped Valdez and made it to Gallagher's quarters. A very bad feeling had suddenly become infinitely worse. Jenna was missing. His heart in his throat, he had gone to Keith's room and discovered that he too was nowhere to be found.

He stalked across the Gallaghers' bedroom and put his hand over the sleeping Marian Gallagher's mouth. The daughter of a general opened her eyes, startled but unafraid.

"What the hell is going on, Marian?" Caleb demanded. "Where are Keith and Jenna?"

Marian climbed out of bed and pulled on her wrapper. "They were both here, I promise you. Keith was talking to that nice Mr. Langston. And speaking of what the hell is going on—how did you get out of the guardhouse?"

A trooper's thunderous banging on the front door was all the answer Marian needed.

"Tell him Keith is already searching the compound for me."

"I'll do it, but only because I know you're doing what's right to help Jenna."

Satisfied with whatever Marian told him, the trooper had gone on his way.

Caleb didn't let Marian off the hook. "You know Keith better than anyone. How far would he go to be a general?"

She jutted her chin defiantly. "I'll tell you this: He wouldn't do anything illegal. Ever."

Joel awoke and began to cry. Marian hurried in to gather him up. "Poor baby, he—"

That was when Marian had found the watch.

"Mr. Langston gave that to Keith."

His stomach churning, Caleb told Marian the significance of the watch. "I'm going to need your help. I can't show my face out there. They'd blow it off before I got two words out. You're going to have to convince them what has to be done. Understand? Just make sure when they follow after me to that hacienda, they come in quiet. Jenna's life and Keith's depend on that."

If they weren't dead already.

But he wasn't going to think that way.

Somehow he got off the fort without being spotted. He knew Marian would convince the troops. He just didn't know how long it would take her. He didn't dare wait.

Caleb hunched low, making his way toward the room at the end of the darkened hallway in Langston's sumptuous hideaway. In his hand he once again gripped his Colt.

"Someone comes!" Iron Fist shouted from within the closed room.

Caleb drove his shoulder at the closed door, sending it slamming back against the interior wall. He instantly memorized the room's every feature, even as he rolled back into the hallway. His shoulder was on fire from the jolt it had taken, but he ignored it.

"Throw down your gun, Langston!" Caleb shouted. "And maybe I'll let you live."

"Kill him!" Langston yelled to Iron Fist. "It's what I pay you for! Kill him now!"

Iron Fist fired two shots down the hallway. "Not see. Can't hit."

"I'll kill the woman, Harper!" Langston shrilled. "I've got a gun to her head. I'll kill her, I swear."

Caleb crawled on his belly toward the door. "Anything happens to her," he said in cold, measured tones, "I can make you one promise: It'll be the Comanche in me killing you, not the white man."

Langston fired one shot at the doorway, splintering wood but nothing else.

"It's a two-shot derringer, Caleb!" Keith shouted. "Watch—"

The small gun popped again. Keith's words were abruptly cut off.

"That was stupid, Langston," Caleb said, climbing to his feet and walking to the doorway.

"Iron Fist!" Langston shrieked. "Now! Now!"

The Comanche leveled his gun.

And shot Elliot Langston in the head.

Caleb rushed to Jenna, catching her up as she started to fall, Langston's body crumpling behind her. Quickly he cut her free of the ropes. Her arms went around his neck. "I was so afraid. I was so afraid he would kill you."

"Hush now, it's all right. Everything's all right." His own voice was tight with emotion.

"Keith—" Jenna said.

The major was struggling to sit up. Caleb made short

work of his ropes as well. "Lousy shot, I'll say that for him." He was holding his hand tight against his upper left arm. "Just a scratch."

Caleb grimaced.

"I always wanted to say that." Keith grinned, a smile more of relief than joy.

Jenna was looking at Iron Fist. "Thank you."

"You took a great chance, Night Wind," the gauntleted Indian said, speaking in Comanche. "You knew I still had my gun."

"And I knew my father's son would not kill me."

"Once I might have, but no more."

It was as close to a confirmation as Caleb would ever get that it was Iron Fist who had shot him in the back the year before.

"Iron Fist lead the People now," the Comanche warrior went on. "Maybe learn to talk with white man. Maybe not." There was no affection in his black eyes, but there might have been just a little grudging respect.

The sound of thundering hooves pounded outside in the yard. Caleb cursed. So much for the silent approach.

"You'd better go, Iron Fist," Caleb said.

The Comanche nodded and was gone.

Sergeant Gibson came blustering in, gun at the ready. He looked supremely disappointed when he found no one to shoot. And then he spied Caleb. "I tried to tell Mrs. Gallagher. I ain't trustin' no 'breed."

Keith lurched past Caleb and slammed a fist into the sergeant's jaw. "Slipped!" He shrugged sheepishly, looking from Caleb to Jenna. "Have to watch my step."

But Jenna felt Caleb stiffen. It would always be this way. There would always be Sergeant Gibsons.

"You need to come home to your wife, to your son," she said softly. "We need to talk."

Just as softly he broke her heart. "I have no home, Jenna."

26

In the days that followed, Caleb remained at the fort but kept to himself, even as he busily dispatched messages to try and locate Jenna's uncle in California. He was just as determined to discover Timmy's whereabouts, telling Jenna through Marian that he was certain something could be arranged with Two Trees. In other words, Jenna realized miserably, he was doing everything he could to bring the pieces of her life together, so that he no longer had to be part of that life.

For two weeks Jenna allowed him his distance, his isolation. Tonight, with Marian's help, she would endure it no longer. Pacing back and forth across the Gallaghers' sitting room, Jenna awaited his arrival. Marian had extended him yet another invitation to supper. He had declined all previous offers, but tonight he had said yes. Jenna was beside herself with anticipation and a wild nervousness she was having no success subduing.

For the fifth time in as many minutes Jenna turned to Marian. "Do you really think he'll come?"

Marian gave an exasperated sigh, but her eyes were kind. "He will. I promise you, he will."

"You didn't tell him I was going to be somewhere else, did you?"

"Of course not. Why ever would I do that?"

"Then someone's probably on the way over with his regrets."

Keith stepped out of the kitchen, where he'd been less than surreptitiously sampling Marian's simmering chicken 'n' dumplings. He crossed to Jenna and gave her a reassuring, albeit awkward, pat on the shoulder. "He'll be here. You'll see."

"The man has avoided me for two weeks—why should tonight be any different?"

Keith looked at the floor, his expression suddenly guilty.

"What is it?" Jenna asked.

Keith sighed. "He heard from your uncle today."

Jenna gasped. "Did he tell you what Uncle William said? Is Caleb sending Joel and me away? Is he?"

"Don't borrow trouble," Marian said, sending her husband a censuring look. "Wait until Caleb gets here."

A soft knock sounded on the door. Jenna's heart leapt into her throat, her hand flying to her hair. "Oh, dear. Do I look all right?"

"You look wonderful," Marian assured her. "If I could be a color, it would be green. With envy."

Marian had helped Jenna arrange her hair in soft, silken waves that cascaded nearly to her waist. The blue taffeta dress she was wearing accented her figure to perfection. She had spent much of the last two weeks sewing it herself. The blue of the dress exactly matched the blue of her eyes.

Jenna drew in a deep, calming breath as Keith opened the door.

Caleb stepped into the room, holding his black Stetson by the brim. He was dressed in a newly acquired buckskin jacket and dark trousers, looking almost exactly as he had the first day she had seen him in Council Grove more than a year earlier. Except for the haunted look that seemed never to leave his gray eyes.

He was steadily regaining his health; her glimpses of him from across the parade grounds told her that he was getting stronger every day. Still, she had been grateful he hadn't been foolhardy enough to go along on the ambush Keith had mustered together hours after the confrontation with Langston. Instead of the *comancheros* surprising the freight wagons, a company of soldiers had surprised the *comancheros*. The battle had been a rout, with most of the *comancheros* captured or killed. With Langston dead, the rest had scattered.

Neither Caleb nor Keith was foolish enough to think that would end gunrunning in the territory, but at least a major source of it had been destroyed.

"Have you heard back on your promotion, Keith?" Jenna asked to break a silence that had grown awkward.

"Sure have," Keith said, grinning. "No promotion for this major. I guess I'm going to be staying on at Fort Bascom. At least for the time being."

"After all you've done!" Jenna said. "It isn't fair—you deserve that promotion!"

Keith shrugged, his grin suddenly sheepish. "Actually I got it. I turned it down."

Marian slipped her arm around her husband's waist. "I'm so proud of him."

"Congratulations, Keith," Caleb said, extending his hand.

Keith shook it. "Got a scouting job that needs filling. You interested?"

Caleb cast a sidelong glance at Jenna, his gaze revealing nothing. "I'll let you know."

Jenna heard the rustle of linen in the next room and went over to peek in on Joel. He was awake, happily kicking in his crib. She brought him out to Caleb, hoping the child could break through some of the awkwardness between them. "Would you like to hold your son?"

Caleb accepted the baby, his eyes filling with such an aching tenderness that Jenna's own eyes burned. She blinked away the tears, saying too quickly, "I understand you've heard from Uncle William."

Caleb shot a mildly annoyed look at Keith, who shrugged helplessly. "Your uncle will be in Sacramento until year's end. I'll go after Timmy, then take you, Timmy, and the baby out to meet him."

"You? You would take us?" Jenna felt suddenly hopeful.

"I wouldn't stay, Jenna."

Abruptly he handed the baby back to her, his face filled with regret, loss. "I, uh, I don't have much appetite tonight," he said. "I'm sorry." He settled the Stetson on his head and was gone.

Jenna started after him.

Keith stepped into her path. "He needs to be alone."

"No, he doesn't," she said flatly. "He's already had far too much time alone in his life. That's the problem." She turned to Marian. "May I ask you to watch Joel for me for a while?"

"Of course, dear. Take all the time you need."

"Thank you."

Jenna didn't bother to saddle the gelding she borrowed from the stables. She just caught up a handful of mane and pulled herself onto its back. The wind felt good against her face as she rode toward the trees that lined the Canadian River. Caleb had been spending every night here alone.

The river, despite its more prestigious name, was

hardly more of watercourse than the creek beside which she and Caleb had first made love. Jenna was counting on the resemblance working in her favor.

She found him beneath a giant cottonwood, his thumbs hooked in the waistband of his trousers. His shirt was open. Wisping strands of his long hair were being teased by a stray breeze to trail across his stunningly handsome face. Jenna felt her blood grow hot just to look at him. It had been so long, so long . . .

She walked up to him, knelt beside him in the grass. "We seem to make our best memories beneath cottonwood trees," she murmured.

"Go back to the fort." He didn't open his eyes.

She smiled. He was no longer so skilled at masking his feelings. She could almost feel the rhythm of his heart beat faster. "Walks With Pride needs his father in his life."

"Walks With Pride is three months old. He'll never remember me. And he'll be the better for it."

She trailed her fingertips across his chest, careful to avoid the nearly healed wound that had almost cost him his life. Her smile broadened when his muscles jumped, his body stiffening with suppressed pleasure. "How can you say that? Would your life have been better if you'd never known Eagle Dancer?" She paused, then added, "I know mine would not have been."

His gray eyes flicked open, searching her face, but she wasn't certain what he hoped to find there. "It'll be easier for him to live in the white world without a halfbreed for a father."

He wasn't going to make this easy. He wasn't going to make this easy at all. "Walks With Pride will know his heritage. All parts of it. He will live an honorable life. That is the best revenge against bigoted fools."

She could feel the tension in him, not anger but desperation. "Go back to the fort, Jenna. Please. You said good-bye to me that night in the guardhouse, remember?"

"And it nearly broke my heart."

"It won't work, Jenna. It can't."

"It won't work only if we don't make it work. Look how much we've overcome already. Caleb, nothing can defeat the love we have for each other. Except you. If you let me go, the bigots win. Don't you see that?" She eased her body down beside his, running her fingers over his flat belly.

He sucked in his breath, arching his head back. "Don't."

"I have to. I love you."

"Jenna, please . . . there's so much that's happened between us. So much pain. Your sister is dead because of me."

"No. No, I was wrong to blame you. Don't you see?" She caressed the strong line of his jaw. "I can blame myself too. What if I'd never taken Bess out of Virginia? Life is choices, Caleb. Bess made the choice to come West as much as I did. None of us can see what's on the other side of our choices. Heaven knows, if we could, none of us would ever come out of the womb." She kissed him on the mouth. "But I know one choice I would never take back."

"What's that?" He groaned.

"Loving you."

He pulled her close, returning her kiss, his hands roving over the beloved curves of her body. He felt himself grow hard, tried to fight it. He couldn't let this happen. For her sake. He couldn't. But he was losing a battle he had already fought far too long.

"Make love with me, Caleb. Make love with me, Night Wind. I love you both so much. So much."

He sighed her name, surrendering, the battle lost.

Reckless abandon. Intrigue. And spirited love. A magnificent array of tempestuous, passionate historical romances to capture your heart.

Virginia Henley

☐ 17161-X	The Raven and the Rose	$4.99
☐ 20144-6	The Hawk and the Dove	$4.99
☐ 20429-1	The Falcon and the Flower	$4.99

Joanne Redd

☐ 20825-4	Steal The Flame	$4.50
☐ 18982-9	To Love an Eagle	$4.50
☐ 20114-4	Chasing a Dream	$4.50
☐ 20224-8	Desert Bride	$3.95

Lori Copeland

☐ 10374-6	Avenging Angel	$4.50
☐ 20134-9	Passion's Captive	$4.50
☐ 20325-2	Sweet Talkin' Stranger	$4.99
☐ 20842-4	Sweet Hannah Rose	$4.95

Elaine Coffman

☐ 20529-8	Escape Not My Love	$4.99
☐ 20262-0	If My Love Could Hold You	$4.99
☐ 20198-5	My Enemy, My Love	$4.99

Outstanding historical romances by bestselling author

HEATHER GRAHAM

The American Woman Series

- ☐ **SWEET SAVAGE EDEN**   20235-3 $3.95
- ☐ **PIRATE'S PLEASURE**   20236-1 $3.95
- ☐ **LOVE NOT A REBEL**   20237-X $4.50

Other Titles You Will Enjoy

- ☐ **DEVIL'S MISTRESS**   11740-2 $4.50
- ☐ **EVERY TIME I LOVE YOU**   20087-3 $4.99
- ☐ **GOLDEN SURRENDER**   12973-7 $4.50
- ☐ **THE VIKING'S WOMAN**   20670-7 $4.50